RED DYED HAIR

A STRADENI   Eugenia.
Fakinou

THREE SUMMERS   Margarita
Liberaki

KOSTAS MOURSELAS

Red Dyed Hair

Translation
FRED A. REED

KEDROS

The translation costs of this book have been covered
by the Greek Ministry of Culture.

Typeset and printed in Greece
by Kedros Publishers, S.A.
3, G. Gennadiou Str., Athens 106 78,
Tel. 210.38.09.712 – Fax 210.38.31.981
April 1992, 3rd reprint Oct. 2003

Title in Greek: Βαμμένα κόκκινα μαλλιά
Cover design by
Kostas and Marina Bostantjoglou

ISBN 960-04-0577-8

TABLE OF CONTENTS

BOOK ONE
Wolves in the distance

BOOK TWO
Pity, we were such a fine, fragile invention

THE CAST OF CHARACTERS

Agis, salt of the earth; fell in love with Martha
Aleka, Louis' first wife
Anargyros, Aleka's second husband, contractor
Anestis, narrator's uncle
Antigone, Louis' sister
Antoniadis, the Stalinist of the group; a good kid
Antypas, Aleka's father, goldsmith
Aristos Krugas, Eugenia's brother, baker
Aristos' brother, cuckold
Athanasia, Louis' step-mother
Athena, Panagos' wife
Bertrand, crazy French-Greek clown
Carmen, or Ophelia, Louis' lover, hairdresser
Chrysanthi Antypas, Aleka's mother, Louis' mother-in-law
Constantine, son of narrator and Haroula
Customs, Fanny's brother
Drakopoulos, tomato sauce manufacturer, married Madonna
Elektra, Maritsa's housekeeper
Eleni, or Twiggy, Moschos' wife
Elias, Louis' father's brother
Eugenia Krugas, almost Louis' wife
Eustathia, Julia's God-fearing aunt
Fanny, Litsa's sister, Louis' sister-in-law
Fatmé, or Sophie, Dutch druggie
Fotis Demenagas, nazi collaborator, heavy
Grocer, Urania's lover
Haroula, Peppas' wife, had affairs with Louis, narrator
Julia, narrator's wife
Kritsinis, major, Corinth Military Base
Lazaris, son of an executed leftist
Lazaris' mother
Litsa, Louis' second wife
Louis, or Emmanuel Retsinas
Louisa, Louis' daughter

9

Maritsa Ghika, Pericles' mother, nymphomaniac
Martha, narrator's great love, Liakopoulos' wife
Martha's mother, fell in love with Louis' uncle Elias
Matina, narrator's sister
Melpo, Anestis' wife, the Smyrna girl
Moschos, Louis' half brother
Narrator, Kostas Manolopoulos, Louis' friend
Narrator's father
Nikolaidis, Julia's father
Nora, narrator's mistress
Olga, narrator's mother
Olympia Krugas, cuckold's wife
Panagos, Louis' sister Antigone's lover, greengrocer
Papadopoulos, police precinct chief
Peppas, tavern keeper
Pericles, son of Maritsa
Persephone Dertilis, Argyris' wife and one of Louis' loves
Petros Retsinas, Louis' father
Polyxeni, Fotis Demenagas' beautiful wife
Quartermaster, Louis' army buddy
Sophia, singer from Trikala
Tassos, neighborhood coffeehouse owner
Tassoula, narrator's old flame, later turned whore
Tatyana, or Madonna, Drakopoulos' wife, Antoniadis' sister
Tormented Man, fell in love with Martha
Tzavaras, Louis' and Moschos' uncle, general
Urania, temptation of the neighborhood

BOOK ONE

WOLVES IN THE DISTANCE

For my children, Michalis and Cleopatra

1. THE BIRTHDAY PRESENT

THE ALMOST MAN. That's Emmanuel Retsinas; Louis for short. Almost ugly, almost good-looking, almost lazy, almost uneducated, almost an atheist. What do I mean by atheist? This: Louis is the kind of guy who never sets foot in church — almost — except for the odd funeral, baptism, or wedding. Including his own. Twice. Three times, almost.

You couldn't exactly call him an upstanding character. Almost, though; almost a man of principles, almost a man without principles. In a word, contradictory, multi-faceted. Trustworthy, almost. Almost OK.

No sooner do I try to describe the guy than I visualize him in my mind's eye getting ready for his first wedding ... No. Not exactly then. A bit earlier. When they sprung the trap on him. Talk about being caught between a rock and a hard place! Just a second, though, I'm doing this all wrong. First, you have to understand just what kind of guy he is. I say "kind of guy" advisedly. It's almost impossible to get a handle on a character like his. If he has one. Putting it bluntly, Louis is larger than life. Think of a river. Think of all the little streams and brooks flowing into a river. That's Louis: the river.

Hold on; I'm still getting it wrong. You don't want to hear about his first wedding. Let me tell you about Fatmé, how I got mixed up with her, how he introduced us. Later we'll get around to the wedding. Better that way. So, Fatmé it is.

Anyhow, I'm at home with Julia, the wife; it's noon on a Saturday. We're eating lunch off trays in front of the TV,

13

watching some soap opera. You know how it is; the same old routine. No surprises, nothing unexpected. For homebodies like us the great adventures only happen in our imagination. But Louis, they actually happen to him. People like us, we have to make do with daydreams. Anyway, there I was, daydreaming when Drrrinng went the phone.

— Cousin?

Louis almost never calls me by my first name. Sometimes he'll call me cousin, sometimes brother, sometimes uncle. He dreams up his own nicknames for just about everybody. He calls Anargyros — him I'll tell you about in a minute — "my good man" because, thanks to him, Louis got rid of his first wife. As a matter of fact, Anargyros stole her. But, back to our phone call:

— I know, cousin, I know. Don't say a word. Got the little woman right there beside you.

Funny, funny, always calling Julia "the little woman" even though she's taller than him, a good 5'10". The athletic type, anything but little.

— You got your slippers on, a tray on your lap, you're watching TV, eating, flopped down on that overstuffed sofa of yours ...

It was as if he could see me.

— Listen carefully. Get up, go to your desk, unlock your little drawer, peel a coupla three ten-spots off your roll, hop into your wheels and tool on down. Have I got something for you — a present, the one I didn't send for your birthday.

My birthday? What's he talking about? Since when does he care anything about my birthday?

— Tell your wife anything, tell her something terrible has happened to Louis. She won't try to stop you ...

When I get there, I spot him on the Corniche, at a corner newsstand just across from a seafood restaurant and the Rodeo Club. Waiting.

Now, this ought to give you an inkling of Louis' style. It's summer, Saturday afternoon. Did I already mention that? Ninety-eight in the shade. Hot enough to fry eggs on the

14

sidewalk. Dust everywhere, and there stands Louis waiting for me, dressed in a suit and tie, with a flower in his lapel. I could hardly believe my eyes.

— Louis?

— Shut up.

Never saw him walk quite so fast before, almost mincing along in his haste.

— Hey, Louis, slow down, you're making like a fairy. What's got into you?

He turns into a dirt lane to the right of the Rodeo. They've paved it now, I think. Along he strides, swaying from side to side, snapping his fingers, glancing warily back and forth. A few yards further and we come to the marina. I never saw it close up before. The place is full of boats; big boats and little boats ... not much water in sight. The boats are crammed in tight, like trailers at a cheap campground. Yachts of all sizes, just like house-trailers, I tell you. Boats with cabins, large and small cabins, and in the front yard — the deck, I mean — are ladies in shorts with tops and without. The only thing missing is the potted plants. The boats all have names painted on their bows, big names, Latin names, foreign names, Greek-sounding names. *Madonna*, *Christiana*, *Lucia*, just like those summer houses with cutesy little names like *Lena* and *Calliope*. Same damned thing. Real romantic. Get a load of the pot-bellies lounging all over that *Christiana* of theirs. And here I am, my friend, watching Louis thread through them at breakneck speed, turning right, then left, down one path and up another.

— Just like your street.

— It is my street, now clam up!

Suddenly he freezes.

— Here we are.

It was a sixty-foot cabin cruiser with what seemed like twenty masts and as many sails ... all wood. I read the name: *Fatmé*.

Before starting up the gangplank he pauses, looks at his watch and glances from side to side.

15

— This is a gangster movie or what?

— Come on, no time to lose.

I follow him on board, where he immediately begins singing the praises of the vessel.

— Amazing! All the latest in computerized equipment, state-of-the-art navigation, barographs, radar ...

Or something like that. He goes on:

— You want the weather anywhere in the world, any time of day; you want latitude, longitude, depth? You got it all, right here.

He punches a series of buttons, lights flash on and computer paper starts to whir out of a slot. Just like an electrocardiogram. He presses the buttons again, the whirring stops, the lights flicker out.

— This way, cousin, for the cabins, four of them.

He leads me through a series of doors, all with polished brass hardware.

— This one here belongs to the owner.

A small bookcase, a television set, mirrors, thick carpeting on the floor, engravings of maps and naval charts hanging on the walls; everything in wood. Dark wood. Everything.

As you can imagine, I keep up a steady stream of exclamations. Amazing! Unbelievable! and suchlike. But the big exclamation, the really big one, comes when he opens the fourth door. In the movies you always get the music at the big moments. Gongs and kettledrums all going off at once. So, he opens the fourth door and there I see a small bunk and on the small bunk a girl, naked. Almost. Ah! I crane my neck for a better look. She's wearing panties. White ones. The rest of her is showing. All of it. Except for her eyes, which are closed. Across the cabin an electric fan is blowing air at her.

— Hey, Louis, she'll catch cold. Turn it off.

— Will you get a load of that, he says.

At that instant she opens her eyes. Almost green. Almost brown. Can't be, you say. Green and brown at the same time? No way. But there it was. You find the most unlikely combinations, the craziest match-ups in the eyes. Can you imagine orange and gray? In a pair of eyes you can.

— Louis, she says.

Or does she. Her voice is like a fine powder. Pure powdered sugar. Louis doesn't seem to notice. He closes the door and leads me to the galley.

— Sit down. How do you like your coffee?

He walks over to the stove. Where did he learn to open cupboards and drawers like that? Find the sugar and the coffee and the coffeepot and the cups and saucers?

— You never knew where anything was in your own house.

— Drink some real coffee, cousin, and keep your mouth shut. Here; it's Italian. The real thing. You can only get this stuff at the Café Greco, in Rome.

That's Louis. Turning up when you least expect him. Figure it out. How come Louis — who lives just behind the dockyards in a place that's more shack than house — is suddenly serving you coffee in a million-dollar seagoing yacht? Who's that again? Louis, the same guy who still hasn't even got a proper roof over that dump of his to keep the rain out.

That must be his secret. Whenever he starts spinning his wheels, that place, that shack of his, seems to give him a charge of energy. You'll find him there nailing, painting and patching away. Every piece of scrap wood, cracked linoleum, warped particle board, rusty sheet metal and tar paper he stumbles across seems to end up there. Every five years, he builds a new addition. With all the add-ons, the place has turned into a long, narrow structure a good seventy feet from end to end. To reach the kitchen you pass through living rooms, bedrooms, bathrooms, seas, valleys and mountains. Hell, he even set up an office.

— Here's where I keep my diary and write my letters.

There's even a well. Yessir. He told me, but I didn't believe him. Right in his father's bedroom. Inside. When I visited him for the first time, it was ten feet deep. He was convinced there would be water in that exact spot.   .

He didn't want to depend on anyone. Wanted his own water, his own power, his own garden. The front yard he turned into an honest-to-God garden. Water was his big worry. When they cut it off because he forgot to pay the bill, or couldn't afford it; being without water himself wasn't his big worry. But the plants were a different story. When he found them withered, it was as if there'd been a death in the family. The electricity problem he'd solved long ago. Set up a home-made windmill, connected it to a rusty old gearbox and some grimy batteries, some transistors or whatever you call them, and began to crank out the current.

— Let's have our coffee in Fatmé's cabin. That's what we call her, after the cruiser. We can speak freely there. She doesn't understand Greek ... only a bit, broken. She's Dutch. From Amsterdam. Come on, let's keep her company.

That's where we go. I sit down at the foot of the bed, next to her feet. He's right next to her head.

— Louis! she says again with that misty voice of hers.

— Like you to meet my pal, Kostas. Kostas Manolopoulos.

— Gus, she says.

— That's what she'll call you. Gus. Your nickname. Don't bother to shake hands. Just grab her foot. Really. It's all the same to her.

Me, I'm still in a state of shock, believe me. I may play it cool, like the guy who's seen it all, but I felt like a greenhorn.

— Grab her foot, idiot. She figured out your nickname, so she's got to like you. Anyway, she's probably soused. Everything looks rosy to her, and a bit blurred around the edges.

So I touch her foot, lightly, as if to say pleased to meet you. And I smile at her. She smiles back, and closes her eyes.

— She's off drugs and onto booze. More or less. Now she's in love, trying to get on the wagon. When she finds someone to look after her, she'll do that. Turns into a little lamb. She wants to be loved. Doesn't really matter who. Just loved.

That's Louis; one surprise after another. I never would have dreamed I'd almost be holding a body like that in my hands. Twenty-six at the outside, a living doll at the very least. You could do anything you wanted with her, that was crystal

18

clear. A woman like that ... it's like hitting the jackpot in a lottery where you haven't even bought a ticket. At night you dream about the number, and when you wake up, there it is. You're reading the paper, you spot the winning number, 3333 etc., and bingo. It's the ticket you bought in your sleep.

— Louis!

— What is it, sweetie? he answered, full of tenderness.

— Just a drop of wine, please.

Louis:

— I'll give you a beating, a good one.

He wasn't joking. She could see it in his eyes. He would do it. Beat her, I mean. Then she turns and looks at me, her would-be savior. I tell him:

— This kind of stuff isn't for guys my age. I'm leaving. Why did you bring me here anyway.

She fell asleep. I look at her again. How did he keep his hands off her, the creep. She was all peaches and cream. All she had to do was open her eyes, move her legs or her body and you'd go numb. It was as if soft, invisible oscillations were creeping over me. That's how it felt.

He'd already beaten her a couple of times; wanted her to stop drinking, save her. So he claimed.

— Louis, I thought I'd seen everything; I never imagined I'd find you shacked up on a luxury yacht!

He laughs. Or to put it more accurately, smiles. Further on, if I can remember, I'll tell you more about Louis' enigmatic smile. How many elements in the periodic table? About ninety, right? Well, that's Louis' smile for you. Innocent, scheming, warm, icy, clever, naive, ironic, criminal, and so on and so forth ... I could find you ninety adjectives, and they'd all fit. Pure chemistry. He smiles that smile of his and goes on with his story.

Seems he found a first mate's job on this very yacht. The owner was an eccentric, a wealthy Italian named Renato who was also the captain. I forgot to mention that Louis' main job of late, particularly in the summer time, is operating yachts. You heard what I said, operating yachts. Louis is no lumpen,

19

no bum, he's a workingman. In his own way, of course.

— Listen, he says. This Fatmé business begins three months ago when I go to work for Renato. He's a fine fellow, Renato is, but he's got one weakness. He likes to travel the world on the lookout for bimbos on the loose. A new one every three months, best I can figure. But this time, with Fatmé, things are getting out of hand. She's a bimbo all right, but she wants booze, and coke. If she leaves a lighted cigaret around and the boat goes up in smoke, then what happens? He could get involved with the police. So he wants to get rid of her, at any price. What's more, he wants her out of here now, today. By the time he gets here, she's got to be gone. That's the problem. What to do with her?

We both look at her at the same time, and see her smile in her sleep. Her smile and Louis' were poles apart. With Fatmé's smile, what you see is what you get. Straightforward. Nothing to hide. Purified. A perfect match for her eyes. No contradictions. Not like Louis. With him, everything is contradictory, at odds with itself. There would be these eyes full of Christ-like innocence, along with a diabolical, indecipherable grin. Then I realize I'm still holding her foot. By the ankle.

I was absorbed by Louis' story. Fatmé was dreaming now, for sure. We could tell by her nipples. Louis was the first to notice. Unbelievable. Suddenly they go erect, as though an invisible hand is caressing them.

— I feel sorry for her, cousin. I can't just kick her out into the street, broke and hungry. But he wants me to give her the boot; he doesn't care how; his mind's made up.

Mind you, if you really want to understand Louis, to find out what makes him tick, we'll need more details, additional fragments of life, to piece together his mosaic. That's how I visualize his life, like a mosaic full of thousands of patterns and colors: churches, whorehouses, birds, trees and sea. Lots of sea. A guy like Louis couldn't last long away from the sea. He couldn't afford his own boat, that goes without saying, so he did the next best thing, bought a lot close to the water, just up the street from the dockyards, where he could build a shack. His only mistake was to build in the summer when there was no rain, and no runoff. Come winter, just as he's putting the finishing touches to his first illegal room he discovers, a bit late, that it's smack in the middle of a small river bed. Everything was a sodden mess. But it was too late to go back. He'd fallen in love with the place, and even planted a few bushes, including the first lemon tree. For three years he worked on a kind of dam. Finally, he forced the raging waters to change course a bit. His battle with the elements was won. In a fit of enthusiasm he hoisted a flag atop the dam, a flag he designed himself. White, with a black patch in the middle. A round black spot, like an ink stain.

Did I mention how Fatmé came into Louis' life? No? It was all very simple. One day Louis and Renato wake up and go topside for their morning cigar. And who should they find, fast asleep on the deck?

— An angel fallen from the sky, exclaims Louis, who was first to spot her.

Renato agrees.

— An angel, he says, and takes her under his wing.

But for Louis, there was nothing religious or poetic about her being an angel; he simply couldn't figure how she ended up on the deck. There was no gangplank — they pulled it aboard at night. There were no other boats nearby at the time, so she couldn't possibly have jumped. The only way to get aboard was by air. But they detected no angel wings on or around the girl; how she got there was a mystery. And a mystery it was destined to remain. When Louis asked her the secret, she broke out laughing. Crazed, wild, hysterical laughter. Her laughing fits were so violent he was afraid she would stop breathing. Naturally he wanted to know how she

21

did it; he'd exhausted all the possible explanations for her landing. I say landing advisedly: Louis' first reaction was it had to be a helicopter. But the noise would have awakened them. Finally Louis couldn't restrain himself; the inexplicable mystery got the better of him. One day he threatened her with a straight razor.

— Goddamn it, spit it out or I'll slice your wrists open. Come on, talk!

He actually cut her. Lightly, by mistake. But by the look on his face, he wasn't joking. She said nothing, then stretched out her hands.

— Go ahead, cut! she said.

But it was too late; he couldn't go through with it. At that exact and precise instant he fell in love with her. As luck and circumstance would have it, her protector was away, so instead of slashing her wrists he embraced her. Kissed her, even.

Of course, it didn't last. Louis' love affairs never last. Always spur-of-the-moment things. A bed wasn't even necessary. Not even. Anywhere would do.

So. In any case — take it from me — from that moment on, Louis began to feel a sense of awe before the boundless unknowability of the universe. And at the same time, he came to discover the absurd, to accept the vanity of all things. He found it inexplicable that despite the existence of death, man insists on living, overwhelming evidence to the contrary. He realized how far he had come, the mystery of Fatmé's apparition had become one with the mystery of existence. It was as though the existence of such mystery means man can live, and find reason to live. Of course when he told me all this, it was after more than a few drinks too many. I had trouble understanding him; it was all a bit unclear.

In any case, it took him several stages to arrive at that conclusion. By then the mystery of Fatmé had become a nightmare. An *idée fixe.* He had to solve the puzzle, or else he could not go on living. It got that bad, I'm telling you. Louis was depressed, melancholy, can you imagine!

22

— Come on, Fatmé, you've got to tell me, you're driving me crazy: how did you end up here?

Not a word. Just that laugh of hers. Renato began losing patience. It was obvious that the joke was getting dangerously out of hand.

— Boss, if she doesn't tell us ...

— One more time and you're gone. Got it?

All this went on in English. Louis could speak English. Another mystery. How and where did he learn it? The razor blade was his last attempt, though. Given the choice between firing and curiosity, Louis finally had to accept that the mystery would never be solved.

— What can you do? Life goes on.

But something inside him had cracked. Not cracked. Shattered. Something crystalline, here, inside the chest, a bit higher; right there, everybody has it. That's what shattered. He even claimed — insisted, in fact — that he heard the noise. Loud and clear. A strange kind of grinding. Crazy things. Like colors collapsing, full of cracks. He wanted to describe it but couldn't find the words.

In any case, as I say, Louis was a changed man, no longer the Louis of old, the Louis we all knew. Or so they say, people who've seen him lately.

First he gave up on the well. Didn't dig another inch. And there it stayed, right in the middle of the bedroom, a huge hole ten feet deep. It's crazy, Louis living in a house with a ten-foot-deep hole in the floor. He still refuses to fill it up. Finally, though, he covered it over.

Because of it his father will also die. He too has discovered the absurd. Now he's reconciled with death. You don't believe me? Up to then, the idea of death terrified him. Now he's calm. Louis' old man. Calm.

What the hell. So, where were we? Ah, yes. In Fatmé's cabin drinking coffee. So when we finish the coffee, we start on the Campari. Strong stuff, and bitter. With lemon and sugar. I was surprised when I see him unlock the liquor cabinet to get the drink. Then he tells me about Fatmé's alcohol problems, why everything is under lock and key.

I've got to admit that after all the weird and wonderful happenings, I'm beginning to feel like someone lost in the middle of a mine field. Impossible to guess what might happen next. No matter how much I'd like to be a liberated kind of guy, without hang-ups, I guess it does matter to me what people think, especially my friends, and Julia. Even aunt Eustathia. Especially her. She's religious, she's rich and she's our benefactress, so to speak. You can imagine what would happen if she found out that her niece's husband, me in other words — Gus, as Fatmé puts it — is hanging around on cabin cruisers with bare-breasted bimbos who sleep with strange Italians, fool around with drugs, who ... Not even Niagara Falls would have enough water to wash me out of her mouth.

— Louis, shouldn't we be doing something about this? Maybe this Renato of yours is right to be worried about some kind of trouble?

One look at him was enough to cut me off. I felt a sharp pang of embarrassment, but I went on.

— Look, for a guy like Renato, life may be on the cheap side. I remember an essay I did on the subject in high school: "Kill or Be Killed." True or false, asked the teacher. Whoever said true got sent home for two days. The two of us said true. Me and you. "Kill or be killed is the rule of life," we wrote. Remember?

Sure he did: the teacher and the punishment.

— Louis, I went on, I don't want to lose my job. I'm a court clerk, which doesn't leave me a lot of leeway. Aunt Eustathia may be helping us out and all that, but she's a woman in her sixties, and she's getting antsy. If she meets the man of her dreams tomorrow and cuts us off, we're stuck with my pen pusher's salary. We lose that, and we'll end up on the street.

24

All this time, Fatmé slept on. Her nipples were back to normal, from time to time her body shifted. Like an artist moving his model until he finds the just right position.

It was dusk by then. Just as Louis got up to switch on the lights, we heard a horn.

— It's the fuel truck, he said and rushed out.

As the door opens, so do Fatmé's eyes. Just a crack. Then a bit more. When she realizes Louis is gone she sits up and, seizing the opportunity, leaps on top of me as if shot from a cannon.

— Gus, you Campari me give.

It was Greek all right. She stretches out her hand toward my glass. I pull back.

— Gus, she says, and wraps herself around me.

All of her. When I say wrapped around, it's no figure of speech. I'm stunned. What she wouldn't do for a shot of Campari. She twines her legs around my waist, snakes her arms around my neck and sits there on top of me. Honest to God. Right there on top of me, all of her, with nothing on but a flimsy pair of bikini bottoms.

— Gus, please, just a little.

— Fatmé.

— Sophie.

— Sophie, you no Campari.

I set my glass down on a side table out of her reach.

— Gus, last time.

She tries to reach it. But can't, and turns back and looks me in the eyes. I look back. She's only a kid. Then, with a mixture of fear and excitement I put my arms around her waist. Carefully. I don't want her to break.

— Gus, just a little.

I can't resist, I'm crumbling. I pick up the glass and bring it to her lips.

25

— Last time? Promise?

— Last time, she says and starts sipping.

When she finishes she takes the glass in her hands, runs her tongue around the edge, then kneels down on the bunk and crawls to the porthole, opens it and throws the glass into the water. It makes a plaff. I'm still sitting at the foot of the bed while she kneels there.

Then she turns around and crawls back toward me. Suddenly she's kneeling upright in front of me. Now her breasts are almost touching my lips. I breathe in and out only a few millimeters from her nipples. "No telling what she'll do to show her appreciation ..." I'm shaking. My cowardice knows no bounds. I think of Louis who'll be turning up any minute now, even though I could still hear the tank truck pumping away; I think of the Italian ... "It's not right for me to take advantage. What should I do?" So I sit there not knowing what to do with my hands. Finally, I put my arms around her waist; I'm almost motionless, I can't make up my mind. Suddenly, after an indeterminate length of time, she leans forward and kisses me. Right on the mouth. Yep. Her. Barely. Then she sits down beside me and starts to cry. At that moment the tank truck stops pumping.

— Gus, I love you, she says, in tears.

Louis comes in.

— Don't bother to get up. As you were.

He pulls up a wicker armchair, sits down and begins to fill in the details! Fatmé is my birthday present, the present he mentioned on the telephone.

— You won't find a sweeter kid. It's the one thing you'll never regret as long as you live, cousin.

I didn't understand. What was he getting at? He went on:

— The dough you brought, we'll give it to her and send her back home. Or you can keep her and lend me the money — right now, I could use it.

Fatmé is still crying. Politely. She knew everything. Understood everything. Everything Louis said.

— What a soap opera, cousin. Her parents are after her but

she doesn't want to go home, not for anything in the world.

— Gus, she says, and looks at me sorrowfully.

Louis goes on:

— You got money, numskull? Rent an apartment. Not for long; six months maybe. Then, if you don't want her I'll take her. I'll be back from Egypt by then. If we send her home she'll get on the shit again; does that and she's a goner. She doesn't want to have anything to do with them; they're real bastards. Me? I'm sailing for Egypt in a few days with the Italian; I can't afford her. Where could I put her? You always used to say I really live my life. Well, now's your ‚chance to live yours ... Your big chance. Grab it, cousin. She likes you. I gave her the whole story. She agrees. At least until she can find work. Worried about that Julia of yours? Not me. Screw her.

Arguments like that. Put me through the wringer. You're gonna let this slip through your fingers? You only get a windfall like this once.

— Take her to a hotel to start with, then find an apartment ...

Scary. Try making up your mind in two minutes ...

— The first twenty years of her life were pure hell. She won't go back home. Scared to death. They'll destroy her. The Italian won't let us take her along. He bought her a ticket. No alcoholics on his boat, that's the rule. I pleaded with him. No deal. She's off the booze, I said, she's cured. No deal.

How am I going to squirm out of this one?

— You think it's easy, Louis?

And he starts all over again. What with his wife and all, he can hardly take her to his place; that would be too much.

— Your old lady won't even notice. But make up your mind quick, before Renato gets here and spots her. Otherwise he'll put her on the first plane home, in person.

What am I supposed to do? What would you do? Keep her? We're talking responsibility here. First off, Julia knows exactly how much I make, right down to the penny, the shrew. I'll have my hands full explaining the missing thirty thousand. What about my job? What if I get mixed up with dope

27

dealers? And the girl, she could just as well end up hanging from a rope, she could ... The possibilities are endless. If aunt Eustathia ever gets a whiff of the story, goodbye goose and goodbye golden eggs. I mean, that three-storey apartment house of hers in the west end, the one in Julia's name. After she dies, of course. But between now and then? She's got me and she knows it.

— No way, Louis. I smell trouble. This is risky business.

— Hey, cousin, you really are a jerk, he finally says. And I always thought you were ready for the Kingdom of Heaven.

— Come on, Louis.

— OK, sorry.

I'm about ready to pop. No kidding. It's not so much the money; I can get a little extra if need be; I have some cash in reserve, but ...

— Look, Louis ...

— Forget it, OK? You're right. It's my fault.

And he embraces her, wraps his arms around her.

— Louis! Fatmé blurts out and begins sobbing again.

No Holy Virgin ever held her Son with such maternal tenderness. He's holding her close, looking her in the eyes.

— Louis, you've got to understand. I just can't run off doing things like that. Sure, I'll help out, but I'm not playing with fire. And this is more than fire.

He sets her down on the bunk so lightly that you'd have sworn she was fragile goods, fine crystal or something, grabs a small suitcase and stuffs it full of her clothing, dresses her in a man's shirt — white, with blue pin-stripes — and a pair of shorts, I can still see them, bright-red like fire, like blood.

As he drags her along, Fatmé stumbles. When I see her going up the stairs, I want to cry out: "Wait a second, Louis, I'll take her, and damn the consequences ..." But I don't. All I say is "Louis." It's all I can do to stuff the money into his pocket. Everything I have. Thirty thousand. He rushes down the gangplank, fires up that indescribable two-wheeler of his and plumps her down behind him.

— Where're you taking her?

28

— To my place. Where else?

I can't believe it. He's taking her where, the sonofabitch? To his wife? From what I hear, his old man is living with them too. He roars off.

From that day on that comment of his, "I always thought you were ready for the Kingdom of Heaven, cousin," stuck in my craw. Her shirt wasn't even buttoned, and as they sped away her shirttails flapped in the wind, like a white flag of surrender.

Just a minute ago I mentioned that indescribable two-wheeler of Louis'. Indescribable because after God knows how many crashes and falls, I don't think there's a single piece of original equipment left on the thing. In fact, if Louis is still alive today, it's because of a string of miracles. Every time he mounts up is another excuse to meet his Maker. But at the last moment his guardian angel intercedes to save him. He doesn't know the angel's name, doesn't know why he does it, but there's something mysterious going on, that much is for sure. You can't just lose your whole front wheel, have the whole shebang collapse under you and then get up and walk away as though you'd only bent over to pick something up. You can't ram the curb and be thrown onto the back of a truck loaded with watermelons, like Louis did — that happened too — and instead of ending up on the ground like a busted melon, the melons were busted. Wild stuff. Not because he's a lousy driver, mind you; not at all. Just that when he's riding his two-wheeler Louis comes up with ideas, makes plans, decisions, dreams. No fear of flying; speed is what makes him go. One time he left home, drove all the way to Rafina and got off his machine before he realized that he'd been driving for two and a half hours.

— Unbelievable, cousin. I didn't know what was going on until I got there. I had no idea I'd been on the road for two and a half hours.

But in those two hours he had — in his imagination, of course — set up a bar. He'd found the backers, his brother's wife, Eleni, the one they call Twiggy, would do the bookkeeping; he never could keep his eyes off her ... What a story. Just get a load of this! As he's whirring along he finds just the spot for the bar, an abandoned house; the owner is a tall, attractive woman who doesn't even want to rent the place — and then ... see how far you can go in a dream. Takes him a half-hour, all the way downtown, to convince her. First he gets her drunk, then plays the harmonica for her — when Louis hasn't got his guitar he makes do with a harmonica — spoon-feeds her grape preserves, one big fat grape at a time. In any case, he gets the go-ahead, so to speak, in bed, with him on the bottom and her on top. With a piercing shriek of "lover!" at the finale she surrenders soul, body and bar.

But the whole thing was concocted as he's piloting that indescribable putt-putt of his toward Rafina. Well, it wasn't entirely his imagination. The place did exist, he knew about it, and the bookkeeper, like I said, his sister-in-law, had studied a bit and kept on bothering him about finding her work so she could dump her husband, she couldn't stand the guy a moment longer. All the rest was made up. All the comings and goings, and most of all the tall lady. Never existed.

Same today. I'm sure that by the time he gets to that shack of his he'll have dreamed up a whole strategy: he'll divorce his wife, if it comes to that, and take up with Fatmé; nope, more likely he'll keep the two of them, Litsaki and Fatmé, both. He'll turn her into a model, and marry her off later, maybe even open up a boutique for her, or a hairdressing salon, or whatever. No doubt about it, for Louis, daydreaming on his motorbike was a throat-gripping experience. What hadn't he dreamed of perched atop the two-wheeler? Even slept with the wives of a couple of uncles of his. Whichever women he liked. Friends' wives too. Whoever pleased him. He stole from make-believe partners, beat people up and ratted on them in revenge. But let's understand each other, plenty of those things weren't all that imaginary. Dreams and reality are so close together for Louis that he's not sure, and neither are you, that whatever he tells you ever really happened or not; like the story of the bar, for instance; even today nobody

30

knows for sure whether or not he made the whole thing up, or whether it really happened. Maybe it happened, because once, in the depths of those centuries of his, he actually ran a bar, so he claims. There's only one thing Louis never managed to do, even in a dream. Kill someone. He never could do it. Even admits it. It's his weakness. In spite of his best efforts, he just couldn't do it. Many times he would bring to mind his worst enemies, or some rotten friends, the kind of scum whose absence would have been a benefit for society and for him, thought of them in such disgusting terms that murdering them would have seemed completely reasonable. No way. Couldn't even do it then.

Still, maybe because of some brain deficiency of his, he confused life and dreams more times than you could count. And remember, these were daydreams, dreams he had while driving his motorbike, or travelling by train, car, or ship. Not in his sleep. Rarely in his sleep. For him, that kind of dream didn't count.

From what I pieced together later — as he explained when I went to see him at the hospital — the accident happened at the precise moment when, in his dream, he was strolling with Fatmé through the refugee district near the oil refinery just as the people were demonstrating in the streets and he was admiring her in those shorts and that open, pin-striped shirt, right in front of Botsaris' glassware store. Just at that moment, the instant of apotheosis, disaster struck. The motorbike plunged through the store window. As it hit, so he said, it was as if he could hear the whispering, the admiring remarks, even some applause. Louis was thrown off and landed in the bedding store next door. His guardian angel was on the job again. Yes, indeed, he said, this time he all but felt the hand reach out and throw him onto a stack of foam-rubber

31

mattresses on display right there on the sidewalk. He got to his feet with nothing worse than bruises and a spot of contusion. Fatmé went right on through the window with the motorbike, shattered the glass and impaled herself on a huge, antique oil lamp. The glass chimney, a tinted affair with pseudo-mythological motifs showing nymphs and satyrs, ripped through her nose and forehead and into her brain, deep in. Nothing happened to the rest of her body, not a scratch. It was a sight to behold!

By the time the ambulance arrived — the fluorescent lights were on and people started to gather, looking on curiously, admiringly; by the time the ambulance arrived — the traffic was awful — it was all over. Before they reached the hospital she'd stopped breathing.

— It can't be, Louis kept repeating. It can't be. Fatmé, my angel! No, it can't be ... me, what an idiot ...

It was the first time I ever saw Louis talk to himself, when I went to see him in the hospital. There he was; injured, and under arrest.

— It can't be!

2. CHALK

LOUIS AND ME, we go way, way back, back to when we were buddies at the Corinth army base. Me, a buck private with leftist leanings; Louis ditto. Our bunks were side by side; we took everything they threw at us — basic training, the harassment and the hard times — side by side. Both of us were from the same neighborhood in Piraeus, both bookworms, Louis more than me actually, even if he never finished high school.

One thing seemed to get on his nerves: I couldn't get worked up about Palamas, the poet. Louis, he'd all but learned the "Dodecalogue of the Gypsy" by heart.

— Can't fool me, it's all hot air, I would say. Big words, sound and fury.

— Ain't so, cousin, ain't so.

Palamas had a big reputation back then.

Louis was surprisingly well-read. Everything from Dostoevski and Gogol to minor Greek leftist authors, not to mention every literary magazine that came his way. It all may have been a bit scrambled in his mind, the way he gobbled things up right and left, but it was tough to catch him off guard. Still, what bothered him most was that I didn't think much of Palamas as a poet.

— Kostas, old buddy, nobody but nobody has a bad word to say about him, nobody except you, that is. What gives?

That was when I introduced him to Kavafy, if memory serves me. Read him a couple of verses. Louis didn't know him; heard the name, maybe. So I brought in a book of his when I came back from leave one time. It almost destroyed

33

him. There, in the light of day, his idol collapsed in a heap of dust.

— Who is this guy, old buddy? Great poet!

That night at Peppas' place, he was fighting to hold back the tears. It was my first time at Peppas', a taverna on the Athens road about three miles outside Corinth. Up to then he hadn't said a word about Peppas or his taverna. Sure, the odd evening I'd see him and the Quartermaster going out, but I didn't know where ... That's what I said; if he didn't have leave he'd simply climb the walls, pay off the sentries and go about his business. The day he heard Kavafy for the first time he dragged me along whether I liked it or not.

— Listen, Manolis, we can't just go running off without leave, how do you expect me to do it? This is the army, not some kind of circus.

But he convinced me. First we worked our way through the barbed wire, then climbed the wall. The Quartermaster, who had a legitimate leave, was waiting for us outside the camp.

That's how I came to know Peppas and Haroula, his wife. Peppas hated the Communists, their party and everything they stood for. Couldn't pay the tab? Call Peppas over, stand him a drink, and start cursing the Communist bandits and their whole evil clan. Don't make the mistake of calling them guerillas, though. Bandits is the word he wants to hear. Curse 'em and keep his glass full. When it's all over, you say, "How much, Mr. Peppas?" and it's all he can do to keep from attacking you for daring to want to pay.

His place was plastered with anti-Communist posters, and bits of shirt cardboard with clumsily lettered patriotic slogans like "Fatherland First," "Know Thyself," "Long Live the Army" and suchlike. They were the work of the village schoolmaster who'd put his pupils to write them.

The most eye-catching poster was the one pinned directly above the radio. It showed a Communist guerilla raping a woman who was supposed to symbolize Greece. No one looked at the rapist; all we looked at was Greece. The whole thing was surrounded by a border of little blue and white flags.

34

Peppas claimed to be a Civil War victim; the Commie bandits had killed his older brother whom he worshipped like a father.

— The bastards, killed my brother did they? God's innocent little lamb ...

And suchlike. It was his only reason for hating them, but it was plenty enough.

— Never bothered me personally; got nothing against 'em.

— Just a second now, Mr. Peppas. If your brother was such an innocent guy, then how come they killed him? Louis asked.

He cut off the conversation with a weird grimace, got up and left. Louis remarked that he seemed confused lately.

Truth is that whenever Retsinas didn't have a cent to his name, he would dangle a baited hook in front of Peppas: funny stories — funny stories are Louis' bread and butter — for a free feed. Not to mince words, he had wormed himself into Peppas' confidence.

We hardly had a chance to sit down before he began the introductions. "Mr. Peppas, his wife, Haroula ..." smiles and handshakes all around. When I heard Louis call the Communists Commies I hardly knew what to think. "Sounds fishy," I thought. "Guy's on the blacklist for leftist sympathies; what's he talking about?"

But he'd hardly gotten the word "Commies" out of his mouth when Peppas ordered the fried testicles. That was Louis' favorite — along with the meatballs.

Some evenings, as soon as Peppas spotted Louis coming into his taverna — he'd named the place "Haroula's" — as soon as he spotted him, he called out the order. "Testicles and meatballs."

He liked Louis; thought the world of him.

— You're a fine lad, Retsinas. A fine lad.

It took me a while to figure the whole thing out. The second time I went, before Peppas came over, Louis had just enough time to whisper:

— Cousin, since you're the educated type, do me a favor, give our friend Peppas a bit of philosophy — he's nuts about philosophy — tell him about life, vanity, death. The Quarter-master here will back you up. I've got some business to attend to. Like I say, Peppas is crazy about tragic tales. Matter of fact, they suit you too. It'll be one big party. You talking, long face like a condemned man. I've only seen you laugh at the movies, you sonofabitch. What the hell, eh. So, like I said, once you tell Peppas "This isn't life; it's nothing but vanity," he'll get excited, start crying, buying rounds and tossing 'em back himself. Just make sure you stand him one or two yourself, don't be a tightwad. He'll pay the whole shot anyway.

That's just what happened. I played the part so well that, honestly, by the end I was weeping along with Peppas. Drink-ing, and weeping. The Quartermaster was taking the whole thing in. "What's going on here," he would've been saying to himself. "Are these guys for real or what?" Couldn't make heads or tails of it. This was when Peppas began threatening to kill himself. After the second plate of food, he started sing-ing the old bouzouki song "Two Doors of Life," and after the third bottle of wine, none of us noticed we were singing a Communist marching song. Frankly, we were in no shape to tell whether it was a drinking song or a guerilla anthem. You remember — sure you do — you could get the slammer for less than nothing if you were a soldier. So imagine what would happen if you're a pinko, singing one of the "enemy's" marching songs. Just then Louis reappeared with a fright-ened look on his face, buttoning his fly. Right behind him, and just as scared, came Haroula. She was plump but graceful. Twenty-five years old at the outside. She shouted at her husband:

— Peppas, the fire, hurry.

She was trying to fix her hair, dark blond hair like pure silk tumbling around her throat. She was a sight to see, a red blush on her cheeks, aroused, trying to fix her hair with one hand and button her blouse with the other.

— You crazy? Making Peppas sing guerilla songs, Louis sputtered.

36

Later, another evening, when the lurching Peppas wanted to show me the rest of his house, I began to suspect the significance of the little scene Louis had dreamed up for me, particularly when I noticed that the kitchen opened directly onto the couple's living room, which you entered through a narrow corridor.

By the fourth time I noticed that Louis always suddenly had to piss in the same bizarre way, at the same moment. "Excuse me for a couple of seconds," he'd say. It occurred to me something was going on, and I got the itch to find out what.

Just as we — the Quartermaster, Peppas and me — were hitting the last verse of the National Anthem, weeping over the glories of the past and the vanity of life — what past, what life? what kind of past can you have when you're twenty-two, what do you know about life? — I left the Quartermaster to keep the show going while I looked for the missing piece of the puzzle.

— Gotta take a leak, I said.

So I did. I look for Louis. Nowhere. Try the kitchen. No luck. No sign of Haroula either. There are two doors in front of me; which one do I open? The pantry or the living room? I choose the living room door and open it. A crack. They don't see me. But I see them. Louis is on the sofa with his pants halfway down and Haroula, with that hair of hers loose, her blouse off and her skirt pulled up, is perched on top of him, rocking back and forth. Rocking back and forth so lightly, so sensually you could hardly believe it. All that weight and all that lightness? It was as if she were in some kind of space-ship, her movements were all air, twisting and turning atop him, in airy, circular movements.

I've never forgotten the image. Can you believe it? Haroula's naked back, her hair all the way down, her breasts rising and falling, an ugly sofa with tasteless wooden legs. Across the room was the buffet and a mirror. A big one. Next to it, a needlepoint picture showing oriental debauchery. I could have sworn I heard music. You know, that improvised,

37

drawn-out, sorrowful music, the kind they used to play in basement dives and opium dens. They didn't see me. I close the door silently and clear out.

I said nothing to Louis. It hurt me that he hadn't let me in on his secret. That night, back in the barracks, I couldn't sleep a wink. I kept remembering the scene, and turning on. Haroula may have been a bit plump but was she ever built! Sitting there on top of Louis with her skirt pulled up, her back naked, rocking back and forth ... Don't even ask. By then, my hard-on was in such a state that all I had to do was touch it and I would have shot off on the spot.

— OK, OK, Kostas, my boy, Louis suddenly piped up from the next bunk. Don't take it so hard. I didn't tell you because I was worried. Not about Peppas, but because you're so afraid to open up, so raw ... You open up for a second and close right up again.

He was wide awake, and alert. He'd spotted me, the sonofabitch. But he had trouble of his own. Big trouble. That very evening Haroula had given him the bad news. She was pregnant. By him, of course. Her husband couldn't have kids. He knew it. He saw doctors to find out if it was his fault; it was. One hundred percent sterile. That was the diagnosis from a microbiologist in Corinth.

Just imagine Haroula, two months pregnant, telling Peppas that miracles can happen; doctors can make mistakes, the kid was really his. But Louis could do even that if he had to. He was capable not only of making Peppas believe the kid was his, but much more. But first he tried to convince her to have an abortion.

— No way. I'd rather kill Peppas, I'd rather die than kill my baby.

That was that, no matter how hard Louis tried, he couldn't persuade her to get rid of the kid. The only alternative was to change Peppas' mind; and change it he did. Maybe it was the Bible story of Sarah, maybe it was because the Corinth microbiologist was a Communist — he was, as a matter of fact — that he diagnosed him as sterile, out of hatred for Peppas'

38

ideological viewpoint, wasn't science always a few steps behind life, wasn't ...

But his last argument was the clincher.

— Mr. Peppas, why don't the two of us visit a real microbiologist, an anti-Communist one. I know just the man, in Piraeus. What do you say?

And so it came to pass. One week later, Louis, me and Peppas were sitting in Dr. Sideropoulos' waiting room in downtown Piraeus. The doctor handed Peppas a wide-mouthed glass bottle without a stopper and led him off down the hall where he told him to ejaculate into the bottle.

We waited, the three of us, Louis, me and the doctor. Peppas was back in three minutes with the sperm. Two days later the doctor called him. He was a Communist too, forgot to tell you, a friend of Louis' father.

— Everything's just fine, Mr. Peppas, you can have as many children as you like. I've never seen livelier sperm.

Peppas just about flipped. From that day on Louis really began to respect me; we became bosom buddies. I forgot to mention, it was me who thought up the whole deal.

— For a thousand we ought to be able to find another microbiologist who can certify Peppas' sperm.

ᐟ That's what I told him. No sooner had I said it than he all but kissed me.

— Amazing! he exclaimed, and quickly turned up Sideropoulos.

He told the doctor what a tragedy it would be when Haroula's baby was born, described the string of murders that would inevitably ensue, that nothing would stop Peppas, the deceived husband, from wiping out the mother, the child and the father. The doctor bought the story. Didn't even want a commission.

— OK, bring him in.

And so we did.

— Kostas, my boy, you're a genius. Ask me anything, and it's yours. What an idea, magnificent, he kept on repeating.

That was how Haroula won a reprieve. That was how peace

and quiet returned to the taverna; because, as you might well have suspected, when Peppas began to notice his wife's belly puffing peace and quiet not only became scarce, but he began to slap her around and kick her.

— Come on, slut, what stinkin' Commie did you do it with?

— I swear to God it's yours; I don't know what you're talking about ...

For Peppas, only a Communist could do such a thing. Her last beating came the day the doctor phoned from Piraeus.

— You can have as many children as you like, Mr. Peppas.

The phone rang at almost the same instant as the last kick. But it was too late; with that kick, Haroula aborted.

And so Louis' and Haroula's baby never did get born. Deep sorrow settled over the taverna.

— God sent me a gift like that and now I've gone and lost it; what a fool I am!

Peppas almost cracked. His hair began to fall out. No. First it turned white, then fell out. Tore himself apart, I'm telling you. For three months he toiled to impregnate poor Haroula. Impossible. Once a month the ovary drops into the woman's womb, Louis told him; that's the trick — the timing has to be right. Just as the ovary drops, you've got to be inside her. That very instant. Imagine, he said; a whole lifetime could go by and you'd never get it right.

Well, Peppas set Haroula up in their bedroom, wouldn't even let her get dressed. She had to be ready, one hundred percent ready. Whenever it happened there could be no delay; he had to attack.

— We can't keep it up, she told him. What about our work?

— The hell with it. First things first.

Even though Haroula was in on the whole thing she had to play along — what else could she do? Not only that, she had to act more convincing as time went by. But she suffered in silence.

Naturally, by the middle of the third month Peppas cracked completely. But before his health collapsed, he cracked ideologically.

Today all this may seem strange, even a little tragicomic, but back then, at the Corinth army camp, it all took on a different dimension.

When Louis broke off with Haroula — when it was all over — something just generally snapped. It was as if the taverna had shrunk, as if the stage sets had lost their color. The testicles and the wine just didn't have the same taste, and Peppas just wasn't the same philosopher. He was a bundle of nerves, nothing could please him.

He began cursing the people who killed his brother; that was when everything began to go downhill, in his life and in his house.

One night Peppas — what got into him? — told us how and why his brother died. He always avoided the subject before. Never even wanted to talk about it. He emptied three glasses of Nemea wine and then began to pour out the details as they'd been related to him by a certain Mr. Fotis, the man who witnessed everything on the night of the murder; the only eyewitness, so he claimed.

So here we had Peppas telling us the story, drinking and weeping.

— 'Cause if my brother was still alive today, everything would be different. And Mr. Fotis wouldn't be enjoying Polyxeni or her dowry. Thirty some acres of orange groves, not counting the olive trees or the villa.

— For the love of God, Mr. Peppas, let's get things straight here. After your brother died, who did you say married her?

Peppas was too confused to get it out. Some things he wanted to hide, some things he wanted to say, and it all ended up in confusion.

— Mean years; nasty, he told us.

One thing was certain. His brother hadn't been dead for a

41

year when Mr. Fotis married Polyxeni.

— The whore, wouldn't even wait till the body was cold.

I don't know why, but the more Peppas peppered his story with those "Mr. Fotis" of his, the more suspicious Louis became. Something had gotten under his skin, something was beginning to smell, something wasn't right.

— And this guy, this Mr. Fotis? Where is he? Anybody know? he asked suddenly.

— Forget it. He's barely alive. Two strokes. One more and he's a goner.

— What about Polyxeni?

— I wouldn't even spit on the lousy whore, I don't ever want to see her again!

Louis was certain that this Mr. Fotis must have played a suspicious role in the whole sad story. In fact, he'd already started imagining the man's appearance, as though he could see his photograph: yellow-green eyes, yellow-green skin, rotten teeth, a scar on one side of his mouth, beetle-browed, skinny.

From what Peppas said, he would have been a man with a domineering manner, a man who behaved like a Gestapo officer, as if the whole world had been created for him alone, the kind of guy who forces you to give him the choicest morsel, the best seat in the house. "Right this way, Mr. Fotis; have a seat, Mr. Fotis."

— From what you say, this Mr. Fotis of yours doesn't seem like such a big shot, Louis hinted with mock innocence.

— He's not; but don't say a word. Still, he's a highly respected man in Corinth, a real gentleman. A man of prominence. One word from him could lose a cabinet minister his job. Every one respects him. Gendarmes and priests alike. You won't get any complaint from me on that score. It's Polyxeni I'm furious about. Him? So what? He liked her, he married her; just looking out for number one. But as for the rest, no problem. Whatever I wanted, I got. Got my taverna permit, and ... and ... One phone call from him was enough to cancel my summons from the health service. That slut can do whatever she likes, but he's always been a fine Christian gentleman. Always.

— Hold on a second, Mr. Peppas. What kind of gentleman did you say. You're telling me this guy ...

Suddenly Louis remembered where he'd seen this very same Mr. Fotis, the man he had imagined. In one corner of the mirror across from the sofa with the spindly legs, the place where he used to sit for his trysts with Haroula, was a yellowed photograph wedged in between the wood frame and the glass. It showed three people. Two men and a woman between them. He remembered the woman too. She impressed him; that's why he looked at the photo in the first place. One of the men was short, soft-looking, a bit naive. The other was tall, proud, overbearing, with scheming, humorless eyes. But the woman was extraordinary, hard to describe. Not that beautiful. But attractive. If she walked by, chances are you wouldn't even notice. But put her under a spotlight and that was it. Love at first sight. Not that fine-featured. Almost stocky, almost plumpish. The more you looked, the sweeter it got. A woman born to betray you, that's for sure. You could tell right away. You'd have to be a real babe in the woods to doubt that for a minute.

— Got a photo of him? Louis asked, ostensibly out of the blue. But he really wanted to know if Mr. Fotis was the tall guy in the photo.

Peppas jumped to his feet, and wobbled off to get it. It was the photo from the mirror, just as Louis had suspected.

— Here they are, the three of them. Friends and neighbors. It's the only one I've got.

I don't recall whether I mentioned it. Louis, he wouldn't go near detective stories or movies, but he had the instincts of a top-notch criminal investigator. Nothing escaped him.

When he looks at you and his little eyes light up and his eyelashes begin to flutter, you'd better realize that he's just zeroed in on you, right down to the thousandth of a megaherz.

— This here's your brother? he asked Peppas, pointing to the short guy in the photo.

— Yes, how do you know?

— And this is Mr. Fotis, right? Louis went on.

— That's him.

He turned to look at me, then at the Quartermaster, finally at Peppas.

— So this has got to be Polyxeni, right?

— That's her, Peppas replied, in a tone mounting wonderment.

Who could have told Louis about the photo? How the hell did he know who was who?

About one minute went by, a minute of silent sizing up. Glances, frowns, doubts. Finally Louis, totally calm, enigmatic, pursed his lips ever so slightly, turned the photo over and read in a loud voice:

— "June 29, 1947, for your name day."

And below, a signature. "Fotis Demenagas." Then he smiled. We stood watching him. Like statues. We hardly breathed. Cooly he turned the photo over and looked it over again. The way an ophthalmologist would examine your eyes, or a cardiologist your heart. That way. It wouldn't have surprised us to see him pull out a stethoscope or a microscope. He held onto it for a few seconds longer, then gave it back to Peppas.

No doubt about it, Louis had the story figured out.

— The day after the photo, the bandits raided the town and killed him, Peppas said, watching for Louis' reaction.

— And the 29th, the day before the murder, was your brother Petros' name day. His name was Petros, wasn't it — or Pavlos?

— That's it, Petros, stammered Peppas, almost speechless from surprise. How did you know?

But instead of answering, Louis got up to leave.

— Come on, men, let's be on our way; we're finished.

At that moment Peppas grabbed him by the shoulder.

— Hold on! Where're you going. You're up to something.

And he sat him down again.

— Hold on, Mr. Peppas. Is this Mr. Fotis still alive or isn't

44

he? Still alive, eh? So, you've still got time. Go ask him. One thing for sure, he wasn't with the bandits. Was he?

— Sure wasn't. He was with the others, said Peppas.

— Fine, that's enough. What do we owe you? We've got to get going.

The devil! He played the role to perfection.

— Manolis, you're not getting out of here alive unless you tell me what's on your mind.

The man was almost blubbering by now. Louis didn't say a word, didn't have a chance. Peppas was so drunk that when he stood up to try and grab Louis, he fell back into his chair, sound asleep.

That night in the barracks we couldn't sleep. Wide awake. Suddenly, I saw Louis turn toward me, nod his head and get up.

— I'm going outside. Come on.

He threw his cape over his shoulders, picked up his cigarets — Santé brand, they were — and went outside. Ostensibly to take a leak.

We sat down outside the latrine on some empty oil drums. First he lit a cigaret and took three or four deep puffs, then he began:

— Listen, cousin ... Peppas' story, it stuck me right here.

And he pulled the photo from his pocket. He'd purloined it.

— Not just the story; the woman.

He pulled out a small flashlight and turned it on. For the first time, I had a good look at her. It was true, there was something bewitching about her. She was one of those women you don't forget. See her once and you'll never forget her.

— I can't believe you believe that jerk-off Peppas, that the guerillas killed his brother. Why would they want to kill a harmless little man like that. Clear as day, something else, something big, is going on here.

— Like what?

— Our pal, Mr. Fotis, probably took a shine to Polyxeni, or to her olive trees, or both.

I looked again at the photo, paying closer attention. He was

45

right. He was devouring her with his eyes. "There was something there already, or the death of Petros created it," I thought to myself.

Meantime Louis had smoked three cigarets. I realized the story was far from over. We said not a word.

I could tell that Louis had already started to move on.

— How old would you say she is? he asked.

— The murder happened in '47, that should make her around ... How old? Twenty-eight, twenty-five?

— About that.

He took the photo, stuck it into his pocket and got up.

We returned to barracks, silent, withdrawn into ourselves. Just as he was lying down, he let drop:

— I can't imagine her kind of woman in love with a blue-blooded creep like that.

And he put his head on the pillow.

From that moment on, the story began to take on mythical proportions inside me.

Five nights went by. On not one of them did Louis sleep in the barracks. He'd managed to get himself assigned to sentry duty every night.

I looked at him over tea in the morning as we sat across from each other on our benches. He was silent, sphinx-like, bent over his cup, with a faraway, otherwordly look on his face. It wasn't until Saturday morning, as I was heading for breakfast, that he grabbed me by the arm.

— Wait a second, you'll find out everything all at once; it'll be a surprise.

I stopped still, with my mess-dish in my hand, eyes pinned on his.

— Just tell me one thing; how did you know Petros was his brother's name?

He smiled.

— That's as far as you got? That's my father's name. Remember? Didn't it say June 29 was his name day?

— Well I'll be damned, I said, instead of embracing him.

Then, smiling enigmatically, he slowly took out his pack of

cigarets, opened it and offered me one. He knew I didn't smoke.

— Take one, it'll make you feel better.

I looked at him, smiled and reached out my hand.

So it happened that there, at the Corinth base, with Louis as my witness, I smoked my first cigaret.

— You'll see how the days roll by.   .

Roll by they did.

I never could figure out why that man took a liking to me. Me, a nobody; clumsy, shy, dull. There was nothing about me, some other aspect of my personality which might stimulate interest. I was honest, though. I was what I was, no mystery, no play-acting. Louis was exactly the opposite. Even a simple conversation with him was an adventure. Wherever you touched him he gave off sparks. The guy was a magician, one of a kind!

Meantime, my curiosity was peaking. I imagined the wildest dreams. In my mind, he was capable of anything. Discovering yellowed letters from Mr. Fotis, letters which would show Polyxeni's betrayal, or her blackmailing him and dragging him by the hair in front of Peppas, forcing him to confess the crime. "I loved her and I killed him," and other unbelievable, melodramatic suchlike. That's what I imagined. I even — after all, the man was at death's door — imagined Louis dressed up as a priest going to take his confession. "Confess-your-sins if you want to go to Heaven," and he would talk. I imagined Fotis Demenagas had asked Polyxeni for a priest for last rites, but in the meantime, Louis had gotten to her, convinced her to bring him in disguise instead of a real priest.

I'd thought of everything because, for me, he was capable of everything. Unearthing fearful stories about Mr. Fotis, documented by letters, witnesses, photographs, he'd prove him a collaborator, a traitor, a German agent, the terror of the town ... I'm telling you, for me, he was capable of anything. There was only one thing I didn't think he could do, and he did it. Listen to this, listen!

One evening several days later, the Quartermaster and I went for a drink at Haroula's. Just imagine what we saw. Peppas and Louis, both drunk as pigs, dancing the tango in the middle of the taverna. Yes, sir. And that wasn't all. The walls were bare. Not a patriotic slogan left. No more "Long Live the Army" or "Communism is the Opium of the People." All ripped down, even the porn poster over the radio.

Nothing really surprised me. But for Louis to turn Peppas into a leftist, well, it took my breath away.

I don't know how long Peppas' ideological rebirth took, but it was about the most staggering thing I've ever heard.

Haroula saw us, and started pleading; I didn't understand what she wanted.

— Mr. Manolopoulos, save our place; do something, they've gone crazy. I went to bed, I wasn't feeling all that well, and suddenly I hear them. Ripping down the posters, busting the teacher's plaques, cursing the prime minister.

Just imagine the scene. A tango playing full blast, Peppas leading Louis, dancing like Rudolph Valentino, with long strides, hands stretched out in ecstasy. They even tried some acrobatic figures, stumbling drunkenly. But if they pulled off the figure, Peppas lunged for Louis and kissed him.

The handful of other customers, under the spell of the spectacle, were throwing plates, clapping, shouting. Pure pandemonium. Then the chants of "Long live Peppas!" started, the retsina flowed like water, and there stood Haroula, begging us to save them.

To tell the truth, it was a nasty situation. No doubt about it; any moment now some friendly neighborhood fascist goons would come busting in, smash everything and beat the piss out of everybody — it was unavoidable — or maybe it would be gendarmes, and they'd arrest the lot of us.

It was then that i took a closer look at Haroula. She'd gotten up just as she was, from her bed of shame where Peppas kept her waiting, to conceive the heir. She was half-naked, barebacked, breasts showing, wearing a cheap bright-red, knee-length nylon nightie; she was well-rounded, a real morsel and her face was gleaming like an August moon.

I never desired a woman quite like that before. I looked at her. She looked back.

— Mr. Manolopoulos, stop them, nothing good can come of this.

I went over to her. Louis, in the middle of the uproar, turned, winked and nodded in Haroula's direction. He knew exactly what he was doing.

— Come, put something on; you'll catch your death, I said.

I actually believed it. She was shaking; it was a cold night. Icy cold with a full moon.

I pushed her toward the kitchen.

— Put some clothes on.

— They'll send 'em off for hard labor.

— But why? They're not doing anything wrong ...

— Nothing wrong! Before you got here, they were singing guerilla army songs, shouting, making a ruckus. You haven't been around for days, you don't know ... All sorts of things have been going on.

I opened the door to the living room — I knew the layout of the place by now — and guided her toward it.

— Come on now, put something on. You can't be like that, you'll catch cold.

And we went in. I let the door close slowly, on its own.

As it clicked shut I reached out and embraced her. Unconsciously. Couldn't hold back. Kissed her.

I didn't really know how people kissed. But the urge was so intense that Haroula, after a few split seconds of hesitation and surprise, let herself go, didn't even try to keep up appearances.

The sofa with the tasteless wooden legs was there next to us; the mirror on the opposite wall. I pulled her close against me. She did not resist. With lowered eyes she settled against me.

Then, clumsily, crudely, I pulled one strap off her shoulder. Her breasts were compeletely exposed. Hard, white, with huge dark nipples. As I tried to pull down her panties I almost lost patience; they got stuck, wouldn't come off.

49

— Don't worry, she whispered. Forget it.

I left it dangling from one leg.

I was overwhelmed. Didn't know what to do first. Kiss her on the lips, the breast, or embrace her? It was like a river in full flood flowing across us, pounding as against a dam, while we struggled against the current.

Then I bent over and kissed her navel, then worked my way up to her breast, to the nipple.

— Tonight's the death of fascism! roared Peppas from outside.

Had I heard him or hadn't I?

— No, don't, whispered Haroula, and pulled my head up by the hair, to kiss her on the lips.

She wanted — maybe she was embarrassed — me close to her face. She felt more at ease when we looked each other in the eye.

At that exact moment, overcome, panting, as though we'd climbed a mountain, I pulled her on top of me as I collapsed back onto the sofa with the wooden legs. She was beside herself by now. So much so that she unbuttoned my fly by herself, pulled down my pants, my shorts all by herself and with quick, sure forward and backward movements I suddenly found myself inside her.

Then she started those feather-light cyclical movements, just as she had with Louis.

I could see everything in the mirror on the opposite wall. Her back, her waist, her buttocks rising and falling rhythmically. It only lasted a few seconds. The shriek she made when she came was indescribable. I was terrified. I'd never heard anything like it before. She seemed convulsed, as if her guts were being ripped out, like a she-wolf whose cubs have been stolen, a moan of pain and release all at once.

I don't know, you can't really describe it, all the magic is gone. You've got to be there, experience it. At that very same instant I came inside her.

I felt her warmth penetrating me, her passion, like a sluggish fluid mingling with my own blood.

50

She had reached her hands under my military jacket and shirt, and was clutching my back. We came to a stop, embracing, panting.

Slowly I came to, regained consciousness of the place and the circumstances.

Hearing slowly returned to my ears, vision to my eyes, fear to my thoughts.

The voices from the next room began to reach us, the clapping and the clanging of the bouzouki, and a rasping voice, Markos, I think it was.

— Whenever I come, it's like I hear bells ringing, she said. You?

— I hear sounds, but I can't tell what it is, or where it comes from. Sounds of all kinds, thousands of them.

I can't recall whether I managed to finish my sentence. It was at that second that the first crashes rang out, like the sound of windows and doors crashing down, wood splintering. It was the Second Coming. Then came the sound of cursing, glass shattering, pitchers cracking on the walls and on the floor, plates being flung through the windows and smashing against the trees and the wall.

Alongside the flying plates you could hear tables and chairs snapping.

— My God! said Haroula, and got to her feet.

She barely managed to pull on her panties. Forget the dress — imagine trying to find one at a moment like that — she yanked a big hand-woven tablecloth from a table and threw it over her shoulders.

Meantime, I was struggling to pull up my drawers and my pants, find my buttonholes, my belt, my suspenders, button my jacket, my fly ... That was it! Game over. I knew it. If the MPs nabbed me, no one could help me. But when the two pistol shots rang out I forgot the buttons and the belts, and holding up my pants with one hand I opened the window and leaped out like a high jumper into the back garden.

I only paused for a second, across the street, to see what would happen to Louis and the Quartermaster. The bullets had punctured the wine barrels above the tables. I saw Peppas' fine Nemea retsina wine pouring out, pale yellow, like piss. Or little fountains, or maybe artesian wells.

I caught a glimpse of Haroula, terrified, coming into the room, the tablecloth covering that bright-red nightgown of hers. In the midst of the uproar, standing there half-naked, she looked more like an odalisque from some other story.

For a second I spotted Peppas, cornered by right-wing thugs who were punching him in the face while the retsina poured over his head.

A handful of other customers in another corner sat there motionless, like wet cats, pretending not to notice what was happening, looking the other way.

— Murderers! I heard Haroula yell, and saw her attack them.

I couldn't see either Louis or the Quartermaster. "Times like this, it's every man for himself," I said, and fled.

Fifteen minutes later I was back at camp. Hopped over the wall, cleared the barbed wire, and was back in the barracks. Ever see a dog running in hot weather, panting? That's what I felt like when I got there. A dog with its tongue hanging out. I couldn't breathe in or out; one more minute and my heart would have snapped like a tightened bowstring.

— What the shit have you been up to tonight? shouted the barracks duty officer as I flopped face down on my bunk.

Only then did I hear the same kind of panting from the next bunk. Slowly, cautiously I rolled over and what did I see? Louis, chest heaving, lying on his back, looking at me with those merry little eyes of his.

Even if we'd wanted to talk, it was impossible. Only deep, gasping breaths came out.

He'd escaped too.

Outside, I could see the moon through the window. Full, round, silvery.

I turned toward Louis. He was staring at the moon too.

No need to tell you that no sooner had I caught my breath than I began to shake. If anyone squealed on me, if any stool pigeon noticed me, I was a goner. I'm on the blacklist, and if it ever got out that I was trying to indoctrinate a peace-loving citizen like Peppas ... I had no idea what happened to the Quartermaster; where was he, what became of him after the barbarian invasion ...

Next morning over breakfast Louis and I kept our mouths shut, and our heads down; I was terrified.

I tried dunking a lump of bread in my tea, but changed my mind. Nothing would go down.

Next to me Louis, as if nothing had ever happened, slurped away at his tea, dunking his bread and eating noisily, enjoying the meal.

It was a fine spring day. Sunshine, a bright-blue sky, no frost in sight. Just a bit of dew. You could see it everywhere. In the trees, the benches, the windows. But it wasn't cold.

— You got nothing to worry about. Did you do anything wrong? Nothing, he said abruptly, as if he had been reading my mind.

— Just a second, Manolis, I said. Can't you see? If the commander's office ever finds out about it ... Don't you realize what you and Peppas were saying last night? What you were singing? Know what? Guerilla songs, yet!

He smiled.

— ·Shut up. You only heard us singing one song, and dancing. And that's all you heard.

I was startled. No, more than that. For the first time I felt a small shudder of revulsion. "All a joke, is it? If that's how serious Louis is, then we're in big trouble." By coincidence, a couple of days earlier my reclassification had come through. From Class "C," for unreliable, I was upgraded to Class "B." I was getting closer and closer to "A," which is reserved for people who don't intend to overthrow anything, people who have made their peace with the regime.

Today, no big deal, you say. Anyway, nobody knows, and nobody cares. But there's no harm in knowing.

The camp commander, Kritsinis, summoned me to his office to give me the news.

— You're clean, Manolopoulos; you're off the blacklist. A year or two, put in a new application and you'll make "A" class, and your problems will be over.

Of course, I never applied for anything; didn't know a thing about it. It was all my mother's doing. Seems she paid a call on uncle Anestis. "If my boy is discharged with that kind of a classification, he's got no future. He can't get a job in the judicial system or the public service ..." Uncle Anestis, who knew the head of the Piraeus police department — they were hunting partners, took vacations together, hung out at the same café — said, "Bring me one of those applications, I'll fix it for him." And he did.

— Something on your mind, Manolopoulos? asked Kritsinis. You should be jumping for joy. Without your loyalty certificate, you know, you couldn't even get a job as a doorman! Let alone that court job you're dreaming about.

Me, I never dreamed of a job at court. That was my mother's dream. Not a lawyer either. She also dreamed about that. The lawyer's job.

— The head of the Piraeus police phoned me, asked me to look after you, said Kritsinis.

Truth to tell, trying to overthrow the system never occurred to me — it just wasn't one of the things I wanted to do — and I sure didn't want to die in poverty. I would have been delighted if somebody else overthrew it, not me.

But the commander's way of putting it didn't make me feel so great. In fact, the blacklist was comforting in a way, because when I got out of the army I wouldn't just not have a job, I wouldn't even have a hobby,

When I saw how casually Louis shrugged off the events at Peppas' place, I began to feel ill at ease. I thought: "That frivolous attitude of his is going to land us in hot water," and I told him so.

— Listen, Kostas, my boy, you're nothing but a bundle of nerves. Relax, let yourself go a little.

I had plenty to talk about: me getting off the blacklist, uncle Anestis, what the commandant said about the future, the chalk ... "There's a piece of chalk, Manolopoulos. Who holds it is unimportant. But whoever does, he has the power to mark out your limits. Within those limits, anything goes. Outside, everything is forbidden." This was the kind of garbage I was getting from the commandant. Only, when he came out with it he was so convincing I almost believed I could see the chalk lines drawn.

— I know all about it, Kostas, the Quartermaster told me the whole story. You did the right thing.

I gaped in amazement. He went on:

— Just watch out it doesn't go to your head. Start taking it seriously and you're out of luck. They'll make a little seamstress out of you.

Then I spotted Karandonis — the battalion stool pigeon — sitting there beside me eavesdropping, pretending to enjoy the spring morning.

— I never made an application for anything. It was mom, I whispered.

— You did the right thing, but like I say, don't take it too seriously, or you'll be at the mercy of stool pigeons like Karandonis.

He said the last few words in a loud voice. It worked. He —

Karandonis — threw down his cigaret, stomped on it in fact, stretched his arms, pretended to glance at his watch, and left.

Meantime, I was dying to ask Louis what became of Peppas and Haroula, what did he find out about Polyxeni, who killed Petros, did he knew her? That kind of thing. No luck.

A few moments later a corporal accompanied by a private came over and stopped in front of us.

— Come on, smart guy, the commander wants to see you; on your feet, march! Louis, a born aristocrat, sipped the last of his tea, picked up his cigarets and lighter, and stood up.

— Come on, you, get moving; this ain't no party we're inviting you to.

And the corporal gave him a push. Louis dropped his cigarets and lighter. He bent down to pick them up ...

— Leave it, you won't be needing that, said the private, and crushed them with the heel of his boot, laughing as he did.

I was about to protest. But the corporal shoved me back onto the bench.

— You, keep your mouth shut.

— Don't bother, Kostas, my boy, Louis chimed in. These are my men, here. We'll get this all straightened out.

He winked.

You can't dislike Louis, or even carry a grudge against him. He's not the kind of guy you pretend not to see when you pass.

As they walked away, with Louis between them, I wagered ''or my name isn't Manolopoulos'' that he'd have them eating out of his hand by the time they entered the commander's office.

I followed them until they turned at the canteen. Just before they turned, I saw the corporal pull out a pack of cigarets and offer him one, while the private pulled out his lighter and lit it.

When I got back to barracks that evening, Louis' bunk was empty. His kit was missing, so was his pack.

No one knew a thing. Not even the Quartermaster.

— He's not in the brig, that's for sure, he said.

— Transfer?

— Nope.

— Think they court-martialled him?

— No way. We'd have heard about it.

— Something worse? I ventured. What with all the suicides. Maybe they suicided him.

— Louis? You believe that? he said with a big smile.

Days and nights went by; not a word. Of course he could have been hiding out on purpose, just to whip up our curiosity.

The ninth night I was in the bathroom; it was bitter cold, the water was so cold it hurt to brush my teeth. Lights out hadn't sounded yet, and at that instant, just as I was bending over the sink to spit out the foam someone tapped me on the shoulder.

— Hey, smart guy, I've got a message for you.

I turn; who do I see but the corporal, the same corporal who escorted Louis to the commandant's office that day.

— Wipe off your mouth, it's still sudsy.

I wiped.

— Where is he? Nobody's seen him since you took him away.

He laughed, the turkey.

— Who's that? Retsinas? Haven't you heard? He's the commander's right-hand man. His odd-job specialist.

He chuckled as he talked. Grossly, stupidly. Finally, when the humor of the situation finally sunk in, I began to laugh too, just as grossly and stupidly.

— Here.

I took the note and read:

"Kostas, my boy, take a bath, put on your best cologne and head for the main gate. Give your name and you'll get a night's pass. There's a hotel called the Belle Vue down at the waterfront. You'll find me there. Bring money. Paradise does exist. You'll see."

Like I said, hang around Louis and your life no longer has a beginning or an end; nothing ever settles down, nothing ever stops moving, nothing ever comes to a conclusion. Years may have gone by since you last saw him, but you'll still be waiting for a sign from him, some news, even the wildest, the most improbable kind. I remember one time — I almost forgot the incident — late at night Drrinng! the telephone. Scared the shit out of me.

— Kostas, my boy, jot this down: 145 Kallergis Street, Piraeus. Got it? Come and see me. Now. And hung up.

Wild stuff, let me tell you. But I went. There was mud everywhere, garbage, deep puddles of dirty water.

Don't know ... maybe in some other society, a different kind of society, Louis would have ended up a bank executive, or a factory manager, or a high-level diplomat, a foreign minister, whatever; a big name, for sure.

What the hell was he calling at this hour for? I was thinking as I made my way along the unpaved street.

Back then, you had to be a doctor, a grocer or a police informer to have a telephone. Grocery stores were the neighborhood phone booths of the era. Thanks to the phone the grocer, or the doctor, were the most important persons on the block.

From the earliest hours you'd hear shouts of: "Calliope, your fiancé! Phone!" "Urania, your father! Phone!" "Catherine, your uncle!" And more.

Thanks to the phone we knew the intimate details of everybody's life: the divorces, the deaths and the crimes. Everything was out in the open, thanks to the phone.

There would be the grocery store at the corner, and you'd see the Calliopes, the Catherines and the Uranias hurrying for the phone.

Sometimes in their nighties, sometimes wearing dresses, hair uncombed or fancily permed.

What a sight! Nothing like it.

Whenever I heard "Urania, your father! Phone!" I dashed for the door.

And now, the star of the show: Urania would come running, hair, nightie, and housecoat flowing in the wind ... One time she even answered the phone wrapped in a bath towel.

As she rushed by you'd melt away at those endless legs of hers, that never-ending neck.

You'd crane your neck hoping the towel, or her dress, would flap open, giving you a glimpse of her leg above the knee, high up, or her breasts, since most of the time she never managed to do up all her buttons or fasten her belt.

I'm convinced that about half the studs on the street would masturbate thinking about Urania lying in her bed.

"Urania, your father! Phone!"

With the shout of "Urania," all hell broke loose. But only for a couple of seconds, until she came running out the door.

When she appeared, everyone came to a dead stop, whoever happened to be on the street at that moment. Passers-by, icemen, coal merchants, fruit sellers, fish mongers. Whoa! Everybody freeze! Like pillars of salt they waited for her.

On her way back she'd take her time, sashaying along, shaking and swaying. There she went, head bowed ever so slightly, as if there weren't a soul in sight, dress held tightly closed with two hands.

Life didn't resume until she closed the door behind her.

But for a few lingering moments you could smell her perfume in the air, the entire distance from the grocery to her house.

Smaragda, the grocer's wife, would foam with jealousy. She couldn't stand any other woman, Urania least of all.

— Now, Smaragda, be patient. Brings in the customers.

Louis knew Urania. Whenever the talk got around to our street and I'd mention her name, he'd smile mischievously.

But in spite of everything, none of us had ever managed to go out with her. She was our unfulfilled dream.

You couldn't get near her. Maybe she looked easy, but there wasn't a man in the neighborhood who could claim to have slept with her.

I guess it was that aura of the unknown that enveloped her

personal life that made us envy her, made us invent dozens, hundreds of rumors about her.

Our imaginations ran wild. She let in her lovers after midnight so no one would see a thing; that's when the orgy to end all orgies would begin. Or so we believed.

But we never heard anything, never saw anything, even though we watched her like hawks, spied on her. We tried to find out who the lover was, as though we were looking for the murderer in an unresolved killing.

The grocer swore her father was real. He could tell by the voice. Always the same voice. Hoarse, an old man's voice.

He never had a bad word to say. Not only about her, not about anybody. But his wife, that was another story.

In the end, we concluded that she didn't entertain her boyfriends in her home. More likely she went to their place. "Every phone call is a date," we said.

So fertile had our imaginations become that we ended up calling her "the Smyrna girl" among ourselves. And she wasn't even from Smyrna, as someone pointed out. But for us, it didn't matter. She was "the Smyrna girl."

Don't ask me why, but we believed the most desirable, sensual, provocative women came from Smyrna.

Our only shred of evidence, the only thing we had on her, was that she spent most of the day in the bathtub. That much we knew for a fact; our neighbor Mrs. Fofo's bathroom was right next to hers.

— Olga, Fofo would tell my mother, all she ever does is take baths all day long. Twice a day, you think it's a little? All you hear is the water running. Meanwhile, her husband works his hands to the bone on some freighter just to pay the water bills. Urania was married to a sailor, a deckhand. They rented a flat, got married, and two months later he signed on for the high seas.

We never saw him again. I did my military service, came back home, and still no sign of him. Later we moved, changed neighborhoods. I forgot Urania and her deckhand husband, until that night when Louis called.

60

— Every time you get mixed up with him, you get in trouble. You've got work in the morning. Stay where you are. Where do you think you're going? said mom.

I was out in the street by then, and she was still trying to convince me to stay home. It was December, icy rain was falling. I'd forgotten my gloves. The sky had a curious reddish cast.

— It's going to snow; button up! she shouted from the balcony.

By the time I found a taxi, the first flakes had begun to fall. The muddy puddles on the street had almost frozen.

My first thought, my first "aha!" came in the taxi, as I tried to warm my hands by blowing into them. I remembered that 145 wasn't Louis' address. Kallergis Street wasn't his street.

It was closer to my old place; would have been Urania's place.

My imagination took off at a gallop. So that's why Louis smiled so enigmatically when we were in the army. Suddenly everything snapped back to life. "Urania, your father! Phone!" and her dashing along in her housecoats — the fire-engine red ones, the bright-blue ones — or mincing along with little steps when the dresses were long and tight and held her legs back.

I lived three or four doors from her. I remember the day we moved; I was plastering a For Rent sign on our front door as she returned from a call. She stopped.

— Hello, she said.

— Hello, I said.

There was fear in her eyes.

— I wanted to ask you, perhaps you're thinking of selling your house? My husband wrote me, asked me to find a place somewhere in the neighborhood ...

— He's still at sea?

— Still. But he'll be back for Easter. He wanted to earn enough to buy us our own place, once and for all.

So that was it. 145 was Urania's place. The closer I got, the more certain I became. Slowly the neighborhood began to perk up. It had hardly changed at all.

The grocery store was still there on the corner. I could almost see the grocer, with that bald head and those beady eyes of his, coming to the door, putting his hands to his mouth and shouting, "Urania, your father! Phone!" Everything was the same, only a bit less well-kept. The houses needed painting, the plaster was cracked and falling, some were in ruins; most houses had metal doors now. The old wooden doors had been replaced. And now there were cars; lots of cars.

From a distance I could see people gathered in front of 145; Louis was there at the edge of the crowd, hands in pockets, pacing back and forth. He only had a jacket on. Had to be freezing. Still couldn't afford an overcoat!

He was waiting for me. Without a word he elbowed his way through the crowd clustered around the open door and went into the house. Just at that moment a photographer arrived. We let him go first, then followed him in close on his heels, down the hall and into the living room ...

— Who are you?... a policeman asked us.

— Reporters, said Louis. The cop left us alone.

We went into the bedroom. How many times had I dreamed of that bedroom! It was done in dark red, floor to ceiling. The blinds, the upholstery, the rug. On the wall, right above the bed, was an oil painting. Reminded me of an old poster, the kind you see at Apotso's ouzo joint, except this one was framed. It showed a plump woman, a popular model of the day, with a look of beatitude on her face, perched half-naked on a divan. Everything was pink! Stockings, cheeks, breasts. Pink! Underneath it was Urania's bed; a wide, massive bed in walnut. And on the bed, a blanket had been thrown over the two bodies, heads included.

At the other extremity a woman's foot was barely visible. The toenails were painted bright-red. Across the room, next to the dresser, was a brazier full of half-burned charcoal.

When he noticed the photographer, a man in civilian clothes picked up one corner of the blanket and lifted it with great care.

First appeared Urania lying face up, naked; next to her, just as naked, was the grocer. Face down. One of her legs lay beneath his leg. His hand still clutched her breast. His body half covered hers. His lips still touched her shoulders, and his other hand was still beneath her thigh, high up her thigh, as if still caressing her, as if still moving.

A perfect work of art, full of color, movement, perspective.

For a split second the flash froze it all.

— Carbon monoxide; it was carbon monoxide from the charcoal that did it; it was burning all night long. I heard them whispering.

That was when Smaragda, the grocer's wife, appeared. She had left for her mother's village in the mountains, but when the snow began to fall she turned back.

It was all the police could do to restrain her. She was cursing, yelling, howling. She was a squat, corpulent woman; must have weighed at least 200 pounds, as massive as he was short.

Then, at the height of the commotion, as they were trying to get her out of the house, the two of us remained alone in the room. I saw Louis, as if possessed, kneel down next to the bed, almost embracing her — can you believe it? — reach out and touch her skin. Then he bent over, ready to kiss her belly. I shuddered.

— Are you crazy? I said, and pulled him away.

We left. From the far end of the street we could still hear Smaragda howling.

We went to his place. A basement flat, more like a dank, melancholy crypt.

All night long we drank ouzo and waited for daybreak, when I left. From the next room, we could hear Louis' father coughing.

— Manolis, aren't you going to sleep? I heard him ask.

At dawn he threw his old army cloak over his shoulders; it had turned colder. He wrapped me in a blanket.

We recalled our army days, when we used to talk about Urania. Louis laughed. Even back then, he knew all about the grocer.

— I knew everything, cousin.

He'd tried a hundred times, but the answer was always no. For a long time she wouldn't go with anyone. Much later, it appears, she got involved with the grocer. Can you imagine?

Just think! There she was, a married woman, but the marriage proposals just kept pouring in. A lieutenant from two streets over, a good-looking, tall blond man. The pharmacist, a bachelor, was wild about her. Not to mention the greengrocer. "Is that sailor boy of yours here or isn't he? You call that life? Dump him."

Finally, believe it or not, she chose the grocer! You figure it out. Lukas was his name.

From that day on, whenever I saw Louis — believe me — there was no way I wouldn't remember Urania.

But we're getting away from our story. Let's get back to the main gate. Remember? I'm supposed to pick up an overnight pass.

The sentry gave me a hard time.

— Retsinas? Who's he? What leave you talking about? This is the army, buddy.

Now what? "One of Louis' jokes," I say to myself. Just as I'm about to turn back toward the barracks, I hear him say:

— Just a second. You say Manolopoulos? Here's your leave. Good luck.

And he hands it to me.

So there I am, walking down the main drag toward the beach in the direction of the Belle Vue and the old fears are awakening, the old hesitations. "What am I getting into this time, what does Louis have in store for me ..." and suchlike.

Me, I'm trying to overcome it, to get myself under control, "bone-head, always wasting your time trying to figure things out." That's what Louis would always say!

— Your mom really did a job on you, cousin. Brainwashed you but good. No way you'll loosen up. Could serve you pussy on a platter, still you won't unwind. Remember how she used to chase you with that long wooden spoon, "eat your dinner, don't fall down, don't get dirty, don't be late. Did you kiss your daddy's hand? Did you say thank you? Give your seat to the nice gentleman." Shit, what's the big deal?

Maybe he wasn't a psychologist or a psychiatrist, but he sure as hell knew me inside out.

— Worst of all, you've got a wild streak in you. Don't try and rub it out. Want to know something? You're crazier than me by a mile. If you let whoever's inside you free, you're off and flying, high and far.

I spotted him as I entered the Belle Vue Hotel — his back, that is — sitting on a couch in the lobby. There were two women with him, he was between them, their backs to me too.

I recognized one of them. It was Haroula. No doubt about it. I could tell by the hair. The other? Didn't know her. Light brown hair, the color of honey. My nerves again. "Stay or go?"

Back rushed the fears, the doubts. "What's he up to, the bastard? If Peppas finds out about this, nothing will save us ..."

I never finished my thought. Louis had spied me in the mirror.

He got to his feet. So did the two women. When they turned toward me and I saw their faces, I nearly fainted. Not at Haroula. It was the other woman. Nearly fainted, I tell you. My mouth gaped open, my eyes like saucers. "I'll kill him, it can't be; impossible!" It was Polyxeni! Just like in the photograph. Yes, sir! Those same capricious eyes, those lips, that mouth. But more beautiful. Polyxeni, one hundred percent!

She was wearing a black beret, a black overcoat, a black skirt and blouse — black from head to toe. Her face was pink, shiny. Like those German actresses from the pre-war movies. Marlene Dietrich maybe.

For an instant no one moved. It was as if a photographer was standing there while we waited for the click of the shutter before moving again.

Nothing could surprise me, right? I'd covered all the angles — everything but that! Polyxeni right there in front of me, standing beside Louis. That, I'd never thought of.

This kind of thing isn't supposed to happen, not even with black magic.

Louis left them standing there and came over to me, took my arm and guided me to a column covered with climbing vines that looked like dark green ivy.

— Don't act like such a hayseed, brother. Don't mess things up. I've made you out to be a big shot. Bring money?

— Yep. Whatever I had.

He took me over for the introductions.

— Just a second, what's going on?

— You'll see.

That's when I begin to ask myself what kind of a jerk Louis is. Makes friends with Peppas, and now he's screwing the guy's wife? Didn't he have any remorse, any sense of guilt? I told him so.

— No, brother, I'm not the rat you think. I don't want you to get the wrong idea. That was no great love I destroyed. All I did was walk into a wasteland; it was barren to start with. I couldn't bear the sight; everything was dry, crying for water. I took nothing from Peppas, didn't slander him to Haroula, didn't undercut him. I like Peppas but — what can you do? — for Haroula he didn't exist, he was already long gone.

Haroula came over and stretched out her hand.

— How do you do?

She looked me in the eye for a split second, then lowered her gaze. When I touched her hand, I felt the same warmth I'd felt then flooding through my whole body.

I remembered the mirror, her back, that cry of hers, "When I come, it's like I hear bells ringing."

Polyxeni did not extend her hand. Both her hands were in her pockets.

— Pleased to meet you, she said, looking at me.

At the little taverna, while the two of them went off to the toilet, Louis leaned over and hissed angrily.

— Don't be a turkey, cousin.

I cut him off.

— Manolis, you're plain nuts. You want a killing or two, and a stay in the brig? OK, whatever happened, happened, but ...

He didn't let me finish.

— Cousin, I've told you before, forget the intellectual stuff, forget your complexes. I've reserved two rooms, side by side.

I didn't let him go on:

— Get ahold of yourself. We're in big trouble. First with Peppas, then Fotis, her husband. If somebody spots the two of them here ...

He was shaking his head. I stopped.

— Peppas? Fotis? He's already gone to meet his maker. You didn't notice she was wearing black? You blind? Peppas? He's in the slammer, in Corinth.

Once again my mouth gaped open. Louis reached over and covered it with his hand. One surprise after another.

Then, talking fast, he brought me up to date.

— A few minutes after the goons trashed his place that night the gendarmes came. They arrested Haroula and Peppas. Her they released, not him. When Peppas finally realized the bandits didn't kill his brother, that it was Fotis' men, Fotis himself, his character went through a quick series of

67

changes. First he was the anarchist, then the maniac — pure-bred loony, no shit. Incredible. You should have seen him. He had Polyxeni on her knees in her basement. "Tell the truth or I'll kill you," he said; he had his shotgun pointed at her head but she kept swearing that she didn't know anything, that she believed to this day the bandits killed her Petros, his brother. Upstairs, Demenagas was breathing his last. He'd just suffered his fourth consecutive stroke. And downstairs, Peppas was playing out that tear-jerker of his. If I hadn't been there to hold him back, he'd have killed her for sure. She owes me her life. That's why I'm telling you, numskull; sleeping with her is the least of it. That's the only thing she'll never regret.

I was listening but I couldn't believe my ears. Especially when he came to the description of Peppas' mourning, to the third phase of his ideological collapse, just before the metamorphosis, complete with saliva running down his chin, blubbering, weeping, banging his fist on the table of the taverna, when he said:

— Me, Louis, deep down, from way back, I was really always with the other guys. Deep down I never believed they killed my brother; maybe I didn't say it — it wasn't a good idea to talk too much — but it didn't take too much brains to figure things out. He never turned against them, my brother; never said a bad word against them. He was even halfway in the resistance, and ... And then, when the Civil War came, he backed off, but he never ... Why would they kill him? I kept asking myself ...

So there you had Peppas drinking himself into a stupor, falling apart ...

That was when he took one of a whole series of decisions. First of all, no way the murderer can go on living when his brother is dead. That was all there was to it. "Andonis, calm down, you're drunk," Haroula said. "Mind your own business." And he wasn't going to belong to the party of his brother's killers. "No way," he said.

— His ideological metamorphosis was complete, and we end

68

up at Fotis Demenagas' place. Peppas storms in, dead drunk, drags Polyxeni out by the hair, and when Demenagas tries to get up he gets his fifth stroke, from fright. When we get back upstairs to see how he's doing, he's already half dead. Peppas sits down and waits. "Nobody moves," he says. Demenagas begs him to call a doctor, and Peppas just sits there, saying "Don't move or I'll kill you." Wild, I'm telling you. "Either he croaks on his own or I'll kill him. He ain't getting out of here alive." Demenagas' death agony lasts twenty minutes.

Louis and Polyxeni were standing in one corner. Silent, motionless, petrified. Louis afraid for his life. The only sound was Fotis' death rattle. In a few minutes, a dog came and began scratching at the door. It was Fotis' dog.

— Peppas gets up, opens the door, gives the dog a kick, and closes it again. Then he yanks the curtains closed and sits down again.

Polyxeni didn't know what to do. She stood there expressionless. But there was a gleam deep in her eyes. You could only have spotted it with a microscope, or by intuition. Meanwhile, Louis was at a loss.

— Cousin, I couldn't tell whether the whole thing was a movie, or whether it was for real. When Demenagas lifts his head for the last time, props himself up on his elbows, Polyxeni grabs me by the hand. I looked at her, she looked at me. She knows if Demenagas survives, if he lives through it, her life will be hell. When he raises himself up and orders her, "Call the doctor, you whore!" she turns her back on him and falls into my arms. She's shaking; maybe, unexpectedly, he's going to pull through. Her fingernails are almost piercing my hands. Demenagas tries to get up, to get some pills from his dresser, but Peppas jumps to his feet and sweeps them onto the floor. Fotis lets out one last "slut!" and falls back onto the bed.

So graphically did he describe Demenagas' death scene that I felt my heart tighten in pain.

Only Louis had the guts to call the doctor, to try and save the situation. Demenagas had a phone. "Doctor, Demenagas is dying. Hurry!"

When the doctor arrived, he found the man stone cold and motionless.

Louis opened the door and told him the story.

It was obvious that no one felt any sorrow. All the doctor had to do was look around, and he would have found relief on their faces, not sadness.

From that day on, whenever Louis told his most colorful stories or tried to put a political twist to his life, this was his most heroic tale. He was there when the wretch was killed.

— You, I said when he'd finished. Haven't you ever had enough? In a month, we're out; what are you trying to do? You want them to lock us up and throw the key away?

Fat chance he'd listen. He was all eyes for Polyxeni.

— Brother, I'm a goner. That's no ordinary woman. Wherever you touch her, you get burned. One night together, and I'll let you know.

At dawn, when the heavy trucks began roaring by along the waterfront outside the Belle Vue, I awoke.

It was six o'clock sharp; wake-up call was at six thirty. No time to lose.

Carefully I slid my legs out from under the covers; I wanted to get up without awakening Haroula.

One of her legs, from the knee on down, was uncovered. She was fast asleep.

I got dressed, picked up my cloak, put on my beret and opened the door. Before closing it I took a last look at Haroula. She appeared to have half-awakened from the sound, but her eyes were still closed. She smiled, then rolled over to face the wall.

When she did her back showed, her buttocks, and the backs of her knees.

I had a curious feeling, a vague queasiness. Her plumpness,

70

now that it lay still, had turned to lifeless flab; suddenly the attractiveness was gone, the lightness movement lent it.

We had forgotten to close the shutters, and in the morning light her body no longer had the magical air it had in the half-light of the room at night; it had become almost threatening.

I closed the door with a feeling of dismay. I felt as though I'd gorged myself on spoiled, rotten food.

I hurried downstairs, and as I was paying for my room, I saw Louis standing there with his hands in his pockets, hopping up and down to warm up his feet.

— So? I asked him.

— Wouldn't let me touch her. Cried all night; I rocked her to sleep, like an asshole. You?

We left. Barely had time to make roll call.

3. THE SEDUCER

I COULD GO ON FOR HOURS; the Louis stories are endless. Never-ending, literally. The people he encounters in his life, and the people who encounter him, they keep running into each other, over and over again.

Louis has a hard time putting an end to anything, but then again, anyone who knows him will have just as hard a time. Can't forget him; most of all, you can't hate him. He'll do his worst and still you'll forgive him. There's a reason behind everything he does; you just have to look at it from the proper angle, then you can accept it, understand why. That's the only way I can explain why I worship the guy. No, not exactly worship. Not only that. Not just admiration. Admiration plus astonishment. Admiration, astonishment and a pinch of jealousy. Maybe. I can't quite find the right words. At any rate, the man sends out uncanny signals. Casts a kind of spell on the people around him.

Say I'm trying to convince someone how wonderful life can be, and I'm rummaging around for arguments; well, I'll start telling Louis stories, stories like the one I'm telling you now. But when I want to warn someone about the slippery slope of life, I always seem to end up talking about Louis too.

He's my example; my negative example too. The kind of guy who leaves a trail of devastation behind him. I guess deadly would be the best word. Maybe that's why some of my friends got burned when they met him. In fact, burned fingers and heartache was all they got, not to put too fine a point on it.

Take the Quartermaster; like me, he was Louis' army bud-

72

dy. From bad to worse he went. Dropped out of university —
he was in med school — left his father's grocery store, abandoned his four-months pregnant wife, and ended up slinging
beer in some Munich brew house, living with a forty-year-old
ex-streetwalker.

Peppas turned into an unrepentant Communist. From the
day they locked him up in the slammer at Corinth, and stuck
him with Demenagas' murder, he never got out. Died behind
bars.

Don't let me get started about Kritsinis, our deputy commander at Corinth boot camp. Instead of bundling Louis
straight off to court martial — remember when he sent for
him? — he ends up keeping him on as his aide-de-camp. Well,
from that moment on, the poor man suffered every possible
calamity you could imagine.

It all began with their first meeting when he tried the chalk
argument on Louis . You know, the invisible hand that holds
the chalk ... That crap.

— You can take your chalk and stuff it up your ass, general,
Louis broke in.

He wasn't even a general. Just a major. Not even that. He
was a reserve major.

When he heard that, Kritsinis froze. One hand remained
there, above his head, finger pointing. His eyes wide and his
mouth open, motionless. He never expected Louis to respond
in quite that way. But Louis took fright when he saw the officer's reaction; maybe something was wrong; if the guy
croaks they'll send him up for premeditated murder. He even
considered making a break for it. But when he saw that the
man's lower lip began to quiver, he relaxed.

Finally, Kritsinis gasped:

— Wh ... wh ... what did you say?

His voice, his bearing, his self-importance had vanished.

— I said, general, that chalk of yours, you can take it and stuff it. Me, personally, I spend sixty percent of my time outside that chalk circle of yours.

Then Kritsinis fainted. First he turned crimson, puffed up and went crimson, face bright as a poppy in full bloom, then fainted. Before he fell, he croaked in a high voice:

— Don't call me general, I'm not a gen ...

At the "gen ..." he hit the floor.

At that instant began Kritsinis' descent; or rather, his ruin.

It's hard to describe his metamorphoses individually, to chart the stages he passed through before reaching the ultimate depths.

When, one night at Haroula's taverna, he announced for the first time, "What do I care about these soldier boys?" his ruin was already consummated. Nothing remained but the official communiqué.

Louis' first step was to transform him into a poet. I'm not sure if he did it to amuse himself or because down deep he didn't think all that much of the military. But he kept pushing Kritsinis to write poetry. "Major, one of these days you're going to have to write a poem; every day you rhyme off these little diamonds in the rough."

Of course, the poetry idea didn't just spring fully-formed from his forehead. He picked up on something the major half-said — "When I was a little boy I wanted to be an artist, and look at me now, in the army" — and made an idea of it. He worked on it, fine-tuned it deep inside himself, and finally brought it out, into the light of day.

They'd get roaring drunk at Peppas' place. Drinking binges like you can't imagine. The major would launch into one of his lyrical transports about his childhood, about a certain first cousin of his — more on him later — and Louis would interrupt him with "Major, you've got to write poetry" and at that precise moment Kritsinis, gesticulating and drooling, would shout out the old refrain: "What do I care about these soldier boys?"

One evening, when he gave Louis his nightly pass, he handed him a sheaf of poems.

— How did you like them? he asked later.

— Major, they're little masterpieces. We'll publish the next batch as a book.

From that day on Kritsinis attended drills and roll calls with growing infrequency. He'd lock himself up in his office, in his room, in the mess hall, even in the latrines, and compose poetry.

Dark clouds began to gather when a certain colonel Papatheodorou made an unannounced inspection; actually, now that I think of it, someone with an eye on Kritsinis' position probably tipped him off.

Kritsinis wasn't in his office; instead, they discovered him declaiming poetry in the officers' head.

When the colonel arrived on the scene, he encountered a bizarre — a mind-boggling — spectacle. It was the only officers' facility in the entire administration building; outside the door, he collided with a reserve lieutenant waiting in the corridor. The man wasn't exactly standing at attention either. In fact, his hands were stuffed in his pockets, clutching his genitals and he was pacing to and fro in a sweat, bent over almost double, doing everything he could to hold back his latrineal obligations, since he was too embarrassed to let Kritsinis know he was waiting outside.

— You can imagine, cousin; our colonel was stupefied, as they say. What does he see? Inside, Kritsinis reading his own poems in that high sing-song voice of his, and outside, the lieutenant is about to piss in his pants.

Kritsinis liked the acoustics of the place; as soon as the battalion marched off on manoeuvres, he would rush off to the head. But this time they caught him; he hadn't realized the lieutenant was waiting outside.

75

The scene turned even more tragicomic when the lieutenant, suddenly confronted by a full colonel, tried to snap to attention and salute. But despite his spasmodic attempts, it was impossible.

Finally, he gave up and let loose. As he saluted, the piss poured down his pant leg. Louis appeared at that instant.

— Cousin, I've never seen a happier man in my life.

The poet within the deputy commander was not all Louis uncovered. He also unearthed the man's repressed homosexuality.

Louis had already put his finger on the role the major's first cousin had played in his life.

In one agonizing night of confession, he contrived to make the major, as only Louis could, relate his first erotic experience with that fateful cousin. From that day on — Kritsinis swore — he'd never slept with anyone, man or woman. "Emmanuel Retsinas, do you believe me?" he asked, again and again. "I believe you," Louis answered. "I've done everything I can to blot out that frigging memory. Three times I've tried with women. Three times nothing."

Louis — by now he'd begun to like the man — told him: "You swear to God, major, past forty and you never ..." "You don't believe me?" "Sure I believe you, but if it's like you say, then you're losing the sweetest thing in the world; man or woman, makes no difference. All a matter of taste. It's yourself you've got to answer to."

The scene I'm describing took place at Louis' house, in Piraeus, in that moldy basement apartment of his. That's how close they'd become. From the next room, his father heard the ranting and raving all night long — sleep? forget it! The two of them tossed down glass after glass, with tidbits of spicy sausages and broiled liver — the major brought that — while

76

they talked about his cousin's prick.

By daybreak, Louis had reconciled Kritsinis so completely with himself and with his passion that the major suddenly became a human being again. Found peace. "Look, cousin" — now he was calling Kritsinis cousin — "that's why I told you to go stuff your chalk. If you don't cross the line, you're not living, and I want you to know it."

So when Louis' sister comes home from work that morning — she's a nurse at Piraeus Hospital — she finds them sound asleep. Kritsinis in full uniform in her bed, Louis in his own.

She nearly breaks into tears. But she holds back. She thinks the world of Louis, but enough is enough. No more of the ragtag and the bobtail sleeping in her bed. Cheap whores, poets, down-and-outers, whoever Louis dragged in, he'd let them crash in her bed. Only thing missing was army officers. Now she was looking at that too.

— Patience! she hears, and sees her father standing behind her.

— I won't stand for it. I've had it. It's time for work, get him out of here. I want my bed, my home; he can get the hell out of here.

On and on she goes. Then she switches on the gas burner to brew up some coffee; tries to calm down.

— I'm sick of you and that son of yours; I'm getting out. Out!

Then she takes a chair and sits down opposite Louis. His bed was in the kitchen, next to the sink.

The father tries to say something. She cuts him off.

— I pay the rent and the light and the water bills around here. The hell with both of you.

Antigone, her name was. She sits down across from Louis and waits for him to wake up.

— Admit it, you bastard. You did it with the major, didn't you? I asked him, when he told me the story the next day.

— Not me, Kostas, my boy; not me. I didn't touch him. He wanted me, he loved me, he said, but I didn't do a thing. Whatever happened, he did it all by himself.

And he tells me the whole incredible tale. The major was telling his life story ... he was from an army family but after the incident with the cousin he wanted to become a ballet dancer; when his parents heard that they shipped him off to military academy, and when he graduated they all but forced him to marry a certain Eleni who left him five months later; he tried to control his impulses with military discipline, but he couldn't get the near-rape by his cousin out of his mind, and so on and so forth ... And as he tells Louis all this, late at night, with Louis' father in the next room, who probably doesn't hear the whole story — probably he fell asleep — the major kneels down on the cold concrete floor and lays his head on Louis' lap, tenderly, like a woman. Then, dead drunk, and finally reconciled with his passion, entirely naturally and spontaneously, he begins to unbutton Louis' fly.

— Kostas, my boy, I've never been in a tougher situation. I hear they can get real nasty if you get 'em upset; I didn't know what to do, honest to God. So I let him go ahead. He unbuttoned my pants, pulled out my cock ... I wasn't wild about it, I swear. For a long time it was limp as a dishrag, like a stalk of wilted celery, I tell you. I was imagining what it would be like to finish my military service with Kritsinis against me; then too, I was ashamed to say no. So I let him do it. I didn't budge. It all began and ended there. For an instant, cousin, I thought — I'm not sure — my old man opened the door a crack. He was awake by then, for sure. I got a scare. I don't know what he saw, if he knew what was going on. Most likely he didn't.

But my sister, Antigone, she had it all figured out, even though she didn't see a thing. From the way the major spoke, the way he walked, the way he held his coffee cup, mostly that

78

— she's got one hell of a sixth sense — she figured out everything.

Meantime I'd arrived. My place was close by, like I said. At daybreak, time for the first bus for camp, I went over. Why, I don't know.

I see Antigone pulling her brother aside in the direction of the old man's room. She doesn't say a word. Just spits on him. I try to talk to her, to be nice to her. I still don't know what happened, I didn't see the major.

And she, as soon as she sees me, she falls in desperation into my arms and begins to sob.

— Why don't you do something to help him; you're his friend aren't you? Tell him! Don't let him do this to himself.

His sister was almost beautiful. I didn't run into her all that often but, yes, she was beautiful.

After that, I always wanted to kiss her eyes when I met her. There was a bitterness there, a sadness. It was as though there was a tear hanging in the corner of each eye, a tear waiting to drop; but it never did.

— Antigone, listen ... don't ... It's all very simple. You can't take everything Louis does seriously. He knows what he's doing. Trust him, I tell her.

Then I realize I'm holding her in my arms, that she's crying. I stop. Don't try to go on. Only caress her hair.

Suddenly she stops crying, raises her head, and with a quick motion leans back slightly and looks at me. A look filled with searching, fear and dreams.

I don't know what to think. I swallow hard, and hold my hand still against her hair.

It's all I can do to look back, even deeper into her eyes. I never could understand why I, Kostas Manolopoulos, never fell in love with Antigone. Never.

— Come on, Kostas, my boy. Let's go. The major's jeep is here. He'll give us a lift.

I climb back up to the street from the basement.

— Don't you ever come back here again! You hear? she shouted after her brother as we pulled away.

79

And I'm still looking into her eyes. Louis let out a deep sigh; a very deep sigh, and pulls out a pack of cigarets.

Ten days later, Papagos formed a government. Twenty days later, the major's reign came to an end.

Six o'clock one morning, a half-hour before wake-up call, two sergeants broke down the doors of the administration building head. Inside they found Kritsinis kneeling on a half-torn blanket, his pants down; the chief camp cook behind him. He hadn't even bothered to take off his officer's cap.

— Don't move! they shouted, pistols drawn.

When they recognized the deputy commander, they didn't know what to do. They tried to back out, to apologize, to close the door, but it was too late. Soldiers had begun to rush over from their latrines. First and foremost, Louis and I.

We were speechless, to a man.

What exactly happened inside Kritsinis at that instant I'll never know, but on the outside he acted as if we weren't even there, as if he didn't even see us.

He was calm, distant and other-worldly. Slowly he got to his feet, pulled up his pants, buttoned them, tightened his tie and moved toward the door.

For a brief instant he became flustered when he couldn't find his glasses. Then Louis stepped forward, pushed us aside, picked them up from the floor and handed them to him.

— Thank you, he said and strode out, the perfect gentleman.

We stepped back to let him pass, and he swept by us as though he had just received a decoration and we were the honor guard. Only the band and the martial music were missing. He exited the building, strode through the main gate onto the road and vanished.

No one ever saw him again. No one except Louis.

4. THE WHOREHOUSE

BACK THEN, after we were discharged, there would be a red alert at my place every time Louis showed up.

No one wanted him around, mother least of all. Sure, in his presence she put on her meekness and servility act, but no sooner was he out the door than:

— You watch out for him. He's bad company, that man. No proper household in the neighborhood even lets him get a foot in the door. They're always calling him to the precinct house, him and that father of his. Now that your papers are in order, don't you go messing 'em up again. Uncle Anestis is really upset with you. And it's all his fault.

Brainwashing, pure and simple — against Retsinas. For her, he was degenerate and parasite rolled into one.

Only later, when word got around that Louis was getting married, did his stock begin to go up in mother's eyes.

— Maybe now he'll straighten out.

Marriage is good for you. Just like regular exercise, according to mom.

— Put's you on God's path; settles you down.

And when she heard the dowry was a one-third share in the Krugas family's bakery, she even began to butter him up.

She invited him over for dinner; the frown disappeared from her face; her voice turned sugary:

— You should be so lucky. She's a lovely girl, the dowry's good, and the family's got good government connections.

It was true. Suddenly Louis had acquired new-found prestige and recognition in the neighborhood.

— Mom, lay off, I said.

But my father wasn't quite so impressed with the forthcoming marriage.

— Your friend always played the independent type, but when it comes to looking out for number one, they're all the same.

Louis' wedding — now there's a tale. I can still remember that frightful afternoon in the courtyard of Saint Sophia's church in Piraeus.

August it was; seemed like the whole world was on fire — make it a blast furnace — and there we stood, waiting for him to make his appearance. But the no-good sonofabitch, he was nowhere in sight. Instead of the groom waiting for the bride, there stood the bride waiting for the groom.

I can still see her waiting, standing there in her wedding gown on the church steps. It was a long gown, high-necked, with a train and veils and long sleeves right down to her finger tips.

"The gown's too long," the guests were whispering.

You had to feel sorry for her. The sun was beating down, broiling us. You wanted to curse the hour and the day that brought you there.

— Retsinas, now you did it. Dragged us out here for nothing, I whispered to Agis.

— I don't believe it, Manolopoulos; I don't believe he's really going to go through with it, he muttered over and over.

We were just the two of us from our gang; Agis and me.

The only one not cursing was the bride. Even though the groom was more than fifteen minutes late; even though the sweat was starting to pour off her.

Not that she wasn't concerned, but a little voice inside her would have been reassuring her, "her Manolis" would appear, and that gave her patience. How much longer, though? Now the sweat was oozing from every pore of her body. Her forehead, her throat, her ears, her nose; sweat everywhere, sweeping away everything in its path, make-up, eye-shadow, lipstick. Her armpits? Don't ask. When she lifted her arm to adjust a wayward curl of hair, everybody could see the sweat-soaked chasm gaping underneath.

By the end of the second fifteen minutes, a kind of generalized, undifferentiated irritation began to set in.

But none of the guests dared displease the Krugases.

Eugenia — that was the bride's name — remained calm and collected in spite of it. And good-looking too. Even though the gown fitted her like a tent — literally — even though her ass almost touched the ground, she was a good-looking broad. Problem was that the sweat made that low-slung ass of hers stand out, and how. By now she was completely drenched; you could read her like a cheap road map, particularly that one spot protruding provocatively, revoltingly. The two sweat-soaked hemispheres were clearly outlined while the slit between them stayed dry.

But it was this slit that turned Retsinas into the Krugas family's would-be son-in-law. Forget what mom said about the bakery. All he wanted from Eugenia was that slit of hers. Not her eyes, attractive as they were; not her breasts, which were not to be sniffed at, not even her pink legs, the kind he liked. He only wanted one thing from Eugenia, that slit. It was the first thing he saw when they met. First the slit, then the girl.

I can see her to this day, lying face down at the beach near the Seashell Club, wearing a swimsuit that looked ten sizes too small, just the opposite of the bridal gown, which was ten sizes too big. Both — the swimsuit and the gown — were from a bridal rental shop.

Retsinas could hardly contain himself when he spotted her.

— Get a load of that ass, will you! he said.

He wasn't far off the mark. I don't know what was to blame. The way she was lying? The tight swimsuit? The way it had worked itself down into the slit? Whatever the answer, Louis couldn't contain himself. We were lying down not far from her, and I could see his prick puffing up inside his gym shorts. He didn't wear a swimsuit; didn't have one. They looked like a cross between underpants and normal shorts. Blue.

But she was not alone. Her brother was with her. Krugas.

Eugenia never went out alone. Not to the beach, not on the street, not to parties. Nowhere.

Personally escorted by her never-leave-home-withouts. Wherever. Mother, father, or one of her two brothers kept her constant company.

— I've seen that guy somewhere before, Louis kept hissing.

He was probing for an approach, circling for an opening.

— I know him from somewhere, I know him from somewhere. Suddenly it came to him. The Krugas bakery, he exclaimed.

They almost overheard.

That was it alright. The family bakery was just a few blocks over from where we lived. Knew him from there. Aristos, that was the guy's name.

Within five minutes Louis struck up a conversation with him. Within ten minutes he knew everything. He simply made Aristos cough it up. Name, job, address, telephone number, politics — that last thing we knew plenty about already.

— You want anything, just come and see me. I'll fix it. The police are my people, the government, the goon squads too, he boasted with a coarse guffaw.

That was another of Louis' terrifying abilities. He could win you over, make you trust him and then make you cough up everything: the things you could say, and the things you couldn't.

Try getting information out of him, though; his home, his work, his spare time — all off limits. But he could make you sing like a bird.

I mean — listen to this! — a few moments later we're standing them an ouzo at the "Romantic," the bar near the yacht harbor, and he manipulates Aristos into confessing his great life melodrama, that he's fucking Olympia, his brother's wife. Eugenia is in the ladies' room washing her hands at the time. He gives a deep sigh, and pulls the hot loaf out of the oven:

— Me, old pal, I'm hiding a terrible secret here, inside, and pointed to his heart.

When we met for the first time, there in front of the Seashell Club, Eugenia played it blasé. Wouldn't even look at us, lying there motionless, face down, which whetted Louis' appetite all the more. From close up though, you could see those two hills — and then some! — rising from the plain of her back. It was all he could do to speak. His mouth had gone dry, his lips were cracking. An incipient basket case.

When she finally does us the favor of rolling over on her back to greet us with a demure little "pleased to meet you," we're just about bowled over, believe me. Suddenly we get a load of those knockers of hers, those eyelashes. Move over, Sophia Loren. Not to mention that mouth, those lips. "Check out the hot buns from Krugas' bakery," we said later. Lousy pun.

We could hardly believe our eyes. If you knew her parents, her brothers, then you'd see why. Her old man and old lady? Pure-bred sea lions. Bellies like beer barrels; arms like heavyweight boxers' gone to flab. But her brothers, they were tall and skinny as storks. Nature gone nuts. What could a living doll like Eugenia possibly have in common with a ragtag bunch like that?

Meanwhile, getting back to our story, the wedding is still on hold.

The second quarter-hour has elapsed and the groom is still nowhere to be seen.

Things are starting to look grim. I feel a pang of fear. Was I the reason Retsinas was standing up the bride? You see, I'm the only person there who knows him. The bastard, he'd managed to convince them that he was an orphan, with no family, no brothers and sisters, no close relatives ... Agis they didn't know from Adam.

Finally, after an hour of heroic waiting, people are beginning to slip away quietly, one by one.

But before total and utter humiliation for Eugenia in particular, and for the Krugas clan in general, we see her brothers pick her up bodily by the elbows and load her into a rented taxi waiting in the street. They're almost frothing at the mouth as they rip the white ribbons from the hood and tear the white flowers from the windshield wipers ...

— We're saved, I whisper to Agis. They're leaving ...

I hadn't finished the sentence when I spot her brother, Aristos, coming toward us in a rage, like a walking telephone pole, the turkey.

He pauses for an instant in the church-yard among the guests who are filing out as politely as they can all the while, looks around, spots me, and heads in my direction. He grabs me by the collar, waggles me back and forth, saying:

— You tell that fairy pal of yours to start digging his grave, got it? Either he marries her or he's a dead man. Next Sunday, same time, same place. Got it?

And turns away.

We break into a cold sweat. It may have been a scorcher but the sweat is pouring off us like ice water.

86

But he hadn't left. Wrong. He takes three steps, stops, turns around. Now his brother, is with him; his brother the cuckold.

Meantime, the taxi driver is getting impatient. He begins to beep his horn TOO TOO TOO ...

He grabs me by the collar. Again.

— Talk! Where's his house? Street, number, district. Spit it out.

One brother's got ahold of Agis, the other, me. Only a few people are left, most of them family and close friends. Help? Not a hope in hell. Over there are the parents and the best man. Ah, and the other brother's wife — I'd forgotten her — Olympia, the one Aristos, "I've got this terrible secret here, inside," is fucking. A living nightmare. Tall, stout, ugly.

— How should I know where he lives, I answer.

Before I can finish, he picks me up by the lapels like I was a feather.

— Forget the funny stuff, talk!

I pretend not to know what he's talking about.

— Honest to God, I only know the guy from the army. How should I know where he lives; he never told me. Agis, you know here he lives? I ask, trying to pass the ball to Agis.

— Talk, you motherfucker and leave your pal out of this. You think maybe I'm kidding? You'll be counting your teeth in a minute. Talk!

The taxi is tooting TOO TOO TOO ... When I hear "teeth" and see my lapels starting to rip ...

— I swear, I don't ...

I make one last effort to wriggle off the hook, but he doesn't let me finish.

A stinging slap on the face brings me back to the real world.

I'd like to see how long you last before you squeal on your friends. I had to choose. I could leave there minus teeth, with a concussion and God knows what else, or I could sell him out. So I sold him out. Crossed the "t's" and dotted the "i's," if you must know. Gave 'em the street, the address, the district, the works. Mine too. I spat it all out, right there in front of Agis. Gave 'em everything they wanted and a lot they didn't.

87

Chapter and verse, I gave 'em. Then they dumped me like a dirty dishrag and stomped off.

As Agis and I headed home, I felt heartsick and humiliated.

Hadn't I warned the sonofabitch in the first place? When he was pursuing her, wasn't she always giving him the "I'm scared" or the "I don't know who you are" or the "my brothers will kill me" line?

— Dump her, she's nothing but trouble, I said.

You think he'd listen? Louis?

That was one of his minor defects, those *idées fixes* of his. Spartan style. With your shield or on it. That's the way he lived his life.

Once he had an idea, he couldn't get it out of his mind; had to carry it to its logical conclusion. A stubborn man; Lenin all over again. Gets it into his head to turn Russians into Communists, and then goes ahead and does it. Couldn't have lived if he hadn't brought it off. The muzhiks and the proletarians and the socialist revolutionaries, probably they could have gotten by quite nicely without a revolution. Not him.

— Unless of course you're ready for marriage. Otherwise, don't mess with the Krugases. Secret police goons like you couldn't believe; they carry concealed weapons, you know.

Me and Agis, we gave him the lowdown; sounded the alarm, so to speak.

— Marriage it'll be, if it comes to that, he told us.

He didn't know what he was talking about. He was almost unemployed. Now and then he'd get in a few hours' work counting frozen Argentinian beef carcasses at the Piraeus cold-storage warehouse, and he's talking about marriage! You figure it out.

Of course, those of us who knew him never doubted he'd dump her in the end.

Rare was the woman Louis didn't end up dumping. But the problem was, what then? The Krugas family wasn't joking. They were killers.

As you see, everything developed with lightning rapidity. Maybe two weeks after their first meeting, one Tuesday noon, Eugenia let him kiss her. Naturally, she fell for him. When you've had a strict upbringing, never been with a man before, and when the first man to kiss you happens to be Emmanuel Retsinas ... Well, don't even ask. You fall for him; you give him everything.

For a whole week, until their meeting the following Tuesday, Louis' kiss burned on her cheek. Set her aflame. And planted the seeds of disaster for the both of them.

Notice I said "next Tuesday" because it was the only day — flour delivery day — that the whole family was away from the house.

Louis had the Tuesday routine figured out early on. It was there at the Seashell Club in fact; he told the brothers: "I'll drop by for a chat one of these days." And one of them piped up: "Any time you like, except Tuesday; that's flour delivery day."

Naturally, he went on a Tuesday. The second Tuesday was even more earthshaking for Eugenia. Along with her soul, she surrendered her body. Now she was his.

Having her wasn't enough for him; he wanted total possession, so back he came the Tuesday after that.

We tried to restrain him: "Watch yourself; what if one of them breaks a leg on Tuesday and misses the flour?" What if? But the possibility of trouble, the thought of encountering those goons, didn't faze him.

We tried to run down the object of his affections; maybe that would turn him around.

— OK, Retsinas, she's got an amazing ass, but how far can you go with an ass? She's completely inexperienced. Leave her be; dump her. Don't make such a big thing out of it; don't get involved.

89

But he insisted. And got his way. The very next Tuesday; not the Tuesday after next.

It was at Tassos' coffeehouse that he described her final and total surrender. We were stunned.

As he talked we could feel the blood rushing to our heads. The three of us had a hard-on.

Just as we were we made a bee-line for the whorehouse, the one at the end of the street, next to the sheet metal yard. The three of us with the same girl. Standing up. She couldn't believe it. First Louis, then me, then Agis, who picked up some crabs in the bargain.

Louis paid the shot. With a thousand-drachma note: his pay for three days' work at the frozen meat warehouse. There was nothing left over. What are friends for, right?

So there's old Tassos serving one round of ouzo after another while Retsinas describes the scene for us in the minutest detail, like fine embroidery.

— It can't be, we said. Can't be.

— Guys, the secret is not to rush a woman. What you want is what she wants, after all. Tenderness is what she wants. Soft movements, feather touches. First, you get her ready. Don't just go roaring in. Do that and she won't enjoy herself and neither will you. After, though, she'll be ready to give you everything. You can make her scream, or not feel a thing. You can bite her nipples and draw blood and she'll let you. You can whip her and she'll just sit there. But first you've got to find out her rhythm, her pace. It's like a play, like putting on a play. The first act, the second, the third, and so on and so forth. Right up till the curtain, you've got to have plot, action, surprises.

We sit there listening, our mouths agape. Even old Tassos caught a bit; he was hanging over us, motionless.

— Didn't it hurt her? asked Agis.

— Painless the first time? No way. But the pain feels good.
Old Tassos tiptoes away at this point, embarrassed.

— But like I say, you can't be rough, you can't push things.
Nice and slow and easy. The whole trick is knowing how to
rub her on the clitoris.

Hell, Agis didn't even know what a clitoris was. When Louis
explained, he began to drool; another couple of seconds and he
would have jacked off on the spot.

— But you start with kissing; crazy kisses, all kinds. Then
you work down to the nipples. But careful, don't suck too
hard. It'll hurt, and you'll miss the boat. And don't get started
unless you're sure there's a bed or a couch somewhere nearby.
Too far away and the whole thing might turn cold before you
get there. It's got to be right there.

Listen, as he tells the story it's all we can do to restrain
ourselves. Agis is beet red. It all seemed totally incredible and
exotic to his ears. He couldn't imagine that an innocent first-
timer like Eugenia would let Louis do all those things to her.

— You know why she said yes? Funny. Because she was
ashamed to say no. I was still sitting there beside her and she
was still the prim little lady; she respected me. But by then
she was so excited she didn't know what was happening to
her; she had no consciousness of space or time. When I turned
her over, she had no idea what was coming next.

The lowdown sonofabitch, first he gives us a detailed
description of the room, and then the main event.

He starts with the family photographs, the walls, the tile
floor, the bed. It all happened on her parents' bed. A wrought-
iron bed with floral motifs, a hard mattress and a rusty spring
that creaked like hell.

Then he begins to describe her body. Like an artist sitting
in front of his easel, brush and palette in hand. Sketching in
color, line, perspective. He sets her up — as he describes it —
in the perfect position: face down, on her elbows. Not on her
hands. Only way to get just the right pitch from the waist
down. Turns 'em into slithering minks or she-antelopes.

91

— Guys, when I put it in her, she grabs the bedposts. She only lets out an "ahh!" Nothing else. Not a word. Just an "ah!"

The comical part of the story is that, as Louis is pumping in and out of her, he lifts his head for an instant and spots, to his astonishment, a photo of King Paul and Queen Frederika.

— You can't imagine what went through my mind! It wasn't Eugenia I was screwing, it was Frederika. With that degenerate smile of hers ... Seriously, I kid you not.

Anyway, a few days after that, things start to unravel.

Suddenly he noticed Eugenia's drawbacks. She was duller than he imagined. Her ass was lower-slung than it seemed at first. She was a royalist to the marrow of her bones, and worst of all, she was fanatically devoted to the institution of marriage. "Hey, sweetie pie, why get married now? What's the big hurry? Marriage or no marriage, we'll still be doing the same thing."

But she was unyielding. Marriage it would have to be. She was terrified her brothers would find out before she could break the news.

— Shouldn't we get engaged, at least.

— Sweetie pie, just be patient. I'll find the right job first, we'll finish our studies; not like gypsies.

But Eugenia wasn't about to be patient. She wept piteously.

Finally — I don't know whether it was the nightmare of a wedding or the low-slung ass, but I do know the ass factor really bugged him — two weeks went by without an appearance by Louis. Two Tuesdays in a row.

She just about flipped. Suddenly she realized she didn't know where he lived, didn't know his telephone number, didn't know how to find him.

In her panic she made two deadly mistakes. First, desperate for assistance, she betrayed her secret to Olympia who then told Aristos. Second, when she was forced to confess everything to her brother, she revealed the secret of Tuesday.

Thus began the tragedy.

— He won't get away, the prick. One of these Tuesdays he'll show up.

92

There was no other way to find him. They changed flour delivery days, and every Tuesday the entire Krugas family lay in ambush, on red alert. One in the kitchen, another in the lavatory. That's what they called their toilets: lavatories.

They set up regular watches. And when Eugenia let drop that he called Queen Frederika an old strumpet, well, the two brothers all but foamed at the mouth.

Finally, Louis fell into the trap. When Eugenia spotted him that fateful Tuesday morning strolling down the street, clean shaven and freshly bathed, she suddenly regretted her betrayal. She realized that everything would soon be over. What was she going to say? "Look out, I ratted on you?" But there was no way out. She had to play the innocent to the bitter end. And play she did.

Louis smelled a rat. The reception wasn't quite like previous Tuesdays. When he asked her, "What's the matter, baby? You're cold as ice. What are you hiding from me?" the two plug-uglies burst in.

Eugenia cried out in feigned surprise, and stuffed her breast back into her brassiere, hands shaking.

Louis played it even more perfectly.

He recalled how many left-wingers had faced the firing squad only because they never had the presence of mind to have their declaration ready. "No sense recanting when you're dead," he thought to himself, "even supposing you'd have a second chance." He had to bow his head, and bow it he did.

When Aristos grabbed him by the hair and slammed him up against the wall, pictures of the executed surged through his mind. The other brother, the cuckold, was only a few feet away, gun in hand. These guys are serious, he thought. No time for bravado.

— Wait a minute, guys, it's all a big misunderstanding.

Eugenia stepped between them, hysterical.

— Don't shoot him! Don't!

What can you do? Louis surrendered; even considered shouting a patriotic slogan like "Long Live the King!" to make it extra convincing.

— What's today, Tuesday? Next Tuesday's the wedding, Aristos suddenly blurted out. Or Tuesday after next.

— No way. It takes a month, according to law.

They would have none of it.

— Don't you worry about the law. That's our affair.

The situation was turning grimmer.

— I'm unemployed, you know that?

— We know. We thought of that too. You'll work in the bakery. One-third is yours, dowry. We'll find you a place. With the workers' housing authority.

They'd covered every angle, the swine.

— After all, you love Eugenia, don't you?

Louis made an ultimate attempt to worm his way out:

— First I'll have to apply for a permit for the house.

— Don't you worry about that. We know how to get things done. You'll get the house; forget the permit.

Lo and behold, Louis suddenly found himself with a house, a job and a one-third share in the bakery ... Take away the rather low-slung ass — alright, alright, nobody's perfect — and the somewhat mediocre mind of Eugenia and he wasn't really in such bad shape.

That was the era, in fact, when a girl with that kind of a panoramic rear deck and a generous dowry was every boy's dream. In America they called it "the American dream" but here I don't know what you'd call it. Me, I'd have signed the wedding papers for less dream than that. After all, in order to inherit aunt Eustathia's three-storey house, I went and married her niece. Fair's fair, isn't it?

— For the time being you'll be staying here with us, until we can get the house arranged, said Aristos, with an air of utter finality.

As Louis stared at the cuckold standing across the room from him with the pistol, an idea flashed in his mind: sooner or later, Eugenia would be mourning her two brothers. They were dead men, one hundred percent. It wouldn't be long before one found out what the other was doing behind his back. As soon as he did, the duel to the death was a foregone conclusion.

94

It was his last hope.

Meanwhile, Aristos was waiting for his answer: would Louis stay at their place? And it wasn't just Aristos; it was the entire Krugas clan.

— Sure, I'll stay, if you take down the portrait of Frederika, Louis added suddenly, essaying a heroic exodus.

Needless to say, that gambit didn't go far.

— Not only we won't take it down, but if you ever call her an old strumpet again you'll be counting your teeth in your hand.

That was Aristos' favorite threat. But when he says "count teeth" he means more than just teeth; I should make that clear.

It was when he heard the words "old strumpet" that Louis realized Eugenia had blown the whistle on him. How else could Aristos have known what he said?

He agreed to everything. Moved in, in fact. With two suitcases. One full of books, the other with clothing.

At his own place, he said not a word. All his father and sister could do was stare as he walked out the door. I went along, to lend a hand. No one asked him a thing. Antigone quickly figured it out.

— They're either sending him away to concentration camp or he's getting married, she said.

What sad eyes she has! All the time, sad. It was evening. We were leaving just as she headed off for work at the hospital.

— Manolopoulos, why don't you say something? she said.

What could I say. I could only look at her.

— You won't tell me where your friend is going?

— To a wedding, I told her. A wedding.

Surely you can understand my position, my humiliation. Here I am, forced to betray Retsinas right in the church-yard by revealing his address to the Krugases.

I'm at the end of my tether. My new suit is ripped, I'm black with bruises, covered with grime. "Good Lord" is all my mother could say as I announce to her that the wedding was cancelled.

Agis is shaking with fright.

— Manolopoulos, we're really in deep shit now. If they tell the cops, we've had it.

When mom hears "cops" she faints on the spot.

She hardly has a chance to come to before Agis comes out with more poppycock:

— Not just the station house. Those guys actually break bones, burn down houses, he tells her and bang, she faints again.

"What's he saying, the airhead?"

Quickly we convene a small family meeting. On the agenda: warn Louis, or lay low?

Mother invited uncle Anestis to the meeting. He was quite a guy. Remind me to tell you about him one day. A contradictory sort of character; the kind of man you could respect. Reformed Communist turned family man. Formerly atheist and card shark. Until age thirty, that is. From that day on, a law abiding, God-fearing citizen.

Formerly a night owl, a bar-, cabaret- and brothel-crawler with three doses of clap on the debit side; time in jail for passing bad checks and permanently sterile thanks to the first bout of gonorrhea.

But, unexpectedly, this same uncle Anestis — the black sheep of the family — transformed himself into a perfectly respectable citizen and a fine upstanding gentleman. He made friends with the Piraeus police chief, and through him, with all the district police officers. He was appointed to a civil service position. He put an end to the cabaret and whorehouse

96

routine, cut the card games and returned like the prodigal son to the family fold.

Mother had been beating me over the head with uncle Anestis' life story for a whole lifetime, or so it seemed.

— See? Even your uncle went straight, made a man out of himself.

I remember how he used to look; tall, well-dressed, light-footed, always dressed in a white suit with a sprig of jasmine in his buttonhole. The spitting image of Alain Delon.

Talk about a flip-flop! When he got the job, that was the end of the jasmine. He seemed to grow shorter. After he took his first bribe, the meaning of the savings account began to sink in. From that moment on he ceased to live. Saving money was all that mattered.

There was only one part of his life that remained dark and unfathomable to us: his marriage. When it happened, we were caught by surprise.

One morning he announced he was being married the following Sunday. The sudden announcement reminded me a little of the old uncle Anestis.

No one knew a thing about the bride. Her name we learned at the wedding ceremony: Melpo, it was. "She's from Smyrna," someone whispered. Been wild about Smyrna girls ever since. Just mention the word, and I start to simmer.

When I saw her standing there beneath the chandelier, tall, fine-boned, round-faced, it was all I could do to restrain myself. The girl was Aphrodite all over again; well, maybe a little on the plump side.

Her eyes were clear and innocent, like a Madonna's; but her body was all woman, provocative, demonic. Her lips were full, sensual, dark red. Her breasts? Don't even ask. Her eyebrows, her neck ... Now that was a sight, that neck of hers emerging from her shoulders. Only seen necks like that in paintings, on old oriental style postcards.

Like I say, from that day on, just say "Smyrna girl" and my mind teems with exotic music, sensual aromas, divans with reclining odalisques and frescoes full of naked goddesses. I

97

baptized those kind of women "Smyrna girls." Mary Magdalene is a Smyrna girl for me; and Urania too.

Matter of fact, aunt Melpo really was from Smyrna. She spoke slowly, with a lilting, tantalizing voice. Just listening to her was enough to get you going. No need to see her even. Phone her and ask her about her flowers, for instance, and if your you-know-whats don't start to heat up then my name isn't Manolopoulos. ⟨

There was an aura of mystery about her life — made her even more attractive. She could have just as well stepped from a passing cloud. Uncle Anestis never said a thing about her. What did she do? Who was she? What was her family like, her relatives, where was she from? Where did she grow up, what did she ... Everything was mystery. Usually people carry their memories around with them; not aunt Melpo. I never once heard her say, "When we were kids ..."

Later, when Louis revealed the great mystery of her life to me, my aunt took on mythical stature in my mind.

She and uncle Anestis had dropped by for a visit. Louis and I were at home.

When Louis saw her he recoiled in astonishment. He said nothing when I introduced them, only nodded his head, said, "Pleased to meet you," muttered something about a headache, and left.

Never did find out whether she recognized him, whether she even remembered him.

— Five years she was a whore on Filonos Street, that aunt of yours. A nightclub dancer, bar girl at the Kit-Kat Club. You didn't know?

He'd slept with her. Frequently.

— I can tell you, Kostas, my boy, that she was the first woman I ever slept with. What a piece. Never behaved like a whore. I was just a kid, but she taught me how to be tender with a woman.

As I listened to Louis, I was lost in wonderment. From that moment on I couldn't look at aunt Melpo without imagining her on beds of debauchery, or perched on a stool in the cabaret waiting for the customers to wander in.

Once Louis took me to the Kit-Kat, the spot where he met her in the first place.

— My very first money, Kostas, my boy, I spent on her. I'd never been in a cabaret with whores in my life.

— She used to sit over there — he pointed to the place — where the girl who's smiling at you is sitting. She's got to have remembered me, Kostas.

Probably did. Now that I think of it, I spotted it in her eyes. Just a flicker, just a hint, when they met at our place.

That may be the reason why my uncle dislikes Louis so much, if we can hypothesize that she mentioned him. Understandably, he didn't want to learn too much about her past.

From then on, I couldn't turn down Filonos Street without remembering her.

She had a gramophone; a huge, elaborate gramophone with an immense horn, and Smyrniote records with music sung in high, nasal drawn-out women's voices. On one of them, I recognized her voice.

At first she denied it, but I was dead certain she was the singer.

We were alone in the house when I mentioned it. I liked visiting her place. Everything about it was voluptuous, sensual. The colors of the upholstery, her photographs, the deep red of the lamp shades, the vases stuffed with sunflowers. Some people like dogs; she liked sunflowers. And perfume. The odor was overwhelming. Everywhere. Even the toilet; in fact it was anything but a toilet. Nothing but lace, pink fur bathroom sets and perfume.

I can't forget one particular photo of hers, just opposite the door as you entered her living room. It was a large photo; caught your eye. In it, she's reclining on a pasha's divan with tufted upholstery. It was obviously a pose struck for a photographer of the day. Only her legs showed beneath her dress. It had to have been from the whorehouse where she worked.

She offered me a sweet, Smyrna style, on a tiny silver plate, also from Smyrna.

She knew I'd come to hear that recording, the one with the breathless, high-pitched voice. She was in her forties now, but still gorgeous.

I still remember that bright-red dress of hers. Just like in the photograph. The dress, I mean.

She finally admitted it. It was her voice. She'd met a man who made recordings. She used to sing then; and dance.

— Don't tell a soul. Even your uncle doesn't know. Promise?

— I promise.

She kissed me. The taste of that kiss slowly became a scent that never faded.

But let's not get the wrong idea here. She adored uncle Anestis. Absolutely adored him.

Naturally, the family meeting — to get back to our story — decided I was to stay put, and not alert Louis. If the Krugases ever suspected I'd warned him I would pay the price, not him. It was also decided that, for the next few days, I was not to leave the house.

Agis cleared out as fast as he could when the meeting wound up.

— As for that pal of yours, Retsinas, he deserves to get the stuffing knocked out of him. He promised to marry the girl, didn't he? Well, let him learn to keep his word. That's what he gets for leading her on.

That last comment came from my uncle. I felt hurt. He, of all people, should know something about love and passion. He was the one who, when all was said and done, had the guts to marry a whore, wasn't he? The arguments flew thick and fast; but I wasn't convinced. I had to save Louis; I couldn't just

100

leave him in the lurch like that, without so much as trying to warn him.

— And don't forget the most important thing; in two months you write exams. If you get involved and they blacklist you again, there's nothing anybody can do. I'm telling you one last time, cut off that no-good bum, otherwise don't expect any help from me, and don't expect any ministry job either.

The final argument brought me to my knees. That shit job at the ministry had become my lifelong dream — a dream and a nightmare, rolled into one. If uncle Anestis had such an important position in the family, it was thanks to the job. Let us all now bow down and praise uncle.

Come to think of it, I still can't figure out why he was so concerned about us. After all, we were just some second-class relations of his. Maybe he liked playing the powerful protector. I can't imagine what he was after because — frankly — I don't have any illusions. There's no such thing as a guileless gesture. Or if there is, it's a rare bird indeed.

Still, to be honest, I was getting scared — rightly or wrongly.

Louis was far beyond Communism, I knew that. Far beyond ideology, even; he was more an anarchist, undisciplined, crazy. Still, I was beginning to realize that sooner or later I'd have to make a choice. On one side stood uncle Anestis, my studies, my little job; on the other lay the unknown, danger, mystery.

My father was sitting off to the side. He said not a word during the whole meeting. He never said anything. Just stared at the sky for hours on end. That's how he would fall asleep, staring at the sky. Now, there he sat, just the same way. In the same place. Mute.

I glanced at him and suddenly something heroic awakened inside me; I thought I could hear distant pipes and drums.

No way I would play Judas to the end.

Just when they thought they'd convinced me and sat down to dinner, I bolted through the living room window.

101

I was too late, of course. By the time I got to Louis' place the cyclone had hit. I beheld a wasteland: books ripped to pieces, shattered furniture, drawers-full of clothing strewn on the floor. And there in a corner on the hard, cold floor, with puffed eyes and broken teeth, motionless, terrorized, burning with fever, crouched Louis. His face had puffed up into one grotesque nose and mouth.

I could barely control myself. If I hadn't stuck around for the family meeting, listening to their dumb talk, maybe I could have averted the catastrophe. Agis was to blame; a gutless wonder if there ever was one! "Are you crazy? If they find us there they'll tear us to pieces." Sure as hell managed to make me think twice.

When I got Louis to the hospital where his sister works, he had bruises on the leg, a broken tooth, sprained hands, and he couldn't see out of one eye. Maybe he'd lose the eye entirely.

Antigone kissed him. Gave him courage. Don't let those apes walk all over you, she said. There at the hospital she finally learned all the details about the wedding, and about how he stood up the bride.

— Serves her right.

When I described what happened at the church, she burst out laughing.

But beating him up wasn't enough for them, the scum. On their way out they set another date for the wedding. "That was just a little taste. If you try and wriggle out again, you'll pay for everything, once and for all," they said. They weren't joking. The Krugas clan didn't mince words. They'd killed people during the Occupation.

102

When I ran into Aristos two days later at the "California," I just about shit in my pants.

The "California" was our neighborhood movie house. Back then, you could catch two movies for the price of one. In at two in the afternoon, out at six.

So, I'm watching Tyrone Power up there on the silver screen when I feel a soft tapping on the shoulder. I turn around and who do I see but Aristos. He was the one who took all the initiative. His brother, the cuckold, was nothing but Aristos' obedient little helper.

— Hey, four eyes, don't go thinkin' you're gonna get away from me. If the wedding don't happen, then you're next. And tell him, don't try blackmailing me with Olympia. If he does, he's a dead man. Him and you both. Ain't no Commies mess around with Krugas' sister. That lover boy pal of yours better watch himself or you'll get it good. Didn't bother you to keep watch for him, right?

That cheap little whore, Eugenia, she really did spill the beans.

As a matter of fact, I did keep watch every Tuesday. That too. But in return for a favor. That was when I was in love with Tassoula.

— Hey, this Tassoula's not for you, Louis insisted. She's a gal from someone else's story. What's she to you, anyway?

She was five years older than me, plumpish, a bit whiney. But I stuck to my guns. It was her I wanted.

— Then make your move. What are you waiting for?

Her brother was a cop. How could I dare, with a brother like that?

All she had to do was set foot on the sidewalk and the would-be suitors would start popping up — and she knew it. She loved being the center of attention. Within five minutes they'd start to swarm, strolling back and forth, eyeballing her. But no one dared go any further.

Back then all the houses in Piraeus had basements, and each basement had a little window onto the street, for fresh air. Many's the time I'd nip on down and wait for Tassoula,

103

who was sitting just across the street from my vantage point, to open her legs.

She sat quite respectably for the first few minutes. But soon she would get tired, go limp, and her legs would flop apart. Or she'd start to scratch. It was one of her favorite pastimes; she'd pull her skirt way up and scratch away.

Finally Louis and I came to an agreement.

— I'll stand guard for you, and you fix me up with her. OK?

I wrote her a fervid letter. He was to deliver it to her. That was my condition.

The upshot was that I broke off with Louis for a while.

He said he handed her the letter but he never did; never breathed a word about me even though he assured me he did.

A while later, when my ardor had cooled, I mentioned it to Tassoula thinking she'd received the famous epistle. She burst out laughing.

— You're kidding, Manolopoulos? You didn't know?

— Know what?

— Retsinas didn't tell you anything?

And she took a step back to avoid laughing in my face. "What's so funny anyway, dimwit?" I was about to say. Which was when she confessed that when I gave him the letter she was already his girlfriend.

— Some friend! He really strung you along!

I couldn't believe it. "That prick, and behind my back ..."

Later, when they arrested her brother, the cop, for narcotics, illegal foreign exchange export and a whole list of crimes, she sublet the apartment and disappeared from our lives, and from the neighborhood. Later on, I'll tell you where and how I encountered her again.

104

Here's how Louis and I got back on speaking terms: A fair amount of time had elapsed since then, much had happened — moving house, exams, etc. — and I'd all but forgotten him. Suddenly, late one afternoon, the doorbell rings. Mom peers through the peephole; it was him. She begins to shake.

— It's that devil again. Shall I let him in?

Instead of answering, I run over and open the door myself.

— Kostas, my boy, that's a hell of a thing to do, cutting me off all on account of some woman.

Mom's nerves are starting to frazzle. She knew that when Louis appears, no good can come of it.

You think she'd offer him a coffee? Hah.

— Ah, cousin, that's quite a mother you've got ...

I'm still clasping his hand, looking at him.

— Get dressed, Kostas, my boy. Don't bring money. I got plenty. I owe you and I'm going to pay it back. Don't ask what or why. Just do like I say. No objections.

I agree. With Louis, never refuse. It'll rebound against you. Might as well deny life, betray everything you hold sacred, your mother, your father ... Every time I refused him, I not only regretted it — as will become evident later — but those ''no's'' of mine gnawed away at my guts, sucked out my spirit.

In ten minutes we're gone. I close the door behind me.

— Where are you going? mom calls out.

She knew. Leave with Louis and it's entirely possible you'll never come back.

We're no sooner out the door than he hails a cab. Louis having money for taxis was like me winning the lottery, say, like an earthquake, like war breaking out.

Inside the cab, he grabs my hand.

— Listen to me, cousin; it's for your own good. Let your mom stew in her own juice. Don't listen to her. She's already got herself and your old man to complain about; don't let her grab you too. What is it? What are you worried about, anyway? Stick with me and you'll be a somebody, a big shot.

Louis was Circe all over again. A pure-bred siren, I mean to say. The wake-up bugle; the resurrection of the dead. That's what he meant to me. He'd lead you down streets and alleys and boulevards; you'd never know whether they led somewhere — or nowhere.

— The dockyards! he orders the driver.

And launches into an apology.

— Cousin, when I saw the state you were in, all because of Tassoula, what could I do? Could I tell you I was already involved with her? I didn't have the heart. At first, I kept it under cover. After — how can I put it? can you really say those things?

I felt no grudge. Instead, I laugh.

— And you just let me go on, making a fool of myself?

— Listen, cousin, she was interested in you too, I could tell. All you had to do was wink. Besides, if I'd wanted to fix you up with her, I could have done it in seconds, no problem. But afterwards, how would you get out of it? Not so easy.

— I don't get it.

— Relax. You will.

As the taxi drives on, I notice how smartly dressed he is. Cool as the proverbial cucumber. Clean shaven, freshly washed, nicely coiffed. Even has a tie on.

Mom hadn't gotten a good look at him. If she had, I'm sure she'd have changed her mind — again.

Mother had a fearful weakness for packages, for wrappers, for the outward appearance of things. The shinier it was, the more she liked it. People and objects. Loose merchandise was not for her; she always chose the individually wrapped piece, the tasteful item. The cellophane wrappers, the bright colors, the baubles and the beads were what won her over. Same for people. Just for instance, let's say you have a full-time job; a house of your own, a doctor relative, or maybe a lawyer. You were a somebody. Why, she'd fall all over herself for you. Particularly if you happened to be a civil servant — not working

106

for some private company — and went to church regularly. More than that, you would become her idol, her master, and she your slave. You could do what you wanted with her. She would even go to bed with you. Not because she liked you — she'd abolished such pleasures for herself long ago — but because she simply couldn't resist, couldn't say no to someone with a few of the social graces.

It's a weakness she's already paid dearly for in life. She, me and my father, but most of all, my sister, Matina.

For the sake of marrying her off to a man of culture and substance, she turned Matina's pudendum into a transit lounge. If a guy was well enough dressed, she brought him home. The wrapping was what convinced her; she could never bring herself to admit that precisely such a proper, well-dressed gentleman would ever dare corrupt a "poor unmarried" maiden.

Fortunately, in the end, she married Matina off to a corpulent olive oil wholesaler from the central market. The simple fact that she was assured of a lifetime supply of free olive oil was enough: the marriage was a success.

And so it was that whenever she mentioned her son-in-law, she crossed herself.

— God protect him, she murmured.

One day, during one of our no-holds-barred arguments, my patience evaporated — it just came out — and I laid it on her straight:

— Your daughter's had four abortions so far, and it's all because of you and your foolishness, and those just-so-proper gentlemen you drag home. They line up, drop their coin in the slot, and leave, and you know it.

Her eyes widened, her mouth, her ears. She shook her head violently from side to side. She refused to believe it.

— Good thing the oil merchant finally married her.

I never spoke to her so crudely before. She kept wagging her head in disbelief, until she fainted. For good reason. Better she faint, better she kill herself on the spot, than admit, for instance, that uncle Anestis' good friend, George, the court secretary, was the self-same man who had taken her virginity.

And the English teacher, when they closed the doors to the study? "She's having her lesson, leave her alone." Couldn't she see he was giving her everything but lessons? Poor girl never learned a word of English. Matina was hoping for a good marriage, of course. "He's such a nice man, and from such a good family ..."

She revived long enough to tell me she didn't believe a word, that it was nothing but my maliciousness. Save your breath, I told her. Stop playing the Holy Mother.

— One look at a so-called nice boy and you lie down and let him walk all over you. Quick, we've got to marry him ... You don't believe it, my eye. Let me tell you a thing or two. Who had to rush her to the abortionist?

— Here, Louis tells the taxi driver, and we get out at the dockyards.

He hands the man a five-drachma tip. Quite a sum for those days. He was a prince, a real prince, the lousy sonofabitch. That's what I call people who pay no attention to money. Princes! I shell out one drachma for something, I think it over. At the taverna, for instance ... Me, I'm wild about shrimp cocktail, but you think I'd ever order it? Fat chance. Mom has injected me with her miserliness, one drop at a time. I can't enjoy anything, not even a sunset with my girlfriend, if the excursion is over the budget. I'm always counting my money, recounting it. Never Louis. He never worries how much a night on the town will cost as long as he has a good time.

I remember one time he dropped by, out of the blue, and took me, my sister and father to see *The Song of the Dead Brother* — everything on him. He did it for dad; knew the old man liked Theodorakis' music.

108

My father admired Louis, really. The two of them would spend hours talking. Louis would spot him sitting there in his corner, sipping ouzo and nibbling bits of cucumber, olives and sardines, pull up a chair, and the two of them would plunge into small talk.

Mother could rant and rave until she was blue in the face — "Get up and do something, forget the chit-chat with that dead-ender" — but he paid her no heed; wouldn't even dignify her with an answer. It was total disdain, lét me tell you.

In fact, those were my father's two triumphs: allowing no one to sit in his corner; and making small talk with Louis.

As for Louis, he totally ignored mother, didn't listen to her. As though she didn't exist.

Like I say, my father liked Louis. That's why the news of Louis' marriage to Krugas' daughter hit him hard. Suddenly, Louis had fallen in his esteem, almost betrayed him. He couldn't stand the sight of the Krugases.

So, you can imagine mom's state when he took the three of us out. Louis struck fear into her; not only on my account, but also on account of father, old Manolopoulos. Don't forget, he was still relatively young then, fifty-five at the most.

She started getting jumpy; maybe Louis would introduce him to another side of life, maybe even to another woman; then he might even dump her on the spot. Never can tell.

Twice she approved of him. Once when it looked like he was about to be married — so finally he's surrendering, she said to herself — and again when he and I quarreled over Tassoula. Both times, she breathed easier.

On a couple of occasions Louis came knocking but I didn't answer the door. When that happened, it was all she could do to keep from bursting into rhapsodies of song. Honest to God, try as I might, I couldn't remember her ever singing before. But now, she came within a hair's breadth.

— I told you so. He's a trouble-maker and a layabout. A snake in the grass, not a friend.

I made the mistake of telling her about Tassoula. But from

then on, I adopted my father's tactics. I didn't listen, and I didn't answer.

But when it came to Tassoula, I couldn't keep my big mouth shut.

— Shut up, will you! I shouted, and kicked the door.

The plywood buckled. Even today, if you visit my parents' place, you can see the patch on the door.

So, Louis came by, picked us up, took us to the theater, treated us to a souvlaki after the show, and brought us home in a taxi.

— We can take the electric, father said.

— Nope, we're going by taxi.

He wouldn't let us put up as much as a drachma. But as we were saying goodnight, he suddenly whispered:

— Slip me enough for bus fare, will you?

Whatever he had, he spent; nothing was left over for bus fare. Now, that's what I call a prince!

So when we get there — back to our story, as I was saying — Louis pays the driver, and we stroll down toward the docks, to Lambros' ouzo joint. Places like that don't exist any more. There were a handful of tables right on the sidewalk; you could watch the ships sailing in and out of the harbor.

Lambros didn't take orders. As soon as you sat down, he'd appear with a tray holding two miniature frying pans with the first course. Baby meatballs. When you clapped your hands and pointed to the empty pans, he brought you the second round. Eggs with sausage. Twelve courses altogether. You could start all over again if you wanted. And he never said a word. Never.

Never even told you what you owed him. Everything was in writing. At the most, you could pry a few words out of him; just the bare essentials if you'd forgotten something, or

110

maybe "Merry Christmas" if it was that time of year.

Sitting there in Lambros' canvas chairs, draining our shot glasses, I knew Louis was about to spring something on me. But I didn't want to ask, didn't want to spoil the surprise.

I told you. With Louis, be ready for anything, anytime. He might turn up in a helicopter, introduce you to a government minister, even fix you up with Greta Garbo. Yep. Introduced me to her one time. It happened on Skiathos, the island. You know the one I'm talking about. Anyway, there I was with my friend, Stavropoulos, checking out the real estate. That was back when Stavropoulos and me were in the hotel business. I was supposed to be a partner and his business was supposed to be incorporated. So, all of a sudden, what do I hear? Louis' voice, from across the water: "Kostas, my boy, you old sinner!" Can you beat that! What do I see? Louis in a swimsuit; a silk one, white and red stripes.

— It's me, cousin. What are you staring at?

He's lolling in a chaise-longue on the deck of a yacht moored in the marina, an elegant looking lady in her sixties is lying on a chaise-longue next to his. Probably English. They're talking English, at any rate.

We go over. He introduces her, and I almost fall backwards into the water.

— I'd like you to meet Greta Garbo.

She holds out her hand. Stavropoulos starts to cough; he can't believe it. OK, maybe it wasn't her. I don't know, really. Sure looked like her, though. Just like in the photographs. The straw hat, the dark glasses; thin, tall, fine-featured. I'm convinced it really was her. Think of it, Louis and Garbo. Hard to believe.

We didn't start talking right away. Just sat there, ouzo glasses in hand, looking at one another.

— Can't go until after dark.

Where, I didn't ask. I wanted to play it cool, to play the guy with adventure in his blood. Which I am, goddamn it; what do you want me to do about it? It's in my blood alright; just that — you see — one after another they grab you, chain you to the oars, force you in between those chalk lines of Kritsinis. Sure you'd like to be free as a bird, me too — who wouldn't ...

So, as we're silently sipping our ouzo, I ask him if he had any news of Kritsinis.

I noticed that as time went by, whenever I encountered Louis, we seemed to talk more about our memories, about the people we'd met together than about the present. It scared me, I didn't like it. I didn't want to lose Louis. I wanted to have a sense of him as he was then, at boot camp in Corinth: handsome, mercurial, mythical. If I lost him, it would mean my own failure.

— See? I'm not asking why you brought me here. I don't want to spoil your surprise.

He looks at me. It's all he can do not to burst out laughing.

— Kritsinis? You're way behind. He's somebody's general secretary at the ministry now. Got his own office, intercoms, secretaries, doormen, the works. A big shot.

The next step was only a short one for me.

— No, Louis! Don't tell me ... This is rich! Work? You've got work?

— Sure do, cousin; sure do.

So that's it. The suit, the taxi, the ouzo. Suddenly he turned melancholy. He hadn't intended to tell me, but now that I'd figured it out ...

— He got me a doorman's job at the ministry. Your old buddy's thick as thieves with the power structure.

Oh no! I was speechless. And now Kritsinis was pushing him to finish school, so he could get a promotion, a permanent position.

— Don't go getting ideas, cousin. Nothing ever happened again. He just likes me, generally, in the broadest sense. He made Antigone head nurse at the hospital. Agis too, found

112

him a job at the water company. Me, Kostas, my boy, I'm leaving. The suit and tie and the job aren't enough. Being a doorman, well, it's a little beneath my dignity. But it's not only that ... I'm just not cut out for being a watchdog. I want to get a few good jobs for my pals, and then I'll cut and run. If there's something you'd like for yourself, let me know.

He was right. Louis just wasn't cut out for the job, for the punch clock and the nine-to-five. For greeting every shit head department boss with a cheery "Good morning, sir."

— Understand? Egotism has nothing to do with it; I'm no swelled head, but ... Look, even the tie is too tight — it's choking me — and they tell you ties are obligatory.

What was I supposed to tell him? What position should I take? But this time I didn't handle it right. Instead of laying it out for him: "Wait a minute, Louis, old pal. Who the hell do you think you are anyway? Everybody has to make some concessions. You want to live your whole life on credit? What about your sister, she's been doing your laundry and buying your clothes for longer than I can remember. What about her?" But I didn't. Deep down I wanted him to stay the way he was, the way I always knew him. I wanted him to stay a nomad, a free man, a bum.

For an instant I felt like a scientist in a lab, performing an experiment. But there were no guinea pigs involved, just people. I wanted to see where a character like that would end up. It was a critical moment. I knew Louis trusted me.

— Nope, Louis, you're no doorman. But what are you going to do? What's happening to your life?

That's all I said.

He drained his fourth ouzo, put down the glass and began to scratch his head. I noticed that his hair had begun to thin. I felt sad.

No, I don't think I betrayed him by not bringing him down to earth. Maybe if I'd convinced him to finish high school, he would have become a proper gentleman by now. But he wouldn't have been the Louis I'm telling you about; the myth maker, the daredevil.

113

He tried that too. The daredevil bit, I mean. But it didn't work out. Never could manage to eat fire or chew iron, or ... He took lessons from a half-French, half-Greek called Bertrand. What the hell; just couldn't cut the mustard. Chipped his teeth, burned his mouth, sprained his ankle. Nearly ended up a cripple, and not a hell of a lot to show for it. But for three whole years he was the third banana in Bertrand's circus.

What a nut case, that guy Bertrand was. I'm telling you! Now it's all coming back ... Wild stuff; straight out of the Middle Ages. Here was a man who had it all — his own business, bags of money, a house, a yacht, and more ... Listen, my friend. His life was pretty as a picture, whatever his little heart desired he had — travel, dough, women ... But he was nuts about circuses and magic tricks. So nuts that he gave up everything and became a daredevil.

Ever since he was a kid he'd travelled the world, not to see the world, but to see the circuses. Years and years he toiled, hours on end, stringing ropes from one end of his backyard to the other, playing the high-wire acrobat. Finally, he got the trick. Then he tried fire-eating, and learned to eat fire. That's when he abandoned his business, his work, the good life, ran off with a French girl — a former mime and fashion model — who was wild about him and started touring from town to town, up hill and down dale. They set up their stage in village squares or in coffeehouses. And at the end of the performance, the ex-model would pass the clown's hat.

Louis could hardly believe his eyes when he first ran across them in Epidaurus. It was to have been his first ancient Greek tragedy, but he ended up at Bertrand's circus instead. The choice was between *Prometheus* and a handful of pathetic clowns and acrobats. But when he spotted the flaming torches and the garish circus posters, it was game over. His wife,

114

Aleka, was dragging him along by the sleeve — he was married now — telling him the tickets would go for nothing, but Louis would have none of it. She lost her temper, started yelling; he wouldn't budge. They split up on the spot, for good. She wiped her eyes, took whatever money he had on him, the theater tickets, told him to go to hell and went to see *Prometheus* by herself. And Louis, he took up with Bertrand. For three years.

For sure, Bertrand must have played a key role in the rest of Louis' life. Must have passed on some of his craziness, some of his philosophy. The French girl lasted two years, then left. Louis three. But he never went back to Aleka. Anargyros had taken his place, as you'll see.

Bertrand? He's still at it. Got a truck now; converted it into a movable zoo, with a huge monkey, snakes, birds and God knows what else, doing the rounds of village squares. He's crazy and he knows it.

Louis introduced me to him once. Really off the wall. No French girls chase him any more. The business was long gone. The tax collectors got half, his brother the other half. Bertrand managed to sell the yacht to buy the animals and the truck. His house? Sold that too. His brother forged his signature, unloaded it. "He's nuts, isn't he. What's he going to do with it?"

Those are the facts you've got to know before you can understand how crazy Bertrand really was.

But let's get back to Lambros' place, down by the docks. We're into our sixth shot by now, darkness has fallen, the harbor has merged with the city. You couldn't tell land from sea. The ships are invisible except for their lights. Yellow lights, moving. The night too. It was walking toward us, coming closer.

I wanted to ask about Polyxeni, the wife of Demenagas, about Haroula, what news did he have about them. But I kept forgetting. Wait, I do ask him about Polyxeni: "What ever happened to her? Ever see her again?" He shakes his head sadly.

— A real bitch, cousin. She knew Demenagas killed her husband. She knew everything, but she kept quiet. She knew it, and she married him. The bitch.

Our speech was beginning to slur. Along with the night came damp and cold. Finally, Louis pulls some money from his pocket, leaves it on the table and gets to his feet.

— Come on, get up. We're late.

He walks off unsteadily.

— Let's make a deal. From now on, we come here to talk things over, to Lambros' place. Agreed? As long as we live.

— It's a deal. And we shake hands.

We stroll down toward the harbor. He's daydreaming again. This time, he's put some money away and opened that dream-bar of his. Coffee, ouzo, eau de vie and little snacks made with everything from smoked meat to Mykonos sausage. Simple, down-to-earth, great-tasting stuff. A workingman's hangout.

— Friends could drop by for a chat. There would be oriental music — Byzantine, Smyrna style — to get the blood boiling.

Now we've reached the port. He comes to stop in front of a handsome neoclassical two-storey building.

— Here we are, cousin, and he points to the open door. Above it is a wooden balcony. At the end of the hall you'll find a wooden staircase. There will be an old lady sitting there. If she asks, say "Retsinas sent me" and go on upstairs. I've got an errand to run; back in a minute or two.

I need a little bit more explanation: what am I supposed to do when I get there, who am I liable to run into, what am I supposed to want if anybody asks — even though, to tell the truth, I'm starting to get a pretty good idea.

— Don't ask so many questions, cousin. At the top of the stairs, you'll come out into a big room. When you get there, everything will be clear. Just take it as it comes.

For him, everything is possible, easy even; but didn't he know me?

— Louis, cut the bull. I'll only go if you come with me.

I know, I know; I was spoiling the show; he'd imagined it differently. Finally he comes along. We go in: a long hall with bare, peeling walls, a bare bulb hanging from the ceiling, barely throwing enough light to see by. At the end of the hall is the staircase, and the old lady sitting there. I look at her as she greets us. Her face is like a page from a history book. You could read the History of Greece in her eyes and in her wrinkles and on her forehead, everywhere. If you look closely, with a magnifying glass, say, you could see the Asia Minor Catastrophe, the Civil War, the Occupation. Betrayals, informers, traitors, heroes. Seas and oceans, Byzantium and Ionia, the marbled king, everyone, everything.

Louis sees me staring at her, long and hard. Who knows what horrors, what scenes of bloodletting I was awakening within her. I'm wearing my black topcoat and prescription dark glasses, for myopia. I probably look like a police informer.

— You're scaring the lady. How come you're dressed like that? Take off your coat.

Halfway up, where the stairs curved, is a landing and a window in the wall. It showed a rainbow set among tiny, tiny multicolored panes of glass. Just like in a church. From above us we could feel a warm, cloying, heavily scented breeze. From somewhere further off we could hear bouzouki music, the voice of Markos Vamvakaris, hoarse and croaking. I look at Louis. He looks at me.

— One day you've got to write all this down, cousin. If you don't, you're a fink.

I'm taken aback. He never suggested any such thing before.

— I read your letter to Tassoula, the one I was supposed to give her. I've still got it. If anything ever happens to me, Agis will get it. When I read it, I say to myself, no way I'm giving this to Tassoula. I kept it.

We enter the main room. One quick look around and I say

to myself: "Just take it nice and easy, my friend, 'cause there's no telling what's likely to happen next."

All around the room are windows and French doors, with small panes. Through them you could see across the inner harbor as far as the break-water, looking for all the world like a brightly-lighted piece of baclava. In the middle distance are a couple of huge smokestacks; that would have been the fertilizer and cement plants. Far away, to the left, the sea had become one with the sky. And if you listened carefully, you could hear the whispering of the waves.

It's the first time I ever set foot in a brothel. In the old days, he used to try to drag me into the whorehouses on Filonos Street. We'd get as far as the door before I'd chicken out. I don't know what it was. I felt intimidated in the presence of whores. Not fear exactly, intimidation. Going by in the street I could see them standing there, leaning up against doorways in their short, short, skirts or dressed in housecoats, bending over wooden balconies with their breasts hanging out in the hope of luring some passers-by, and I felt a kind of pang deep inside. A mixture of stage-fright, shock, shyness, curiosity. Part of me lusted crazily after them, another part couldn't imagine what they could possibly be like.

— Hey, sucker, for fifty drachmas you can do whatever you want. On the floor, face up, face down, whichever way you want it, they'll do it. What you waiting for?

My problem was that when I was a kid, women had assumed mythical dimensions for me. Everything about them seemed remote, legendary.

— Come on, have a seat, he says, and pulls me over to a small couch.

We've all seen rooms like this in the movies, where the plot includes a bordello scene. But when you're up close, when you're right in the scene yourself, it's a lot different.

— You finally did it; got me inside, I whisper to him.

When the initial shock wore off — up until then I hadn't really seen anything, I couldn't make out faces or things: everything was confusion, one big jumble — my first impres-

118

sion was of suddenly staring at a bizarre, variegated fresco. One girl's legs seemed attached to another's, like some immense surrealist canvas. My eyes leave one whore's — Litsa they called her — bright-red lips and come to rest on the bright-red lips of another. Some are strolling around, others are sitting, dressed in scanty black lingerie and long, transparent red peignoirs. Red was the dominant color. But put all the colors together — the black, the red, the white, the green, the pink — and you plunged into a whirlwind of hues. Your head started to spin. But slowly I begin to focus on faces, features, eyes.

My gaze comes to rest on a soldier. He's seated in a corner, bent over, eyes popping, flicking back and forth trying to choose. You could tell. He's winnowing out the unusable material, and keeping the best: That one's got nice legs but zero breasts — I follow his glance and his thoughts — the other one's got good breasts and legs but she's full of varicose veins. The one standing up, she's more than forty. Too bad; her body, her legs, her breasts, terrific. Too bad she's not younger. He's weighing the pros and cons. His eyes leave her, and come back again. "She's the one," I say to myself.

— Hey, you looking at the soldier boy or the girls?

Then he turns toward Litsa. I liked her looks too. Couldn't even have been twenty, wearing a pink peignoir which she opens and closes methodically every few seconds. He looks back at the older woman. Sizes her up again. Then he stubs out his cigaret and gets to his feet, strolls right in front of the forty-year-old, winks at her, and walks off. I knew he'd choose her. There was a look of fear in his eyes, something only a forty-year-old woman could understand. Litsa might have made fun of him.

— What's going on, Louis, why did you bring me here?

— Shut up.

— I'm really not interested, how can I ...

But his mind was far away, that much I can see. Just then, Litsa comes over and sits down beside us. Let's say you're dreaming about the Holy Mother and suddenly she begins to unbutton her blouse and show you her breasts ... how would you feel? Well, that's how I felt. Awe, veneration, carnal desire all rolled into one. Here's the Holy Virgin dangling her breasts under your nose while you're still saying your prayers.

— Your friend here, he doesn't like company? she asks.

— He's a bit shy. Wants it to come naturally.

Then, suddenly turning demure herself, she closes her peignoir.

— Why are you wearing dark glasses at night?

— They aren't dark glasses. I'm nearsighted.

She smiles and, all of a sudden, takes them off.

— Isn't that better? My name is Litsa. You?

— Manolopoulos.

— Not your last name, your first name, and she laughs.

— Kostas.

Just then a fat man who's been watching her for the last few minutes gets to his feet. Fiftyish, pudgy, short and sweating.

— You busy? he asks.

She smiles at me again, as if to say "What can you do? he seems to like me, ..." puts my glasses back on my nose and steps out into the hall.

— Louis, why did you bring me here?

— Promise me you'll behave like a gentleman right until the end, and I'll tell you.

— What do you mean, gentleman?

He meant I couldn't be shocked no matter what; I couldn't back out.

— Just imagine, cousin! Imagine I bring you to one of these rooms and there, on the bed you see — let's say — Urania. Or whoever you want. Your aunt Melpo? Her? Let's imagine she split up with Anestis and went back to work. And you see her there on the bed, nude, waiting for customers.

My imagination begins to churn. "What if aunt Melpo was really here," I think. He makes me promise: whoever it might be, even his sister, I'm not going to back out. Meanwhile, curiosity is beginning to get the better of me.

120

— Give me your word? No wheedling your way out when you see her.

— My word, I said, and we shook hands on it.

I begin to study the room more closely. There are pots of half-wilted flowers, an oil-burning heater with its chimney going through the ceiling, brass oil lamps on the walls ... I must have been staring for quite awhile because suddenly I spot the soldier coming out again, with the gorgeous forty-year-old whore right behind him.

He was walking smartly, with a sense of assurance. He'd done it. Probably. Meanwhile, she's back at the same old place, waiting for the next customer.

Only then do I realize Louis has vanished. No sooner did I give my word than he seemed to vaporize. "This is it, Manolopoulos; the chips are down," I mutter to myself and began to look for someone I can recognize. There's one girl whose face I didn't see. Must have just arrived. She's plastered up against the heater, wearing a wide skirt and a sea-green blouse with a red scarf knotted around her neck. All I can see is her back. Her legs are spread apart a bit as she rubs her hands to warm them. I wait for her to turn, to get a look at her face. In a few minutes, the fat man comes out, pauses, wipes the sweat from his brow, and leaves.

"What's he dreamed up for me now, the sonofabitch?" No way I know that woman. The bare back and shoulders against the sea-green and red give her an alluring, provocative look. One thing for certain, it isn't aunt Melpo, it isn't Urania and it isn't Antigone.

Suddenly she turns. Just a second, I'll get a look at her face. Impatience, curiosity. She turns to leave and I see her. Tassoula. I'm not dreaming. She's changed, of course. Thinner, more svelte; she's dyed her hair, changed her hair-do, now it's short, permed.

When she lifts her head and spots me, she freezes in her tracks. The great moment. We look at each other. She doesn't say a word. I remember my promise to Louis. She walks toward the door. I follow her. What else can I do. I manage to

121

pretend to be relaxed, stay cool. She comes to a stop in the middle of the hall. Then opens a door and goes in, leaving it open. I go in and close the door behind me. She's standing there, motionless, erect in the middle of the room, her back to me.

— Retsinas brought you?

— Yes, but he didn't tell me who I'd be meeting.

— I knew; I was expecting you.

And then, without a word, she pulls her blouse over her head. She didn't have a brassiere on. She sits down on the bed. I'm still standing there, staring at her, speechless. My little acting job had come to an end.

— Don't ask me anything. Don't get involved. Better that way.

She makes a gesture to sit down beside her. I sit. She begins to tell me her story; how it is she ended up here. I stare at her breasts. She didn't notice. Her nipples are long, pointed. Later, when I sucked one of them it gave milk, just a tiny droplet.

— From the abortion, probably, she says. Don't worry about it.

There are tears in her eyes.

But wait. Seems we've lost track of Eugenia and the wedding, and the whole Krugas clan besides. If I remember rightly, we left off back when I encountered Aristos in the "California" — the movie house, that is — and he told me that if Louis didn't marry his sister, there was no telling what he'd do to me.

From that point on, though, events unfolded much more rapidly than anyone could have expected.

Naturally, I was in no mood for a movie for the rest of the day. I had to piss every ten minutes I was so scared. Then

122

came the stomach cramps and the diarrhea. I left. A few minutes more and I'd have choked to death.

By the time I found Louis, I was just about at wits' end. When I finally did turn him up and told him what had happened, he advised me to stay calm till next Sunday, the date of the wedding. "We'll see; I'll think of something by then," he said.

"He's stark roaring bonkers," I said to myself. I told him:

— Are you out of your mind, Louis? You're not going through with it, are you?

— I don't know. But don't you worry about it. If she hadn't ratted on me to her brothers, I'd have married her, OK? But how do you expect me to marry the same person who ratted on me?

Meanwhile my own folks, terror-stricken by Krugas' promises that we'd have nothing but trouble, quickly decided to move. Father disagreed.

— Leave me be. I'm not budging from this place.

On the third day, they convinced him. We moved; a few streets over. All for nothing, as it turned out. A few days later, at noon, two pistol shots rang out. You could hear them as far away as Tassos' coffeehouse.

The news didn't take long to catch up. Krugas, the one they call the cuckold, had shot his brother and Olympia. He'd caught them in bed, in the act, in the most disgusting position the human mind could imagine.

So, instead of attending the wedding of Louis and Eugenia, we attended the funerals of Aristos and Olympia.

I never got around to asking Louis if he put the bug in the cuckold's ear, that Aristos was screwing his wife. Louis, needless to say, didn't attend the funeral. We went instead. Eugenia spotted us. She hoped to see Louis. When she didn't she probably felt hurt. For sure she did.

123

5. FRAGILE MATERIAL

WHEN I TOLD MOTHER Louis had a civil service job, that he had real pull, that he could even get me hired if he wanted ... well, let me put it this way: to say she just about tumbled over backwards would hardly describe the impact. The astonishment devastated her health. The way I see it, at any rate, that was the cause of her sudden collapse, the diabetes, the heart murmur and the mild case of thrombosis. Couldn't believe it; simple as that. Suddenly black was white and white was black.

— Retsinas? A ministry job? Impossible, she said.

In her eyes he was such an incompetent, such a loutish and contemptible character that ... And when she learned that he'd gotten Agis a job at the water company, well, she was struck dumb. She began stammering, crossing herself.

— I ... I just can't imagine ... what can I say?

Then she began to back off, gradually. Well, she admitted, maybe he did have some good points.

— He's not so bad, after all. Look at those eyes of his, how clever they are.

Then, sniffing the main chance, she quickly put aside her old fears, fears he would lead father and me astray; she even made the dramatic concession of inviting him to dinner. For only the second time in her life.

She visualized new horizons stretching into the distance. For my sister — the oil merchant hadn't yet made his appearance — for me, since I had yet to choose where I would make my career, for father who would soon be pensioned off — maybe Louis could look after him too.

124

Mother had trouble sleeping at night. When I happened to wake up early I would see her lying there, eyes wide-open, through the open bedroom door. She was designing our lives, just like an architect. And not just our lives; everybody's. The lives of people we knew and people we didn't. All they had to do was come within range. Of course, those nearest and dearest to her got top priority. That's why she never took a job, never did a thing around the house. She was destined for other roles; sure, she did a bit of what passed for cooking, but only the bare minimum. There wasn't enough time. She never had enough time, since her plans stretched well beyond our own life spans, generations into the future, to her great grandchildren and beyond. Her brain had become a fully functioning computer, loaded with data, with programs; all you had to do was press a button, and out would churn the answer.

Mother was more than an architect. She was a prophet. Tassoula? She had everything figured out. Aunt Melpo, ditto. Everything.

— I don't like the smell of it, was her line.

For her, there was a connection between the sense of smell and someone's character. She was the first to pick up on the shady side of someone's story. When, by mistake, I told her about aunty's past, she didn't panic. She'd already figured it out.

— I'd like to see what you're going to do about it, I said. You, the virtuous woman — you're going to allow that sinner in your home?

Tell the truth, it was a dilemma of major proportions. But in the end, not only did she not throw her out, she actually began to butter aunty up, to sweet-talk her, to wait on her. What could she do? Uncle Anestis knew certain gentlemen who carried a lot of weight back then; he knew the Piraeus police chief. We only had one protector, and we could hardly afford to alienate him.

— I don't know what your aunt used to be. But she's certainly no sinner now. She's devoted to her home and her husband.

That's how she squared things with her principles and with her credo. But her way of squaring things all but turned my father into a being without backbone. From a certain moment onward, he gave in to her; bowed his head.

During the early years of their marriage, he resisted. He even tried to involve her in his own interests. Big deal. She followed along halfheartedly for awhile, marking time. But when her predictions started coming true, he began to lose his best arguments. For instance, she suggested that they use the dowry money to buy a second place; she wasn't keen on the idea of going into business with Thanassis. "You'll lose your shirt. Just stay put, don't go looking for easy money." He wouldn't listen. "Thanassis this and Thanassis that," father rattled on. Within three years the business was gone, the dowry was gone, the job was gone. He was unemployed. Three years, three disasters. "You'll see; he'll take our money and run." And so it was. Thanassis became a big shot in town; the biggest lamp shop in Piraeus. "And now he pretends not to see us, fine gentleman that he is."

The only "profit" we ever got out of the deal was the olive oil merchant. She stuck us with the man. Please, don't ask me to tell you what she predicted, or what finally happened. With the oil merchant, I mean. Mom was an honest-to-God Cassandra, a Delphic oracle. She never missed. Only Louis threw her for a loop. When she came to him, the computer broke down. Her predictions kept falling apart.

Anyway, after the episode with Thanassis — "that no good swindler!" — father never raised his head again.

He knew by now that she'd be proven right in the end, so why bother, why fight it? Slowly he retreated into his ouzo, and into silence.

Only Louis could pull him from the fast-flowing stream of the inevitable. Like I said, he adored Louis, but didn't dare hold him up as an example, as someone to be emulated.

Sometimes, late at night, I eavesdropped on their whispered conversations.

— What are you wasting all your time on that no-good bum

126

for? What are you after? You want him to lead your son by the nose, is that it? Get him mixed up in politics? He's nothing but a useless layabout. I'm right and you know it!

On she ranted while my old man said not a word. What could he say? But when word got around that Louis had a civil service job, dad spotted his opening.

— There, what do you have to say about that? The no-good layabout, remember? But you invite him over for dinner, hoping he'll fix up your son. So now he's Mr. Retsinas; so he's not a deviant and a pervert after all. Now you'd just love to have him as a son-in-law, isn't that right?

He got it off his chest, all of it. Not a word out of mom. That's when her upper lip began to quiver, like I said. Faintly, but perceptibly. When you're mom, when you think you don't have anything to answer for, you'll end up with a stroke, or something like it. That's exactly what happened.

I felt sorry for her. Deep, deep down she was right and I knew it. For the first time, I started to feel twinges of regret. Poor thing, spends her whole life lying awake nights, trying to fix up everyone else's life — and always forgetting about herself. On top of all that, whenever we caught her in a moment of weakness, like now, whenever she didn't have an answer, we went after her viciously. We took dead aim and shot to kill. The lot of us. Didn't she used to say "Who laughs last laughs best?" So why was she inviting him over for dinner? To admit her error? Not likely. It was far from clear that she was in error. She knew her antennae could receive signals we couldn't. But she couldn't prove it.

Funny. At that stage Louis proved her right, and she proved him right. If you used her tactics, you couldn't lose. But you would never earn that other paradise, the one Louis held out for you. Follow Louis and you wouldn't lose either, but there would always be that nagging doubt: were you sure you did the right thing.

Now, though, two minutes before he was to arrive, we had her in the dock — father and I — and we were reading her the list of charges.

127

— When will you finally admit nothing is all black or all white? What makes you think your life is better than Louis'? Is he a thief? Did he kill anyone? Is he a pimp or something? So, what is it?

To this day I can see her standing there with the platter of fish, staring at us with those big round eyes of hers. That would have been when the tremor began, the one I mentioned earlier. She was standing exactly in the doorway between the kitchen and the dining room. My sister was in the living room, leafing through a photo-romance; all she could say from time to time was "Shut up, will you, I'm trying to read." The numskull! Didn't it occur to her that we were trying to redeem her? If she had been more careful, she would have known better than to marry the oil merchant in the first place.

At that precise moment, when I saw her lip began to shiver, I felt the first twinges of regret. But by then I had a full head of steam. There was no stopping me:

— What do you know about life? What makes you think you're right all the time? Because Louis got a civil service job, overnight he's a fine gentleman?

On and on I went, more out of orneriness than conviction.

— You know who got him the job? Who appointed him? Kritsinis, that's who!

No holding me back now. I let her have it with both barrels.

— You know why? Because he's a fairy and Louis laid him. Hear me? That's how he got the job; because he got laid.

That did it. Her heart murmur suddenly reached a crescendo, the shaking of her lips spread to her whole head; she dropped the platter of fish. Her best platter.

All hell broke loose. There was fish all over the floor; our best tablecloth was a mess. We'd gone too far. No one had time to react.

At that very instant the doorbell rang. Father didn't hesitate; he didn't want to see a soul; and locked himself into his room.

— I'm not hungry, leave me alone; I want some sleep.

Out he walked. I had toppled his idol. Now it was my turn to get upset. After all, I was happy he liked Louis and I didn't want to diminish Louis in his eyes. Besides, I was lying. Louis never laid Kritsinis, as you know. "Don't worry about it; he'll get over it," I thought. "He'll forgive him."

Like I say, you can't bear a grudge against Louis. Even Pericles — a friend of ours from the coffeehouse — forgave him, despite the fact that he caught Louis in bed with his mother. Unbelievable, you say? But it happened, I swear.

Sure, Louis was involved with Pericles' mother for a while. Not that there was anything abnormal about it. In fact, if you knew Mrs. Maritsa Ghikas, Pericles' mom, you would have found it not only normal, but inevitable.

For us, all of us, Pericles' place had always been a setting for fantasms, for fervid speculation. None of us had as much as set foot there, but, from a few whispered remarks, a word here and a word there, it had taken on exotic proportions. My mom called it "the house of sin." Agis called it a bordello until he got the job with the water company. After that, though, he changed his tune.

— Remember what we used to call it? Well, it's just another house.

Much later we found out what made him change his mind. One day, just as he was describing Mrs. Maritsa's bordello to some people at the office, who should walk in but the department supervisor who just happened to know Mrs. Ghikas well, very well indeed. Try that for diabolical coincidence! In addition to supervisor, he was a huge, powerful man, with bulging muscles. A slab of beef on the hoof, as it turned out later, when the two found themselves in a tête-à-tête situation. Mr. Beef goes over to Agis, grabs him by the shirt collar with the clear intention of nailing him on the beezer, and says:

— You stinking little fart, one more word about Maritsa and I'll bust your balls.

And lets him drop. If the hulk's sentence had been a few words longer, Agis might well have breathed his last.

From then on Maritsa's place became "just another house."

As it turned out, Mr. Beef defended Mrs. Maritsa's reputation so zealously because he happened to be her lover at the time. Later he became her husband, and when he kicked the bucket, he became "dear departed Leander." Stroke. He was the third, or was it the fourth, husband — no one knows for sure — to croak on her. All from strokes. The first was Ghikas. Probably.

You could have filled a small dictionary with all Mrs. Maritsa's nicknames. Blondie they called her, fire and water — that was Tassos', the coffeehouse owner's, term for her. "How's fire and water these days?" For still others she was the dark lady, the sinner, the nymphomaniac. Louis explained to us exactly what a nymphomaniac was:

— A woman who wants sex all the time, but can't ever reach a climax.

— Wrong. She wants sex, and she can come, differed Andoniadis, another member of our group.

But our main source of information about Maritsa was Agis, our chief gossip:

— Guys, they say when she wants it and there's no man available — she doesn't masturbate; not her style — she calls Electra, the maid, flops down on the bed, spreads her legs and has the girl diddle her. Unbelievable stuff. The girl knows what she likes by now, so she just goes to it.

Still, part of the story must have been true. Before Electra went to work for Maritsa, she was a workaday little woman who minded her home and her job. But later she turned into a flaming lesbian. In fact, a few years later, after her divorce, she ended up living with a Viennese woman in Kastella, an archeologist. After that, we lost track of her.

The only person who made an effort to find her was Louis. The whole story had made a profound impression on him; par-

130

ticularly her daring. She was just a simple woman. I still remember her. Uneducated, kindly, almost God-fearing. He wanted to find her, to ask her, to understand where she found the courage to take that kind of "social" leap.

That's Louis for you. He doesn't want the people he meets to drop out of sight. Wants to be in touch. Not so much for the sake of company. More to find out what happened to them, how they changed, how they developed. He's endlessly fascinated by the possibility of following the course of their life at close range. If he knows what you were, he's itching to find out what you've become.

When he discovered that the Quartermaster, our army buddy, was living with a German ex-whore in Munich, he burst out:

— Now that's what I call revolution, Kostas, my boy! How can you ever pull off the big one if you can't handle the small ones? Didn't know a word of German, a married man, timid, complexes up to here, and now look at him. We'll have to go look him up one of these days.

Even if nothing in your life had changed, even if you simply let it go to seed, Louis still wanted to know about your mind's inner workings, about your soul, how you came to accept things, how you made peace with the idea that it's game over, no more wild oats, now it's home sweet home. Time and time again, years later, someone's name would suddenly pop into his mind, someone's story.

"Kostas, my boy, you've got a car. Let's go see what happened to Polyxeni. Is she alive, dead, remarried?"

Louis' relationship with Mrs. Maritsa was a landmark event for our whole gang. She would have been in her forties then; he was twenty something. We could hardly believe it.

Like I told you, Pericles, even though he was part of the group, had never invited us over; that alone was enough to fuel the rumors. It was crystal clear that some of the stories had to be true.

Whenever Agis had a bit of fresh news, we could see it coming miles away. As soon as we spotted him, we knew: from the

131

way he walked, the way he swung his arms, the way he moved his legs, his ears.

— Shhh! He's got some news!

He walked with rapid steps, you know, hands swinging to and from, ears too. How the hell did he do that? But his trademark was the way he bit his lips, mainly the lower lip. And if there was really interesting news, he gnawed at them until they almost bled.

— Calm down, Agis, you're slicing off the meat, we cautioned.

— Guys, you'll never believe it. Maritsa's husband's dead; from a stroke. He's putting up his brother, Menelaos, and one day he turns up earlier than usual and what do you think he sees?... Wild happenings, my friends. Wild.

We sat there, gaping.

— Come on! Out with it! What did you see?

— Guys, he catches 'em, doin' it in an armchair, stark-naked. Just as he's abut to grab her by the hair and yank her away from Menelaos, he keels over. It's all she wrote for Ghikas.

We weren't laughing. It was frightful.

— Some of the neighbors called Pericles; he was at night school. Something snapped inside him. They say he grabbed a butcher's knife, went after his mother and uncle. Was gonna kill the both of 'em. The Orestes story all over again.

To be honest, though, many people didn't believe the stroke story. Ghikas, they said, had caught her in the act more than a dozen times and nothing like this had ever happened. Naturally, the butcher's knife never got used. Pericles handed it over to his mother when, in a dramatic scene, she confessed that if he killed his uncle he wouldn't simply be a murderer but a parricide. She'd been having relations with the uncle for years; he was Pericles' real father. Not Ghikas.

The Louis-Maritsa story began one day when Agis, panting and lip-biting, announced he'd finally managed to get inside Pericles' house. He'd seen it. We all grabbed chairs, sat him down in the middle and waited.

132

I don't think I described Maritsa to you yet; maybe it's not even necessary. Short, plumpish, blond with blue eyes and hair, lots of hair. She had hair on her arms, her face, in her armpits. Her lips were extraordinary: fleshy, plump and rounded. Both cheeks had dimples. The spitting image of Ava Gardner, only shorter. One look at those eyes and those lips and you fell under her magic spell.

— Guys, she gives out magical vibes. Three, four feet in all directions. Maybe more. Don't ask me how exactly, but if you get too close, you get burned. Seriously. Electro-magnetic radiation.

— Agis, Louis suddenly declared, either you find a way to get all of us into that house, or we're going to have you charged with slander.

He stared at us like an idiot. But finally he buckled under.

— Alright, but first I've got to invent an excuse.

But Louis was in a hurry.

— Now. We want to go now.

And he did.

Maritsa opened the door, wearing a white silk slip.

As she walked, you could hear the rustling of the silk and of her eyelashes. You never saw eyelashes like that before! Long, auburn and definitely not fake. They were so long they rustled. You could hear 'em. She didn't seem to mind us seeing her in her slip.

— She never wears clothes in the house, said Agis when he noticed our astonishment.

The rooms were shrouded in half-darkness. She didn't like too much light. Heavy purple curtains covered all the windows. The inside doors were all in etched glass, with scenes of swans and satyrs.

— I like shady things, she told us.

Her voice was husky, soft, enticing; it seemed to be coming over hidden loudspeakers. Up to that moment we had only caught the odd fleeting glimpse of her as she hurried by in front of the coffeehouse without turning to look; we'd never had the opportunity to chat with her. At the most, she gave us a sidelong "How are you?"

The house was crammed with sofas and couches, and folding screens made of wood and canvas. Dark red wool carpets covered the bedroom floor, blankets of the same color covered the bed; above it hung a painting of a reclining semi-nude. Later we learned it was a reproduction of *Madame Recamier*. There were table lamps with red glass shades on the night tables.

She liked classical music, the theater, and romantic fiction. So she told us. Funny. Never met a "loose" woman who didn't like the fine arts. She noticed me staring at the painting.

— I bought it in France, she said. I like it.

She'd been to France. Quite an accomplishment in those days.

— Don't get so bloody curious, Agis said. That's where she goes for her abortions.

Now that he mentioned it, not one Easter would go by without Maritsa taking a trip to France. Agis was throwing us one surprise after another. And all the while, as Mrs. Ghikas gave us the guided tour of her house, we were falling under her spell.

She put a record on the gramophone — you know, the kind with a huge horn and a winding handle, just like aunt Melpo's — and we listened to piano music. Later on, when I heard the same piece, I learned it was Beethoven's *Moonlight Sonata*. Add the scent that enveloped her to all of the above, throw in the piano, and you'll get a fair idea of what the atmosphere in her house was like.

— My dear lady, Louis said. I don't know what my friend, Kostas, here, or Agis, intend to do, but there's no way I'm going to leave your house. I'll bring my shaving gear and pyjamas; all I want to do is watch you, listen to you.

Or words to that effect, half in jest, half serious. He stayed. Can you believe it? He stayed. He wasn't joking. We left, he stayed on. For three nights.

Later, Pericles came home from night school — they had completely forgotten about him — and discovered them in bed,

134

asleep in one another's arms. He closed the door quietly, and waited for them to wake up.

When Louis got up he found Pericles in the study, sketching sailing ships and stormy seascapes; he pretended nothing had happened.

— You here, Pericles? Manolopoulos and Agis just left.

That's exactly what he said. Pericles didn't seem concerned. He was resigned to the fact: his mother was who she was. He even started talking with Louis about Chinese poetry; read him a few poems, as I recall.

After those first three nights, Louis became a regular visitor at Maritsa's. For a good year this went on. I think he had to repeat his school term. Much later, Maritsa herself told me it was the very first time in her life she'd been so much in love; and the first time she'd been faithful to the same man for six months running.

But after six months, she couldn't resist. "Family friends" began to come visiting. Even uncle Menelaos would put in an occasional appearance. Pericles never spoke to him. If Louis happened to be around, the two of them would ease out.

Once Louis described Maritsa's love-making style.

— I'm telling you, that's why a woman like her never gets abandoned, cousin. Maybe you're ready to drop, but she resurrects you. It's not just love, not even an orgy; it's a feast. All that — plus the unexpected, the impossible.

On and on he went.

— If that's how it is, you'll get sick from exhaustion. Look at you; you'll wind up with a case of TB.

And so it was. It was all his sister could do to rescue him. When he started to spit blood, she bundled him off to the hospital.

The story of Louis and Maritsa was my mom's strongest argument against him.

— Is nothing sacred? She's what she is, alright; but him, jumping all over your friend's mother?

But the weirdest part of the whole thing was Pericles. He turned silent, remote, enigmatic, unapproachable. Shortly after Louis began to spit blood, he went into a profound depression. Then he plunged into Chinese poetry. He quit drawing ships and seas; now his subject matter was black birds and bats. Then he dropped out of night school and locked himself into his room; he painted the walls red, let his hair and beard grow; washed more and more infrequently; only went out after midnight. We chalked it up to the "family friends"; he couldn't tolerate them.

Agis insists that many things happened before Louis finally broke off with her. He claimed that he caught her in the act not with "family friends," but with Pericles himself.

— Are you crazy? What are you saying? You know what you're saying?

— There's no other explanation, Manolopoulos. She could seduce a saint, let alone a kid.

The sonofabitch had to know something. But the idea didn't really bother me; it all seemed perfectly normal. Her sleeping with her son, I mean. Maritsa was like ... like the earth having intercourse with the universe. If she could have copulated with all of mankind she would have done it, and never wondered why. She was an immense pelvic cavity in a state of constant arousal. Restraints, taboos? Not her. If there had not been certain technical difficulties, she would have happily let the whole of masculine humanity march through her. Her vagina was like nature itself in a state of perpetual springtime.

Later, Louis confessed:

— Kostas, my boy, if you're out of sperm, she can make you bleed. I've done it.

Finally, Pericles moved to Salonica, whence he never returned. Never wrote her again either. He abandoned Chinese poetry and took up foreign languages; opened a language school. Didn't open it himself, actually. He married a hairy forty-year-old woman from Salonica — Maro was her name. The school was hers. No one could ever figured out whether he married her because of the school or because she reminded him of his mother.

When Louis ran into him twenty years later, he'd turned fat. In his twenties, he'd always been thin, nothing but skin and bones. "The ghost," we called him. "Here comes the ghost."

But the truth is, Louis and I owe that woman plenty. Primarily because she taught us to love good music, and the theater. She was the first person to take us. By the hand, literally; took us by the hand and led us there. I remember, we came back to her place. It was nearly midnight, but we were enchanted; we talked on until dawn about Vania, Astrov and Sonia. The play was Chekov's *Uncle Vania*. God bless Chekov and God bless Maritsa.

There I go again, off on a tangent. Now, where were we? Ah, yes; just as Louis was scheduled to arrive for mom's dinner invitation.

As she collapsed to the floor, the doorbell rang. We were expecting Louis; but Agis appeared instead. "He's got news," I thought. He could hardly restrain himself, that was obvious. He was winking, gesticulating; had to see me in private.

— Louis sent me. He can't make it. Something came up.

I took him aside; didn't want mom overhearing.

— What happened? He's not coming? How come?

— He's waiting outside. He's furious; fit to kill.

Before mom could piece together what was happening I pulled on my jacket, put on my shoes and we rushed downstairs. Maybe Louis wasn't coming because he couldn't be bothered climbing the stairs: for a split second the thought crossed my mind. It wouldn't have been the first time. "Kostas, my boy, I'm not coming to your place any more. Too many stairs," he once told me. He could walk from here to Timbuktu and back, but don't ask him to climb stairs. You'll kill him.

137

— What stairs? Let him tell you himself, snapped Agis when I told him what I was thinking.

We found him pissing — early afternoon it was — behind a parked truck. Obviously, he was having frequent urination problems. Must have been emotional stress; every ten minutes he had to run off for a leak.

— Look at the state I'm in, will you!

From there to our destination, about three-quarters of an hour on foot from my house, he stopped to piss another five times . Twice in regular urinals, the other three times behind parked trucks or fences. Meanwhile, he was in full flight, oratorically speaking:

— If I could kill him myself, I'd do it. But he's too strong. Maybe the three of us could do it.

I still didn't know what in the world he was talking about. The only thing that filtered through was that we were going to kill someone.

I'd never seen Louis quite so excited before. His normally debonair manner had deserted him, along with his self-control.

— Where are we going?

— To Argyris' place. Now shut up.

Argyris was part of our coffeehouse crowd. He was a Communist party cadre and the man of the moment for our group, not so much because of his ideas, as because he'd shacked up with poor little Martha, the orphan.

— Why, that piece of shit! Why doesn't he mind his own goddamn business. Just carrying out the party line, is he? A defenseless girl, he claims. I'll look after her, my mother will take care of her, muttered Louis as he hurried along.

But Argyris' mother soon died, and he began to take care of the girl himself. Louis was still hanging around the party in half-ass fashion, Argyris' half-comrade, so to speak.

— Hey, Louis, fill me in, will you; what's going on?

For an answer, he pulls a photograph out of his pocket.

— Get a load of this; you'll understand everything.

I looked. Kritsinis! It was Kritsinis, our deputy commander

at Corinth boot camp, hanging from the neck, in his home. From the ceiling chandelier hook. Hanging from the ceiling in his dressing gown. I was stunned.

— Claims to be my friend, Argyris does. Used to be my cell leader. The asshole. Thirty years old and still hasn't got a clue. Anyway, a couple of days back we're having a drink at Lambros' and I get a bit carried away ... and I spill the beans about Kritsinis. Like a fool, I lay it all out for him: how Kritsinis found work for me, how he likes to dress up in women's clothes at night looking for lovers, how he goes around in disguises to avoid hurting his political career. I told him everything, all the details. When you come right down to it, he never hurt anyone. Only himself. Let him be, the poor devil. He minds his own business, doesn't he? How was I supposed to imagine that he'd go through with it, that he'd actually rat on the guy.

Louis was beside himself. With remorse, tension, guilt.

— Why did I go and tell him everything? What a fool! How did I know he was such an asshole? So goddamn bloodthirsty? Mostly I told him for the hell of it. How was I supposed to know?

By the time we reach Argyris' house, Louis' description of the situation has us fired up, and then some. Our clear intention is to strangle the guy. Not me so much, to tell you the truth; in fact, I was lobbying for a lesser punishment.

— Come on, Louis; the death penalty's a bit much.

— Manolopoulos, you don't know what you're talking about. As far as I'm concerned, Kritsinis was a gentleman. He didn't always look at things from the party angle, he didn't always ... So what if I was on the blacklist. He helped all of us out, selflessly. Thanks to him, ten guys are putting bread on their table. Not to mention Agis.

139

— A real screw job, Louis. No doubt about it. Deserves to have the shit knocked out of him.

That's Agis talking.

We draw near on tiptoe, go through the wooden door which opens onto the courtyard and come to a stop at the front door. It was cracked, the paint was peeling.

We look at one another, then Agis gives it such a powerful kick that the door not only gives way, it splits right down the middle. A woman's shriek rings out and as we rush in we see the "defenseless" Martha grabbing a blanket to cover her nakedness — she's wearing a short, miserable nightie — while Argyris, clad only in his shorts, dashes off to hide in the bathroom.

— I knew it, I knew your little fairy pal would kill himself, I knew it! the raving revolutionary is howling from his safe haven. It wasn't me. A guy I know, a reporter, guy named Karalis; he did it. Not me. But what's it to you, anyway? He's your brother or something?

And he launches into an explanation of how the enemies of the Party must be crushed by all possible means. Kritsinis is the son of an informer, isn't he? A quisling; someone who fingered people right and left at Corinth.

— How many guys did he send off to desert islands for holidays? You check that out? He was nothing but shit. Right or wrong? The people that came back from Makronissos, how many of 'em came back thanks to him? When you get down to it, that's one less reactionary.

Louis listens, trembling with rage. Then he lashes out at the door with his feet, spitting, shouting.

— And what makes you think I give a shit what his father did then or what he does today? Ever since I met the guy, he was OK — or wasn't he? Did he turn human or not? Why did he help me out, anyway? roars Louis.

— I don't know. People say ... I don't know. People ...

— You, you're going to judge him? Us you're going to judge? You're better, you? So why don't you marry the girl instead of just shacking up with her? Taking care of her on Party

140

orders, eh? Now who's going to wash the shame off me, for selling out my friend? The man trusted me, he opened his heart and I double-cross him, is that it? Whoever told you I put the Party ahead of my conscience? Shit head! Expel me, go on ...

Louis is foaming at the mouth.

— Come out of there! I'll light this dump on fire and you'll roast, right where you are. Who's going to pay for my emotional distress when the man phones me up to spit on me because I betray him? What am I supposed to say? Stuff like that doesn't bother the right wing; that's what you think, asshole! Don't kid yourself. He's not dead today because he was exposed; it's because I betrayed him. That's why he hung himself. You piece of shit! And they had to have pictures, right on the scene? Was that your bright idea, or maybe your cell leader told you what to do?

— No one, I swear it, The reporter, he did it. Don't get the Party involved. What does the party have to do with it?

Meantime, Agis and I locate the master key and a screwdriver. We batter and push, but the fucking door won't budge.

All the while, Martha is huddled in a corner of the sofa, wrapped up in her blanket, staring at us with those perpetually astonished eyes of hers.

— Open up, shit face; you're only making it worse for yourself. Open up and take your licks or there's no telling what will happen. We ain't leaving, get that through your head, howls Louis.

He's almost at the point of banging his head against the wall. Just couldn't get over it.

— The man entrusted me with his secret, treated me like a friend, and me, like an idiot ...

He starts kicking at the door again. I try to calm him, but he keeps right on:

— Lucky he hung himself, otherwise I would have beaten him to it. What could I say to him? How could I look him in the eye. How could he believe I wasn't in on it myself?

141

Louis was right. All the opposition papers had dragged Kritsinis through the mud. Ran photos of him wearing wigs and women's clothing showing his legs, right downtown.

— What about the Second Coming? What'll I tell him when I meet him on judgment day? You asshole, you shit head! All so that sleazy reporter buddy of yours can get his scoop?

Always the practical one, I try to calm things down by asking Martha to make some coffee. She goes into the bedroom to put some clothes on. A second later, Agis nudges me.

— Lean over a bit, Casanova, and you'll see a woman that is a woman.

He points to the bedroom door. No need to lean over. There's a mirror across from the half-open door. Naked, Martha looked even thinner. If you were to ship her off as a package, the label would read "Caution! Contains Fragile Material." Pure glass. All except her eyes. Those immense black eyes of hers, like dark coals.

When Louis comes in from the front yard — after taking a leak — he catches us peeping through the door. Even sneaks a look himself.

We all knew Martha ever since she was a little girl. She never saw her father. Killed by the Germans. Can barely remember her mother: a lifetime of jail, exile, one holding cell after another. Woman gave everything for the struggle. Only her life she didn't give; too late for that. A three-wheeled motorcycle took it for her. That makes two left-wingers killed by three-wheelers! Lambrakis and her. But before her eyes closed for good, she entrusted comrade Argyris with protection of her daughter. Suited him just fine. A fat, disagreeable slob like him would never have met such a woman in his whole life. So when they evicted Martha from her mother's place, he took her into his own miserable dump.

But, as you'll soon see, the coffee I asked her to make would prove to be fateful. Argyris is still besieged in the toilet while Martha is making coffee, tears pouring down her face. And Agis is rinsing out the coffee cups next to her in the kitchen, whispering in her ear.

142

Louis comes over to me.

— Save the girl. You like her? You like her. Take her away from lard-ass. He'll squeeze her dry and throw her away. Marry her if you have to.

I stare at him. Never expected that kind of advice.

— What are you staring at? What's marriage for anyway? With Martha or without her, you'll never be happy unless you listen to the voice inside you. Hell, if it's only cold logic, might as well clip our wings, and our craziness and our friendship. Cut me off first of all.

What am I supposed to say? Things just don't happen that way? Anyway, how am I supposed to persuade her?

— How, Louis? Where am I supposed to take her? If I had a job, OK; a place; maybe we could discuss it seriously.

He shakes his head; he's about to call me "jerk-off," but he doesn't. Instead he turns his attention back to Argyris, and begins kicking at the locked bathroom door, cursing:

— You're no human being, you're a snake! You're not even a man. If you were, you'd come out of there and say, "Hit me, you're right."

He stops for a second. No answer. He turns, looks at me, and asks me again if I like Martha.

— You know I do. Sure, I like her. But what am I supposed to do with her? Why don't you tell my mom to let me bring her home. Will you?

He turns his back on me, kicks out at some bags lying on the floor, half-lifts his arms and spits toward the heavens.

— Well, fuck me! And he calls himself a man?

He turns back to me wild-eyed, aggressive.

— Cousin, mark it down: you're going to regret this. You're going to cry. That's something precious you're throwing into the wastebasket. No, make it the garbage can.

Better he punch me, spit on me, curse me than say what he did. It was a direct blow to the heart. A bullet couldn't have done a better job. I freeze in my tracks.

I look again at Martha. My kind of girl! She brings in the coffee. The fear is gone from her eyes. She's relaxed now. Agis

143

is close beside her.

— This one has extra sugar. I don't know how you take your coffee.

I start to speak, struggle to find something intelligent to say, something that will impress her, something like "If you made it, it's got to be right." Something along those lines, but by the time I can muster the courage to say it, Agis has already dredged up one of his dreadful wisecracks:

— Even if it's poison, we'd drink it.

Martha blushes scarlet.

— Cut the smart cracks, Agis, says Louis.

If Louis was the general, Agis was the foot soldier. Next thing you know, he'll snap to attention and say, "Yes, sir; as you will, sir!" He would do anything for Louis; respected him more than you can imagine; ran errands; played the yes-man; worshipped him. He was convinced that Louis was destined to become a Very Important Person.

— Us, the best we can hope for is some crummy office job with a shit salary and a cheap dowry. But Louis, mark my words. He'll be running the show one of these days.

That's how he looked up to Louis. Swore by him, in fact.

— Come on, Agis, you got money. Run buy us some smokes, will you, Louis suddenly blurts out.

So, before I know it, I find myself alone with Martha. The more I look at her, the better I like what I see. Her eyes are sucking me in. Just as she is about to take the cups away, I dare to ask her to sit down. Louis eases out of the room, ostensibly to wash his hands in the kitchen. But he's watching from a distance. She sits down, and in a few moments, turns toward me.

— You should get out of here. It's not for you, I manage to say.

She smiles. Must find my remark naive, to say the least.

— I'm finishing school this year. Where can I go? she says.

Now she's more than looking at me. She's provoking me. There is a curious daring in her eyes. Her lips too. You might think that being an orphan, living such a miserable life would

144

have transformed her into some kind of fearful, irresolute creature. Not Martha. The more you looked at her, the more you could feel a strength about her, a stubborn streak.

Then I realize that her eyes aren't the only magnetic thing about her; her legs are too; from the ankles on up, long and straight. She may be thin, but I don't think I ever saw more perfect legs. Fortunately, the couch we're sitting on is a bit saggy; we've sunk so far back into it that her blue skirt is well above her knees.

What to look at first? Lips, eyes, legs? I feel myself melting, I can't move. In any case, when she says, "Where else can I go," I feel myself collapsing at her feet. "What do I say now," I wonder. "What do I suggest? Where should she go?"

— I don't know. There's got to be a way; you'll find a job, something will come along ...

I'm spouting nonsense. What am I telling her that for?

— First I want to finish school, then go to the Polytechnic Institute. I like drawing. Maybe I'll become an architect. Argyris isn't all that bad.

I try to drive a wedge between them.

— It's awful, what he did to Louis.

— Really awful. I told him so myself. I knew it. You shouldn't do it, I told him.

I try to reveal a little more of myself, to tell her something a bit erotic, a bit more ...

— You know, I remember when your mother used to send you over to our place so I could give you a hand with your homework.

That's the best I could do. The farthest I could go. I want to add "I really like you" but ... Oh well, I guess it was a kind of baring of the soul, as far as it went.

— I remember you, she says. It was my first year in high school. They assigned us subjects, and you used to tell me what to write ... Just a second. What was it now? Now I remember, "My Day at Home." I wanted to put down all my crazy ideas, all the stories I wanted to tell. But you said: "No, maybe you really did all those things, but maybe you didn't.

All of a sudden, when you're alone with yourself, you might find out you don't know what to do with all your free time. Better tell the truth instead." So I did. The teacher gave me the oddest look. But he liked my composition. Gave me top marks. I never wrote a bad one again.

While she spoke, something Louis told me long ago, when we encountered her at a movie theater, rushed back into my mind. "Kostas, my boy, she's in love with you. Don't tell me you can't see it?"

In the meantime, our hands have fallen to the cushions, almost touching. As she talks about her school compositions, about how everything we said that day influenced her life, all I can think is: "Do I take her hand or not? Take it or not?"

From the kitchen Louis is egging me on. "Go after her," he seems to be saying, gesticulating. Suddenly I grasp her hand. Barely touch it ... It's burning now. How soft it is! Frail, just a wisp, a baby bird. A baby bird you could cradle in your palm. She leaves it there, and at the same time looks away from me. As if she's embarrassed, but her hand doesn't move.

That touch! If I told you it was like an electric current surging through me, that wouldn't be the half of it. I'd taken my jacket off, now my pants are starting to bulge. I don't know what to do. I'm mortified. I try to think of something else, try to calm down, but nothing works ... As long as we're in contact, the current keeps flowing. I can see her legs, see the outline of her breasts. She's not wearing a bra. They're small, firm, round, like tennis balls. Inside me the confusion is growing. I want her. "What should I do now?" I wonder. "What now?"

To make my job easier, Louis eases the kitchen door closed, ever so gently.

My fingers begin to move, gently, across her palm. Like a faint caress. Again she doesn't pull away.

Then, without knowing why, I turn to her and with my other hand touch her chin and lift it up, bringing her eyes level with mine.

— Tell me ...

146

I stop. As she raises her eyes, I drop my hand from her chin and bring it to her back. Then, gently, softly, I pull her toward me; in my mind is the "Caution: Fragile Materials" label. Except that in the space of a few seconds the fragile has suddenly turned inflammable.

— I like you ... always have liked you, I say.

She, with her first finger, strokes my lips.

— It's not true. You like Tassoula too, and Urania. Your mother wouldn't let you see somebody like me ...

She can't complete the sentence. We hear Louis trying to hold Agis off.

— Easy there, big guy. Just wait a second. He's helping her solve some mathematics problems.

Then Argyris starts to wail from the john. He can't take it any more.

— Get out of my house. I'll call the cops. Retsinas, you mangy hound. You hear me?

Now it was his turn to bang on the door. But the second he says "mangy hound," Agis and Louis burst in. They find us seated like plaster saints on the couch. They head straight for the toilet. Agis is first to speak.

— If you're man enough, come on out of there. Come on out, go tell the cops.

Louis turns toward Martha and me, looks us over. Now he's enjoying himself, the bastard. He always did want to break me out of the goody-goody mold — been trying for half a lifetime in fact. Always did want to "corrupt" me. Call it his obsession. He leans over to Martha and points toward the toilet.

— You're going to stay here with that creep? If you do, don't expect to see me again.

She turns first to me, then to him.

— I don't know, she says.

— I'll try and convince mom to let you stay with us, and we'll take it from there. First of all, you've got to finish school.

What the hell do I mean, first of all? Agis butts in.

— Look, I've got space at my place. I'm still living at mom's.

147

We've got a whole spare room.

Without a word, Martha gets up and goes off. We look at each other in puzzlement. "What happened? Where's she going?"

— You want to call the cops? I'll let you out; I won't even hurt you. But only if you turn us in to the police. Otherwise I'll burn your house down, Louis tells Argyris.

— Know something, you're crazy. Why don't you go find the reporter, that guy Karalis. I only mentioned it. He's the one that blew the whistle. And don't go dragging the Party into this. Don't put me in a difficult position, please. The Party doesn't know a thing.

By the time the Louis-Argyris dialogue was over, Martha had stuffed her things into a suitcase. When we see her standing there in the doorway, ready to go, our jaws drop. She's even wearing her beret. I always remember her that way. With a beret on her head, I mean. Sometimes a blue one, sometimes red, sometimes black. Standing there in the open door, surrounded by the door frame, she looks for all the world like a painting entitled *Woman with Beret.*

My legs are starting to shake, I have difficulty moving. "She's got the guts to walk out," I think to myself, "to walk out on security, and me, I'm to blame." She comes over to me.

— Don't worry, Manolopoulos, it's not your fault. Don't let it bother you.

She could read my mind. Agis stares at us. First at the one, then at the other. I don't know if he realizes what's gone on before. But in the midst of the general embarrassment he walks over to her, takes her suitcase and says:

— I don't know what you think, but I've got room to spare at my place.

And out he goes. Agis' gesture moves Martha so much that, tears aside, she decides to follow him.

I make one feeble, halfhearted effort, "I'll try to see what I can do at my place ..."

— Don't worry. I'll stay with Agis, she says.

In pantomime, Louis tells us to leave the house silently. We

148

tiptoe out, leaving Argyris in the toilet. Besieged without besiegers. He never even knew exactly when we left.

We were a good two blocks away when we heard him. It was more than a shout; it was a howl.

— Martha! Martha!

He called only her name. Fortunately, a taxi was going by; we jumped in, the three of us, along with the suitcase. Otherwise he might have caught up with us.

Much later, I encountered Argyris. Three times, in fact. Once at his wedding, once after his wedding, and once at his funeral. It was only then I learned he'd been expelled from the party. Him and Louis.

In the taxi I tried to talk to Martha.

— Look, tomorrow ... I'll talk to my mother. I'll twist her arm, I'll ...

She took my hand tenderly.

— Don't bother. There's no need to get mixed up in my problems. Until I know what I'm going to do, I'll stay at Agis' place. Then we'll see.

Maybe Louis didn't beat up on Argyris, but he was delighted to have taken Martha from him. It was vengeance of the worst kind. Or so he told us, at any rate, in an explosive outburst of laughter:

— He won't be forgetting this overnight, the scum, he said, suddenly turning reflective.

As we sped away in the taxi, Louis explained how it would be better for Martha to spend a few days in a hotel. Argyris was likely to go looking for her; she couldn't take any chances. Better for her to cover her tracks.

We took her to the Mycenae Hotel, on the harbor front, next to the John Bull pub. First floor, room twelve. Agis was still toting her suitcase.

6. LOUIS' FIRST MARRIAGE

"BELMONDO, ONLY SHORTER. Plus blue eyes. Pure blue eyes." That was Louis as described by his first wife, Alice.

Us, his friends, by the time we found out about the marriage — and the daughter — the party was already long over and the break-up was at hand.

— I could see it coming, Kostas, my boy; never could tolerate that "Alice" of hers. Mommy calls her Alice, daddy calls her Alice. But me, it stuck in my craw from day one. As far as I'm concerned, she's Aleka; for them, she's Alice. Maybe if they'd agreed to Aliki ... you never know. But Aleka all the way to Alice, well, that was a joke and then some. "What's the difference, Aleka, Aliki or Alice?" was all that dimwit father of hers could say.

It was back in the Maritsa era. Louis had just gotten a job as a book salesman when calamity struck, like a one-two punch. Calamity one was Alice.

— It was just after I saw *Lolita*, cousin; she was Alice all over again, I swear. "You've got to be the one who plays Lolita in the film, sweetie," I tell her. She didn't know what to say, Kostas, my boy. No, no, she stammers, giggling. "No way, sweetie, got to be you ..."

Calamity number two was his bankruptcy — the financial variety, I mean. Even though he sold a good five hundred editions of the collected works of Dostoevski and Eugene O'Neill, at least two hundred cookbooks — author unknown — and more, much more in less than four months, he went bankrupt just the same. Stunning success — all for nothing. He could

150

never collect anything more than the down payment, and it was always the last.

Actually, there was a third calamity. Before he turned book salesman, he may have read the odd book; but when he began to sell books, reading became a kind of cocaine. Impossible for him to sell a book — didn't matter what book — without reading it first. Even read the cookbooks, cover to cover. That's why, if you ever got a dinner invitation at Louis' place, you'd come away licking your fingers. Plus, he got involved with the sea; took on as a cook on the *Elli.*

In any case, it didn't take him long to conclude that one lifetime would probably not be enough to read all the books he wanted to. But a certain disdain for any kind of work that called for a specific schedule — any kind of dependence at all, in fact — may have also played a part in his downfall. Once he'd picked up Dostoevski, was Louis about to put it down and show up at that shit doorman's job of his at the ministry? No way. That was the main reason he quit; not so much because of Kritsinis' suicide, not even because of the tongue-lashing he got the moment his protector departed. The main reason was that they forced him to punch a timecard.

Those were the days when all the government offices — one after another — began installing those accursed punch clocks. Louis endured it for three days. After the fourth day, he never set foot in the place again.

Before the arrival of the punch clocks things always went smoothly. If he was an hour or two late, he smoothed things over by sweet-talking the bitch who ran his department. "Just missed the bus, dearie." He even used traffic jams as an excuse, even though there weren't any traffic jams back then. He'd simply foreseen the future. Whatever it was, the bitch excused him.

151

Agis said: "You think it's the 'dearies' and the traffic jam stories that keep her off his back? Don't be a sucker, Manolopoulos. You believe everything he says?"

Louis — he insisted — for whom, as everybody knew, nothing was sacred, was well and truly screwing the "dear" lady, screwing the bejesus out of her, in fact.

Louis wouldn't admit it; not right away. Later. Sure, he'd give me one of those enigmatic half-smiles of his, but the full and complete confession only came later.

— I'm telling you, you can't believe him, said Agis.

And so it was. A cloud of mystery obscured half of Louis' life; entire blocks of time were filled with events unknown to us. Then there are the parts of his life which are known to some of us, and not to others. Take the episode with the half-Greek, half-French freak, Bertrand; the time he played the fakir, for instance. We only found out about it years later.

— I'm telling you, Manolopoulos, he screwed the good lady's feet right out from under her. Believe me or not. That little office of hers at the end of the hallway was a regular chamber of cries and whispers.

She wasn't that old. I met her once when I went to pick up Louis at work. "Angel face, I'll be away for a couple of hours, OK? Have to lend my writer friend here a hand." He'd started to call me a writer. Now "writer" was added to the name list, right up there with "cousin" and "Kostas, my boy." Of course, the good lady gave him all the time off he wanted. She was maybe in her forties, with a truly canine face. All the features of a dog: broad nose, receding chin and narrow forehead ... Dogfaced, yes; but not bad looking. Ever look closely at a dog's face, look him in the eyes? Have a close look and you'll see what I mean. Sure, she was still a dog, but the more you looked, the better you liked her. And her appearance wasn't the only thing canine about her. She acted like a dog; even barked like a dog, so they say.

— Louis, don't tell me you're ...

He looked at me.

— No way. Are you crazy?

152

But when she stood up and walked toward the door, I could hardly believe my eyes. Dog-lady had the body of a ballet dancer. Perfect. Legs, waist, buttocks. Her face was one thing, her body was another. That's when I began to believe Agis. Of course, I didn't say a word to Louis, but I believed Agis. "The bastard, he's doing it to her. For sure."

In fact, they say that the lady bore a son, courtesy of Louis; a son who died soon after birth. That's not all they say, either. I heard that after Louis left the ministry, even after she'd retired on pension, no matter where he was, no matter what he was doing, whether he was married or single, she would seek him out. He was the first man she ever had, they say. She would track him down, call him up, and beg to see him.

— And he agreed?

Agis was emphatic.

— Sure did.

To top it off, he described a meeting between Louis and the dog-lady, a meeting he observed at first hand, when the two of them paid her a visit one day.

— But he made me swear not to tell any of you.

Her place was an enormous apartment not far from downtown. She lived with her mother, a paralytic eighty-year-old.

— Guys — even though we were grown men by now, Agis still called us guys — that place was a mausoleum. Everything dark, and gloomy: walls, furniture, curtains, paintings, floors — everything somewhere between light black and dark brown. There was a long central hall, with doors leading off to the sides, right and left. The whole place was panelled in mahogany. No glass anywhere, nothing but wood. It was an old building, with high ceilings, the walls were almost bare. Only a few paintings — landscapes mostly — a few pieces of furniture, a scattering of trinkets. The bookshelves were almost empty; the only thing in them were stuffed birds. Not just on the bookshelves either; the whole house was crammed with stuffed birds. Her father's. A hunter, he was. Shot the birds and had them mounted. A taxidermy nut. A painter too. The landscapes with the trees and mountains, that was his work. When we came in, her mother ignored us. She turned her wheelchair around and rolled off toward the back of the house. The wheels squeaked; they were rusty, hadn't been oiled for ages. Then she turned off into a side corridor and disappeared. "Must be some fallen aristocrats, some kind of has-beens," I said to myself. Me, after the introductions, they left me cooling my heels in the living room. Her, the lady, she'd lost that canine look of hers there in the half-darkness. She had so much make-up on — her eyes, her lips — that you'd have sworn the whole thing was some kind of stage production, especially the way she made her appearance, coming out from behind some heavy curtains between the living room and the dining room. Seriously. It was like she'd stepped out of a play, like she was wearing a mask. Reminded me of some English actors I once saw at Epidaurus. She was a dead ringer for their Clytemnestra. The atmosphere was stifling. So was her body. Supple, tall, bony. Pure Clytemnestra. The only white in the whole scene was her dress. The darkest thing was her stockings. Jet-black, fish net stockings, pure harlot.

I heard the squeaking of the wheelchair, metal grating on metal. "It's her mother rolling up and down the hall," I said to myself. "Dearie, why don't you open some curtains, let a little light in? Why don't you air the place out?" said Louis. And suddenly, guys, I noticed the cobwebs, on the tables, the ceiling, in the corners. Cobwebs everywhere. You'd have sworn she left them there as decoration. Then she offered me a piece of chocolate and a drink. I didn't touch them. The two of them left, Louis and the lady. They stepped through the curtain and vanished. Left me standing there. The walls were hung with old family portraits. And a law school diploma with her name on it. Persephone Dertilis. That was her name. Dertilis. Suddenly, I sensed a presence in the room. I turn and who do I see? Her mother, in her chair, halfway between the hall and the living room, watching me, motionless. "The hell with you, you old bag," I wanted to tell her. Just looking at

154

her turned my stomach. She was wearing necklaces, lots of necklaces, and a medallion, the kind you keep photos in. And she was glaring at me wild-eyed, vicious. I turned toward her. "How do you do?" I asked. At that very minute, from far away, I heard something like a moan, a long, drawn-out ahhh ... "O, the creep, didn't waste a second, did he? Already he's humping the lady." When the old lady heard the sigh she vanished. Swung the chair around and disappeared.

I couldn't make up my mind whether to go or stay, but just then I heard Persephone moan again, longer, more drawn-out this time. The empty, high-ceilinged house magnified the noise, just like a loud-speaker. Guys, it was just like a detective movie, I tell you. Imagine, the old bag with those jewelled necklaces of hers. I tell you, I counted a good fifteen of 'em. You can see how crimes get committed. Out of the blue, as if she's daring you to finish her off, grab the loot and run. When I heard Persephone moan for the third time, I stepped over and closed the door, went through the curtains, opened another door slowly, cautiously, and came to stop just outside where the moaning was coming from, the last door, the one Louis and his "dearie" were sure to be behind. Now, there I am, the show's in full swing, and I'm not going to take a peek? I bent over. Unfortunately, my angle through the keyhole didn't show me the entire space, only half, or less. Half the room, half the couch. On it half of Persephone lying face down —.that's all I could see of her, from the waist down — with those black stockings of hers, her white dress pulled up, and behind and above her, half of Louis — that's all I could see of him — with his pants and shorts halfway down his thighs. The shorts were blue with white stripes, that I remember. So there he was, heaving up and down in her behind, puffing and panting like a steam locomotive on an upgrade. What if he keels over in the act, I thought. I'm telling you, it was worse than a steam locomotive. "He's getting old," I said to myself. Persephone's moans were becoming a roar. Hey, guys, it was all I could do to hold myself back. You can't believe how I was getting turned on. You know, those classy blue-blood broads

155

who pretend they don't know a thing about murder, above all suspicion, just watch 'em crank up their asses for some sex-starved punk like Louis, some stud from the other side of the tracks.

Agis went on and on; we were beside ourselves from his blow by blow account.

— So, where were we? Ah, yeah; right at the big moment, when her groaning was just about out of control, I felt something licking my fingers — I was kneeling on the floor. What the hell? I leaped to my feet! It was a cat, a black cat, rubbing against my leg. He'd ruined the best part. Before I could get back to the keyhole, I heard another soft murmuring, but from another direction. "The old lady," I thought. "Looking through another keyhole somewhere." I turned around to look, then changed my mind and went back to the keyhole. Too late. It was all over. I saw Louis standing there while she wiped his penis with a towel, with infinite tenderness, like a mother washing her baby. Oh so tenderly, so gently. From far away I heard the squeaking of the old lady's wheelchair. When I tell you it was like a crime movie, you'd better believe me. Black cats, darkened rooms, crazy old hags, cobwebs, mounted birds. Only the murder victim was missing. Add the old lady's necklaces and there you have it, your perfect crime on a silver platter. Kill her and buy that car you've always had your eye on, plus help Persephone get rid of the ghost that's haunting her house.

I didn't leave. I could hear whispering, with an accompaniment of crying and snivelling. The two of them were sitting on the couch. Above her head I could make out a portrait of a naval officer in full dress. An admiral, with a moustache. Had to be her old man, the one who shot and stuffed the birds. Suddenly she got to her feet and disappeared from my field of vision. Louis began to button his pants. An instant later the lady comes back and sits down beside him. "Your friend, do you think he?..." she asks as she pulls a wad of bills from the pocket of her housecoat and hands it to him. Seriously, no shit; a real wad of thousand notes. He never even said thanks.

Just stuck it in his pocket, like it was his salary. We're talking money here, not just a couple of bills, the going rate kind of thing. Then she turns toward him, takes his face in her hands and forces him to look her in the eyes. She's crying, but you can't hear. The tears are running down her cheeks, dead silent. Crocodile tears, maybe? Finally she started to tell him weird things: he's got to marry her, she only has a few years left to live, her health is failing, he shouldn't be stupid, those useless nephews of hers may inherit the estate; but they treat her rotten, she's scared they'll try to kill her, she ... she ... That kind of stuff. I wanted to yell at through the keyhole, "If you don't want your nephews to get the family fortune, will it all to Louis. Spit it out. You want to buy him, isn't that it?"

Later, we all tried to figure out how far we could go on the lady's fortune. Hell, the house on the corner alone would have brought us twenty million easy. Not to mention the wooded lot in the suburbs, another apartment, and a store downtown. Not to mention the bank accounts, the pensions. Hers — the one she'd get — and her father's, the one ...

So when Agis broke his word and sprung the marriage and will story, everybody climbed all over Louis:

— Marry her, fool. What have you got to lose? It's not as if you don't spend time with her anyway, not to mention the sperm you throw her way; what else can happen? Sure, she's a few years older. Big deal! Just get her to sign over the corner place, and then sit back and enjoy life.

Agis wracked his brain for arguments. It was Louis' only chance for happiness, he was convinced of it, and us along with him. One plan on top of another. Open a textile factory, a thread-making factory. That was all Agis could think about lately. Leaving the water company and starting up a thread-making factory.

I listened and laughed. I knew they were wasting their time. Even Argyris — when word got around — put in an appearance ever so gingerly. He'd opened up a tiny refrigerator repair shop; but he needed cash, so he could "go after the big boys."

Louis let them talk. That's what I think. I never believed there was any doubt in his mind. But Agis was frothing at the mouth:

— Fool, he told him, you'd rather play the gigolo; you'll give her the works for a lousy couple of thousand but not for a couple of million?

He simply could not comprehend. The controversy dragged on a good six months.

— The lady's got what she's got, after all. What have you got to lose? You're robbing her or something?

In the meantime, they'd learned all there was to know about Persephone's health; even knew the date of her death. They found her doctors, bribed nurses for copies of examination reports. It was crystal clear. The lady's heart had come to the end of the line. What didn't she have? Emphysema, myocarditis, acute ischemia? Name it.

— She'll croak on you in bed before you even marry her. In fact, you'll probably be suspected of murder.

Not much later the controversy turned to panic when her mother, "the ghost," kicked the bucket. That meant Persephone's real-estate holdings had doubled.

After the mother's funeral which, let it be noted in passing, we all attended, the group held its highest-level confab ever. Twelve of us were there, in total. Everyone's emotions had reached such a fever pitch that Agis came out with "either he marries her or I'll never speak to him again. What a fool! Who does he think he is? The opportunity of a lifetime, and he's just pissing it away."

He wanted to save Louis, by force if necessary. Once or twice I sat in on those heart-to-heart sessions of theirs. Today, Louis might have handled the problem a bit more realistically, but back then it was almost like a game for him; everything went in one ear and out the other.

— Louis, you let 'em talk; you even get involved. How come? You know you're not going to ... why?...

He laughed.

— Cousin! Let me tell you something. I'm not dead against

158

it. I'd be happy to marry her and she likes the idea, but I'm certain that when it's all over we'd both end up with broken hearts, and I'd end up with no money. Her nephews will get it all. What do you take her for? Talk is cheap; when you come right down to it, she's her mother's daughter. If she gives you something, it's to get something back. Let it drop. Better that way. Whenever I need pocket money, the girl comes by and nurtures me.

How I relished those highfalutin words Louis would drop into the conversation from time to time.

— Why should I spoil our story, Kostas, my boy? Those black fish net stockings of hers are enough for me. Drives me wild, Persephone face down with those stockings on. When you get right down to it she's lonely. A couple of kind words, a nice fuck: what more do I need? Marry her and she'll give me the heave-ho the minute I don't perform on schedule. Why bother?

He was right. Ultimately, their story ended in a way that no one had anticipated. We never suspected a thing until one fine day we spotted the announcement in the papers: Persephone was marrying Argyris, the fridge man.

— Just what I always said, Kostas, my boy. As soon as money is involved, it ain't worth shit. Stick around and watch what happens now.

Agis was a bit more direct.

— Didn't I tell you so, Manolopoulos? The broad's starved for dick, no two ways about it. Soon as she sees Louis ain't selling, she buys another dead-end kid. The lady knows how to shop. Not to mention that now Argyris is stuck with a bottomless pit.

Naturally, nobody from our gang was invited to the wedding. So when they spotted the twelve of us standing there on the steps of Saint Dionysios church, not far from her house, they turned so yellow you'd have sworn it was a sudden attack of jaundice. The church was crawling with cops. Word had gotten out that her nephews were going to knock her off from a distance, à la Kennedy, before the rites of holy

159

matrimony were over — anything to stop Argyris from in-heriting the family fortune as surviving spouse.

In the end, Persephone survived the ceremony, even though we expected her to keel over any minute, what with her weak heart and all. She survived her wedding night, survived the honeymoon. Argyris chose Singapore for the trip. "How long will we survive, anyway?" Singapore was his dream. Where the hell did he come up with such a far-away dream?

Right at the "Do you take this woman," Agis whispered:

— Needs a slave to fan him, the fat slob. He'll die of overeating any day now.

As it turned out, overeating wasn't the cause of death. Burp-ing was. Yep. Some people burp for relief; him, one burp and he was a dead man. That would have been seven, maybe eight years later — I can't recall exactly — when he was fat, really fat. One day — it just happened to be a Friday the thirteenth; what's more, he was the superstitious kind ... As I say, there he was, sitting in his easy chair sipping whisky from a Bohe-mian crystal glass when the burp came. When he opened his mouth he died on the spot, in his chair, motionless, comical. All the guests laughed, in fact. They thought he was about to tell them a funny story. It was only when he collapsed face down on the floor that they realized it wasn't a funny story at all; he wasn't joking.

The whole group turned up at his funeral. All twelve of us. There was Persephone, looking like Marlene Dietrich, the bitch. Her body was as young looking as ever. With the veil over her face, and the black mourning clothes — black was always her color in any case — you could only see her legs, and you felt sorry for poor departed Argyris. There were two short speeches, one by a short, ugly man, a representative of the refrigerator industry, another from the Party; Argyris had re-joined after his marriage. Agis was standing there next to me; he couldn't help himself, came out with one of those dumb jokes of his:

— So, it's Louis' turn again.

He wasn't far off, actually. Even today, I hear, he visits her

160

every so often. Twice I saw him in her neighborhood. That's where he was headed. I didn't speak to him. But I did follow him. He went up the street, climbed the stairs and then took the first right, straight to her house. The third time I spotted him, just as he was about to ring her doorbell, I called out. He turned toward me.

— Hey, cousin, don't go getting ideas. She's a lonely lady, almost sixty. We're not so young ourselves any more, and he pointed to his head.

What little hair he had left was almost white.

But Persephone couldn't buy him. She visited him once at his place, down by the dockyards; could hardly believe her eyes. With her, he could have been sleeping between silk sheets and featherbeds; he preferred privation.

But, back to Louis' marriage with Aleka. The whole show lasted about two years, if I remember rightly. Round about the third year he dumped her, lock, stock and barrel. It was at Epidaurus, as you recall, the time Louis ran into that bizarre clown, Bertrand. He never tried to look her up again. When her lawyers finally traced him and handed him the divorce papers for signature, not only did he not object, he thanked them.

— She asked me to get married, after all. It's her right to ask for divorce.

Made sense.

Aleka was wild about those blue eyes of his back then. "Belmondo, only shorter." With his jokes and his bohemian ways, she bought all the books he could deliver. He was a book salesman at the time you'll recall.

— Read this one, little cousin, and that one. Take 'em all. They're good for you, full of vitamins.

Ha-ha-ha-ha laughed little cousin, and bought the books. Imagine; later, she discovered he'd sold her the collected works of Dostoevski and O'Neill twice over. She never touched them, of course. Not one. Didn't even glance at the cookbook. So, one fine morning when Louis discovered that Aleka's bill was more than twenty thousand — an unbelievable amount back in those days — only then did he begin to appreciate the seriousness of the situation.

The first to become alarmed was the wholesaler who noticed the accounts receivable multiplying at a breathtaking rate; then Louis noticed it.

— Little cousin, what gives? Better tell daddy to start coughing up.

But Aleka was a spoiled, obnoxious kid to start with. "Pure Lolita, Kostas, my boy; no shame. Always got a wad of gum in her mouth." So, that day, with a mouth full of chewing gum, she shot back:

— Marry me, and we'll fix everything up. You want?

For Louis, everything in this world was normal. He agreed.

— Sure, why not.

Her parents would rather have killed him than given him their daughter's hand in marriage. But she was an only child. What could they do? How could they change her mind without upsetting her?

Finally, after her third suicide attempt, her Belmondo became a part of their household.

— I had to ask for her hand in person, cousin. So I bought a bouquet of flowers and off I went. Wanted to knock 'em dead, so I bought the biggest, the fattest and the cheapest I could find. Gladiolas, more than three feet long. Twice I almost poked her mother's eyes out. Never saw parents so disgusted with their would-be son-in-law. Mostly the father.

Louis attended the engagement ceremony with his sister.

162

The father was so sure the marriage would never take place — just like with Eugenia — that he didn't bother to show up.

But after they got to know him better, her parents should have been just wild about Louis.

— Mr. Antypas, when your daughter asked for my hand, I accepted; no questions asked. No house, no cash.

At first Antypas didn't know what to say, then turned as red as a fresh-boiled beet, and said:

— My daughter asked for your hand, you say? You've got the gall to ... to ...

He searched for the right word; couldn't find it. Aleka, who was getting the coffee ready in the kitchen, was cracking up. She loved Louis' vulgarity; it was enough to silence the toughest audience. But she intervened in timely fashion, and smoothed the ruffled feathers.

— Daddy, all Manolis is saying is that he's not marrying me for my money.

Later, of course, she had occasion to call that Belmondo of hers an asshole one hundred times over, for not demanding money and a house. That skinflint father of hers, he never gave her anything faintly resembling a dowry.

— We'll just wait and see whether it's you he's interested in, or your money.

His father-in-law's proposal was direct and unambiguous.

— I'll take you on at the store — he was a goldsmith — and you'll learn the trade. Drop the books. No future in books. You'll never become a businessman unless you've got a place to call your own.

Louis didn't beat around the bush. He explained that his own goals were a little higher, and began to talk about that dream of his, about the bar cum coffeehouse; then he talked about the sailor's life, and his plans to get his seaman's papers ... Putting it bluntly, he gave the father to understand that perhaps he shouldn't get his hopes up about the jewelry store idea.

— The man you want to marry is crazy, Alice, and you ought to know it. Me, I never heard anything like it. Someone

163

offers to make you a business partner and you just shit on him?

Her mother, Chrysanthi, was dismayed by her husband's behavior.

— Panos, what kind of language is that?

But her Panos kept right on ranting:

— But he's shitting on me, Chrysanthi, what else do you want me to call it? You heard him. Shitting on me, that's what. Here I'm handing him a job and he just sits there blabbing about coffeehouses and ships ... bullshit!

Chrysanthi had a higher opinion of Louis. She found him rather likable. In fact, she enjoyed his company. She also had a couple of propositions herself:

— First he should finish high school — just two years to go — and after, he can become a lawyer. We can get him in without exams. The dean is a friend of your uncle. With that eloquence of his, he can go far. He's a natural. Got a head on his shoulders ...

She almost convinced him. Seriously. If they hadn't separated so soon, Louis might even have finished high school. But in the meantime, it was their marriage that almost came to an end then and there when the book supplier appeared on the scene, uninvited. On the day of the engagement he began legal proceedings against Louis. I've got the impression the whole thing is still in the courts, thanks to that bankruptcy of his. When the wholesaler, who was a clever man, realized Louis' enormous talent for selling books for one thousand and up, he loaded him with collected works of the great authors by the ton.

But what can you do? Louis and he never hit it off. The man buried him under an avalanche of cards to fill out, signatures to get, ledgers to complete.

— Whoa, Mr. Whoosits, we're drowning in paper. Paper paper, nothing but paper.

He never once called the man by his name. Hatzaras it was Called him Mr. Whoosits. Whoever he's really not fond of, he calls Whoosits.

164

— The turkey! How can someone spend so much time around books and still be nothing but a greengrocer? All he ever does is pore over the ledgers, enter figures, keep accounts. Never read a page in his life. Sunup to sundown in that basement office at that metal shit desk of his, ruining his eyes, his heart, his legs. There's nothing left of him, the asshole.

All of us were certain that Louis would never give him a thing. From the moment Louis spotted him, Mr. Whoosits was 'ated to fall to Louis, and fall he did.

No one ever knew, and no one will ever know if the customers simply refused to pay or if Louis pocketed the balance. At first, Mr. Whoosits said he would let the matter drop, all Louis had to do was hand over the customer cards; he would collect on them himself.

Naturally, no one ever found the cards. They disappeared into a great black hole, or else Aleka threw them out when she came steaming back from Epidaurus.

— Just get off my back; I never saw any cards. Probably forgot 'em on one of his nights out, she said.

One thing for sure, from the moment he took legal action against Louis, Mr. Whoosits' life went downhill fast. That miser — money was everything for him, more important than life — slowly abandoned his business; gradually he stopped ordering new books, forgot to renew his old stock, started to ignore his employees who soon began to pilfer from him. Destroying Louis soon became his only purpose in life. He left the bookstore, lost his fiancée, hit an old woman with his car — cost him a small fortune — and burnt his country house to the ground in distraction. His life had become an unending succession of disasters.

Try as he might, he couldn't stop Louis' marriage, even though he plied Aleka's father with the most scurrilous rumors he could think of. Louis was everything from a white slaver and a drug-pusher to a homosexual hustler or a pimp, or both.

— Mr. Antypas, save your daughter. The man's depraved,

unscrupulous. You'll be fortunate if all he does is turn her into a streetwalker. And he's an unrepentant Communist, what's more. A Hydra. But I'm going to crush him! He won't get away from me.

When word got out that Alice was four months pregnant, it was too late to cancel the wedding. The local parish church, the neighbors and their own good name in business would not even let them contemplate the prospect.

So after a dramatic examination of the entire situation, the Antypas couple decided on marriage.

— No, Chrysanthi, the wedding will go ahead, don't argue with me. Abortion in the fourth month is risky; we can't take a chance. And we're sure as hell not going to have any bastards in our household. Let's hope he straightens out. What can he do, anyway? We'll make sure he straightens out.

But straighten him out they did not, even though for awhile he attended night classes to finish high school, as I told you. He might have straightened out eventually if he hadn't been overtaken by events. Louis' one great weakness was events. He lusted after events.

— Kostas, my boy, dream up something. Don't let time pass while you just sit there. Get on the phone, meet people, go out onto the streets, knock on doors. You never know, maybe you'll flush out a hare. Sit on your rear end and you start to go under; you start to think about the vanity of life, about death, you dry up. Better take a nap than ... But if you're not asleep, put your tongue to work, your feet, your hands, your brains.

Once — I was married by then, on my way to the health club for a workout — I remember bumping into him on the street. Where was I going? he asked, and before I could even open my mouth:

166

— Kostas, my boy, I never thought you could be so dumb, trotting around the park in your underwear. Take it from me, cousin, it's one big jerk-off. What's in it for you, anyway? Instead of running around all by yourself, better you should chase after some nice round little chambermaid or some well-preserved high society dame, if it comes to that. At least you might get some reward for your efforts.

I never worked out again. Wrote off the health club registration fee. Maybe I went once or twice, all together.

— Let me find you a girlfriend, Kostas, my boy; someone you can do all your exercises with. The athletic type, preferably; then the two of you could head for the hills. No way that pathetic, dull-witted wife of yours could keep up. In fact, come to think of it, let me introduce you to Nora — now there's a broad who's wild about mountain climbing. Her husband's a stick in the mud himself, a fat slob to boot. Gave it up after a couple of tries. Now the lady gets it on with mountain climbers. The call of the wild, know what I mean? Mountain streams, pine trees, bees buzzing, birds chirping. I couldn't even keep up with her. Tried it twice; that was enough. But you, you're a health nut ...

This was not another one of Louis' tall tales. There really was a Nora. An existing person. One hell of a lady, what's more. The sonofabitch even introduced us. At first I didn't believe he would go through with it. But one afternoon I suddenly found myself seated prim and proper in one of her husband's easy chairs with Nora across from me. Not only did I finally believe Louis, but it was too late for me to back out.

— Doubting Thomas! I tell you something, you believe it.

Nora was certainly not to be taken lightly. She was pink-cheeked from all those mountain streams and pine trees, her flesh was firm from all those mountain trails, her breasts jutted out, no doubt thanks to all the healthy exercise in the fresh air ...

— I've always liked keeping fit, ever since I was a little girl, she told us.

She was like a mink, the broad. I never saw a body quite as

supple as hers before. And Louis was sitting there telling me:

— Kostas, my boy, if ever you get the urge to do it un-
naturally, no need to turn her over. She's like rubber; all she
does is stick her toes in her mouth and lo and behold, there
you have the choicest white ass you can imagine looking you
in the eye. That's what I call a well-trained gal. There's no
position she can't handle. All you need is the imagination to
ask.

The more he talked, the hotter I got.

— I'm telling you, if I wasn't against hiking on principle, I
wouldn't have given up those bucolic delights for anything.

So intensely had he piqued my curiosity about this "juicy"
woman that I was just about ready to overcome remorse,
hesitations, fears.

— What's the big problem, anyway? I'll cover for you. Let
Julia stew in her own juice, as far as I'm concerned. We'll give
her a story about some land. That's it, tell her you've found
some land at a good price, and she'll send you to hell and back.
Woman's a born bargain hunter.

He all but convinced me. It would have been the first time
I'd cheated on her since we married.

— What more can I say, cousin? Want me to tell you the
worst? Imagine, you keep your nose clean — and she's grab
bing the first chance that comes along. Instead of tormenting
yourself when it happens, act now; then you won't end up crying over what you missed.

Whenever Louis talks about Julia, he always lets drop the
odd remark; vague, hypothetical.

In any case, without exactly knowing how or why, I ended
up in this tête-à-tête with Nora and her husband, at their
place not far from downtown.

— Don't worry about the husband. He'll die sitting there,
simmering in his own fat and sucking in smog, Louis said
right in front of him.

The husband was munching chocolates, pistachios, hazel
nuts, whatever was within reach.

— I like smog. Besides, why should you worry, anyway? My

168

body can't live without it, he said, laughing.

He was an intelligent man. An operatic baritone. Nora had her reasons. You couldn't really condemn her for running around on him, even if she did it one hundred times. For him singing and sex didn't mix. Total non-participation was the rule. He had discovered that after intercourse his voice lost some of its timbre; was he going to risk his career for the sake of Nora's uh, um?... "Sorry honey, but I ..."

So the lady became a mountain climber. Pure coincidence, of course. The first man to make a loose woman of her was a director at the opera company, a guy called Lakis, who just happened to be a mountain climber. He introduced her to the lure of the summits; she who had always loved the sea.

Later, Lakis began to display some alarmingly homosexual tendencies and the two of them were forced to break off under extremely dramatic circumstances. But nothing really changed. The two of them kept up their expeditions to the high country. He with a former script-writer, she with a former gymnastics teacher from a girls' academy. Her husband trusted her. Not so much her as the people who adored the peaks and the canyons. He believed that above a certain altitude people not only became healthier, but more moral.

— Hubby here is a fine fellow, Kostas, my boy. A true modern. No grumbling, no jealousy, Louis assured me right there, in his presence, while the man giggled.

— I believe in nature's restorative powers. Pity my legs won't carry me; I'd love to be able to climb mountains and scale rocks.

And so it was that I became a mountain climber. Not for long, though. After a couple of times, Julia up and tells me she's coming along; she wants to see the land. I had to scramble to put her off. Louis bailed me out that time. He notified Nora that I couldn't make it, and I asked him to find out from her if any mountain land was for sale, something I could show Julia. Luckily she knew of a place. And so it happened that one Sunday, just for laughs, we bought — she bought, I mean — the land on Euboea. The place is probably worth a fortune

169

today, but we got it for a song back then. Six acres of fruit trees.

I never saw Nora again. From Louis I found out that she had returned to her first love, the sea.

— The sea air is really good for you, she told him, when he ran into her with a rowing enthusiast one day in a semi-deserted cove, and the two of them laughed until they cried.

.

.

Louis was right, as it turned out, when he counselled me to let things happen. I told him so.

— It's not only me who says so, Kostas, my boy. That's what your poet says, the one you introduced me to, that Kavafy of yours, with that Ithaca of his. It's the voyage that counts. That's all he says, over and over. But you don't seem to have gotten the message. For your information, that's what saved me from Aleka. If I hadn't been on the lookout, I would never have taken on with that wild man, Bertrand.

Well, that's not exactly what happened. Even if Bertrand had never appeared, Aleka would have left Louis; she couldn't take it any more. Not Louis. The way things happened.

— The truth is, cousin, that the girl was accustomed to three square meals a day, to the movies, to the occasional ice cream cone. Our habits were different. She didn't like walk-ing, didn't like a cold house, didn't like doing the laundry by hand. What did she expect from me? With me, one day a week there might be food, the other six days, there might not be.

The first few months of the marriage her father gave them pocket money. Then he cut them off.

— That's it! End of the line. I'm not going to slave so that sultan of yours can loaf around, he told his daughter. Mean-while, she was discovering that hearts and flowers weren't enough.

When she realized that living with Louis was not the same

as living with daddy and having Louis for dessert, she panicked. Suddenly it was clear that all those jokes of his, the stories that left people in stitches, weren't only meant to pass the time. He actually intended to live that way; that was how Louis was. Only that and nothing more.

In fact, he outright refused to go to work in her father's shop. It seemed so foolish, so ...

— Are you out of your mind? How are we going to get by? The kid is due in a month. You've got no medical insurance. Who's going to pay the hospital? Or maybe you think I should give birth in the indigents' ward? Father means it. He's not giving us a thing. What are we supposed to do? Come on, you tell me.

Daddy would not relent.

— Let him show up at the shop and learn a trade. He'll earn a good wage; I'll sign him up for medical insurance. What else does he want?

Aleka had become the intermediary between spouse and father. Then came the destructive quarrels; even today, when Louis thinks back to them, he suffers momentary paralysis of his lower extremities.

— Come on, speak up. Father wants to know what you intend to do; what your plans are. No way he's going to work while you loaf. Unless you want me to work while you loaf around.

Louis was upset with Aleka for not being enough of a feminist.

— A real feminist would never, never tolerate it, cousin; I mean, sitting around at home while her husband works, he said bitterly after recounting the whole story of his marriage when I went to visit him in the hospital.

It's true. At the height of his feud with Aleka, he suffered a curious paralysis of the lower limbs. Ended up in the public ward with an indigence certificate. Simultaneously, his wife was giving birth to a daughter in a modern maternity clinic in downtown Athens. Paid for by daddy, of course.

Finally, the brutal realities caught up with Louis; he became a goldsmith.

— What the hell, might as well try my hand at it, he told Aleka. And so he did. He actually became a goldsmith.

The ultimate concession came neither easily nor painlessly. It was preceded by several melodramatic suicide attempts by Aleka, efforts by the parents to starve him out, and endeavors to win him over to the capitalist system:

— Don't be an idiot! Gold is gold. It never loses value.

That was his father-in-law's favorite line, his old sweet song.

When Antypas cut the allowance, their household finances went into a tailspin. Rent went unpaid, the water was cut off, then the electricity ... Paralysis of the lower extremities was inevitable. Then came admission to the hospital, the birth of their daughter, and finally, his exodus from the hospital.

The first pre-quake tremors began to register on the seismograph when, arriving home from the hospital, he attempted to unlock his door and realized, stunned, that the key no longer matched the keyhole. "That little fucker, ..." he mumbled over and over. Finally he rang the doorbell; a civil servant opened the door. For Louis, anyone who looks reasonably contented, with pyjamas, slippers, slip-covers on the furniture, plump pink cheeks is automatically a civil servant. He's never missed yet.

— You can smell 'em from a mile away, Kostas, my boy. Placid, self-assured, absolutely certain that as long as they live, no world war will break out, nothing will ever disturb their peace and quiet. Maybe they used to be leftists; but they end up conservatives. They change the way they look, the way they move, their tastes. They paddle along like frogs, as if they had webbed feet. Wearing masks, even at home. And not just one mask. Several. One for their children, one for the

172

boss, another for the wife, another for the mistress, another ...
Sure, there's the odd exception, but a mask is a mask.

Louis had the man figured out the minute he opened the
door. "Works in the registry office," he said to himself.

— There's something about 'em, cousin. You can spot 'em
right away.

Louis divided people according to department, or depart-
ments according to the people who worked in them.

— Cashiers don't look the same as desk clerks. In depart-
ments where you can get bribes and under-the-table payoffs
people end up looking different, Kostas, my boy. Just look at
'em, you'll see what I mean. Their noses get longer, droopier;
they go bald, their smiles turn sardonic. They've all got thin,
tight lips, rotten teeth, a sharp eye and a hunched back.
Cousin, I've never seen a guy you can bribe who hasn't been
a bit of a hunchback, with a crafty smile. I'm serious ...

So our man from the registry office — probably had inside
information from the landlord on what kind of depraved in-
dividual the previous tenant was — gave him a cock and bull
story about the apartment being vacant. He was the tenant
now, he said, telling Louis to get off his back because frankly
he was sick and tired of being bothered. He handed him a
fistful of letters and unpaid bills and all but slammed the door
in his face.

No way around it. Louis had to move in with his father-in-
law. There he met his daughter for the first time. All his
Lolita said when she saw him was:

— So you want things to happen, do you? Well, get a load
of this, and turned her back on him.

Appears he'd also expounded his "let things happen"
theory to Aleka, but back in the carefree days before the wedding when it would have made him attractive. She liked it

173

then; in fact I daresay the theory captivated her.

Anyway, his reception at the Antypas' place was halfway between dubious and distrustful. It wasn't that Louis had any objection to living with his in-laws. He would do them even that favor if he had to.

— Don't you worry, pops, he said. I'll make myself comfortable; it's your daughter I'm a little worried about.

Antypas' blood began to boil. Two hours of Louis was enough to send his blood pressure and cholesterol levels soaring.

— I can't stand it, Chrysanthi. I can't take that son-in-law of yours anymore.

But the sad part of it was that Louis still liked Aleka.

— One look at her, Kostas, my boy, dressed in that miniskirt of hers — brown leather — what can I tell you? A gift from the goldsmith. I couldn't hold back, couldn't wait for the chance to climb all over her.

— What's this "your daughter" routine, Mr. Retsinas? "My wife" is what you should call her. Wake up, you're married. You've got responsibilities, a child. Fine, so I paid the maternity clinic. I was wrong, but I wasn't about to have her giving birth on the street, like a tramp.

Louis couldn't hold back.

— Where does that leave me, old man; I was in the indigents' ward. What's that got to do with it?

Louis never called him dad or father, only old man or pops. Antypas turned beet red in anger. He looked like he was about to burst.

— Calm down, calm down, Chrysanthi urged him as she swabbed the sweat from his forehead.

Couldn't even complete a sentence with that man. All his arguments turned against him, stood on their heads. Suddenly he was revealed as backward, self-seeking, and malevolent. After an entire lifetime beyond reproach, living the life of the Good Samaritan, "suddenly this guy appears" and humiliates him in the eyes of his daughter and his wife. Worse yet, he couldn't dismiss Louis outright as a dowry

174

hunter or a shakedown artist. Louis was neither. Antypas may have had a sneaking suspicion he was dealing with a unique case, that he didn't have much room to manoeuvre, that he had few weapons available. I tell you, Antypas suffered the comeuppance of his life. But the comeuppance gradually turned to horror when he realized in astonishment that his wife, Chrysanthi, was not only not repelled by her son-in-law; that she actually enjoyed his company. The situation was turning dramatic. Worse; tragic. As you will see. But one thing was certain; Antypas was not about to give up.

— Maybe you'd like I should pay your rent? Maybe you think Alice moved out on her own, on a whim? Well, think again. When they evicted her, what was she supposed to do? What did you expect me to do as her father? Leave her sitting there on the street with all her belongings, waiting for you?

Another fight was more than Aleka could stand. She stamped out, slamming the door behind her, and retreated to the room her parents had given them, off the kitchen. The room held all their worldly goods: crates of books, papers, bags of junk, suitcases, the sloth's guitar — in his father-in-law's eyes he was a sloth — and, of course, the baby's cradle. The only thing new and clean in the room was their bridal bed, a gift from Antigone, Louis' sister.

When he went in to speak to her, he found her face down on the bed, pounding the pillows with clenched fists, weeping.

— What could I do, cousin? I'd made up my mind to get out; I'd had it up to here with the nagging, and then I noticed her thighs and I just couldn't help myself, I jumped on her. She couldn't hold back either. We didn't even manage to close the door. Took me like earth thirsting for water.

Louis was certain her mother had seen them. Not only had he heard footsteps, when she avoided looking him in the eye as they sipped coffee in the living room while her husband growled, "Don't even give him poison," he was certain.

— Mom was a little up-tight, cousin; when she saw us in that position, who can tell what was going on inside her.

The act was not consummated immediately, though. The

175

baby started to howl from the cradle.

— Stuff the pacifier in her mouth, hurry up! hissed Aleka.

Pants at half-mast, Louis scoured the floor, found the pacifier, stuck it in his daughter's mouth and ...

— Shut the door! You left it wide-open.

He closed the door and turned back to Aleka. Knelt down behind her, stroked her belly briefly, then the groove between her little buttocks and, for a few seconds, remained motionless, ecstatic, drinking in the sight. Then he grabbed a pillow, stuck it under her to elevate her rear end a bit, and ...

— One heavenly piece of ass, cousin. World without end.

Louis never held anything back from his friends. He liked details, all the details. His wife or a one night stand, it was all the same to him. No playing favorites.

— When I tell those stories, cousin, it's like I'm experiencing them all over, again and again. I get the feeling they'll last, that somebody's writing them down somewhere, that they'll go on, into the future. The broads don't go for it much, of course. They don't want me talking about them to my friends.

It was true. Louis never hesitated to give us every version, every variation of each and every one of his erotic exploits. Later, when we actually met the women he slept with, we knew everything there was to know about their bodies, how they behaved in bed, up to and including how they reached orgasm, the color of their nipples, whether they were tight or slack, wet or dry, their weaknesses, their secret vices.

We even knew how big Aleka's clitoris was.

— Enormous, guys; size of an acorn. Just lay her on her belly, and put it in her from behind, and then, if you so much as touch her clitoris, just touch it, whoosh, she comes. But first she wants you to put it in soft, sweet and gentle. Once you're inside, then you turn into a barbarian, you can do whatever you want, but before you're in, she wants gentleness, tender loving care, blah, blah, blah. But with a pillow everything fits in the right place, lined up to perfection.

— Louis, that's a hell of a way to talk about your women, jeeze.

176

He flared up.

— Why, cousin? If you think they should be ashamed of what they're doing instead of being proud of it, then I agree ... Me, I glorify 'em!

— You lead us into temptation, put ideas in our heads ... Aren't you worried maybe ...

— I'm a man, cousin; I know the score. You don't think I know Aleka is, shall we say, a bit of a tease. You think I'd be surprised if you looked her over once or twice, or even thought about screwing her. Forget ethics, and friendship for the time being. It's a chance I take, cousin. If it does happen, if she wags her tail at you I don't doubt for a second that you'd screw her. Let's not kid ourselves. And if you don't do it, don't tell me you won't regret it one day ...

Meanwhile, Antypas was tightening the noose. And after the love feast with Aleka just after he got out of the hospital, there was no way Louis could leave her.

— She drives me wild, guys, what can I say? Everything about her turns me on. Even her toes. You name the position, there's something exciting about it.

And so, after the third day, he fell into line like a good soldier. Agreed to everything. It was a goldsmith they wanted? He'd become a goldsmith. Wake-up time was seven o'clock? Seven o'clock it would be.

Antypas was so confident that he didn't even bother with the niceties.

— On your feet, loafer! We leave in ten.

The house was more like an army camp. Before Louis could finish his coffee he heard the car honking. Beep, beep, beep. Washed his face, put on his shoes, coat, cursing and spitting. "Jesus Christ almighty, what a mess," and dashed off to do his duty.

177

They even cut off his morning cigaret. No time. And even if there had been time, Chrysanthi's headaches would not allow it. "Don't smoke; gives the lady a headache." So he butted out, cursing under his breath, and left. Meanwhile Aleka would roll over in bed, while their daughter, Louisa, wept in her cradle.

— Let her cry! How much longer can she keep it up? She'll finally wear out.

Before Louis could shut the door of his father-in-law's Austin, the car was underway.

— Late again.

Within two months, Louis had become an accomplished goldsmith. I kid you not. Antypas hardly knew what to think. Louis even began to turn out his own designs, and people started to buy them; they sold like hotcakes, in fact. Ever seen those rings with the snake motif and the inset diamonds? That's his design. Later all the other goldsmiths copied it. I'm telling you, he became a really first-class craftsman. The father-in-law couldn't believe his eyes. Finesse, speed, attention to detail! His work was like fine embroidery. Us, we saw neither hide nor hair of him. Spent all his time with the father-in-law. They closed at midday, grabbed a sandwich, then went back to the shop to get the next day's orders ready: the rings, the necklaces, the gold chains. Come evening, they would open up again. Then at eight, back into the Austin and home. Not a word from Louis. A model of good behavior. Not a protest, not a curse.

Gradually, the financial situation improved. They rented the shop next door and expanded the business.

— Let's wait a bit, Manolis. When we move out of here, let's move into a place of our own instead of paying rent.

Said Aleka, happy and contented, in bed at night, planning

178

for the house, for the baby, for a new coat, "You should get something for yourself" for a new dress. Don't you think lamé suits me, off the shoulder ...

— Later we'll get our own car, what do you think?

He listened in silence. Just listened. For the first time in his life, Louis was in danger of being swallowed up by routine. That was when none of us really knew whether he'd decided to "clean up his act" or whether he had reasons for keeping away from everybody.

In the meantime, from the other end of the living room, from papa's bedroom, came another conversation:

— I've never been so mistaken. That son-in-law of yours is a real artist. He can create angels, the sonofabitch.

He wasn't exaggerating. Louis had designed tiny angels which were so perfectly formed that they set the whole market abuzz.

— Never saw that kind of detail work before.

Antypas began to worry. What happens if he asks to become a partner tomorrow?

— But you promised, said Chrysanthi.

— I did, but I really meant after I die, or when I retire. Then he can have it all. Let's say I agree now. Do you trust him? Sure, he seems to be acting honorably, I admit it. But what if he has some say? Will he be the same, or will he try to throw us out? In the back of my mind, I still think he may be up to something. He's been making the rounds of government offices, talking to the police, the way I hear it.

But her husband's misgivings didn't bother Chrysanthi.

Of late, Aleka and her father had begun to quarrel; she didn't like Louis being paid only a straight wage; she wanted him to become a partner. Chrysanthi said the same thing.

— Take him in; you promised. Otherwise he'll leave. We

179

need something to keep him and Aleka together ...

But Antypas wasn't buying.

— Where's he going to go, now that he's found the goose that lays the golden egg?

But statements like that increased Chrysanthi's disillusionment with her husband.

— Cousin, we never did find out what was bothering her. Was it because he was a tightwad, or because their sex life was on the rocks? Louis told me later.

Antypas had not been sleeping well. He would get up at night, stroll up and down the hall, go out into the garden as though he'd seen a vision of evil; and always, before returning to bed, he would close the second hall door, the one that led to his daughter's room. He couldn't stand the sound of love-making every night. Got on his nerves.

From what Louis told me later, I deduced that Aleka's mother had probably confessed to her daughter that daddy's sex life was in a shambles; what's more, his full-scale impotence probably dated from when they bought the country house in Aegina. Ever since, as she explained it, he would get the urge twice a year at the most. But what was the connection between the country house and daddy's impotence? Fresh air is supposed to perk you up in that respect. But instead of perking up, it was the reverse.

So, one night, as Antypas was wandering through the darkened house, his wife dared to ask him what was the matter, why was he so upset.

— Nothing. Go back to sleep.

He sat, not lay, beside her. But from the way he said ''nothing,'' she knew Louis' and Aleka's love-making was driving him to distraction. But he wouldn't talk about it. She rolled over, and began to cry. But a few minutes later he touched her on the shoulder; enough is enough, he said; he couldn't stand it any more, time for them to find their own place.

— He's an animal. Day in, day out, that's all he can do? They can clear out, the both of them.

180

"Why, you don't like it?" she wanted to say, but bit her tongue. He refused to lie down, and sat there on the edge of the bed, trying to remember what he'd forgotten. "Ah, yes, the alarm clock!" It was Sunday morning, they were going to Aegina for the first time and here he'd forgotten to set the alarm.

— He's driving me crazy, I almost forgot.

But Louis had already realized that his presence in the house had become a catalyst. He had a feeling, a premonition, a sense that the relationship between Antypas and his wife, which had once looked for all the world like a watertight dike had begun to crack, that water was pouring through the cracks.

Next morning, when the alarm clock sounded after Chrysanthi's night of tears, a bizarre sequence of events unfolded.

— That was no normal clock, cousin. More like a shrunken grandfather clock. Enough to wake the dead. A real alarm system.

After the fact, Mrs. Antypas confessed she always believed the clock was the principal cause of her headaches. She mentioned it once to her husband, but he told her to stop being foolish; he was not going to give it up for anything in the world.

— It's English; you can't find movements like that anymore; besides, it's a family heirloom.

Entire generations had grown up with that clock, he claimed. His grandfather, his father, himself, their daughter.

All the great events in his life were connected with the Mermaid, he claimed. That's what he called it: the Mermaid. It had a mermaid for a trademark, just above the inscription "made in England".

181

Waking up in the morning in the Antypas' house to the sounds of the Mermaid was like waking up on religious or national holidays. The clock did not begin to chime softly, as it might well have, picking up volume as it went. No. Just the opposite. It struck thunderously, like a twenty-one gun salute. Then the ringing gradually died down, when it was too late to make any difference.

So, the first bong echoed through the house like the crack of doom.

— First, cousin, the kid wakes up. You never heard a kid bawl like that in your life, take it from me. Aleka lets out a yelp, then buries her head under her pillow till the alert is over. Me, I wrap myself in the blanket, but usually I manage to stay asleep. Mrs. Antypas leaps up like a coiled spring, panicstricken, flailing around trying to stop the ringing, but her husband is holding tight to the clock until the chiming stops and the Mermaid falls silent. He's the only one in the house who can stand that infernal din. Reminds him of his childhood years, the parades, the Albanian campaign, when he was a group leader in the National Youth Corps and the self-same grandfather clock would awaken him for outings. But what transpired that Sunday was ... let me tell you, cousin, it was totally unexpected. For starters, Mrs. Antypas didn't leap to her feet like a coiled spring. Imagine, day in, day out, the same reaction, time and time again; now when he reached out to grab her hand, he was astonished to see that she hadn't budged. For a second he shuddered when he saw her lying there wide-eyed and motionless. Maybe she was dead. But when he saw her eyelids fluttering, he drew a sigh of relief. "On your feet! Time to get going!" It wasn't a request, it was an order. Kostas, my boy, that morning I realized I'd done a job on the old gaffer. When his wife refused to follow the cortege departing for Aegina, when she told him, "I've got a headache, I'm not coming," Antypas almost had a seizure. Couldn't believe his ears.

For the first time in their married life Mrs. Antypas did not follow her goldsmith husband. As you can imagine, he started

182

to shout, to drag out the old standbys, "Come off it, what do you mean you're not in the mood? I work like a slave all week long, I can't do what I feel like on Sunday?" but he never finished. Two things stopped him. First, the look in her eye. It was clear that she was not going to change her mind. Second, Louis' trip to the toilet. Just as he was about to tell her, "Oh, come off it, ..." he spotted Louis in his underpants scurrying pigeon-toed down the hall toward the toilet, holding his you-know-whats. At that moment it hit him, just who the hell got up that night and opened the hall door, the one he remembered closing.

— Couldn't hold back, cousin. When that Mermaid of his went off, I just about wet the bed.

But Louis' leak stopped Antypas from taking drastic action against Chrysanthi. He felt slightly ridiculous. And she repeated: "I'm not coming; go by yourself."

Now, Antypas was at a loss. He glanced at his life partner, in Louis' direction, thought it over for a split second, and decided to go by himself, without a word.

Within three minutes he dressed, mumbled a short prayer and walked out the door. When Louis, in the act of pissing, spied him from the bathroom window striding down the street with that midget knapsack on his back and those one-of-a-kind short pants of his, the ones that came down to the knees, he broke into an old Boy Scout marching song. Antypas probably heard him. Louis saw him glare daggers in the direction of the bathroom window, purse his lips and crawl, humiliated, beside himself, into his Austin. Only when the car had vanished, and Louis had shaken the last drops from the end of his penis, did he begin to truly appreciate what had happened.

— Kostas, my boy, for days I'd begun to get the notion that all was not well with the good lady. I don't know if the whole situation was my fault, or whether it was bound to happen anyway.

His friendship with the mother began earlier, one evening when Antypas had taken Aleka to the doctor. That was the evening Louis asked to see the family photo album.

Just between us, one of the first things Louis does when he visits someone's house is to unearth their old photos. It's an obsession with him. Then he tries to piece together their story.

— That's how you get to know a man, Kostas, my boy. He can pose all he wants in his Sunday best, but you can still get a feel for a man's qualities, for his life story, for who he was and how he became what he is.

I remember how delighted he was when once I took him to a show by a painter friend of mine, named Migadis, who painted pictures that looked a lot like photographs.

— Amazing, Kostas, my boy!

— I knew you'd like it; that's why I brought you along.

And he tried to explain why he liked them so much:

— It's because, Kostas, my boy, a painter can strip away the pose and the masks and give you the person beneath, show you his thoughts. That's what I like. I can understand more about a woman from looking at a painting of her; the flesh and bones are real, her feelings show. In a photo she's hiding, pretending to be a saint, expressionless.

As he leafed through Chrysanthi Antypas' photo album, Louis suspected that this prim and prudish little homemaker once must have been another person. At age twelve — it was clear from the photos — she was a regular nymphet, fetching and flirtatious.

— And innocent, cousin. You could see it in her eyes. By fifteen she developed breasts like Sophia Loren. I couldn't believe it. There she was, leaning over a baby stroller on a muddy playground, with some dry olive trees in the background. Her skirt had come up. Just a schoolgirl.

Mrs. Antypas was abashed; she blushed crimson as Louis leafed through the album.

That was before he taught her to drink ouzo.

— But what's a glass or two of ouzo going to do to you? he said as he filled her first glass.

From the photos it was clear she had known poverty and

184

misfortune. Her parents were respectable people. But suddenly her father had fallen in love with a showgirl.

— He drove a taxi for a living. One night he picked her up from a show in his cab; the girl, I mean. She was drunk, flat broke. It was three days before he showed up at home. Came back for a few days, then left again; we never saw him again. Just a second, maybe I can remember what the girl's name was ... No, she wasn't a chorus girl, she was a singer.

Afterward — as Louis pieced the story together — began the decline. He could see it in the photos which followed. The clothes got progressively poorer, they kept moving to ever-smaller houses.

— Mother began going to church a lot. But God never abandoned us.

So by age twenty-four our dear Mrs. Antypas had become unrecognizable — and for the worse. Her features had become hard-edged, her eyes most of all. Her mother had begun to dress her like a nun. Long dresses with collars up to the throat. Long sleeves, long and wide. Ugly skirts, ugly blouses. She couldn't shave her legs. "Nice Christian girls don't shave their legs." The only remains of her former majesty were those breasts of hers.

Chrysanthi's mother — her husband ran off with a showgirl, remember — began to hate the theater, to hate music, to hate love, and life.

— You never had a love affair? Louis asked her.

No. Never had a chance. Maybe once. She couldn't remember, never really knew what was going on.

— My God, why am I telling you all this? My husband will kill me if he ever finds out.

The album was just about finished when suddenly Louis spotted a photo of Aleka in a bathing suit.

— But that's not Aleka; it's ... me.

Louis hardly knew what to say.

— Ah, mother-in-law, you're hiding things from me. Here you're one very pretty woman.

— Aleka and I look alike. Dead ringers. See?

185

For the first time, for a split second Louis noticed a sensual sparkle in her eyes.

— I saw it, cousin. I saw love in her eyes.

Then she met Antypas. He wasn't a goldsmith back then. He was still sacristan at the parish church. It was just before a public ceremony to be held in Piraeus ...

— We had Metaxas back then.

Louis burst out laughing.

— Our Best Worker, our Little Father you mean?

— Him. That's what we called him. I remember that afternoon like it was yesterday. I think he wanted to sign me up in the Youth Corps. A wedding was just winding up in the church. "Are you coming?" he asked me and my mother. Mom helped out cleaning the church back then. That's where I met him. And off we went.

Louis recoiled in surprise.

— When?

— August 1936, it was. People running every which way, Youth Corps members, cops everywhere, confusion. I can see it as clear as yesterday. Then they lit a bonfire. It was a huge stack of books. They were burning unpatriotic literature, someone said. It was getting dark, and as we stood there watching the flames, he took my hand.

Louis put down the album and stood up.

— I remember that bonfire too. I was six years old. My dad took me. "I want to get a look at those bastards," he said. We lived close to the church ourselves; just a few streets over.

— Imagine that, she said.

That night, Mrs. Antypas began a process of metamorphosis which continued until she had become unrecognizable. Five or six evenings alone with Louis were enough to turn her world upside down.

First off, he convinced her to shave her legs.

— Gams like you can't believe, cousin.

For that, Antypas never forgave her.

Meantime, Louis, who didn't think much of her in the beginning, began to warm to her.

Then he persuaded her to dye her hair. Blond.

— You can't imagine what she looked like. The spitting image of Rosa Ashkenazi, you know, the bouzouki singer. But she wouldn't cut her hair. Antypas insisted she keep it long. And she did.

After that, Louis started the psychoanalysis. One session every afternoon, culminating in that fateful Sunday when Antypas departed for the country house in Aegina all by his lonesome.

That was the Sunday Louis finally convinced Mrs. Antypas that her headaches had nothing to do with either the clock or menopause.

— My dear lady, whatever do you mean? For years you've been buried alive in this place, and you're telling me it's menopause? You've got so much life left in you to live that ... that I can see you remarrying.

He didn't really believe that last remark; it was more designed to shock. But she had become accustomed to him by then; she didn't shock easily.

Louis not only worked like a psychiatrist; he worked like an archaeologist.

— If you can unearth things one layer at a time, cousin, you may end up with the walls of Troy.

Day by day he became more and more convinced that down deep an entirely different woman was hiding. It was plain to see. Her features slowly softened, the sadness left her eyes; the fear and the nervousness vanished. For Antypas, the changes were inexplicable; but even though they terrified him, he created no scenes; in fact he almost accepted them.

She felt strange that evening; stranger than ever before. The two of them were alone in the house. Aleka had gone to visit a certain Anargyros — remember that name, I'll get back to him — and Antypas, as you'll recall, was in Aegina. Something earth-shattering was about to happen; everything seemed to point in that direction. Yes, she felt strange that evening. Perhaps that's why she blushed more deeply than usual at Louis' leading comments on her long lost love life, perhaps that's why, when she saw his eyes examining her from head to toe, she was suddenly at a loss for words. In her confusion she spilled ouzo all over her good dress. But in spite of everything, she was not afraid. Louis had begun to gain her confidence.

When she got up to change her dress in the bedroom she felt giddy, her legs shook ever so slightly, a sign that the combination of "revolution" and ouzo was beginning to take effect. When she came back and sat down in her chair she made an effort to speak, to excuse herself; but she couldn't hold back, and burst out weeping.

— Crying like you'd never believe, cousin. Sobbing. "It's never too late," I say to her. But she just keeps on bawling. Blame it on the ouzo.

Louis had taught her well. The glass she spilled on her dress was her third. He poured her a fourth. She drank it without protest. And dissolved in tears.

— I don't have anything against my husband. I don't know what's come over me. He just doesn't seem the same to me any more. Trouble is, he promised to give you half the shop as a dowry and now he won't make good. All he ever does is fight with our daughter.

Louis was so touched that he caressed her hair to comfort her. Tenderly. It was like soothing balm to her.

— Don't you worry your head about me. I knew he wouldn't do it. Today, even if he gave me the whole shop I wouldn't accept it. Just between the two of us, I can't stand your husband.

— No, don't say that; he's not a bad man, but ...

Her tears stained the second dress. She got up, went to her bedroom again. "I'm going to wash my face," she said. Her sobbing could be heard through the closed door, right there in the living room. Louis didn't know what to say, how to bring her out of it. Those were the days when he borrowed a book by Freud from Liakopoulos. His head was full of syndromes and rejection theories, libido and hysteria. He knew — Aleka told him — that her husband never touched her. "Hysteria!" It was clear what was happening, but what was he to tell her,

188

what to do? The more theories he tried on her, the worse her situation became. "Instead of helping her, she got worse."

At that exact and precise instant Liakopoulos rang. He was beside himself with joy; Zahariades had been expelled from the Party.

— Finally, they kicked him out, the idiots! Did you hear the news?

Expelling Zahariades had become his obsession

— What a jerk-off artist!

Wherever you ran into Liakopoulos, in people's homes, coffeehouses, in the street — even at Hatzis' funeral, another old friend of ours — it was always the same old refrain.

— The guy's an asshole. Hasn't got a clue. He's such an asshole he couldn't possibly be a foreign agent.

He had Zahariades on the brain, I'm telling you. He'd have killed him if they gave him half a chance.

— Didn't my father get shot, Manolopoulos, because of him and his errors and dumb-shit decisions? Didn't I get blacklisted because of him; can't find a job anywhere?

Eventually — soon enough in fact — he found a small-time job, as you'll soon see. It wasn't long before he built that jobbie into an empire which almost covered the whole of greater Athens. But the sorrow and anger over his father were genuine. He really loved the old man.

— After that fuckin' abstention campaign in the '46 elections, they wouldn't let my old man alone; he took to the mountains, and that was the end of him. What the hell abstain for, the turd-head? Never could get his act together.

Liakopoulos talked so fast that each word seemed to swallow the next — I doubt Louis understood half what he said — and with Mrs. Antypas weeping in the next room the only thing he could remember clearly was being told to go get

189

Manolopoulos — me, that is — and come over to his place to celebrate over some drinks. Louis preferred talking with him in person; he liked watching him talk, seeing the flecks of foam at the corners of his mouth. He preferred Liakopoulos, spittle and all, to listening to him over the telephone and only understanding half of what he was saying.

Last time I saw Louis was ... wait a second ... Ah, yes. I dropped in at Antypas' shop. There he was. I remember it was just before my sister's wedding to the olive oil wholesaler; mother had sent me to pick up gold jewelry for the wedding in hopes of getting a discount.

Louis slipped two rings into my pocket, one for the groom, the other for my sister. He also gave me a bracelet, and two or three of those miniature angels of his, on fine gold chains. Didn't charge me a drachma.

— We can't go driving poor old Antypas under. Here, take this ID bracelet too.

And he bared his soul to me.

— I've had it, Kostas, my boy. Sure the money is good; I've got a respectable nest egg now, but I just can't stand that man any more. He's exploiting me for all he's worth, and Aleka seems to have found out about Persephone. The old man ratted on me. She came to the shop once or twice and he recognized her. Shit! I want my freedom, sonny boy. Can't even tell my friends from my enemies these days. Everybody tells me — even my father, that saintly man — to stay put, just stay put, they say.

He talked on and on, but people kept interrupting us. Buying trinkets and tiny crosses, or bracelets and necklaces ... I watched him work. Everyone who entered the store would leave with a purchase. A wrinkled woman in her mid-fifties came in, her face was covered with pustules; she turned to

190

putty in his hands. "Dearie, you'll like this bracelet so much you'll never take it off. Take it, try it on for a few days. I don't even want your telephone number. If you like it, and if you remember, come back and pay."

He gave it to her, wouldn't take money. Then came another, and another. They wanted one item, he sold ten. Finally he lost patience, grabbed the padlock, pulled down the shutters and locked the shop.

— To hell with Antypas and his business. Come on, he said, and we left.

He took me a few doors down the street to a little bar called "Dorothy's." That's what the sign said, in capital letters: DOROTHY'S.

I took a seat. As I lifted my eyes to look around I froze. Dorothy was not Dorothy. She was Haroula.

— You remember Haroula from Corinth, with Peppas and Polyxeni, he said.

— You crazy? How could I not remember Haroula?

I had barely gotten the words out when I saw her looking at me. Then she came over to us and gave me her hand.

— How are you, Mr. Manolopoulos?

Wow! The memories that smile touched off.

— Fine. And you? I said, gaping at her like a bottom-dwelling fish.

I couldn't believe my eyes. She hadn't changed that much. She had lost a bit of weight. Dressed as she was, with a little imagination — red silk blouse and pleated blue skirt — she was still the same Haroula; recognized her immediately. But at the same time, it was like meeting someone new. Her lips were the same, of course; the face was the same, she had the same glitter in her eye, but she was someone else. Now, with a brighter shade of lipstick and longer hair, she was even more attractive, even more delicate. She reminded me of Speranza Vrana, the actress, from a musical review I saw in '55; she played a whore, I think. Anyway, I didn't expect this kind of surprise. How was I to imagine I would meet Haroula at Dorothy's bar.

After so many years, I still didn't have Louis figured out. He'd been working on it for weeks, for sure, the scoundrel. Everything had been carefully planned.

— How is Mr. Peppas, I asked her.

— From the day they arrested him he never got out of prison. Then they seized our taverna. He's dead now. Died in exile. What was I supposed to do? I couldn't stand it in the village. I wasn't from there. And I had the kid little Constantine.

Louis was sitting next to me, chain-smoking and pretending to be busy looking at something else. Pretending. "What kid?" I wanted to ask but before I could open my mouth Louis kicked me in the shin.

— What are you doing now? Are you still in school?

— Still. Still waiting.

I could tell Retsinas was about to say something, but instead he sent her off to get a round of ouzo. Which gave him a chance to fill me in:

— So she shows up with the kid. Who's she going to turn to? "Dorothy's" happened to be for rent. She killed herself a few days earlier Didn't you know her? Dorothy wasn't a woman. She was a man.

I cut him off. I couldn't endure hearing yet another story.

— Just tell me about Haroula.

Meanwhile, she brought us our ouzo.

— Let me tell you something about Manolis here; not even my own flesh and blood would help me like he did. He found me some money, helped me with the fridge. He's even the kid's godfather.

She stopped. Her eyes welled with tears. Without a word she turned and rushed to the back, looking for a handkerchief.

— Let's get out of here, said Louis climbing down from the bar stool.

He left money on the bar, tossed back his drink and went out, dragging me behind him, almost forcibly.

— Just a second, Manolis; what is this?

— Come with me; I know what I'm doing.

192

We left. And began walking up the sidewalk. I expected Haroula to appear at any moment, to call us back, but no; she did not.

— I was keeping that meeting as a surprise for you as I'm sure you realize; but since things didn't work out ...

I wanted to find a way to talk about Haroula.

— Go ahead ...

— What can I say, cousin? It didn't occur to you? Why she baptized the kid, Constantine? Born exactly nine months after your night at the Belle Vue, in Corinth. She swore up and down she never slept with another man. Nine months to the day, it was. Counted 'em. Give or take a day or two each way. Up till then she only had three men in her life: Peppas, me and you. Circumstantial evidence — who needs it? One look at the baby's picture is enough; it's the spitting image of you. Me, what did you expect me to do? She shows up with a baby in her arms ... She wants to find you, wants you to know. Still has hopes. "Forget him," I told her, "he's still going to school. Later, maybe." I didn't want to complicate your life. Besides, stories like that aren't your style. Said I didn't know where to find you. I did the right thing. Didn't I?

I was more shocked than moved. In fact, I was almost terror-stricken.

— You should have told me.

He stopped, stared at me.

— So you can do what, fool? Marry her? Recognize the kid? Take her into your home? Like you took in Martha back then? So there, I'm telling you now. Forget the big talk, Manolopoulos. You made your choice, and you've got to live with it. You want more trouble on top of it? Don't give me that stuff? I should have brought her to your place with the kid, just for laughs, to watch you squirm.

That's what you call rubbing it in. Made me feel like a piece of shit. All I could do was squirm, like he said.

— You're not cut out for stuff like that, Kostas, my boy. I thought we already agreed.

193

— Why didn't she tell me when she found out she was pregnant?

— You crazy? That was all she ever wanted; a kid. And the best you could have done was offer to help out with the abortion expenses. And to think she was in love with you ...

I began to feel chilled. We'd reached the square. In the distance we could hear voices; probably newsboys calling out the headlines. Louis perked up his ears. He was hoping desperately the government would fall, there would be elections, the democratic parties would win, and he could finally get his seaman's papers, the ones these bastards wouldn't let him touch with a ten-foot pole.

— Still dreaming about your papers, Louis?

— What do you think, cousin? You think I'm going to piss my life away with Antypas in the goldsmith shop? But these assholes? I've got a bad reputation, they say; don't inspire confidence.

As it turned out, the government did not fall. The criers were touting an extra; they'd just captured a murderer in Salonica.

We sat down on a bench in the square. He pulled out his cigarets and offered me one. No thanks. Couldn't get Haroula's baby out of my mind. I asked him for more details.

— Forget it. It's all over. Her mind is made up. You think she's going to come begging to you for support.

Again a pang of fear.

— Who's to say she won't come knocking one day down the road.

He turned again and stared at me. First he smiled that murderous smile of his, the smile that could mean he'd like to cut your throat, that he's sorry for you, or that he's had it up to here with you, depending on the circumstances.

— Kostas, my boy, what I wanted to do was ... You know what I'd like? For us to meet at age eighty, and you tell me how much you've regretted in your life. I mean, really. Would Haroula have been so bad for you? With Martha you ran like a rabbit. Now with Haroula, same old rabbit. She's not asking

194

you for support payments and stuff like that; it's your own life. But you're dumping her pretty damn quick, if I may say so. And I'm telling you this because I know you like the both of them. Give me one good reason why shouldn't you live with Haroula? Don't even marry her. She makes good money. Whatever you want is yours. She'll help you finish school. Or maybe she's not good enough for you as a mistress?

On and on he went ... I'd lose her just like I lost Martha; everybody and his brother was after her; a shipowner was drinking to her health. But she kept on refusing, she was still waiting for me. She's an intelligent woman, knows all the great authors, more cultivated than most smart ass college grads ...

I heard him out, but back then it all sounded incomprehensible, frightening. Leave my home and my studies and shack up with a ... a barwoman? Let a woman who was almost a ... let her pay the rent and put me through school? Who knows how many beds she slept in, no matter what Louis says. Of course, I didn't tell him what was on my mind; but he understood.

— OK, Kostas, my boy, forget it. I'll never mention it again. But I'm telling you, you're always taking a wrong turn. Mommy says get your diploma? So get it but you'll end up sticking it up your ass. Mark my words. You're not the career type. You're wasting your time. Your blood is telling you to go one way, and you, you're pissing your life away going in the opposite direction. OK, so forget your son, forget Haroula. Forever, he said with an air of finality, and spat.

7. THE METAMORPHOSIS

LATER, MUCH LATER, Louis told me that by the time
Liakopoulos and I reached his in-laws' place that fateful Sunday, the following earthshaking, awe-inspiring events had
transpired: to wit, not only had he succeeded in calming
Chrysanthi Antypas, but in completely transforming her.
Then, in full awareness and with malice aforethought he
decided to make her drunker still.

— The voice of experience, Kostas, my boy. Never try to
liberate the tongue and the passions of a woman without a
stiff dose of ouzo beforehand.

"Tell me," I asked him the following day, "just what were
you trying to do, anyway? Why?"

He wouldn't say. Hemmed and hawed. But he categorically
denied he had any particular strategy. As I understood it, he
liked the idea of Mrs. Antypas' metamorphosis in a vague,
abstract way.

— Things started to happen, Kostas, my boy, when I went
to get her in the bedroom, to help her calm her hysteria.

He found her sitting at her dressing table in front of the mirror, elbows resting on the glass tabletop, face cradled in her
hands, weeping. Tears were streaming from her eyes as she
stared at her reflection. When Louis entered the room she
turned toward him and launched into a monologue: "Good
Lord, what's wrong with me? I'm not well. What's come over
me? Why am I crying?" Louis sat down close to her on the bed
and let her talk. "I'm not well. What will I tell my husband?
I promised him I wouldn't drink ouzo and, look, I did. He

196

made me swear I wouldn't tell you he was for Metaxas and I went and told you. Didn't want me to shave my legs and I did. Didn't want me to dye my hair, I did that too. I didn't go with him to Aegina; why? What's gotten into me?''

On and on she went, not even noticing that Louis had gotten up, left the room, and returned with the ouzo bottle in his hand, the two glasses, and most of all, that she'd tossed down her fifth shot. In one gulp.

— I don't want you thinking I was starting to get ideas, cousin. Not on your life.

When he got to his feet and stood behind her, their eyes met in the mirror. At that exact instant she stopped talking, stopped weeping. She even gave him a crooked smile. Then, naturally as can be, Louis bent over and picked up a comb and hairbrush from the glass-topped dressing table. She remained motionless. He was at a loss, but only momentarily, until a wild idea came to him, an idea which he quickly put into action. Suddenly, totally unexpectedly, he released that outlandish pigtail of hers, one of Antypas' last bastions. The blond hair flowing free was breathtaking. Louis couldn't restrain himself. He began to comb her hair.

It was too late for her to resist. She accepted her fate. How could she have known that Louis had once been a ladies' hairdresser?

You heard what I said. A ladies' hairdresser. Right after his discharge from the army, I think it was. The police refused to give him his political loyalty certificate; he couldn't get his seaman's papers.

— Retsinas, don't let anyone kid you; you'll never get that certificate You should be thankful to be alive.

Papadopoulos, the police chief, brandished the thick file under his nose to underline the point.

— You ought to thank your lucky stars your brother is well connected. With a file like yours, you should have been dead long ago.

I don't think I mentioned Louis' half-brother, Moschos. By another father. The distance which separated Louis from his brother was multifaceted, covering everything from class to metaphysics. Almost intergalactic. What I mean to say is, they were like people from different galaxies, let alone different planets. The brother was a career military man — that should tell you all you need to know. A childless uncle of theirs, one of his mother's brothers who was a touch on the aristocratic side, something of a coupon clipper, a bit the blue-blooded conservative, adopted him young. In brief, the shame of the family on his mother's side. General Tzavaras was his name; a military magistrate he was.

Anyway, we'll talk about that some other time. Now back to our main subject, police chief Papadopoulos, who adamantly refused to give Louis his certificate despite the fact that he, Louis I mean, was quite prepared to sign a loyalty oath and even repudiate Zahariades, the Party general secretary.

— Not a chance, Retsinas. Don't try and kid us.

— And what am I supposed to do, chief? How am I supposed to live? Want to be a truck driver? Got to have a certificate. A priest? Same story. Longshoreman? You guessed it. Can't even work as a ticket-taker on the bus. Did it for a month, then they fired me. Wanted to see my papers. How can I finish my studies? Your papers, please. What will I do? Office work, collect garbage? Forget it. Can't leave the country. First you need a passport. Can't even get me a license to drive a motor-cycle, do deliveries. Where will it all end?

As he spoke Papadopoulos was picking his nose and gazing idly at Ophelia through the open window. Ophelia was what people in the neighborhood called Miss Carmen, who a mere six months earlier had opened a new hairdressing salon called "The Head Beautiful" just across from the station house. No one knew for sure just where the Ophelia came from — maybe they confused the play with the opera.

198

In any case, the police chief was daydreaming as he picked away at his nose. It was crystal clear that Louis' survival concerned him far less than the tall, slender silhouette of Carmen who was, at that very instant, leaning provocatively in the doorway of her salon.

Then Papadopoulos removed his finger from his nose and began to arrange the pencils on his desk.

— How can I convince you I'm sincere, chief? I don't want to overthrow your regime, and even if I wanted to, I couldn't. Whatever you want, I'm your man.

And he launched into a ringing denunciation of the Communist Party and its sundry front organizations, proudly proclaiming his readiness to die for the motherland, for her skies and seas.

— Give up, Retsinas. You can't convince me. Bring your father in to swear a loyalty oath and I'll give you your certificate, but with a father like yours ...

Just as Louis was about to repudiate his father and mother, he noticed in which direction the chief was looking. He was wasting his time. Once again he would have to go cap in hand to that asshole half-brother of his. Otherwise, goodbye seaman's papers. He got to his feet.

— Alright chief, I give up. But what the hell am I supposed to do? Steal?

And then, midway between nose picking and arranging the inkwells on his desk, the chief absentmindedly let drop:

— Well, try hairdresser. Why don't you become a hairdresser? You probably don't need a certificate.

When Louis made the announcement that night, in the midst of one of those epic games of hearts of ours at Tassos' coffeehouse, everyone was thunderstruck. I was the only one who laughed. A loud, boisterous laugh. The thought of Louis as a ladies' hairdresser just about drove me to hysterics.

Liakopoulos, the oldest of the group — about the same age as Argyris — who styled himself a real man because his prick was ten inches long, stood up angrily and turned on me:

— What're you laughing at, Manolopoulos? He's just crazy

enough to do it. His father was a barber in the army, so what's wrong with being a hairdresser?

Agis didn't know whose side to take. Truth to tell, he couldn't bear the thought of his idol doing ladies' hair, brandishing a comb limp-wristedly in one hand, mincing around with rollers and hairbrushes, shampoos and conditioners.

— It's just not right, Manolis, he said, but Antoniadis wouldn't let him finish.

— Why not! Let him do it! He should take the job, the papers should write it up, put it on page one. Let people find out what you have to do to make a living if you're a leftist.

Antoniadis was the Stalinist of the group, after a fashion. More fanatical than Argyris, an unrepentant hard-liner. Believed in comrade Zahariades and the dream of the third round.

— The leader tells us to put our weapons down, so we put them down . If we have to become hairdressers or deliver coal or haul ice then we'll do it. Our main job is to stay alive.

Liakopoulos began to froth at the mouth. What seemed like two thousand insults poured out — more like rapid-fire spitting — within the space of a minute; then he let fly a final and entirely comprehensible "fool" and got up to leave.

Antoniadis wasn't that much of a fool. He had inherited a tiny old calendarist church from his mother, so he scraped by on the take from Sunday collection baskets and votive candles lighted by the faithful, all of which gave him the spare time and the money he needed to believe in the revolution and in the struggle of the Greek proletariat. They couldn't close his church down, you see; it was protected by the constitution.

Before Liakopoulos walked out the door, he hesitated, then let drop something worse, and a good deal more provocative, than "fool."

— So speaks the man who lives off the opium of the people.

By opium he meant the church. Having spoken, he stalked out. It was the first time anyone had rubbed Antoniadis' Achilles' heel in his face, so to speak. He grimaced, swallowed hard, opened his mouth — but nothing came out. Then picked up his cigarets and headed for the door, mumbling to himself.

— Sit down, piped up Economides, the group conciliator and my mother's idea of the ideal son.

— By the time you figure out what's wrong, it'll be too late. You'll all be reactionaries.

So he spoke, and left.

That evening, Louis dropped out of sight. For a long time — almost a month. Maritsa — remember her? — was the first to uncover him at Carmen's "The Head Beautiful" when she went for her monthly dye job. The news spread like wildfire through the neighborhood. Retsinas, doing hair at Ophelia's! His sister, Antigone, wasn't surprised, although she didn't see anything funny about it. When she broke the news, their father happened to be listening to the finance minister announcing a devaluation of the drachma.

— They say your son got a job at the hairdresser's. Did you hear?

No response from Louis' father. Maybe he didn't hear what she said; or perhaps he thought the drachma devaluation was more important. Probably the latter.

Be that as it may, after three months Ophelia was so impressed by Louis' skill, and by the number of customers he brought in, that she suggested they become partners. He would think it over, he said. Come the sixth month the proposal had changed. He had to choose: "Partners plus marriage or abortion and we'll see." He opted for abortion. It was then that the baneful Papadopoulos again intervened. The day after the abortion, when he went to visit her at the clinic, who should he run into but Retsinas.

— What's this Commie bandit doing here? he asked.

Same for Louis.

— What's this rascal doing here?

201

The encounter turned out to be a fateful one, both for Louis and his professional career. He had a gut feeling: the minute Carmen left the clinic, the cop would give her an ultimatum: "Fire the Commie, or I leave."

Sure enough, that was the ultimatum. At which point Carmen, as you might expect, opted for state power instead of Commie banditry, which in turn obliged Papadopoulos to escort her to the altar slightly earlier than anticipated.

The wedding took place the very same day the taller of the Krugas brothers, the one they called "the cuckold" — you remember him, don't you? — shot Aristos, the other tall brother, along with his ugly wife, Olympia, in their bed of shame.

You could hear the gunshots from the church just at the climax of the wedding ceremony. Louis was in attendance. We'd gone together. Afterward, when we found out about the murder, Louis said: "One less rat." I didn't fully grasp what he meant at that moment. Later I had to laugh. Still later, when it occurred to me that the killing suited him perfectly, helped him escape Eugenia in fact, I realized he may have had something to do with it. Then I shivered.

But back to that fateful Sunday in the bedroom, when Louis began combing Chrysanthi's hair. A bit before that scene — the combing part, I mean — I forgot to mention Louis' and Aleka's afternoon quarrel over whether to buy an apartment or not. Possibly, if it hadn't been for that spat, events would not have unfolded with such dizzying speed and with such devastating impact on the Antypas family.

— Come on, Manolis, don't be so stubborn, Aleka whined. We can get a bank loan, and Mr. Anargyros will give us credit. I want a house of our own. What's wrong with that?

But Louis hung on doggedly, telling himself, "You asshole,

202

don't let those thighs and that ass of hers distract you, not this time."

With that girl Louis could never rise to the occasion. Kept falling on his face; couldn't say no. She knew it, of course. She was fully conscious of the power of her weapons, and for that very reason she held them in reserve, for the final assault.

— Dearie, don't keep on pushing. No way I'll go that deep into debt. When your old man dies, we'll take over the place; I don't mind sharing a house with your mother.

Aleka wouldn't budge. Neither would Louis. "Don't give an inch, asshole, or you're finished," he kept telling himself. She pulled off her garters, but he remained motionless. Nothing she could do would catch his eye. He insisted on talking without looking at her. "Get thee behind me," he muttered over and over, as he stared at the trellised grapevine growing in the back yard. He had on nothing but his undershorts. The moment he turned toward her he knew he would be transformed into a pillar of salt; surrender was inevitable.

— Aren't you going to look at me? All I see is your back.

But the danger of succumbing was not only a matter of sight. The rustling of her lace nighty, the smell of her perfume were enough to start his pulse pounding. The truth of the matter is that for Louis, all his senses were a source of torment: sight, hearing, smell, they all rolled over him like a millstone.

— Sweetie pie, let's just imagine that something happens to your old man tomorrow; hypothetically, let's say he kicks me out. Then what? How do I pay off the debts? I couldn't survive long, and you know it.

Aleka opened a jar of scented cream.

— Tell daddy to make you a partner, that way he can't fire you. I told him so already; we even had an argument. What can he do? He has to agree.

She began to apply the cream.

— Seriously, you think your father will make me a partner?

The aroma began to besiege his nostrils.

— Why shouldn't he? But he doesn't trust you. He found

out that you're trying to get your seaman's papers, that you're seeing that nymphomaniac bitch, Persephone.

Louis was pleading for her not to make any enticing moves in front of him, because the way she was now, slathered with scented cream, wearing that baby doll of hers, his fall would be ignominious, diametrically the opposite of glorious.

— The minute she shows up, they say, you run off with her to one of those cheap hotels where the whores go.

— He's telling you that to drive us apart.

— They spotted you behind the church.

— You believe that nonsense? Me and her, in a hotel?

— No?

— Absolutely not, he said curtly, cutting off the conversation abruptly.

Back she came to the burning question, whether to buy an apartment or not. She already found a place, she said, and Mr. Anargyros, the contractor, would sell it at a good price. He answered with some stock phrases that would have done his former cell-leader, Argyris, proud: "Comrades, bank loans are a trap. You start playing the game without even realizing it. First they hook you with the idea of private property, a little place of your own, then they reel you in. You scrape together a down payment, then comes the mortgage, the taxes, the bills; fifteen, twenty years, however long it takes to pay off, you hope and pray the system survives and flourishes, 'cause you know that every disturbance, every strike — it only takes one — and they'll take it all back. And you, like any house-owner, you'd rather die than have them take it back." That was roughly what he told Aleka, in the manner of a party study group in political economy. Aleka didn't understand a word, of course. Not only was it all way over her head, but also because, reflected in the half-open closet door mirror, she noticed to her surprise that Louis' penis, as he spoke, had begun to spring to life. Her only response was "Forget all that crap," and she crawled across the bed, pulled him toward her and began to pull down his white undershorts as he droned on.

204

Aleka's offensives always ended with his unconditional surrender. He accepted all her conditions. They would borrow
money, buy the house from Mr. Anargyros, and that evening,
when daddy returned from Aegina, Louis would finally ask to
become a partner. The following Saturday they would go to
Epidaurus so she could finally see a Greek tragedy. That was
the only way she would agree to swallow his sperm, she said.
He had to promise. He promised; she swallowed.

By the time Liakopoulos and I got to Antypas' place in
response to Louis' party invitation, Aleka, smug in triumph,
had rinsed out her mouth; put on a tarty blouse that half-
exposed her breasts and back; put her stockings and garters
back on, topped off with a tight-fitting mauve skirt which set
off her pert little body to perfection; awakened their daughter
and set off with a song for her meeting with Mr. Anargyros
to finalize the apartment deal.
— He'll be there on Sunday?
Louis had only seen the man once. Could barely remember
what he looked like. Bald, short, paunchy, with blotches on
his cheeks, his hands, around his eyes. He was a redhead to
boot. That was all he could remember. Oh, yes, rich too.
— I'm meeting him at his place. He's holding the apartment just for us. Tomorrow may be too late. He's expecting
me.
— Bitch! She knew all along, thought Louis as he watched
her leave. But slowly he came to terms with himself. "When
you get right down to it, everyone ought to have a place of his
own. It's no big deal. Let's see what happens."
As she closed the front door, Aleka called out:
— Don't wait up for me. After I'm finished at Anargyros',
I'm going to see your father, show him his granddaughter.
That was game over. Believe it or not, Louis was actually

205

moved. Almost cried. After that, to the best of his recollection, he had become so reconciled to the idea of the house deal that he began thinking in whose name they should buy the place. "I didn't want to get stuck like poor Bolas. His wife, Sophie, screwing everyone in sight, while the poor SOB spends years paying off that lousy three-room of theirs, the one they bought in her name, the one he left just as soon as he finally paid it off."

Louis would never admit that his sole purpose in inviting us that fateful Sunday was to wreck Antypas' domestic bliss, even though — that much, he did admit — the blockhead had it coming. Sure, he used every trick in the book to unlock Chrysanthi Antypas' heart, but he never imagined it would destroy her.

So, as he was combing her hair — remember? — he sprang the latest on her: he was expecting two good friends of his; Aleka would be back late — she'd gone to see Mr. Anargyros' apartment — and only a few moments earlier her husband had phoned from Aegina to say he wouldn't be back that night, he had missed the last boat.

— Why didn't you let me talk to him?

— You were crying; what would you have told him if he'd asked you why you were crying?

— You're right. What would I have told him?

Then he began telling her stories. First the one about his pal, Thrasyboulos, and the wreck. Was the whole wild tale true, or simply a figment of Louis' imagination? None of us ever found out. Nobody ever saw the man again. One thing for sure: Louis had the hots for his wife, Anait, but since Thrasyboulos was a friend, he never let her know it; avoided them in fact. He was afraid of what he might do.

— Cousin, that Anait is one exotic lady. Armenian, you

know. Sings operatic arias. Everything about her is spherical: cheeks, boobs, ass.

No sooner had Thrasyboulos bought the new Volkswagen than he drove by Louis' place to show it off. The plan was for the two of them to zip down to Corinth for a cup of coffee. But Louis came back alone, black with grime, blood-stained, his clothes in tatters.

— Forget him, he told Anait when she opened the door. Your husband and his new car, they're on the bottom by now. When I come to, there I am, hanging from some rocks on the cliff. They're still looking for him. That's how fast we were going.

She had been sleeping; it was after midnight. She stared at him wide-eyed in amazement. He wouldn't let her cry out, or tear her hair. She was still half asleep. He calmed her, comforted her. "Such is life; we're mere mortals," stuff like that. For about two hours he comforted her, until she fell asleep on the couch. Then he took a bath to clean away the dirt. It was about two-thirty in the morning.

Later Anait said that when Louis awakened her, the whole thing was like a dream.

At daybreak, when Thrasyboulos walked through the door, clothes in tatters, face covered with grime, he found the two of them naked in one another's arms, sleeping blissfully.

Mrs. Antypas recoiled in shock.

— What are you telling me, Manolis?

The story was too much for her. She lost her bearings. The compass points of good and evil — the dos and the don'ts — had disappeared. Now what? Lose her temper, or laugh? Of course, as I'm telling it to you now, it all seems incredibly vulgar. But believe me, the way Louis told it, right down to the tiniest detail, was so convincing that if you were to hear him, you could only conclude that everything that happened later was bound to happen.

— Manolis, those are immoral things you're telling me. With your friend's wife? How could you?

After, when he told her about Maritsa and Eugenia, she just

about went over the edge. Christ spoke in parables to save his flock, didn't he? Well, Louis told stories to rebaptize souls. It was clear as day: resist as she might, those stories of his were opening Chrysanthi's horizons; opening them dangerously wide.

— But, Manolis, what did they teach you in school? What made you take that road?

— A bit inherited, a bit of luck. From my mother, maybe. Her first husband was an army man; left her after a year of marriage, in '30. That's when my brother was born. She filed for divorce after he took part in a military coup attempt along with some other officers. He was arrested in a pigsty just as they were taking an oath to assassinate the prime minister. That night mother took it on the lam with father's former major-domo. Nine months later I was born. The major-domo, he was my real father; a Venizelos supporter, and the camp barber, a reserve lieutenant by rank. My old man always claimed he told the prime minister about the plot himself. Heard about it from mom, the two of them had an affair going all the while. He was a good-looking man, my dad. Three years later Antigone — my sister — was born. Five years later, at another former prime minister's funeral, the two of them were arrested. Mom and my old man. The funeral had turned into a demonstration against Metaxas. There was a downpour that day. By some devilish twist of fate, they were arrested by her former husband, who had become a big shot in the regime. Ten days later mom died of pneumonia, from the soaking she got in the rain. My father kept on working as a barber. Then he got work on the railroad, as a sleeping car porter. They claimed he was a Communist and fired him. Her first husband died from a stray bullet during the fighting in Athens, as he was climbing over a wall ... But it's all too much to keep track of, I'm afraid. Probably I take after my mother.

Mrs. Antypas had become so engrossed in Louis' stories that when he asked her to look at herself in the mirror to see how she liked her metamorphosis, she almost fainted. The last traces of her former self had vanished. From head to toe she beheld a new Chrysanthi. Not only outwardly, but inwardly, too; deep within herself. She could see it! Her eyes had a fresh gleam. They had become deeper, more melancholy, more thoughtful.

Louis remained dead still, letting her stare at the image in the mirror. He knew well what was going on in her soul at that moment: the final phase of metamorphosis. He knew it, and left her alone. The mystical process must not be interrupted. Yesterday and today were clashing in ultimate collision. Recollections, memories, rejections, everything was struggling within her. Any minute now she would sigh deeply. Any minute now she would say, "I've wasted my life. What happened to my life?"

— Cousin, I was so certain I just waited for her to say it, and she did, exactly: "I've wasted my life. What happened to my life?" The same words. Can you believe it?

Then, as she turned to look at him, he told her very diplomatically that his visitors were due any minute; perhaps it would be better for her to change. At first she didn't understand — she was still lost in her memories. When she returned to the present, she was quick to agree. He suggested — where did he get the idea? — she put on one of Aleka's dresses.

— Just for laughs, we'll see what she says when she comes back and sees you in one of her dresses.

Still half-drunk, Chrysanthi raised no objections.

— But you have to let me choose, he said.

She let him. He went over to Aleka's wardrobe and chose a red skirt slit up the thigh and a white blouse with fine gold piping. She put them on. The skirt was tight-fitting, the blouse showed every square inch of her bosom. He knotted a bright-red kerchief around her throat. Then came high-heeled shoes, black stockings, a black necklace and black earrings. Her hair cascaded over her shoulders, pure blond. But there wasn't quite enough time for her to do her eyes. If it hadn't been for a few wrinkles on her face, you couldn't have told mother and daughter apart.

I'll spare you the details. You can fill them in yourself. We get there around sunset. And by seven o'clock the four of us are well and truly soused. Louis, Liakopoulos, Chrysanthi and me. And when I say soused, I mean soused, literally! Maybe Louis not quite so much, since he's the one who remembers all the details I'm telling you now. All I can remember is Liakopoulos bawling like a baby; two days earlier he gets called down to the police station and they make him sign a loyalty oath; sign it, they say, or that's it for you and your future.

— So I sign, I sign ... What am I supposed to do. I sign.

Me, I'm slurring my words; take me to Haroula's, I ask Louis. I want to see my son, I want to marry her, to ... Can't even remember what I said.

Chrysanthi is laughing loudly, continuously. Uncontrollably. Then Liakopoulos starts complimenting her eyelashes. Louis overhears the last of the sentence; he thinks he wants her to sing the song about a lady's eyelashes. I overhear Liakopoulos ask Louis: "Where's her husband, anyhow?" and Louis answers him in a whisper: "Aegina; he won't be back tonight." And then Chrysanthi begins to sing the eyelash song. Sounds just like Stella Greca, the bouzouki singer. Liakopoulos crawls over and embraces her legs. She loses her balance and collapses on the couch. He starts speaking to her but no one can understand a word. Least of all Chrysanthi. All this while, I'm thinking of Haroula.

— Come on, take me there on your motorbike. Won't take us two minutes. We'll pick up some ouzo. We're all out. And a couple of beers.

I'm intent on seeing Haroula, even if we have to bring her here.

— Why not; tell me why not?

Chrysanthi is giggling, chuckling, coming out with the odd

210

"Ah! What are you saying?"

Liakopoulos is wild about Chrysanthi.

I never knew just how I ended up on Louis' motorbike, nor how we ever managed to make it to Dorothy's bar.

— Closed, idiot!

— Closed on Sunday? Funny.

We look around; maybe she's somewhere nearby. No one. Shut tight.

— The shipowner probably did a job on her. Shacked up with her, for sure. Too late, you asshole. She's long gone.

On our way back Louis lets fly a long string of curses.

When we get back to the house with our armload of ouzo and beer, there isn't a soul in the living room. The room is empty; the silence, total. Curiosity gets the better of us. Louis motions to me to keep quiet, and tiptoes toward the bedroom door. It's closed. The only way for us to see inside is from the garden window.

We move stealthily, carefully out into the garden. It's all we can do to restrain our laughter. What we see is quite literally indescribable. We haul over a concrete block to stand on, bringing our eyes up to counterpane level. There is Chrysanthi, standing with her skirt pulled up, clutching the wrought-iron bed frame while in front of her Liakopoulos is toiling to fit that enormous ten-inch prick of his into her. First he lifts one of her legs, then the other.

— Come on, sweetie ... Where you been hidin' all this time? he mutters, his words slurring from the combined effects of ouzo and arousal. Your leg, sweetie, just a little higher. Come on, baby, just a little ...

By then no one can understand a word; almost a quarter-hour has elapsed and still he hasn't succeeded in getting it into her. He's sweating, puffing, but it just won't go. Louis is

211

about to yell at him, "The bed, you idiot. Throw her on the bed!" when he lifts her tenderly, sits on the edge of the bed, and pulls her down on top of him. Speechless and awe-struck, we watch the entire scene, to the end. With that enormous prick of his, we're worried the poor woman will end up with a perforated uterus.

In the meantime, Liakopoulos has become a raging beast. He rips off her blouse and brassiere, her breasts pop out like lightning flashes in the darkness. He hardly knows what to do first, whether to grab or suck. For an instant we catch a glimpse of Chrysanthi's behind; it's mottled with red marks from where she's been leaning against the bed frame. The whole spectacle is, put succinctly, beyond description.

Then she begins to let herself go, to move back and forth rhythmically on top of him; we can hear her whispered moaning slowly gaining in volume. The whole wild scene lasts for a full fifteen minutes. Liakopoulos has another major asset: he can hold off coming for as long as the woman needs, and that just about drives Chysanthi wild. Like a gigantic stopwatch, the bastard. Her last cry is partly a sob, partly the groan of a slaughtered animal as you plunge the knife into its throat. First she sucks in her breath as to gasp for air, and then comes the scream.

When finally he returned, around eleven, Antypas found himself face to face with fate, with the raw stuff of events. No way I can begin to describe the shock; the chain reaction of shocks. He was hardly over the first when the second hit him.

From a few doors down the street he could hear dance music; that was a surprise. Being a suspicious type, he didn't ring the doorbell. Instead he let himself in with his key. As he came from the hall into the living room, he got shock number one: he saw Chrysanthi, but he thought she was Aleka.

212

— What's going on here? Where is she? Your mother? he asked but before he could complete the sentence he realized that the woman dancing with the urangutan, with Liakopoulos I mean, was not Aleka; it was her mother, his wife, Chrysanthi.

But put the "his" in quotation marks from now on.

Shock number two — stronger still — came when, tearing her from his embrace, he became aware of her "filthy" metamorphosis. But it was just an impression. Before her torn blouse had a chance to register, shock number three came, the ultimate shock: horrified he beheld the tumescence rising beneath Liakopoulos' trousers which, due to the unreconstructed monstrosity of the man's notorious prick, were bulging at the seams. Even if he hadn't seen it, there was more than enough evidence from the way the "ugly son-of-a-bitch" was embracing "his" Chrysanthi. She dashed off to the bedroom and locked the door behind her. He kicked us out of the house, the three of us. What could we do? We said not a word.

We stand there for a few moments, right outside the front door, looking at one another. What are we supposed to do? Nobody knows.

— You no-good rat, I thought you told me her husband was in Aegina, wouldn't be back tonight? Liakopoulos fumes.

Even today — I'm telling you — no one knows for sure whether or not Retsinas was lying when he told Chrysanthi her husband had called from Aegina to say he'd missed the last boat and wouldn't be home that night What's more, we never found out if it was all, as I say, a carefully designed strategy to eliminate his father-in-law. Of course he denies the whole thing to this day, but for those of us who know Louis, the denial means nothing.

A split second later Louis' bedroom window comes crashing open and all his worldly goods come flying out. I can't recall seeing a more spectacular eviction. The first thing to fall at our feet is his guitar. And within a few minutes, the front yard and the street are littered with everything from shat-

213

tered mirrors to Aleka's torn bras. Antypas' destructive rage envelops even his own daughter. Everything becomes rubbish at our feet. The baby's cradle, their bed, the mattress, her clothes, lace nighties, hangers ... soon a small mountain of variegated colors is taking shape, right before our eyes. The last things to come flying through the window are Louis' books and cards. Come to think of it, that's probably what happened to Hatzaras' cards; you know, the book installment cards. So, he had them all along and refused to hand them over, out of spite, the SOB. Liakopoulos is foaming at the mouth.

— You asshole! Now look at us! he wails, over and over again.

We leave the stuff lying there in a heap, and set out to try and find a truck. Antypas is still heaving the odd item out the window. We turn the corner and pass Louis' in-laws' bedroom window. In the corner of the window we catch a glimpse of Chrysanthi's face half-hidden by the curtain; her eyes are full of terror and defiance.

Liakopoulos pauses for an instant and looks at her with boundless sorrow.

— The poor woman, he says. Life just ain't fair.

— Every revolution starts with a little bloodshed, answers Louis, and walks off.

One corner over it occurs to us maybe Louis should keep watch just in case Aleka shows up, while we go find a truck to cart the rubbish away. That's what Antypas called it, as he roared from the window: "Here, take your rubbish, you little fucker."

We return with the truck, load it and are just about ready to leave when what should pull up to the curb but a limousine that looks at least thirty feet long. But before we can react, who should climb out but Aleka and her daughter. I'd never seen her before. What a heavenly piece of ass — truly — was Aleka. Louis was right. Anargyros, the redhead, is sitting at the helm with a flower in his lapel, wearing dark glasses, the kind blind men wear. We don't know what to think. Dark

214

glasses after dark? Patent leather shoes with spats, and a gold watch chain dangling from his vest pocket?

As Aleka is about to introduce us Louis picks her up bodily and plumps her down on the truck, right next to his motor-bike. Liakopoulos takes the kid on his lap in the front seat. Anargyros stares at us, mouth agape. What's the point of trying to explain? They almost forget me; I'm trying to be polite to the developer, "this thing and that thing, you know," and before I knew it, they drive away leaving me standing there.

Liakopoulos continued seeing "his" Chrysanthi on and off. Roughly once every three months, when Antypas would go for his cardiac examination. You can appreciate that after the sequence of shocks of that fateful night, his heart suffered irreparable damage.

She rang him; Liakopoulos, that is.

— How are you?

Always the picture of politeness.

— Are you alone, sweetie pie?

— All alone.

Aleka lived with the developer, Mr. Anargyros, for some time before she married him — until her divorce from Louis came through, that is.

— The two of them were probably at it before, cousin. Possibly even that Sunday when we got kicked out. Not because she loved him. Nope. Mostly for that shit apartment; she wanted to get a good price, easy payments. I knew something was going on when I took her to Epidaurus and we just happened to run into him. The whole thing was a set-up. That's probably why I dumped her and ran off with Bertrand's circus. Come to think of it, that's probably the reason. I was hurt, no kidding. Deeply hurt.

Whenever Louis visits his daughter, he spends two hours

215

living like royalty. She lives in a semi-palatial house in Psychiko, a place with an immense garden, a swimming pool, landscape lighting, lawn furniture, fountains.

— Cousin, if you could see how the servants pour whisky for the redhead, in the finest crystal glasses, you wouldn't know what to think! Not to mention Aleka. Might as well be the queen of something or other, strolling through the statuary like some half-ass empress. But that daughter of mine! I may have abandoned her, but she's wild about me.

Personally, I don't think Aleka ever stopped worshipping him. That's why she paid such a high price for her double-cross later on. You'll see.

8. THE LAST SUPPER

LAZARIS, THE WISE GUY of the gang, had a blunt way of putting it:

— Childhood trauma ... that's why he's the way he is.

He was insistent. With Louis, it had to be a case of childhood trauma.

— No, really? That traumatic?

— Absolutely. When you get right down to it, he never knew his mother; now she's an almost mythical figure for him, he idolizes her. Just because she leaves her royalist husband who happens to be a Metaxas sympathizer — so he claims — and blithely puts the horns on him with a left-wing barber, that makes her some sort of heroine for standing up to the establishment? Big deal. Who did she think she was standing up to? That's why she died young if you ask me.

When Lazaris got started on that psychology bullshit of his, that heavy-handed pseudo-psychoanalysis, the gang would break up in less than ten minutes.

That particular time, Agis was the first to get up to leave. We were sitting on the sidewalk, outside Tassos' place. The weather was lousy: cloudy, humid, rain in the air. I tried to convince him to stay.

— Let me go, Manolopoulos. We're going to listen to this shit? Louis remembers what his mother was doing when he was eight years old?

Agis' remarks got a rise out of Lazaris.

— Of course he remembers, you illiterate. Why wouldn't he? Even if he doesn't remember the events themselves ...

217

well, he would have heard people talking, he would remember what they said, subconsciously, which ... But then, what can you expect from someone who's never opened a book in his life. Mark my words, my fine friend, it's the childhood years that ...

Agis cut him off in mid-sentence.

— Go on, go and kiss your pal, professor Big Shot, on the ass, and spare us the highfalutin bullshit.

Big Shot was the nickname of one of Lazaris' university professors. Agis had hit the nail on the head. Lazaris was the professor's full-time ass-kisser. Day and night, visions of academic careers and scholarships danced in his head. All his spare time he spent running errands for Big Shot, scurrying around like a fourth-class gopher.

Lazaris' mother had contrived to get herself a cleaning job in a big office building downtown. What she wouldn't do to keep her darling boy in pocket money and good clothes for his academic career! So it was that Lazaris managed to give the eminent professor the impression that he was a well-to-do emigrant's son. But it was all a sham, as we later found out.

— So ashamed of your father you bump him up a notch, Lazaris? Better he should be a well-to-do immigrant? Well, blame it on your mother. She knows everything and still she puts up with you instead of popping you one on the snout.

That was exactly how Agis put it, much, much later — we were grown men by then — at Drakopoulos' wedding. Humiliated him. Could Lazaris bring himself to admit, back then at university, that it was the nationalists who shot his old man, alongside Liakopoulos' father, at Trikala?

In real life, mother and son lived like cave dwellers in the refugee quarter of Piraeus, not far from the former jail. But if you were to spot Lazaris emerging from his subterranean

218

lair and making his way towards Athens, dressed in a smartly cut suit, carrying a leather briefcase, his hair brilliantined, wearing patent leather shoes shiny enough to see your face in, you would hardly know what to think.

At the sight of him, Antoniadis turned his face skyward, spread wide his arms in fake ecstasy and came out with the most blasphemous thing he could think of.

— Perfidious God, how can You tolerate such injustice?

In order for Lazaris to play the big shot, his mother just about turned consumptive, blind and crippled. She was so nearsighted she could barely see, but she had no glasses. Her arms and legs were all but useless from arthritis. Undernourishment had turned her into a living skeleton.

— That no-good skunk, he's made a slave out of her. Won't even stand beside her in his doorway; can't have her miserable appearance creating a bad impression. Who knows what kind of tall tales he tells the prof, how many pairs of boots he has to lick.

— Hey, fool, no way you'll make assistant professor as bullshitter and boot-licker. How low can you get, unless you're some kind of genius. But a genius Lazaris was not. Just a phony; and the child of his parents.

Whatever the reason, he hadn't put in an appearance for quite awhile, for which Louis was probably to blame. Last time he kicked him right out of Tassos' coffeehouse.

— Clear out, you no-good liar! Get going! he said.

We looked on speechless as the eviction proceeded apace. With nary a word, Lazaris skulked off, tail between his legs.

— What is it, Louis? What did he do?

We all thought it had something to do with women, maybe he ratted on Louis to a girlfriend we didn't know about. But Louis avoided answering.

And now, what seems like ages later, this fine gentleman, when he hears about Retsinas' divorce from Aleka, suddenly reappears at the coffeehouse — Sunday noon it was — with his tie, his brilliantined hair, his leather briefcase, "Just passing by; so I thought maybe ..."

He was insanely jealous of Retsinas; simply couldn't under- stand how a punk like him had managed to snare a looker like Aleka, and from a well-to-do family yet.

— Sure, sure, Retsinas, he said. You make like Mr. Non- chalance, but you sure know how to bait a hook.

And now here he is, the asshole, dumping all over Louis in- stead of acknowledging his greatness for turning his back on the easy life. "Who the hell does this mister Retsinas think he is anyway? Is he crazy or what, walking out on that kind of girl, on that kind of future, on a shop which prints money ..."

— What was wrong with the father-in-law anyway? So he was a Metaxas man, big deal. What did he expect? Just leave it lie. But while we're on the subject, Manolopoulos, didn't he all but screw the guy's wife — didn't the guy almost croak? — and how the hell do you walk out on your wife and child and suddenly become a circus daredevil?

It was from Lazaris that we learned of Louis' latest craze, that he'd left Aleka in the lurch at Epidaurus and joined that pathetic travelling circus. We were speechless, lost in wonder- ment, as I recall.

— You, Manolopoulos, you're buddy-buddy with the guy, why didn't you stop him. Even the prodigal son returns. You don't just walk away from that kind of opportunity.

We didn't know what to think. Why was he so interested in Retsinas all of a sudden? Before then, the sight of Louis was enough to turn him green with envy. That's when he came out with his famous outburst about Louis' childhood traumas.

No one replied. It looked for all the world like a conspiracy of silence. When Agis lashed out at him, I tried to calm things down. I ended up loathing myself that day. Once or twice, in fact, I almost ended up agreeing with him; it was about time for Louis to sober up. Not only did I behave underhandedly,

I also put Agis on the spot. I'd found out that Lazaris had joined EKOF, a paragovernmental student group; that he'd become Big Shot's number one stool pigeon in order to get scholarships and good behavior certificates. But I kept my mouth shut; didn't say a word. See, back then I wanted to get into law school pretty badly myself, and he was one of those people it's "better for me to be on good terms with." But he would have gladly turned me in if he could. The only way the son of an executed leftist could get ahead was to give continuous, living proof of his loyalty to the system. "What's gotten into that jerk, Agis, going after him like that? Guy used to shit in his pants when you said 'boo,' and now he plays the hero?"

— Look, Lazaris, back off or I'll hang your dirty linen out to dry and you along with it. If you've got something against Louis, then tell him to his face, Agis snapped angrily, then stood there, waiting for his answer.

Lazaris was cornered. Finally he shut his mouth, pursed his lips, looked at us, shook his head scornfully as if to spit on us, and got to his feet, picking up his leather briefcase — he never left home without it — and walked out the door. I tried to smooth things over.

— Just a second, Lazaris, I cried. You don't have to be so ...

I tell you, I didn't want him lumping me in with his enemies. I was afraid of him. I got to my feet, started after him, but Antoniadis stopped me. Then I turned to Agis:

— Are you nuts? What dirty linen are you talking about? You know who he is? What he can do to us? Who are you to put us on the spot, anyway?

Icy silence.

— I just don't want the guy around our group.

Then the probable cause of his hatred came out. Lazaris had made a pass at Martha, tried to make Agis look bad in front of her; that was why.

— Is that it, Agis? That's why you went after him?

— That's not the reason, I swear to God. I've had it. If Martha likes him, she's welcome to him. She'll be the loser. His

221

prick can't be more than an inch and a half full-out. If that's all she wants, he's welcome to her.

Then, to save face, he had to explain what he meant by dirty linen, and reminded us of the time Louis kicked Lazaris out of the coffee-house.

— What's that got to do with ...

— Plenty. Remember '55, when the twenty Communists broke out of prison? Well, one of the fugitives knew his mother; tried to hide at their house. Lazaris happened to be out at the time, but when he came back and found the man, know what he did? He turned him out, in broad daylight. It was clear that once he stepped across the threshold — a full-scale manhunt was underway — his chances of surviving were zero. But that didn't stop him. He swore at his mother: who did she think she was, messing up his future; and besides, who said he had to follow in his father's footsteps?

We were bowled over by Agis' fugitive revelations — and about Lazaris' little birdie. Just at that moment, it began to rain cats and dogs. Lazaris would have been drenched, for sure. No way he could have made it home in time. Never saw rain like that before. Within five minutes the streets had turned into rivers. You couldn't tell where the sidewalks ended and the streets began; all you could see were raging torrents rushing toward the sea. We had time to grab the trays with the ouzo and the coffees and seek shelter inside the coffee house.

From behind Tassos' windows we drank in the spectacle. That day both Louis' and Lazaris' basements flooded.

In the public square at Trikala, roughly three days after the downpour, just as Louis was sawing the half-French, half-Greek daredevil's latest lover in half — the French girl was long gone — who should he see, standing right there in front of him, but his sister, Antigone. She was staring at him, icy and expressionless. He was so startled that he abandoned the woman, dropped the saw and ran over to her, and took her aside. They stood there awkwardly, looking at one another.

— I was embarrassed, cousin. Never been so embarrassed in my life. OK, OK, Antigone, I tell her, nobody's killed your father.

Without a word she opens her purse, hands him the house keys, a handful of unpaid bills, turns her back on him and walks away. All she says is: the basement flooded, their father almost drowned, he's near death in the hospital, most of the furniture is ruined, someone better pay the bills she's just handed him, and she's had it, she's leaving.

— I just can't take it any more. I just can't take it. Enough is enough.

Before he can say, "Hey, wait a minute, what is all this?" he sees her stalk angrily off and climb into a Volkswagen parked about thirty feet away. He even catches a glimpse of the driver. It's Panagos, the neighborhood greengrocer. Played accordion in his spare time. Everybody knew Panagos. He was a financial whiz; his money-making schemes were as complicated as a five-year plan. First appeared in the neighborhood in '45, just another guy down on his luck, tall and skinny. By '46 he started to get fatter, and shorter. I think he worked in a taverna just down the street; one year later, in '47 I think it was, he made the jump from the working class to the ruling class. The disappearance of Liakopoulos, the father, was his chance of a lifetime. The mother of Liakopoulos, the son — you remember him, from that wild night at Chrysanthi Antypas', Louis' mother-in-law — couldn't hang onto the family greengrocery after the death of her husband; so she rented it out to Panagos.

In '50 he fell in love with Urania — we all know her, right? — asked her to leave her seagoing husband and marry him. When she refused, he arranged a brokered marriage with Athena, the daughter of our neighborhood butcher, a fat woman with a substantial dowry who was so nearsighted she couldn't hit the broad side of a barn. At the same time, the Liakopoulos' grocery store went up for sale. With Athena's dowry he could afford the store, but he would lose respect. "Sold out, did you?" people would say. It came down to a choice between Athena and his own store versus respect and no store. He chose the store. Athena was simply the means to an end.

In around '55, if I get my dates straight, in addition to the greengrocer's, he'd succeeded in adding Krugas' bakery to his empire. When the one Krugas brother killed the other and was sent up for life, Krugas, the elder, decided to sell.

So, Panagos' dizzying climb gave him the right to a car, a house, a wife and several mistresses he kept in a two-storey place in Kastella which also belonged to him. Athena's near-blindness made his infidelities easier. She was so myopic she couldn't see straight. Not even the hands of the clock, to tell when he came and went.

And so, when Louis sees his sister getting into Panagos' Volkswagen, he can't believe his eyes.

— No way, Manolopoulos, no way she's going to go out with that opportunist, he told me a few nights back when I met him at the souvlaki stand at the corner near the church, just down from Lazaris' place.

He couldn't get over his sister's downfall. The whole thing was totally unexpected.

— The guy's fifty-five and she's not even thirty; he's married even.

When he runs after her to find out where his father is, Antigone has just enough time to tell him:

— Don't wait around for me to show up, hear? Never again. Never.

— Which hospital?

— The General.

I tried to get to the bottom of things, as I recall, when I met him the next day at the souvlaki stand.

— Don't let it get you down, Louis. It's not as bad as it looks. Panagos is no crook, after all. He's OK. Antigone was

224

fed up. Something had to give ... What was she supposed to do? He turned up, she went with him. Don't go looking for the whys and wherefores. Anyway, Athena is on her last legs, didn't you hear?

He hadn't heard. How could he, after so many years away.

— Well, that's something. Everybody wait their turn, right?

And he tossed back his fourth ouzo, with one gulp.

After his sister's departure, Louis abandoned Bertrand's circus and took the train to the Piraeus station. The moment he arrived — even before he went to the hospital to see his father — he called, asking me to meet him at the souvlaki joint. I could hear the sound of trains in the background, over the telephone.

— You're coming, right? I got to see you. Can you make it? Just got in. I'm at the station. If you smoke, bring a pack of Santé, or whatever. No filters.

Louis only travelled by train; airplanes weren't his cup of tea. In any case, he never had enough money for an airline ticket. He wasn't wild about buses either. Boats and trains. Nothing else.

He grew up with the smell of coal smoke in his nostrils. As a kid he spent long hours perched on the viaduct near the church, watching the trains puff by beneath him like huge black snakes.

— Manolis, you a masochist or something? What is it about this place?

He'd take me along with him. Most of the streets weren't paved back in those days, and the passing trucks covered us with layers of mud, coal dust and assorted grime.

Further along, to the right of the tracks, was a wall of corrugated metal panels; that was where the prostitutes hung out. Just across from the viaduct, near the station, was the souvlaki joint. You couldn't find tastier souvlaki in all Piraeus. Not now. Then. We once tied one on in that very same souvlaki joint before calling on Katerina. Actually, it was Louis that took me. My first time!

Her place was one street over, on a street with no houses; in fact the street was nothing but a series of roughly whitewashed walls on both sides, with open-air storage yards behind them. Huge sheets of metal were propped up against the walls; inside the yards were piles of scrap metal; immense, useless ship's engines, propellers, anchors, boilers, gears. The doors hung half-open on rusted hinges.

Until seven o'clock in the evening, the din of traffic was earsplitting: trucks, pushcarts, three-wheelers, horse-drawn wagons. After seven, in the space of five minutes, the streets, the scrap yards and the offices emptied. Offices? Hah! They were nothing but lean-to's with broken windows, made of corrugated iron too. Rusty. Earth and rust. Everything seemed to be painted a dark brownish red, like menstrual blood. Faces, windows, streets, walls. Even the sky; when traffic was at its height the passing trucks and carts stirred up the dust until the air itself seemed reddish-brown.

There was no lighting to speak of. Only a handful of dirty street lamps on power poles at the far end of the street.

After seven, around about sundown when darkness fell, those same streets filled with stillness, with silence. Only the whistling of the trains shattered the quiet. You couldn't even hear your own footfalls because of the thick rusty dust. But from time to time you could spot dark shapes vanishing behind the corrugated iron sheeting or slipping through the gaping doors of the scrap yards. And if you came closer, you might be able to hear deep breathing, the sounds of love-

226

making. Under a full moon you'd be spellbound! A tall, dark green poplar tree stood there beside one of the power poles. Just add the sounds of train whistles in the darkness, and you've got a ready-made fairy tale.

Katerina and Rosa, both from Smyrna and both in their forties, were the area's full-time whores. All the young guys from the surrounding neighborhoods got their first lessons in love from them, and their first doses of clap.

Me, when Louis took me the first time, I couldn't do a thing. I was shaking like a leaf. No erection, no desire. Even though Katerina handled the whole thing very tactfully, still I ... Maybe it was because it was cool that evening and I was wearing a short-sleeved shirt. Maybe too because I couldn't see a thing in the darkness. Neither her eyes nor her face.

— You're right, Manolopolous, that's the reason. When I can't see the woman, just to get an idea of what she looks like, I can't do it. Don't let it worry you.

The second time, everything went perfectly. I chose Katerina again. She led me straight over to the streetlight. Louis had probably put the bug in her ear. So there we were, in the sickly gleam of the streetlight. When she unbuttoned her blouse and her breasts came cascading out, I forgot everything else. She was tender, so tender.

— Come on, little man, don't be shy.

She unbuttoned my trousers herself and began to rub me. The poplar tree was only a few yards away, standing there alone, like a discordant note, its leaves rustling in a gentle breeze.

It cost us fifty drachmas a head. Louis paid the shot. Both times. Not that he had anything to spare, but back then his father still had his job on the railway, assistant porter or something like that.

Often, I would be reading at home when his old man was working the night shift; I would hear Louis' whistle, climb stealthily out the living room window, and together we would make tracks for the station.

His father would give him whatever money he had in his

pocket. They exchanged neither greetings nor small talk. Only the basic stuff: don't attract any attention, don't forget the keys.

— Be careful not to wake your mom when you get back.

Except that she wasn't his mother. She was his stepmother. Athanasia was her name. Louis' old man loved him, even though they didn't say much.

The odd time I went to Louis' place and found only old man Petros there. The fake casual chit-chat most parents engage in, things like "Tell that loafer to get serious about his schoolwork, will you," or "Does he say if he's going to finish school or go to sea?" was not his style. Nothing of the kind. He had confidence in Louis. That would have been the reason.

He treated Antigone the same way. Only a few words; the bare necessities.

— I really like your old man, I told him in admiration when we met at the souvlaki joint one evening.

He did not reply. Something was wrong, I could sense it.

— They fired him, cousin. End of the line for the pocket money and the free rides.

His dad also got him free train tickets as far as Larissa. And I, like a know-it-all, I pipe up:

— But he's a tenured civil servant, they can't do that.

— Sure they can. If you'd read the papers you'd see what's going on. Not just literature and schoolbooks.

When our great and good friend, Papadopoulos, hauls old man Retsinas down to the police station and tells him to sign a loyalty oath saying he wasn't a Communist, Louis' father says: "I don't know a thing about it. I just mind my own business." Papadopoulos sees things differently, of course, and he proceeds to prove it: the old man took part in Party activities, paid dues, boycotted the '46 elections; sure, maybe he

228

wasn't a criminal, but his ideology, well, that was worse than any crime, besides, he was too dangerous for them to let him keep his job, and what did he mean he can't do anything to the trains; he could if he wanted to, that was the point, and in any case, either you sign or goodbye job.

That discussion took place on a Wednesday afternoon at the police station. On Friday morning they informed him of his dismissal.

Panagos was a regular visitor at their place back then, around when he'd rented Liakopoulos-the-father's greengrocery and a little before he fell for Urania. Old man Retsinas may have been a good deal older, but Panagos got a real kick out of his company. Close-mouthed as he was with his own kids, Louis' father was talkative and charming with friends. In fact they nicknamed him "the philosopher." Wasn't a problem he couldn't find three solutions for. Only a handful of people — no kidding — know that Panagos is the creation of old man Retsinas. He gave him the idea of renting the greengrocery, he came up with the Athena solution when Panagos almost ran out of money, he put the notion of buying the Krugas' bakery in his head. "Hurry up, put the screws to the old man, grab it. You think he's long for this world with one son behind bars and another six feet under?"

Anyway, Panagos, in an attempt to repay some of his obligations, did everything he could to persuade old man Retsinas to sign that shit loyalty oath like Papadopoulos wanted. Signed one himself, he said, and it's no shame and besides, he was no Party big shot and anyway, where would his next meal come from if they fired him and after all, they only want his dues money anyhow.

Louis' stepmother, Athanasia, kept up the same refrain. What a royal ear-fucking they gave him that Wednesday afternoon. Louis overheard them from his room. He wasn't taking his father's side. Maybe he was a member of the Party Youth Movement at the time, a card carrying, dues paying member at that, but he quickly understood that Panagos' and Athanasia's arguments were stronger and more logical.

229

That was when he learned that Panagos had suffered two bullet wounds, that he'd been beaten and driven out of his village, and that if he hadn't signed two loyalty oaths, one on top of the other, he'd be a dead man by now. The first one was to a lieutenant in the gendarmes, not far from Corinth: "Just ask 'em about Panagos, and they'll tell you. Here are the scars, if you don't believe me." And he showed them. Louis saw them too.

How could I have ever known that Louis' source of information for the weird tale of Haroula, Peppas and Fotis Demenagas was none other than Panagos. So, all the while he was playing the sleuth, the bastard!

The other oath he signed right here, in front of Papadopoulos.

— It's my fault things turned out this way? Just because they're a bunch of jerks who let the other guys screw 'em, I should take the rap? You tell me. Did they have all of Greece in their hands or didn't they? They did? So why did they hand it over, in gift wrapping yet?

Poor old Retsinas just didn't have a leg to stand on. All he could mutter was "ideology's one thing, mistakes are another."

— Don't be so pigheaded. I am talking sense and you're off in the clouds. You know who grabbed me and dragged me down to the police station when I first came here, in '45? Who? The cop with the split lip, the guy named Vulgaris. You know who he is? A nazi collaborator, that's who. Yep. And no sooner do I set foot in the neighborhood than who do I see? Vulgaris wearing a police uniform at the precinct house. The whole damned police force is full of quisling bastards trying to avoid going on trial. When he spotted me and called for my ID, I was stunned. We were from the same village, but he didn't give a shit, the rat. Instead of letting it pass, he hauled me in on the spot.

Louis' old man sat there listening with a saintly smile on his face. He was thin, and he looked like an ascetic, a holy man.

— I'm not betraying my ideas, Panagos. The rats will always be rats, and they'll grab our jobs, all of them.

Panagos started to lose his temper.

— Excuse me, but you're spouting nonsense. Let 'em torture you and beat you with no hope of getting something out of it? No bloody way. Unless you're expecting posthumous rehabilitation or something. But until then, what do you do? Me, I don't believe in God and rewards in the afterlife.

He was no believer, but he later became a church warden in order to persuade Papadopoulos to remove his name from the blacklist.

— OK, so I won't commit any crimes, so I won't bother anybody; but I shouldn't look after my own house?

Louis interrupted them when, suddenly, he thought of his half-brother. He stuck his head through the door and told them so.

— Why don't you go see Moschos or uncle Tzavaras, dad? He's mom's brother. If he wants to, he can make sure they don't ask you for signatures.

At the sound of the name "Tzavaras" old man Retsinas nearly dropped dead.

— Me, Tzavaras? Me?

He began to choke on his own saliva. Athanasia came running in with a glass of water, Panagos pounded him on the back.

— What happened? He killed your father or something? Just because he's on their side?

Athanasia finally spelled out just what happened.

— Not his father. My brother. My sister's husband. Sentenced him to death. Twice over. Killed him.

Everybody froze. Old man Retsinas was a man of few words to begin with — up till that time he had never told them the life and times of Tzavaras — and now, when they heard the story, their blood ran cold.

My first encounter with Tzavaras came when Louis and I visited his place to meet Moschos.

That was where I also met Moschos' fiancée, Eleni. Later we nicknamed her Twiggy — she was a dead ringer for the famous fashion model of the day. Slender, frail, not bad looking, just like her namesake; she seemed to be in a perpetual daze — dazed and smiling. And almost nauseatingly polite. Whatever you said, whatever you did, her reply would be "Thank you so much," "What can I get for you?" "You're too kind" or "Have a seat." Perpetually spooked. One mysterious woman, let me tell you.

— The atmosphere at your uncle's place is thick enough to slice, I tell Louis as we're leaving.

Tzavaras was a short, fat, bald man, grim-faced and cold as ice. One look at him was enough to strike terror into your soul. He scared the shit out of Moschos and Twiggy, that's for sure. They might as well have been his servants. You've got to remember, too, that Moschos was on the verge of graduation from military school. He was wearing his cadet's uniform that day — it was too tight — with the sabre dangling from his belt.

Seeing him running to and fro like a costumed lackey in front of Tzavaras, it was all I could do to keep from laughing.

— I'm really sorry for Eleni, I told Louis after we'd left.

— Me too, cousin!

And his eyes sparkled.

— One thing for sure. Your uncle's getting it on with Moschos or Eleni, I said.

Uncle wasn't home right that minute. But as we were doing the introductions, the door opened and in he came. Red alert. Moschos rushed over to take uncle's hat, she brought him a glass of water; then came the phone messages, the mail, some flowers which had been delivered. Oh so polite. "Don't tire yourself out, uncle!" "Here uncle, let me do that." "You had a call from Mr. Papagos, uncle." He listened all the while, impassive.

232

When he spotted Louis he shook his head, uttered a curt "Grown up yet, you?" and retired to the back of the house. Me he didn't even notice.

Back then, of course, Louis knew only his uncle's good side, so it didn't really bother him. But now, as his father revealed the real Tzavaras for the first time there in front of Panagos with that "sentenced to death, twice over," he froze; literally.

— What did you take Tzavaras for anyway? Just because he claims he's a fine Christian gentleman, you believe him? Even death would have been better than what he put me through after I married your mother. His own sister, leaves her to die in a jail cell instead of getting her out. "Drop that bum" — me, that is — "or I don't even want to know you." That's what he told her. You want sleaze? He's your man ... done it all. Started out as a royalist thug; worked for Metaxas' secret police, then informed for the Germans. Know how many people he sent to the next world with one simple stroke of the pen?

In spite of all that, Panagos tried to convince Louis' old man to sign a loyalty oath.

— Leave Tzavaras out of it, Mr. Retsinas. OK? You're right, but there's a big game being played here. You've got to pay, isn't that what you're saying? Say you don't sign, that's going to hurt Tzavaras? It's yourself you're hurting. People who minded their own business during the Occupation, they were the smart ones. Ditto for later. What are you trying to say, anyway? We should always be getting the shaft? It's not only your job you'll lose. That'll be the least of it. They're executing people for nothing around here. One day they pick you up on the street and the next day, before you can say boo, you're facing the firing squad. And when you get right down to it, who the hell asked me if we should put our guns down?

233

And now dear mister Zahariades is telling me to dig 'em up again! Give me a break, will you? It's not enough that these rotten scum kept their noses clean, never lost so much as their lap-dogs; now I'm supposed to be extra nice to 'em, let 'em stand me up against the wall? No thanks, mister. I've had it. No more.

Old Retsinas listened, but no matter what Panagos said, it was all the same to him.

— In the end, he only convinced me, cousin. And not entirely, at that. But he did start me thinking.

True enough, Panagos' outbursts stuck in Louis's mind, and ended up turning his world topsy-turvy, which is why it struck me as odd when he called Panagos an opportunist over the matter of his sister. As it turned out, Panagos wasn't half as naive or oblivious as he looked.

— Whatever you say, Mr. Retsinas. I own up; I didn't join the Liberation Front for ideological reasons. I was just a country boy. Just doing my duty, but there are limits. You want me to live like a hero out of spite? I can see which way the wind is blowing as good as the next guy. The second round is a goner; they've knocked the shit out of us. It's time to lay low, and see what happens.

It was on that note that Panagos ended one of his greatest harangues. From then on, he gradually cut back on his visits to old man Retsinas, until he ended them entirely.

When Louis's father was dismissed, shock waves radiated through the whole neighborhood. One by one, people cut him off. Wouldn't even greet him on the street.

— You want they should put us on the blacklist too?

First the parents turned against him, then forced their children to follow suit. That was when mom did all she could to convince me to break off my friendship with Louis. I didn't. Probably because I hadn't realized yet what it meant when the powers-that-be put your name on their list. Still, let's not kid ourselves; I was a little spooked myself. I did everything I could to find ways to avoid drawing attention to myself. Whenever Louis and I got together, I gave the police station a wide berth, or tried to arrange to meet him after dark. At first, I didn't really visit his house too often. Don't know whether he noticed. Naturally, the first one in our gang to cut him off was Lazaris. Crossed the street when he saw him coming.

Anyway, after Panagos stopped coming, old man Retsinas lost heart; he gave up looking for work, stopped talking to people, didn't even want to go out. The odd evening we would spot him, walking the darkened streets like a ghost. The only one who wasn't on his case back then — what was he going to do? where was he going to get work? — was Louis.

Slowly his old man settled into the basement. He stumbled across an old wreck of an armchair, with tattered, bright-colored upholstery, on the sidewalk. One night Louis spotted him dragging it toward the house, then trying to squeeze it through the narrow door frame. He almost wept.

— Don't worry, dad; I'll give you a hand.

For a month the old man tinkered with the chair. Then he placed it opposite the high basement window and sat down. He wouldn't let anyone move it from that spot.

I don't know who lives in Retsinas' basement today, but if the house is still standing and you drop by for a visit, you'll see the marks on the floor where the chair legs — fat, stubby legs — wore away the concrete.

Let's be fair, though. Old man Retsinas suffered more than his share of calamities. Number one was when they put a price on his brother Elias' head, a price of 50,000 drachmas. The brother was a former schoolteacher who escaped from an exile transport; no one had seen hide nor hair of him since. Then came the execution of the elder Liakopoulos and Lazaris; both pals of his. Used to play hearts at Tassos' place, the three of them. Old man Lazaris worked on the railroad too.

Next to the armchair stood a wrought-iron table with a marble top. The elder Liakopoulos gave it to him back when he was trying to spruce up the greengrocery, just before he left to join the guerillas.

— Take it, and remember me when you're drinking your ouzo.

That was where he kept the radio. A pre-war vintage Dutch Philips. Louis bought it for him from a Piraeus junk dealer. Bought it with the first money he made working in the frozen meat lockers, counting Argentine beef carcasses. Bought his guitar and the radio at the same time. He plopped it down on the marble table top and switched it on as everybody stood around in anticipation. When the husky voice of Sophia Vembo came through the speaker, the old man's eyes lit up.

— Works just fine, said Louis with a wink.

Old man Retsinas said nothing. But there were tears of gratitude in his eyes, for his son.

From that day on, he would wake up and go to bed with the radio at his ear. His hearing had begun to fail, so he kept the volume cranked up high.

One evening Panagos came bursting into the house like a wild bull, rushing down the steps two at a time.

— Are you crazy? What are you doing? Playing Free Greece Radio at full volume? Have you gone bonkers? Where do you think you are? You're just going to sit there and let him do it, Athanasia? A stool pigeon goes by and we'll all be in concentration camp tomorrow.

As he was about to turn it off, old man Retsinas grabbed his hand.

— Just a second!

At that very instant they were announcing the execution of Liakopoulos' and Lazaris' fathers. No one said a word. When Athanasia realized the radio was still playing at full volume, she hurried over and turned it off.

Athanasia had changed of late. She'd become a bundle of nerves, always talking to herself. But now she acted as if the execution of their friends was no big deal, turned on her heel and hurried off to wash the dishes.

— My stepmother's just not right, Manolopoulos. The old man's getting on her nerves. She's worn to a frazzle.

After a while Panagos began visiting Louis's father again, carefully, taking all the precautions. It wasn't long before his wedding with Athena, the butcher's daughter, and one year before he bought the greengrocery. Slowly but surely old man Retsinas came back to life.

It must have been one evening in October, 1949 — I'd dropped by Louis' place — when I saw them all huddled around the Philips listening to Free Greece Radio. I caught the last few words of the news bulletin myself. By then, in spite of Louis' efforts to keep me posted on the latest developments, I'd kind of lost interest. I heard a voice — a hoarse voice full of bitterness with a tinge of sorrow — saying that hostilities had ended and that the Democratic Army was laying down its arms, but it was only a truce, and before long monarcho-fascism would meet its ultimate defeat ...

I can still remember Louis, hands in pockets, pacing back and forth, sputtering, and old man Retsinas' wiping his eyes on his pyjama sleeve as the tears ran down his face. Then Panagos launched into still another harangue: what's this bullshit they keep on feeding us, what do they mean only a truce, who the hell is keeping his powder dry, what the hell powder anyway?

Old man Retsinas said nothing, just shook his head slowly. Louis nodded at me and we went up the stairs. He never went to another Youth Wing meeting, never scribbled another slogan on a wall. Three days later when Papadopoulos summoned him to sign his first declaration, "How many would you like?" Louis asked as he signed, without getting his certificate, of course.

Athanasia really raked old man Retsinas over the coals about that goddamn declaration.

— She's made a wreck of the man, cousin. Sign the damn thing and get it over with, she can't feed all of us, how much longer can she go on ...

She worked at the same downtown office building as Lazaris' mother. She was still a youngish woman, in her early forties.

— Petros. I can't take it. I'll walk out, that's what I'll do.

The last and greatest fight happened on old man Retsinas' name day. Louis finally took a stand.

— Let him be, Athanasia. You're right, but if he doesn't want to sign, don't make him sign.

Athanasia was about to answer, but she held back. She could see her husband sitting there, mute, in his armchair staring out the basement window night and day, and her taste for argument dried up. But something had died inside her, and she knew it.

Antigone was there too. All she did was open wide those enormous eyes of hers and stare. Then, at the worst possible moment, she told them she had decided to become a nurse. Panagos had put the idea in her head. "Why not be a nurse?" he said, "you'll have food, wages and medical care. Free."

— Shall I, dad?

But instead of dad, Athanasia spoke up.

— Do it. Someone has to work in this place. The hell with your politics, the lot of you.

And abruptly she pulled the small brown purse she kept her money in out of her pocket and plopped it down on the marble table.

— That's it — everything I've got. Take it. As of tomorrow, I'm unemployed. They fired me. Because of your father.

It hit the Retsinas family like a thunderbolt.

Anyway, in spite of the doleful atmosphere, Athanasia insisted on going ahead with the dinner they'd laid on for the name day celebration. She invited everybody. Even me. I counted twelve people at the table. It was the Last Supper all

238

over again. I was so obsessed with the idea of the Last Supper that I started to wrack my brain, imagining who was Judas.

Agis was there, along with Argyris. Panagos and Athena had arrived before anyone else. Just as dinner was being served Liakopoulos showed up, wearing a black arm band for his father. As soon as he spotted Panagos he turned on his heel to leave. Couldn't stand the guy; hadn't he sweet-talked his mother into selling the greengrocery? Louis grabbed him by the sleeve.

— Sit down, forget all that shit. What's done is done.

— Nope, I'm leaving. You've got undesirables here.

Panagos took offense, got up, grabbed Athena's arm and said:

— Come on, get your purse. We're leaving.

She didn't know what to do. Where was her shoe? Athena always takes one shoe off, wherever she goes. "Excuse me," she says, "it's that damned corn on my toe," and off it comes. But by the time she located the shoe, Argyris forced them both back to their chairs.

— I paid you good money; hard, cold cash, he kept telling Liakopoulos, who was still frothing at the mouth.

— You crook, you double-crossing creep ...

You know Liakopoulos. When he gets carried away, no one can understand a word he's saying, so his curses fell on deaf ears.

Just then the appetizers appeared, sizzling hot and spicy. Just the thing to put an end to the shouting match. A strong wind began to blow. Louis got up and plugged a crack in the window.

I almost forgot Lazaris. He was there too. Showed up without an invitation, looking for Moschos' address, and stayed on for the party. Or so he claimed, and we believed him. So maybe he didn't really fit in with the crowd, but Louis invited him in for a glass of wine anyway. "I'm in a hurry," he mumbled. "Just for a minute," and took a seat.

Martha's mother was there too; she was still alive back then. She'd been released from prison camp a few weeks

239

earlier, under some kind of amnesty. She was still the same sweet, good-natured woman; pale, ethereal. So ethereal that even the wrinkles on her face seemed to vanish in the aura that enveloped her. Even they were ethereal, the wrinkles, I mean. She had the carriage of an aristocrat. If you'd have guessed "a countess down on her luck" you wouldn't have been far from wrong. Her movements, her walk, the melodic way she spoke, gave her a kind of nobility, a strange air of natural superiority. She always ate with knife and fork, and only used linen napkins. Who would have believed that until she married, she worked as a maidservant in the homes of the wealthy? In '35 she was a maid for Kondylis, a big shot politician. She could still remember him. Once, in fact, she saw him with her own eyes pounding the wall with his fists and cursing King George, the man for whose throne he'd sold out his own beliefs; and now, that self-same "wretch" had shown him the door. "That was my reward?" he howled. Was it true? Was she confusing Kondylis with someone else? Remember, she'd never been to school; couldn't even sign her own name.

That's what she told the torturers on Makronissos when they tried to make her sign the declaration so she could go back to her daughter.

— I can't read. How can I sign?

Once, twice, three times she told them ... Finally, a smart-ass camp guard looking for a way to relieve the boredom piped up:

— You mean, if you could read you'd sign?

— I might.

Big deal. Just when she thought they'd forgotten the whole thing, one morning the same guard burst into her tent with an older gentleman in tow.

— He's a teacher. In a month you'd better be able to sign your name, otherwise you're both goners.

When Louis told me these stories, I could hardly believe my ears.

— And if I tell you, cousin, who that older gentleman was, you'll say it only happens in storybooks. Try this on for a coin-

240

cidence, will you. It was my uncle Elias. Yessir. My father's brother. She didn't recognize him immediately, didn't remember him all that well. First he fell in love with her and she fell in love with him, then they discovered they were neighbors, that they already knew each other.

In less than three weeks she learned to read and write. The first letter she read was from her daughter. The girl was eight then.

In a month they brought her in to sign the declaration. But she never did. Just as she was signing — as she was putting her signature on the paper, in fact — she began to cough up blood. The torture specialist, a buck sergeant called Ioannides, was on hand to witness the ceremony. When she saw those faces all around her, like characters out of a nightmare, she began to vomit. But there was blood mixed with the vomit. Ioannides started howling like a hysterical old woman, "Get her out of here, out!" Believe it or not, she got out without signing. By mistake.

But let's get back to the dinner table. Not all twelve people are still accounted for. Sometimes I counted twelve, sometimes eleven, sometimes ... Just as I was counting, there came a knock at the door. We weren't expecting anybody. A shudder went through the room. Wild rumors of large-scale executions and arrests were everywhere. We'd just finished a discussion about Zahariades, the Party leader, and general Plastiras, the prime minister. Argyris, the senior member of our gang, started it all off with a slashing attack on Panagos, along the lines of: at least he could have the decency not to go slinging mud at real heroes, now that he's decided to shut his mouth and sign.

— Get off my back, will you, Argyris? What do you mean, heroes? The guys who signed everything over to the Brits and got exactly nothing? That's who I'm talking about.

241

Liakopoulos began caterwauling at this point, joining the fray against Argyris on the side of his sworn enemy, Panagos. Argyris was shaking, literally. Sitting there at one end of the table, shaking, and staring at the window. If a neighborhood busybody were to happen by, bye-bye university, bye-bye career.

Louis and I looked and listened with a mixture of wonderment and bewilderment at the anguished dispute without getting involved. Argyris put on a brave face. "Come on, who gives a damn?" he said, but in a whisper. Martha's mother was the only one to keep cool.

Once again came the knocking, but no one made a move to answer it until Athanasia got to her feet. When she opened the door, our jaws dropped. The man who walked in was like someone straight out of the Bible. I mean it. For a second I though it was Aris Velouhiotes, the dead guerilla leader. A dead ringer. The same heavy beard, short in stature, flashing eyes, thick fingers. A dead ringer. Seeing him standing there on the landing, most of us thought it was some kind of resurrection. All that was missing to complete the Aris portrait was the rifle and the greatcoat. And the forage cap.

The first person he embraced was Martha's mother. True love stood revealed. What an embrace that was. Naturally, it was uncle Elias, the fugitive. You probably guessed it before I could get the words out.

Argyris rushed over to the wall, switched off the light and closed the curtains. There was a sudden chill. Athanasia couldn't stand her brother-in-law — she knew he was an influence on her husband — and she never even said so much as "welcome."

No need to tell you how terrified I was, how I thought of mom who called out to me as I left, "Now don't you go getting into any trouble."

If they caught you hiding a hunted person back then, the least you could expect was prison camp. Why, only a year later they shot a man for circulating a peace petition. Can you imagine that now, today?

242

There was minor confusion in the gathering until we could make room for him, find a chair.

— Anyone see you? asked Athanasia.

— No one. Maybe Tassoula, but she didn't recognize me.

Old man Retsinas was about to say that now, with Plastiras as prime minister, things would be looking up, "We'll be able to breathe easier," but Argyris was telling everybody not to have any illusions, he was just the same as the rest.

I was trembling with fright. "If they've picked up his trail ..." Once again I thought of the Last Supper. For the sake of accuracy, there had to be thirteen. I counted, counted again. Twelve. As I was counting, Athanasia began serving the second course. Was there any beer? someone asked. None.

— I'll nip over to the grocery store, she said.

She put on a jacket, took her good purse and went out. The wind had picked up. It was June, but winter was in the air. A real gale; the wind was whistling through the basement window.

— Get toothpicks too, Athanasia. Don't forget the toothpicks, piped up old man Retsinas as she went up the stairs.

— I'll bring some. Go ahead and eat, all of you. Don't wait for me, the food will get cold.

We started eating. But we'd lost our appetite, our spirit. Panagos tried to crack the odd joke, but his fat wife, Athena, was the only one laughing.

The main course was over, and the salad, and the wine was just about gone when Panagos asked: "What happened to Athanasia? She's not back yet."

Pour ice water over Louis' father's head and you couldn't duplicate his expression. Pure terror.

— Athanasia! Athanasia! he called out.

Nothing. Silence. Antigone got up and looked through the house. Not a soul.

— She's gone. Gone for sure, declared old man Retsinas.

Nobody wanted to believe it. "No way. Where to? What for?" Louis ran down to the corner grocer's. They hadn't seen

243

her; she hadn't even gone into the store.

— Don't waste your time. She's gone. I know it. I could see it in her eyes. Now that I think of it, I saw it. I shouldn't have mentioned the toothpicks.

Louis discovered that there were beers in the fridge. She was lying. So, her departure was premeditated.

Someone suggested trying to catch up with her on the street.

— Don't waste your time ... She's gone. It's the toothpicks ... muttered old man Retsinas, ready to faint.

He got up and walked over to his chair. Didn't look at us. "It's the toothpicks," was all he said, over and over.

Antigone burst into tears, and covered her face with her hands. Panagos started to caress her hair, lovingly.

Then I discovered that Lazaris was also missing. He'd snuck out during the commotion. That's why I could only come up with twelve, not thirteen. The bastard! I felt a stab of fear, but I kept my mouth shut. I let it pass; didn't want to stir up more trouble.

The Philips was playing a tango at full volume. Agis, always the bumpkin, wanted to break the ice, so he asked Antigone for a dance. Meanwhile Martha's mother managed to calm old man Retsinas down, telling him "She'll be back any minute now, I'm sure of it," and suchlike.

But suddenly, old Retsinas broke into a guerilla song. Panagos jumped to his feet in horror.

— Are you nuts? You want to ruin all of us? Stop!

But he kept on singing, as if he were beyond time and space. He could no longer see nor hear. It was only when Louis shouted a plaintive "Please, father" that he broke off the song in mid-verse. At the same moment Agis noticed Lazaris' absence.

— Hey, guys, Lazaris is gone!

Panagos turned pale. In a panic he shouted at us to get our things together and clear out. Athena went looking for her shoe. Then we got into a discussion of what would be the safest place for Elias to stay. We all stared at one another.

244

Everyone had an excuse. Even Argyris, Mister Tough Guy.

— Don't worry about it, I'll look after him, said Martha's mother.

She never finished her sentence. The door crashed open. Both doors in fact. They didn't even bother to knock, for the sake of appearances. Three guys in civilian clothes, it was. "Police!" they shouted.

They only left Antigone behind. And Athena. The rest of us they threw pell-mell into a waiting police van. Martha's mother was opposite uncle Elias. She wasn't crying. She was smiling. Her hands were in her dress pockets, and she was trembling.

As the jeep pulled away I caught a glimpse of Antigone there on the sidewalk staring with those enormous, frightened eyes of hers, and behind her Athena, with one shoe off, holding it in her hand, a tasteless blue pump she never had the chance to put on.

For an instant the van's spotlight played across their faces. They held up their hands in front of their eyes against the blinding light.

9. FLIGHT

WHEN LOUIS PHONED asking me to meet him at the souvlaki joint, I was more than a touch irritated. I hadn't seen him for a long time. Not since the day his former father-in-law, the ineffable Antypas, threw him into the street.

The souvlaki joint, too, had suffered the ravages of time. The place was run-down and dirty, the walls were coated with grease, the floor peeling, the ceiling covered with mold and water stains; a real mess.

And when I saw him alone in a corner, unshaven and slouched over, dark despair flooded over me. A portrait of Karamanlis hanging just above him, covered with fly specks and faded, rounded out the picture of wretchedness.

Pinned to the wall next to Karamanlis was a large color photo of the Olympiakos soccer squad in their red and white jerseys. Further on, a stopped wall clock. He was staring at it.

— Three years ago it was stopped, same time. Remember?

It was December; the weather was chillingly damp. The last rains had permeated everything. The door wouldn't close; the kerosene heater wasn't working; it was freezing. I remembered the basement window in Louis' old apartment the night they arrested us, remembered how he'd tried to stop up the cracks — "Manolis, for God's sake, what are you doing?" — standing on her good sofa with his shoes on! His stepmother couldn't stand that wreck of an armchair her husband had dragged in. "Petros, it doesn't match anything ... and that awful little table! Wrought-iron? With wooden furniture? My God, this isn't a home, it's a hellhole!"

246

Louis pulled out a cigaret and lit up. I watched him. His forehead was broader now, his hair was beginning to thin, even turning white in places. He was dressed in an odd mixture of clothing: gray bell-bottomed trousers — narrow cuffs were in fashion then, he was wearing bell-bottoms — a long, double-breasted plaid jacket, a plaid shirt with a blue sweater, no topcoat.

When he crossed his legs I noticed his socks — another oddity, them. Green. And black patent leather shoes. He saw me looking him over.

— Don't stare at me like that, cousin. I've been robbed. What's left is what I'm wearing.

He bent over and opened his suitcase.

It was almost empty. Some socks, some books, a few pairs of those long undershorts of his — he'd gone back to boxers, it appeared — and his shaving gear.

— Catastrophe, cousin.

There was a knapsack lying next to his suitcase.

— That thing, it's yours?

— Belongs to Sophia.

"Oh oh," I said to myself. "A new character in the story." He picked up my surprise, or rather, my displeasure.

— I'll tell you the whole story, Kostas, my boy. You'll meet her in a minute. She went to the toilet.

The train must have been delayed — I can't recall just how he explained it — but it was scheduled to leave the following morning.

— To tell you the truth — believe it or not — I can't remember exactly how it all happened. I remember the two guys, though. Dark, with mustaches. Ran into them in a taverna in Trikala. Knew me from the circus. Come on over, let us stand you a drink. Sophia was with them, the girl I mentioned. She was on the road too. From then on, Kostas, my boy, I barely remember a thing. I told them I wanted to find a hotel for the night. "Us," they said, "we'll fix you up in our truck 'Alexander the Great.'" We'll this and we'll that, they said. I remember we changed places so I could get closer

247

to Sophia. Was it ashes they put in the wine? Dunno. But I wasn't drunk, that's for sure. More like sticking my head in ice water. I heard 'em telling me I was in luck, she was one hell of a piece of ass, pointing to Sophia. I heard and I didn't hear. In any case, I didn't even know it when they dumped me at that twelfth-class hotel. But this much I can tell you, when I woke up in the morning there was a half-naked woman sleeping next to me; the blankets had fallen half onto the floor. I just about went nuts. She was sleeping with her mouth open. Adenoids, she told me. She had enormous nostrils. When I saw them opening and closing, I panicked. And to top it all off, she was as thin as a rail, nothing but skin and bones. Her knees looked like a cross between a goat's and a horse's. But what hair! It was long, silky. That's what did it to me in the taverna, when the two guys invited me over for a drink. All I could see was her back, and her hair. "Why not?" I say to myself, "what do you have to lose?" So I went over. Good thing I bought my ticket beforehand. They cleaned out my suitcase and my pockets. Stole everything I had. I cleared out of there in a hurry, before what's-her-face could wake up; all hell would have busted loose. I couldn't even remember if she was the same woman as in the taverna. Had me stoned cold, the bastards. The hotel keeper didn't know who they were. Never saw 'em before in his life. "They brought you in, you and the lady, and left you there in a shambles." Must have been vegetable wholesalers or something. I remember, their truck was loaded with piles of empty crates.

As Louis was telling me all this, unconsciously I reached my hand into my pocket to see if I had any cash on me. He noticed.

— Don't worry, Kostas, my boy. If you can pay for our ouzos and my phone call ...

I was embarrassed, for God's sake. There was money in my pocket. Money mother had given me to pay some bills and my examination fees. Four or five thousand, all together. Talk about a pickle. What now? The court clerk exams were three weeks away. If I didn't pay, I'd lose my chance. Should I give him the dough? What should I do? He changed the subject back to Sophia.

— As for the little slut — get a load of this! — just as the train is about to pull out I see her rush onto the platform and leap into the last car. Like a pole vaulter, I swear to God.

Suddenly, as though he'd just thought of something, he broke off the narrative and glanced over toward the ladies' room.

— Come on, get up! he told me suddenly. Pay the drinks and the phone call and let's get out of here.

— What about the girl?

— Forget her. Quick. No such thing as a lost woman.

I threw the money on the counter and we rushed out. The owner hurried after us with her bag.

— Belongs to the lady. Tell her we had to leave in a hurry.

He shook his head. We turned to the corner and walked rapidly uphill, past the "Balkan" theater.

— Did they get a lot?

— Everything I had.

— Sophia didn't know them?

— Never saw 'em before. Probably they picked her up in the truck along the highway from Kalabaka. She's a bouzouki singer. Said she had a deal to sing at the "Romantic" in Amphiali. Anyway, let's not exaggerate, she's not quite as monstrous as I described her. Only her knees, but even then, if she put on some weight ... Maybe thirty-five years old. After she washed her face in the train washroom and put on a bit of make-up, she was a new woman. Missing a tooth, she was. Busted it on the clarinet. The clarinet ruined her life ... the guy who played clarinet in the band, that is. When she decided to stop singing folk songs, he beat the shit out of her.

We reached the edge of town, where the shanties begin. Call it the refugee district or the slums, it all amounts to the same thing. One tumbledown hut after another. The bus line ran up the main street, but the laneways between the huts were so narrow only the iceman's pushcart could pass. In fact, due to lack of space inside, most of the huts had their iceboxes outside the front door. The streets were full of puddles and little rivulets of muddy water, summer and winter. Behind the shacks were rows of trees, and beyond them the port and the open water. Off to the right the sky was invisible, hidden by smoke from the fertilizer factory. A bit further and you could start picking up the stench. This was where Botsaris' light store and Jordanidis' bedding store were located. In fact, I remember we stopped for a second to admire an antique kerosene lamp in the window. It could have been the same one that killed Fatmé later.

I kicked an empty tin can. I was at the end of my tether.

— Look, I've got about four thousand on me; I've got some bills to pay. And an exam fee. Take a thousand for the night, and we'll see.

He wanted to go to Liakopoulos' place, but Liakopoulos wasn't answering the phone.

— Don't even try to find him. They're picking people up again; he's gone underground.

I don't know what made me look behind us.

— Louis, the mystery woman is following us. It's got to be her.

— I saw her.

She caught up with us and tagged along without a word. No introductions, nothing ... She was just as he'd described her. Halfway between not bad looking and ugly. With a short green skirt and a cheap imitation fur coat. In her high-heeled shoes, it was all she could do to keep her footing on those muddy streets, let alone walk straight. She bobbed from side to side like a rowboat on the swell.

— They robbed her too?

— Did they ever. And not only robbed.

Louis figured that the two guys in the truck had screwed her somewhere between Kalabaka and Trikala. Got her drunk first, then raped her. They left her the bag but stole her leather purse.

— Got at least forty thousand off her. Along with her ID card. And her costume jewelry. Not to mention that they most likely knocked her up and now she'll be stuck with somebody's bastard.

The word "bastard" made me think of his sister. But where was I to begin? When she gets knocked up by Panagos? When he picks her up in Trikala and they head for Salonica to have the kid? When Panagos insists on keeping the kid — his wife Athena was infertile, wasn't she? Wasn't it only a matter of time before she dies and they can marry? Where to begin, what to leave out? Should I tell him he had her shacked up in the villa in Kastella, with their father? That the old man couldn't put up with the idea of his daughter being a kept woman and pregnant to boot? That he ran out, went back to his armchair in the old place five days before the storm?

Anyway, I gave him the gist. Louis listened, pursing his lips and scratching. He didn't much like the idea of family matters intruding on his life. "I've only got one life to live. Not several."

— The downpour gave Antigone the solution, if not the opening, she was looking for. All of us were there until midnight, bailing the place out. Everything was floating. We just got to your old man in time. Antigone came crying to the coffeehouse. But she didn't take him to her hospital. She was too embarrassed. Instead, he ended up in the General Hospital, and from there Panagos picked her up and they came looking for you.

— And when was it the two of them ...

— When they fired her from the hospital for left-wing sympathies. He'd started hanging around her earlier. One day he took her to see his place in Kastella, maybe she'd be interested in renting ... That was where ...

Night had fallen. The lights went on. The sickly yellowish street lamps on the power poles cast a faint light over the refugee district, reflected dimly off the stagnant puddles and the muck.

Then the shop signs lit up, and the lights went on in the shacks. One after another, curtained windows and cracks in the tar paper began to gleam. Most of the doors were made of

251

planks crudely nailed together. Through the cracks came the cloying smell of cabbage, tobacco smoke and frying, something halfway between rancid hot oil and burning sugar. And in the distance, we heard music. It must have been an old record, a broken one. We could barely pick out the words: "Hold me tonight, fill me with kissing. Tomorrow I leave, it's you I'll be missing ..."

— Remember that one, cousin? Who wrote it? Where did we hear it?

I stopped, tried to remember. Then, for the first time, I heard Sophia's voice.

— It's Hiotis.

— You can sing it too, sweetie? I hear Louis ask her, ever so tenderly.

— Sure, she answered, and suddenly, for no good reason, broke into tears.

I began to feel strange. She rummaged through her pockets for a hanky. Didn't have a purse, remember. Louis gave her some paper napkins. Suddenly she was convulsed with sobs. What had gotten into her all of a sudden? She blew her nose, wiped her upper lip, her eyes, her cheeks.

— Go on, have a good cry, don't worry about it. Kostas here is one of us.

We went on. Through the hand-embroidered curtains, inside the shacks, we could see people. Some seated around tables, others in bed, still others drinking, talking.

The sounds of music led us on; this time it was an oriental rhythm, slow-moving, slurred. We came up to a blue-framed window with half-closed shutters and peeked in. A dark-skinned, curly-haired man with a mustache was sitting on an ottoman playing a string instrument with a short neck — I'd never seen anything like it before — which gave out a peculiar sound.

— It's a saz. Turkish, great for melody, whispered Sophia.

On the wall was a mirror, an antique mirror with a gold frame. The table had been pushed aside and I saw a girl wriggling to the rhythm of the music, in the middle of the room.

Was she sixteen years old? At the outside. She held a shawl stretched across her throat, brought it down to her breasts, and back up to her throat. It was as if there wasn't a bone in her body. She danced, watching herself in the mirror.

Sophia had stopped crying, and looked on.

The damp cold was piercing me to the bone. If I'd had any idea I was going to be out so late, I would have brought my topcoat. I hadn't managed to tell Louis a thing about me, about my studies, my possible civil service appointment; nothing about my relationship with Julia which was rushing at breakneck speed toward engagement and marriage.

We had no sooner made our way back to the main street when Louis hailed a cab. It screeched to a halt beside us.

— Give me the thousand; we'll square things later. I'm going to the hospital to see my old man, then home. Coming?

I just managed to slip him the bill as he climbed into the cab with Sophia.

When I got back home, I couldn't stop thinking about the thousand note. No way I was going to ask mom for more money. She might have come across, but first I would have to listen to the old song and dance about Louis. More than that: I would have to agree with her. What arguments could I possibly muster in his defense?

I remembered Sophia's expression as she climbed into the cab; the anguished look in her eyes when she turned to wish me goodnight, and remorse flooded over me. "You think just like your mother," I muttered to myself angrily. I didn't know whose side I was on. Lately, Louis' don't-give-a damn attitude had begun to grate on me. "He's made his bed, so let him lie in it. What comes around, comes around." "Oh yeah, smart guy? What did Louis ever ask of you?" went my dialogue with myself.

253

As mother was serving my dinner — a hot fish soup — there in the warmth and security of the home, I began comparing my life with Louis'. Damn it! I didn't want to be so goddamn petty. Self-loathing welled up in me. "Forget him. You, you turkey, you've got it all; just because you slip him a thousand, you start whining, start raking him over the coals. But when he gave you fifty for the whores? When he took you along on those free trips with his father's train pass?" "Sure, sure, but where's he headed? What's his future? What's his life plan?" Things were becoming less and less clear. "What the hell is he after, anyway? OK, a loafer he's not. So why doesn't he get a regular job? He's just wasting his time, wasting his energy, wasting his life ..."

I was eating so nervously, so clumsily that my mother cried out:

— Calm down! You're getting soup all over your shirt. You'll have to change it tomorrow.

Would she bring up the money? I was quaking at the thought. But before I could even get that far, she blurted out:

— So, what happened? You pay the fees?

Was she a medium or what? I pretended not to hear. What was I supposed to say? That I knew you could buy five shirts back then with one thousand drachmas, not just one. Tell me, what could I possibly say? "Throwing someone else's money around, playing the philanthropist and the big shot? What? You never noticed your mom hasn't bought a new coat in ten years? It never occurred to you that your father nearly went blind working at the tailor shop to put you through school?" "Yeah, yeah; go ahead, put a price on the Retsinas family's bad luck, the persecution; Louis especially And now — go ahead, deny it! — you, you look like a lousy cheapskate beside him. Would you ever have the guts to take on a woman like Sophia, for no good reason? All he knows is her first name. Just plain old Sophia. Not a thing about her, nothing about her past, zero ... Imagine she turns out to be pregnant in the bargain; what then? You'd bring her home? Sure you would. Let Louis pick up the pieces. Hospital bills, rent overdue, out of work and broke, in an unheated house with a woman called Sophia on his back.''

I could see our own kerosene heater pumping out the heat, mother was bustling to and fro, preparing tomorrow's meal. "Creep! What more do you want? Maybe you lived the same life? You've got it all, you do. Even a father who makes you your suits.''

I was starting to feel queasy. I left my food half uneaten, wiped my mouth, put on my jacket and my topcoat.

— Where are you going? mother called out. Watch yourself! I don't want you getting mixed up with those people.

She meant the Retsinas clan. My sister would be dropping by with the olive oil merchant, mustn't be late; and if Julia comes what should she tell her ...

— He's gone, tell her. You don't know where.

I left on the run, grabbed a cab, drove down to the old neighborhood, got out at the souvlaki joint next door to Tassos' coffeehouse, bought souvlaki, bread, wine, and made a beeline for the Retsinas' basement.

When I reached their house, I found old man Retsinas flat on his back on the sofa, while Sophia was slouched in that old armchair we all know so well, wrapped in a blue and yellow plaid blanket. She was cold. Her teeth were chattering. It was like a piano solo for the keys only.

Louis opened the door.

— What's going on?

— Screw it.

What did I see in the semi-darkness? The only light came from a kerosene lamp. The power and water had been cut off. The room stank of iodine and decay. Everything was warped, even the picture frames on the wall. The floor was thick with slime and garbage, like a muddy unpaved street. Everything

255

was rotting. Everything. The furniture, the clothing. The walls were green and bulging. I touched the plaster; an entire piece fell off.

Sophia tried to turn on the Philips.

— No current, remember?

Even the neck of Louis' guitar was warped. A write-off.

And then, in the gloom, I began to make out other faces. Silent, motionless.

— You're among friends, cousin.

Antoniadis and Liakopoulos. Present.

— I thought you went underground, I said to Liakopoulos, more for the sake of something to say than ...

— Me? What for?

You'd think I'd insulted him. I looked at them, one by one. It was like a wake. I took a seat. No one spoke.

— What's the matter with you guys? You're about as lively as a fridge full of stiffs. What's your big worry? It's my problem.

Nothing could take the life out of Louis. I put the food and the wine down.

— Anybody hungry? I said, here's some souvlaki and wine.

— No way we can last the night in this place, said Antoniadis.

Louis began to pass the souvlaki around. Two each.

— I just ate, I told him. No thanks.

— Look, if your old man spends the night here, he won't see the light of day, said Liakopoulos as Louis handed him the food.

Then Agis arrived, with candles and blankets. Martha was behind him. When she saw me, she hesitated, as if she didn't want to see me, as if she'd seen a ghost. She took the candles from Agis and began lighting them, one by one. The whole thing reminded me of the Easter vigil.

When she reached me, she gave me an ironic glance and said:

— Mr. Manolopoulos, congratulations on your engagement.

I winced. Why did she have to say that just now? It hurt. She said it out of spite, I was positive. I wanted the whole business over with as quickly and as quietly as possible. Engagement? What engagement? She was lying, just to hurt me. But what hurt even worse was that "Mr Manolopoulos" of hers.

Just as I expected, Louis, as he was trying to cover his father with a second blanket, overheard and turned to me:

— Who's the lucky girl?

— Julia, said Martha, taking the words out of my mouth.

— So, you've been concealing things from us, cousin. Mom's got you set up just fine, alright. But let's see how you handle her in bed, wise guy. Aren't you the guy who likes 'em tall and thin?

Better the earth swallow me up than have to answer to Louis. The whole time, at the souvlaki joint, on our walk, the whole time I wanted to tell him about me, about my problems, but I kept putting it off, forgetting to bring it up. But what hurt worst now was my humiliation in front of Martha.

Louis hardly knew Julia. Never really could warm up to her, though. To start with, no one could stand her father, and peoples' dislike for him seemed to extend to Julia even if, for a while, she was apparently interested in Louis; even been seen in his company a couple of times.

— Louis, don't bother covering your old man; forget the candles. I'm telling you, there's no way we're going to spend the night here. Are you nuts? shouted Antoniadis as he went into the kitchen to get wine glasses.

— One of these days you'd better get serious. You've got responsibilities. He's dying. ·

Liakopoulos was losing his temper.

— You can't keep this up. I mean, excuse me!... I don't know how you managed up until now, but now things are really tight. It ain't like it used to be.

The advice flew thick and fast, until for an instant we all fell silent. It was a nasty silence, the kind that made the cold and the damp even more intense. You could almost hear them stalking the room. I shivered.

Sophia's teeth continued to play. Louis sat down at the foot

257

of his father's bed and looked at us. All of us. And as I saw him there, across from me, gripping the mattress with both hands and nodding his head, I felt awful, really awful. For an instant I pictured him as a sixty-year-old man — maybe it was the light, I don't know — imagined him with white hair, bald, wandering aimlessly, unthinkingly, through ports, public squares, cities and villages, making a living as a beggar, greasy and unshaven. And then I imagined him differently. Dyed hair, the eternal ladies' man, chasing widows, older women and female tourists above fifty through the streets of downtown Athens, from Omonia to Constitution Square and everywhere in between, proud, miserable, exhausted.

— Maybe you can't see what's being going on, out there in the countryside where you've been eking out an existence. Things are changing here, fast. Everything is harder, and easier. It all depends.

It was as if we'd planned the whole thing. And the whole downpour of prophecies and free advice started all over again. We had to bring him down to earth.

— Take the grocery store. The little scraps of paper, the easy credit; gone, all of it. Tassos' coffeehouse, demolished; now they're building an apartment house. If you don't have dough in your pocket, you're nothing.

— What the hell were you doing for three years? Where were you? No lack of opportunities around here, that's for sure.

Unconsciously, at the question "What were you doing?" everybody looked at Sophia. As if to say: "That's all? That's all you've got to show for it?"

— The party's over, Retsinas. Come down to earth, or you're in big trouble. And don't go making fun of Manolopoulos. He wants to marry Julia? Good for him. She's good-looking and ... You think maybe he shouldn't wake up one fine morning with a nice fat dowry and a summer place and a fistful of cash? Give us a break. Work like a horse so you can finally buy a second topcoat at age fifty? It's not like he was in love with someone else and dumped her, right? The guy's

258

a walking blank check; so now he's cashing in.

As Liakopoulos ranted on, Martha was glaring daggers at me from the kitchen. As if to say: "So, we're not good enough for you, fathead. You'd rather have the easy life and a nice dowry."

Antoniadis got to his feet, started to pace back and forth.

— Better I should keep my mouth shut. We're worse than animals.

It wouldn't be long before he and Liakopoulos come to blows.

— Spare us the Stalinist crap, smart-ass. You messed up your own nest pretty good, the way I hear it. Why not just keep your big mouth shut.

— Why should I? You think it's just fine, don't you? Him marrying the black marketeer's daughter. You think she even comes up to Manolopoulos' ankle? He's doing it for her money, isn't he? That's all he ever cared about, isn't it?

— Wait a second. He's marrying the daughter. What do we care about daddy. And what's more ...

I stopped listening. And looked at Louis in amazement. The bastard, he'd forgotten about his own problems and was watching us in delight, a broad grin on his face. I could see it, as plain as day. Meanwhile, the quarrel continued to swirl around us. Now it was Antoniadis' turn.

— All it takes is a couple of ten-spots ... goodbye ideals, goodbye friends and friendships.

Nothing could hold him back! It was a frontal assault.

To tell the truth, everything had come up roses for Liakopoulos, and then some. How could he have imagined what would become of the lousy ten-spots he got when his mother sold Panagos their greengrocer's.

In fact, with those miserable five-and ten-spots and with a bit of pushing from a sharp uncle of his, he invested — along with the uncle — in some land in one of the northern suburbs. And so, before we knew what was happening, Liakopoulos became a real estate developer, right before our eyes. A real big shot. As I recall, he used the lot as collateral to buy three or four apartments. Not much later, almost before the building was finished, he sold two of them and bought land in Neo Psychiko. Which became collateral for a few more apartments. Antoniadis weighed in belligerently:

— Got it, Mr. Retsinas? Our fine friend, the big shot developer is sitting there telling us we can't spend the night here, instead of offering us one of his houses.

— If you had 'em, would you do it?

— Me? If I had?

— Yes, you? If you had apartments, would you do it?

From this point onward, naturally enough, Liakopoulos became increasingly unintelligible, foam-specked and incoherent. Now he was trying to demonstrate that "friendship is one thing" and "living your life" is something else. Besides, he had no objection to putting them up; but where, how? First of all, he didn't have anything free right this minute. And anyhow, what was so wrong with people looking after their own lives?

— Look after your life, fine; but don't go overboard. So Panagos buys the grocery store for a slice of dry bread back then; that's no excuse for you to start gobbling up other people's land and making a killing in the bargain.

— Who, me?

— Yes, you. You sold Agis' land to buy two lousy apartments, did you or didn't you?

That was news to me. Agis tried to keep the discussion from going any farther. He was afraid of Liakopoulos, for other reasons.

— What did you expect? It's Piraeus. Depressed area. Buy cheap, sell cheap.

I said nothing. And looked at Martha. Throughout the whole shouting match she stood there with her back to us, staring through the basement window at the night sky. As good-looking and fine-boned as ever. I glanced over at Agis. "Don't worry, something's got to give," I thought. "They can't go on much longer." We could all see it coming. He was just a desk clerk at the water company, uneducated, un-

260

cultivated — that was the general impression — and, sure, he was a sweet guy, really, but how was he supposed to keep up with Martha? She'd already finished architectural school — on Agis' money, of course, let that not be forgotten — and now she was working as Liakopoulos' assistant in his new office.

Hired her six months ago, in fact, at three thousand a month; Agis barely made two. It was an unfair fight, and a futile one. Not so much for economic differences as for intellectual ones, mostly. All that was missing was a cause for separation. It wasn't long in coming: Agis' notorious insomnia. But more on that later.

Anyway, nobody could figure out Antoniadis' sudden hatred for Liakopoulos. Probably had some dirt on him we weren't aware of; that might have been the reason for the threats. Or maybe because he'd screwed Agis over the lot?

— Retsinas, you can't trust anybody farther than you can spit these days. Do what you have to do, Antoniadis intoned in warning.

Liakopoulos leaped to his feet and grabbed him by the collar, ready for blows.

— What are you trying to say? I owe you something? Maybe I screwed you? Or is it because I gave you a hard time about that private church of yours? Well, excuse me, mister. My mistake. There, is that good enough for you?

And he let go.

"Whoa!" I thought. "Liakopoulos, the prime egotist, says 'excuse me'? Something wrong here." Meantime, the fire from Antoniadis was withering, implacable.

— My lips are sealed, Liakopoulos, and you know it; otherwise I'd tell you just where you can stick those "excuse me's" of yours.

— No, come on, if you're a man. Say it.

Louis picked up his guitar and started to tune the strings. Suddenly his father got to his feet.

— Manolis, let's go to uncle Elias' place. When I was in the hospital he said, "When they let you out, come right on over."

Louis didn't answer. And kept tuning the guitar.

Liakopoulos seized the opportunity to be helpful:

— We can use my truck. I'll take you wherever you want. If you need a place, honestly, I don't have anything free right now, so you can stay at my place, no questions asked. But there's no way you're going to spend the night in this place. I've got three rooms. One's empty. I don't know about the lady ... If there's room for all three ...

And he looked at Sophia.

— Manolis, don't worry about me. Go wherever you want. Me, I'll just wrap myself up in a couple of blankets; I know where to go tomorrow.

— What's the big deal, anyway. It's not exactly the end of the world. Just another night. We'll survive.

In spite of the cold, Liakopoulos was starting to sweat.

— You figure it out. Mr. Antoniadis here wants us all to feel guilty. So I made some money. Big deal. I'm supposed to be ashamed? Or would our fine friend prefer us to wear rags and beg in the streets?

— I said, My lips are sealed. That's it. Period.

In an effort to change the subject Agis — for some curious reason he was becoming irritated himself — tried to swing the conversation around to Lazaris, saying what a turd he was, how he still blamed Louis for dumping his wife and kid for no good reason ... Martha didn't let him finish.

— Shut up, Agis. Who needs it? Who cares? What's wrong with you, anyway?

Agis retreated into his corner and didn't let out a peep for the rest of the evening. Louis began to pluck away at the guitar, and slowly, a melancholy melody took shape, a faithful echo of the melancholy atmosphere that reigned in his house.

I'd become so lost in my own thoughts that my mind turned to Julia, to our own story. Louis' tune faded out, along with the small talk. His words — "Let's see how you handle her in bed, wise guy. Aren't you the one who likes 'em tall and thin?" — burned into my brain. Needless to say, Julia was both tall and thin.

One thing's sure, if mother really did set a trap —, me getting involved with Julia, that is, as Louis claimed — she had to be one hell of a schemer. She may have set the same trap for Julia; you can't rule it out. A regular procuress, is what I mean to say.

The minute details are coming back to me now, the facts. I would be chatting with mom about this and that and she'd throw in an offhand, "Did you hear, Julia got her teacher's certificate?" "Who's Julia, mom?" "Nikolaides' daughter, you know."

So began the matchmaking. Not that I noticed. Every day or two she let drop a new dollop of information. "Her aunt Eustathia is leaving her a whole three-storey building." "Her father is going to set her up with a nursery school." "What father? He's her stepfather." "Turned out better than a father."

Whether she intended it or not, the idea took root in my mind. I was short of women at the time. It was one of those situations where whoever crossed my path, the result would have been the same. I would have fallen for her. For a moment the idea of approaching Martha crossed my mind, but I didn't want to offend Agis. "He's just about to marry her and here I am, trying to ... It's not right." I started to feel pangs of guilt, of cowardice, of embarrassment. No way. I throttled the thought. I thought of Haroula, but when I went to see her, ostensibly to visit the bar, she couldn't even be bothered shitting on me. Haroula had taken on airs; she was self-assured, well-groomed. I couldn't get over it. She was in a hurry, she invited me over to her place. Gave me a card, with her address and telephone number yet. The whole thing was quite formal though, and just a trifle malicious. Not to mention distant and

263

indifferent. "How are you, Mr. Manolopoulos? How is school going?" There I was, looking for a nice, easy woman, and she hangs me out to dry. On my way out, she let me have it: She'd married the owner of the bar, no need for me to worry about our son, he was growing up like royalty. I was speechless. I got out of there as fast as my legs would carry me. She never said a word about our son before.

I remembered Louis: "Kostas, my boy, you're trying too hard to toss your life in the wastebasket." He could have just as well spat on me.

My life is a story of precautions, of fallback positions. Being trapped in compartments and cages and walls. "Full speed reverse," I thought. "Set your course on Martha."

Believe me, the woman problem was really tormenting me back then. Martha, in particular, I was infatuated with her. Every day she passed by our place on her way to Liakopoulos' office, dressed so extravagantly that she looked more like a fashion model than a girl from the neighborhood. It wasn't long before my infatuation had turned into an obsession.

At any rate, let me tell you — you need this information — that just before my final assault on Martha, we had an unexpected encounter, at Drakopoulos' wedding. He was the first guy in our group to make it big, as a tomato sauce canner; a classmate of ours who didn't take long to move on to other neighborhoods and other schools. He was going to marry Antoniadis' sister, a good-looking girl named Tatyana.

At the reception I just about went to pieces when I spotted Martha standing there among all the guests, pretty as a picture.

As usual, she stared at me provocatively, almost insolently. I still remember the torment when we danced. A blues, it was — she was the one who asked me! She draped herself all over me, worse, twined around me, squeezing me like a boa constrictor.

The harder I tried to conceal my erection from her, the tighter she stuck to me. It was as if she wanted to see how long I could hold back. I was afraid Agis would see what was going on — he was there — and her, she was behaving as if there wasn't another soul in the room, clinging to me like a leech.

When, despite my efforts, I finally did ejaculate — unexpectedly — she reacted with real concern. She knew very well what had happened. We remained motionless for a couple of seconds. Then, danced over to the hallway that led to the toilet. All without a word! I slipped out the kitchen door. No way I could get the stain off my pants; I was terrified the others would see it. That's why I left. Never even said goodnight to her. I think her dress got a bit stained too.

The days went by; I didn't know what to do until my humiliating dismissal, not to say outright removal, by Haroula, that is, at which point I said to myself, "Full speed reverse; set course on Martha."

I abandoned the niceties, abandoned my own hesitations, and made straight for her house. Agis, providentially, was out of town at the time. He'd gone back to the village to see his mother, which helped stir up my sense of guilt just fine. "I'm going to get it off my chest, come what may." I knew she wanted me; no doubt about it. I just knew it.

I took a bath, shaved, splashed on cologne, put on my new suit, a fresh shirt, a blue tie, and left the house.

Mother recoiled in fear. Schemer that she was, she had to have sensed what was behind my elaborate preparations.

Now, after the fact, I can understand her panic. Her "marriage with Julia" strategy was on the point of collapse.

I heard her calling me to come back, uncle Anestis was coming, she said. The louder she called, the faster I walked. I couldn't wait to get to Agis' place.

Good thing I didn't knock. Once again I'd come in second. No, not second. Third. Nope, not even that. Fourth. First was Argyris. Remember him? Then came Agis. And now, the third man was Liakopoulos. Him. Just as I was about to knock, I spotted him through the living room window, caressing Martha's hair. She was seated in a canvas chair, while he stroked her head as he talked and talked ...

265

"Why don't we get married?" poor old Agis would ask her, when all the while storm clouds were gathering. How could he have known back then why Martha kept putting off the wedding.

Now, when I think of it, I understand why Antoniadis hated Liakopoulos. He knew just who was undercutting Agis. Now I realize why he never could stand Martha, because "she treated the man who stood by her like shit."

When I saw her eyes through the window as Liakopoulos caressed her hair, my legs just about gave way. Sure she saw me. At the very least, I felt like a complete idiot. But she didn't let on; didn't even turn her gaze away from me. She seemed almost to enjoy that I'd seen them together.

Our encounter at Drakopoulos' wedding had truly been my last chance. Instead of grabbing her and taking her with me then and there — forget about Agis and Liakopoulos — there I was again, indecisive, pathetic.

And so I fell into mother's trap even earlier than expected. She'd organized it all, perfectly, and I hadn't suspected a thing; what an asshole I was! She knew exactly when and where the fatal blow would fall. It would be at Julia's step-father's country house, and that's exactly what happened. Right by the seashore.

Not that I couldn't have backed out. But Nikolaides had clout; he was a prominent Piraeus politician, a gynecologist who had made a fortune as an abortionist. By then, I was in his clutches. Thanks to his connections, I passed the Justice Department exams; more than passed them, in fact; he also lined up the job I was to be appointed to.

Now that I'm telling you the story, I recall that the only one who didn't come along on that fateful outing was my father. He couldn't stand Nikolaides. If he was coming to visit, dad would hide like a hunted mouse. He was allergic to the man. It's true; his face would puff up. Must have been a medical curiosity. And the funny thing is that as much as my father loathed him, Nikolaides kept asking after him.

— Isn't Mr. Manolopoulos here?

And without even asking, he started nosing around the house. It even happened that he would uncover him, sometimes on the back porch, sometimes in the kitchen.

Anyway, on that fateful outing, Julia surrendered to me, body and soul, in the cellar of their country house, where we'd gone to get a few bottles of daddy's "incredible" home-made wine. Everything was "incredible" to Nikolaides. "We've got some incredible wine." "Our country place is incredible." "What an incredible car."

Later, Louis asked me how the whole thing started.

— You're a bit shy; she's a bit cool, a bit stuck-up, a bit hoity-toity. So how the hell did you get mixed up with her?

— You figure it out! Before our trip to the wine cellar, no one ever said a thing about any relationship; less so about marriage. Just the odd passing reference.

— You really must have been feeling loose.

— Sure was.

But what he really liked was the part about the rat.

— So, as we open the cellar door, this enormous rat leaps out at us, Julia lets out a shout and falls on me.

— Don't tell me your mom planted the rat!

— No. The rat was the wild card of the story. And the mark of fate, believe it or not. If it hadn't been for him, I probably would never have found the courage ...

— So in spite of everything, you actually did it, cousin? You surprise me.

— Surprise? Wait till you see how she surprised me. When I kiss her, it's like she's having a fit. Something else, let me tell you. Like I'm not even there, like she can't hear a word, can't see a thing. Blind, deaf. I speak to her, but she can't hear me. She opens her mouth and just about swallows me whole. For a second or two, I'm afraid she'll tear out my tongue by the roots. Never expected anything like this, especially from such a prissy young lady, so snooty, so goody two shoes. You know how she is, right? Anyway, before I know what's hit me we're on the floor, me flat on my back and her on top. I never manage to pull down my pants. Frankly, I'm getting a charge

267

out of the idea that a God-fearing girl like her can suddenly change into a raving sex maniac.

To tell you the truth, later it occurred to me that she was really a bit too wanton to be true. Some women, the kind with the lofty moral standards, the highfalutin "honor and reputation," turn out to be the biggest prick-eaters of the lot. Women like that, hell, you end up wanting to blow your brains out when, years later, you suddenly discover that they've spent their entire married life fucking every pair of pants in sight.

Once I mentioned to Retsinas that I could never be sure about that woman.

— Can you believe it? I look her right in the eye and I still can't be sure if she's leading another life. What I mean to say is, I wouldn't be in the least surprised to find out, twenty or thirty years down the road, that she was getting it on with the guy I least imagined. Her stepfather, for instance.

I must have been completely caught up in my own memories, when, all of a sudden, I see Liakopoulos opening the door to Retsinas' basement and leaving.

— Wake up, Manolopoulos. You dozed off, or what? We're on our way.

Then I saw that everyone was on their feet, picking things up, moving around. Seems that while I was daydreaming, they'd decided to abandon ship.

— Come on, dad, get up, we're leaving. We're going to uncle Elias' place, and he took him by the hand.

We all came to a stop. It was the first time any of us had seen Louis act with such tenderness. Old man Retsinas picked up his clothing and started to get dressed. Louis sat down across from him; so did we. Nobody moved a muscle. He was emaciated and yellowish, his legs were white, completely

268

hairless, as if they'd been sandpapered smooth.

First he put on his shirt. The cuffs were frayed, the collar half-worn away. Half the buttons were missing. Then he pulled on his trousers; unpressed. They fit him like a tent. His belt had a huge, rusty buckle. And his jacket was buttonless, almost worn-through at the elbows, the lapels shiny from filth and wear. Most of his teeth were gone; he hissed instead of talking; he needed a shave. I turned my eyes from the father to the son watching his father dress. The bitterness in his eyes! My God! I shivered. Reminded me of Antigone's eyes.

He asked for a comb, and as he was combing his hair, Martha broke into tears. Couldn't hold back.

Sophia was gathering up the blankets for Agis, and when she saw Martha burst into tears she hardly knew what to think. There she was, weeping, trying to wipe the snot from her nose and the tears from her eyes.

Agis went over to comfort her, but she slapped his hand away.

— Leave me alone, she snapped.

Antoniadis didn't know what to do either, so he went over to the electric panel and ran his hands over the switches to see if the current was really disconnected.

Agis, insulted, gathered up all the blankets in his arms and went up the stairs through the open door. In two seconds he'd become an old man. Hunched over. Can you believe it?

I started after him, but Martha suddenly stepped in front of me.

— Let him go. Just mind your own business.

Her eyes were throwing off sparks. She looked me right in the eye, standing there in front of me, and it was as if she was spitting on me. And suddenly, before I knew what hit me, before I could react, just as she stopped crying, out of the blue, she hit me with such a violent slap in the face that I staggered backwards and almost fell over. Her eyes were still riveted on me, still glaring daggers. I saw it clearly now: she hated me. She was about to let fly with an insult, something like "half-wit!" perhaps, but when she saw old man Retsinas gaping in

269

amazement she turned toward the door and left on the run. I'd never been so humiliated. I wanted the earth to open and swallow me up. At that moment I lost her forever. I knew it. Go after her, I told myself. Go. But I lost my nerve. Again.

The first horse cart went by in the street, with a horrific racket. It was almost dawn.

Louis went back to gathering up his things, whistling "Kiss Me Tonight, ..." the song we heard earlier that evening there amid the refugee shacks.

When Liakopoulos returned with his truck, we'd already hauled the goods and chattels of the Retsinas family up to the sidewalk. The last thing to go was the portrait of Louis' mother that hung on the wall. It's paper backing was sodden from the damp. I handed it to Louis.

Antoniadis, the last one out, closed the door. The two of us stood there on the sidewalk, waving goodbye. Agis and Martha had left. Sophia was sitting in the front seat. As the truck pulled away, she turned and looked at me.

The roar of the departing truck drowned out the noise of the horse carts as they clattered single file down toward the harbor.

BOOK TWO

PITY, WE WERE SUCH A FINE, FRAGILE INVENTION

For Kiki

10. SOIRÉES

JUST AS I'M ON MY WAY OUT the door, the phone rings. Julia answers.

— Where's your husband? Tell him to stay right where he is. I'm on my way. Catch him before he leaves.

He caught me. It's Lazaris. Why in the world do I have anything to do with the man? Don't ask me. The harder I try to cut him off, the friendlier he gets. We no sooner scrape together enough to buy a place in Athens than there he is, in Athens, two blocks down the street. Even before I can think of getting a new car, "call me," he says, "just tell me what you want and I'll get you a discount." And he gets me eight percent off. Guy's got his nose into everything. But I still can't stand him. Makes me want to puke. Know how dad lights a candle whenever he meets that slimy father-in-law of mine? Well, when I hear Lazaris' voice I can feel — no shit — my blood pressure and cholesterol going up.

Same thing this time. Sitting there waiting, I begin to itch with the same queer irritation. Finally I tell Julia I'm going, I'm in a hurry; I get to my feet.

— Wait a while. Maybe it's something serious. Her voice is trembling.

Julia is his prime defender. "What did he ever do to you?" is her line, her slogan. Sounds just like my mother. Should I tell her what he did; what I went through thanks to him after the last supper at Retsinas' place, when he blew the whistle on the whole gang — I don't doubt it for a second — and they arrested the lot of us. Six months in jail. Economides lost his

273

life in the bargain — he was at the supper too — the perfect example of the good boy, said mom: "That's the kind of boy you should be friends with, not that troublemaker." When she found out he'd been shot — turned out he was up to his neck in the underground wing of the CPG — she admitted for the first time that she'd miscalculated. Julia shakes me out of my reverie.

— If he makes you sick, then do whatever you like. Cut him off. Who'll be the loser. Me? You. Whenever you need him, you seem to find him.

Never gives up, the bitch. Dumps all the responsibility on my head, makes me out to be a first-class ass-kisser; meanwhile, she's all sweetness and light with him, always organizing those little get-togethers of hers. And he's not the only one. His little pal, Moschos, tags along right behind. One look at him in his lieutenant's uniform and the blood rushes to my head.

— How much more am I supposed to put up with? Be friends with those crapheads?

That's how most of my dialogues with Julia end whenever we're about to call on them; Moschos or Lazaris, what's the difference?

— I'm sick of always hearing the same old song, over and over.

Julia wouldn't give an inch. Truth is, no matter what rotten log you roll over, you'll find Lazaris or Moschos underneath, or the both of them. Worst of all, they drag Tzavaras, Moschos' uncle, along. He's on pension now, a toothless old monkey.

She may pretend to be nothing but an onlooker, but Julia's hooked on those soirées of hers. That's what the general calls our evening get-togethers.

— Ah, these soirées bring back memories!

No evening would be complete without a bloodcurdling story straight from his career as an army magistrate. The worst had to be — it still sticks in my memory — his account of the time he was serving in Trikala, when they hung the

274

severed heads of Velouhiotes and Tzavellas from a lamp post in the public square. If you can imagine; his description was so nauseating that Moschos' wife, Twiggy, ran off to the toilet to vomit. Couldn't take it.

The only thing worth remembering about those evenings was Twiggy; ethereal, dainty, timorous, rarely speaking. Occasionally, when no one was looking, she'd ask me in a whisper about Louis. I realized he was the forbidden subject of discussion at Moschos' place; perhaps, for her, he was a piece of forbidden fruit.

But let's not beat around the bush, I'd gotten myself into deep shit. Better never get involved. Take the first step and it's all downhill; there's no turning back. The fact that they had enough pull to stop me from being transferred to the provinces was enough to make me their full-time errand boy. Just think, before I could move to Athens on my own, they had me relocated from Piraeus. Before my turn for promotion came up, they had me promoted to court secretary. Like lightning. Of course I was utterly helpless to do anything about it; couldn't even lift a finger. If it hadn't been for Julia, no way I'd ever have been promoted, much less transferred to Athens. I would have spent the rest of my life rotting in some provincial courthouse.

— Forget it, Kostas, my boy. Don't make such a big deal of it, Louis told me one time, when we met for a shot of ouzo at a hole in the wall across from the central post office. Soft peddle the sob story. Fact of the matter is, you enjoy it.

— Not me, Louis; Julia. She thought it all up, she organizes everything. Happens every time; nothing I can do to stop it. As soon as I make a move to break away from the pack, she trots out the next five-year plan and me, I end up going along with it, waiting for next time. Sure, sure, I put up with it, let's

275

face it; I go along, don't I? But still ...

I encountered him, as I recall, on the sidewalk across from the post office. Hadn't seen him since that indescribable night that he hauled his father off to his uncle's place in Liakopoulos' truck. No, wait! I'm talking nonsense. I saw him at my wedding, and somewhere else, too, always when I least expect it, like the day he led me to Fatmé, on the yacht.

So, there I am strolling along with my head in the clouds when suddenly I see a small crowd gathered around a short, fat man with a mustache declaiming in a loud voice, rhyming off the miraculous virtues of some new stain-removing powder. In front of him was a table full of all sorts of weird and wonderful gimmicks. "Step right up, ladies and gentlemen, step right up; this is the answer to your life's dilemma — the invisible spot."

I stopped for an instant to watch when, all of a sudden, who do I see but Louis, throwing down a handful of bills on the table and buying three packages of stain remover. Nothing surprises me anymore, but I will admit that the sight of Louis buying stain remover, well, I never thought I'd see the day. Before I could wrap my mind around that one, I saw him moving off toward Omonia Square. I followed him. The sidewalk was crowded — high noon in downtown Athens, you get the picture — and I lost sight of him a couple of times. My plan was to surprise him.

Suddenly he comes to a stop. Just as I'm about to call his name, he disappears. I start running, trying to catch him. "I'll be damned! He was right here!" Just then I spot him. He's turned around and is walking toward City Hall. With a hat on. Imagine that! Louis wearing a hat.

From the back he looked like quite the gentleman. Right down to the briefcase. "What if he's not the rebel he used to be? What if he's decided to take the path of Righteousness?"

I remember the time Liakopoulos turned up at my place, cursing him up and down:

— Manolopoulos, I've had it with that Retsinas of yours.

After the flight from the basement, he'd gotten Louis a job

as supervisor of the apartment block he was building on Agis' land.

— I'm going to can him, I swear I am. OK, nobody's going to go drinking the blood of the workingman, but him, instead of supporting me, he's doing everything he can to bankrupt me. Fine, don't get me wrong; we were all lefties, still are, in fact, but — you tell me — if I do things the way he wants, I'll end up on the street before I know it. Workers today, they're not the ideologues we used to know. You can't imagine what a shit-ass bunch they turned out to be. Sit on their ass and eat the grass. Give 'em an inch and they'll throw you a mile. Day after day, all I ever hear from him is "What do you need it all for?" One insult after another. Don't tell me he's doing it for the Party. No way. The guy's a vagrant, been expelled from everything. Gives me lectures on surplus value, and his own life is pure anarchy. What's he after? Listen, mister, just earn your daily bread and keep your mouth shut. No way, Manolopoulos. Your pal's getting on my nerves in a big way. Making me look bad. When you get right down to it, he's not in the Party, I am. I'm the one who keeps pumping in the big bills, not him. What does he want, that I should be a jobless beggar?

So he fired him, slap-bang. Never wanted to see him again. That incident was the reason — or the cause — why the whole gang shat on him.

I remember a million things and I keep forgetting where I am. Just about lost track of Louis. Ah, there he is! Just as I'm about to call his name, he plunges back into the crowd gathered around the table. Now the fat prestidigitator with the mustache has whipped up a whole little tub of suds to show how his miracle powder wipes out the stains. I follow Louis in, close behind. "Same old Louis," I say to myself. I don't speak to him right away. Better wait. The magician's little packages aren't exactly moving like hot cakes.

Then, Louis timidly pulls a handful of bills from his pocket and buys three more packages. Immediately the rest of the crowd starts buying.

277

When he moves away again I let him go for a couple of paces until, when he stops before crossing the street, I rush up beside him and give him a big wink. He recognizes me.

— Manolis, still at it, eh? Shilling, are you?

We sit down at the ouzo joint I mentioned earlier. He gives me the packages of stain remover.

— Take 'em. It's on the up and up. They really work. We just buy 'em from the corner store and sell 'em for a little more. That's all there is to it.

We look each other in the eye.

— Kostas, my boy, I missed you.

His eyes had lost that glitter of theirs. They weren't as blue as they used to be; they looked washed-out, cloudy. And his skin was harder, rougher. Then I glance at his briefcase.

— Don't. I managed not to become a pen pusher.

He opens it, right there in front of me. Empty, except for a few newspapers to plump it out.

The magician I'd seen a few minutes ago? His brother-in-law, he tells me.

— No, Louis, don't tell me you're married again.

— Sure am, to Litsa. Her sister, Fanny, is the wife of the fat guy you saw. Used to be a nurse. Came calling at uncle Elias' place to give my dad his injections. When time came to pay, plus some money I owed her from before — why am I telling you all this, anyway? — it turned out to be easier to marry her little sister, Litsa, and cancel the debt than pay her back ...

— Wait a second, Louis, you don't get married for life just to wipe out a debt. That's what happened with Aleka, the same damn thing. You forgot? You wouldn't marry Persephone, who could have given you everything you always wanted, you could have lived like a king, and you went and ... What did you say her name is?

— Don't say it, cousin, maybe I didn't quite make it to king, but I married a princess. Litsa is my princess Cissy. You saw the movie? That's her. A real princess, from top to toe. Come on by and meet her.

And he draws me a map on the flap of his cigaret box.

278

— You won't believe it, but I've got a place of my own now. Your old pal is a house owner. A house with a yard, and a garden. Come on over. Bring your wife and come on over.

Not only did Julia not want to go, she did everything she could to stop me from going. Same old song and dance all over again. When are you going to get serious, things were so nice and quiet, and now you start hanging around with a man like that. When she saw me grab the car keys, close the door behind me and walk out, she changed her mind. From the balcony she called out:
— Wait, I'm coming.

So that's how I came to know Louis' house. Not a house, really; a shack. And not exactly a shack either. A stage setting of a shack.

It was crazy. Julia couldn't believe her eyes. It wasn't just your common garden variety stage set, either; it was a work of fantasy. Surrealist stuff, let me tell you. Instead of walls, the madman used entire sections of secondhand stage scenery. Doric columns alternated with tar paper, royal boudoirs with concrete blocks and roof tiles, the walls of Anne Frank's house with crudely painted bright-red bricks, a balcony door leading to a half-ruined balcony straight from the love scene in *Romeo and Juliet* with a whole windowed wall from Chekov's *The Seagull* ... The more you saw, the crazier it got. Most of it was made of massive fake wood panelling. The living room would have been from a brothel scene; it reminded me of the *Three Penny Opera*. There was

279

a whole room straight out of Dostoevski's *The Idiot*, the scene where Ragozin kills Anastasia Philipovna The staircase to the roof had to be from some medieval castle. Gray, and overpowering. When I put my foot on the first step it caved in. Rotten.

The entrance was a cross between an ancient palace, a whorehouse and a church, mostly due to the windows, with their arched frames and stained-glass panes.

Better not say too much about the furniture, nothing about the remains of the royal thrones of all the ages and all the kings. The curtains were frayed and worn, remnants of former theater curtains, most of them deep purple in color. Statues and masks were everywhere. Only when you touched them did you realize they were all hollow, made of papier maché.

— Louis, are you nuts? Where'd you get this stuff?

I still hadn't figured out what it all meant. An entire wall — just now I spotted it — was covered with a huge painted canvas showing a scene from the *Comedia del Arte.*

— Found all of it, along with my brother-in-law, Customs.

That's what he called him, I swear. Customs. The man worked once at the customshouse, so Louis baptized him "Customs." So, the two of them threw some of the stuff together themselves, salvaged some from abandoned theater warehouses, borrowed some more never to return, and bought the rest.

— Get this, cousin; it wasn't even my idea. Customs had the inspiration. Once he had a job as prompter in a theater. We had the lot alright, but we needed to put up a house quick, so he put the idea in my mind. He knew I'm a bit crazy. "Know what I say?" he says, "fix it like a theater, make the walls out of stage sets. Free material." Customs himself had just squatted on the lot next door. And so we became more than relatives, we became neighbors.

But overall, the shack had an estheticism, a style; deep down, it wasn't in bad taste.

— Fine, Louis, but one morning you're liable to wake up

and find it blown away by the wind, I said, noticing how crudely put together, how ephemeral the whole place really was.

As Louis showed us through the house, Julia almost fainted at the sight of the magnificent, worm-eaten backdrop. She must have felt like she was breathing in the dust of centuries; there were swords, masks, torn wall-hangings, sagging chandeliers, and, most of all, fake mirrors made out of silver-painted paper. It was all she could do to stay upright. When she saw the skull hanging from the wall, she grabbed onto me to keep from falling.

— See that skull? Straight out of the original production of *Hamlet.* And that's Hamlet's sword.

He was improvising, straining to impress us. As if it could be the same skull!

When he lifted his hand to touch it, Julia turned her face away.

— Don't get upset, he says, its clean.

— This is a real museum you've got here, Louis. Charge admission and you'll make a fortune.

By now, Julia's abhorrence was getting on my nerves. Here I was, overcome with enchantment as, slowly, I entered into Louis' world, and she's hissing, "Let's get out of here!" into my ear.

— It's clean, Julia, he told you. What's the matter? I ask in irritation.

It was all I could do to avoid slapping her.

— And now, I'll show you Marguerite Gauthier's bedroom ... When I saw Verdi's *Traviata* at the opera, I said to myself, that's the kind of bedroom I want for my little Litsa to sleep in.

So it was. The spitting image.

We entered Marguerite Gauthier's boudoir. When the door swung open, the delicate fragrance of violets made our heads swim. In the half-darkness, we could barely make out the contents of the room. There was an enormous bed made of bronze and wrought iron, the kind with huge bedposts at the four cor-

281

ners, and curtains like diaphanous mosquito netting. Next to it was a luxurious cherry red lounge chair and next to it, an antique telephone, the tall kind with hanging earpiece, sitting on a marble-topped commode.

Julia even tried to pick it up, but there was no dial tone. Dead.

— It's all stage sets, Julia. Didn't you hear?

She put it down. Red was the dominant color, fire-engine red. Same for the heavy velvet curtains: bright crimson.

We paused in the doorway and stared at the decor in wonderment. Even Julia was at a loss for words. An enormous copy of a painting depicting a reclining nude covered one whole wall.

— Over this way, Kostas, my boy, I'd like you to meet my little Litsa, my princess Cissy.

In astonishment we saw Retsinas' princess Cissy, to our right, behind the door, seated in another cherry red lounge chair. She was reading a Harlequin romance under a Chinese table lamp with tiny white and yellow glass facets.

— Ah, Manolis, more of the same? Why are you making fun of me?

And she got to her feet and held out her hand.

— Please excuse me, I didn't know, she added, trying to gather up the clothing from the floor around the bed.

Honestly, for an instant I had the sensation I was in a palace or perhaps a high-priced bordello. The way she got to her feet, that dark green silk nightgown of hers, the way she held out her hand to greet us, the way she spoke, almost slurring her words with a touch of tremolo in her voice, the way she looked at us — and then there was that distant fragrance of violets — I couldn't tell exactly what it reminded me of.

— Well, cousin, when I invited you to my place to meet a real princess, was I right or wrong? Here she is ...

— Don't pay any attention to him. He doesn't know what he's talking about. Manolis is full of crazy ideas.

I don't know if I've ever seen a more gorgeous woman. Honest to God. A stunner. Her eyes were moist, perpetually

282

moist. And green. All she had to do was look at you for an instant, and you were drawn to her eyes. When she got up, threw a red shawl over her shoulders and walked over to open the window, there, in the light, I caught a hint of the contours of her naked body through the diaphanous folds of the nightgown.

Next to the lounge chair was a low table with a gramophone, the kind with the big horn.

— What am I going to play for you, eh, old buddy? Go on, take a guess.

I couldn't.

— Remember our night in the refugee district?

He wound up the gramophone and put on the record, while his princess Cissy sat waiting, ill at ease, on the bed. It was as if she wasn't alive. The way she sat there, motionless, it all looked like a carefully arranged stage setting with her more like a life-size doll. - ·   _ ·

— Come on, we'll go chat in the kitchen until Litsa can get dressed.

He brought out ouzo, olives, cheese. In a few seconds the song began; it was "Kiss Me Tonight ..."

The first notes brought our walk through the refugee district back to me, along with Sophia from Trikala, and then, the night at his place. · · ·

— Whatever happened to Sophia?

— Nothing. A cold fish. Sang six nights at the "Romantic" and made a pile. They paid her off and sent her back where she came from. When she got the money, I grabbed her and took her straight for an abortion. Those two guys, the ones who picked her up in Trikala, just about made a mother of her. I dumped her at the clinic and left. Haven't seen her since.

He interrupted his narrative because at that moment Litsa entered. Her hair was carefully combed, and she was wearing a dark green knit dress; she was smiling, and beautiful.

— She lives the life of a princess. Hardly ever leaves the house, my little Litsa. No farther than the front yard. We all work for her. Well, to tell the truth, not exactly everybody.

283

Fanny, her sister, is our resident saint. Used to be a nurse, I think I told you. There isn't a bicep or a buttock in the whole district she hasn't pricked with those needles of hers. Leaves first thing in the morning, comes back at night. What a gal. What would we ever do, Customs and me, if anything happened to her?

As Litsa crossed the room toward her throne, with her first steps I realized she walked with a limp. It was barely noticeable, but, yes, she walked with a limp.

Julia noticed it too. I felt a pang of sorrow. "No, goddamn it," I wanted to say. "Pity! Why?"

— She's gotten over it mostly, cousin, Louis whispered as if reading my thoughts. Kostas, my boy, I've taken little Litsa here to a dozen doctors. But she won't listen to them. She's afraid she'll die young. Think of it, could a living doll like that ever die?

I looked at her legs as she crossed them, admired the perfection of her right calf.

Later, when Louis took me into the front yard to inspect the windmill, he told me she was seated when they first met.

— When her sister introduced us, and suggested I marry her, I was overwhelmed. But it was no joke. It was too late to turn back. She spends all day reading, or knitting.

The yard was full of flower pots. He cut off a sprig of lavender and handed it to me.

— A mystery woman, cousin. Still can't figure her out. You never know what's on her mind; she won't let you. Pure enigma. No way you can dominate her. That's why she's pure bliss in bed.

He had to say that, the bastard. The way he described her, you would have thought he was talking about a whore instead of his wife. But he was right on one count. She wouldn't give you even a hint of what was on her mind, if there was anything on her mind. She was full of half-finished sentences, and giggles.

— Ever since she hurt her leg, she's never gone outside. Only to see the doctors.

Then he took me into his father's bedroom. The old man was lying flat on his back, staring at the ceiling. He didn't recognize me. The Philips was beside him on a night table; it was playing popular music.

— How are you, Mr. Retsinas? It's me, Manolopoulos.

He turned, looked at me, and slowly his eyes brightened, as if he had just heard music from the depths of the ages.

— Fine, he said.

— Hey, how's your sister, Antigone?

— Still shacked up with Panagos at his place in Kastella. They've got a kid now. His wife, Athena, is still alive. Weighs more than 250 pounds and she's still alive, my friend.

As we were leaving, his princess Cissy opened the window overlooking the street, the one that looked like a stained-glass church window. As it swung open, we caught the scent of violets. Louis shouted out:

— Keep in touch!

Then stuck his head out, while she waved and smiled at us.

— Bring your friends and come on over, you creep. I don't hold anything against anyone, and you should know it. But them, they don't even want to look at me, the assholes. What did I ever do to them? If you find out, let me know.

Really, what did he ever do to them? I never could figure out why they all began to hate Louis so intensely. It's crazy; if you don't count Drakopoulos, who had a reason, after all — assuming it's true that Louis knocked up Tatyana — nobody else had any reason at all for that senseless hatred.

You know something? I finally got my seaman's papers. You're looking at a captain now. Yachts my specialty. If you run across anyone who needs a skipper, you know where to find me.

I don't know what got into me; I stuck my hand into my pocket, pulled out a fistful of thousand notes — beats me how many — and gave them to him.

— Look, I forgot to bring sweets to wish you good luck for the house.

He made no objection; held onto the money, in fact.

285

— Call up the guys, don't forget. Come on over, tell 'em; I forgive 'em all.

Even before I'd turned the corner, Julia poured out her bile.

— You had to give him the money? You pick it up off the street or what?

She kept on blabbing until we were home. But I wasn't listening. I was smelling the violets. The scent had rubbed off on my hand.

It began to rain. In my mind I still had the image of Cissy as she waved goodbye from the window. The image left a curious, astringent feeling in my mouth. Like chewing bay leaves and nutmeg. Julia blabbed on. Crabbing, nagging, just like the time before when I went to meet Louis and didn't get back before dawn. What a going-over she gave me then! I said I'd be back by nine, and who should I run into but Louis.

— Why run yourself into the ground, old buddy? Who are you trying to catch up with anyway? Come on, let's sit down and talk things over.

— I promised Julia; I can't.

— So what. Beats me why you don't slap the odd horn or two on her, freshens up the cells, they say. Lost your nerve? What's happened to you? So you promised, so what?

I got back home at daybreak; at five. Tieless, vestless — I was wearing a vest.

That was when Julia handed me the ultimatum: "Me or him. Take your choice." Once again I chose wrong. Her.

Now, where did we leave off? You recall? Ah yes, I interrupted our story with Lazaris' phone call, where he tells me to wait, he'll be right over. Anyway, it did give me the chance to bring you up-to-date on Louis, and that ineffable shack of his.

So, when Lazaris finally appears, I'm standing at the open

286

door, on the point of leaving, while Julia is puffing nervously on a cigaret. Strange she should be so nervous. Clearly had nothing to do with the circumstances. I'm the one in a hurry; I've got to get to the office, not her.

— Where you been, Lazaris? I was just leaving.

— It was all I could do to keep him here, she piped up.

— Quit griping, Manolopoulos. Your great and good friend, Emmanuel Retsinas, better known as Louis, is under arrest. In the hospital, what's more. Seems he killed a foreigner with his motorbike. A Dutch girl. She was with him, he crashed; but he won't get off easy this time. This time he's finally killed someone.

He stops talking and asks for coffee. That's Lazaris: starts a sentence but never finishes it. It's a trick, an attention-getter. He'll come out with two or three words, and then stop. The idea is to pique your curiosity, and to test your reaction at the same time. Then he'll start up again with bits of information, dribs and drabs. If you're lucky, you'll live long enough to hear the end of the tale.

Naturally when I hear the words motorbike, foreigner, Dutch girl, my blood runs cold. "He must have killed Fatmé," I say to myself. It's all I can do to hide my distress. I begin to shake. He picks it up, the rodent.

— What's the matter? You're shaking, he says.

— See? That's his man; it's only him he gets shook up about, answers Julia.

The bitch. Just had to say it.

— Seen him recently, Manolopoulos? he asks me, knowingly but offhandedly. Ostensibly.

But instead of me answering, she chimes in again.

— Day before yesterday, at noon, while we were watching TV, the phone rings. It was him.

— Now that's what I call a coincidence, he says. He kills her the day before yesterday; day before yesterday he calls you up.

Panic. I hadn't said a word to Julia. Nothing about Fatmé, nothing about the yacht, nothing about Louis' birthday present — Fatmé was the present, you'll recall. I didn't really tell her much, in fact. Something about his seaman's papers, getting them renewed. And now everything is unravelling. Look out. Lazaris is just the guy to blow the whistle, what's more: "So, you knew the Dutch girl too?"

Meanwhile,the commotion had awakened auntie Eustathia. Another story. She's our full-time house guest now.

One day when I get home from the office there she stands, surrounded by a pile of luggage; I just about shit in my pants. That night, our bedroom is more like a boxing ring:

— Who the hell told her she could move in with us?

— Daddy.

— Daddy who? Daddy runs my house, is that it? Doesn't even bother to ask me? You're telling me that we're stuck with that old scarecrow in the next room? Not on your life.

Cool as a cucumber, Julia lets me blow off steam then tells me I'm the man of the house, I'm the boss.

— I am. Aren't I?

— Sure you are. Just call daddy, tell him off, ask him who gave him permission to dump her on our heads, then tell her to pack her bags and leave.

That did it. Me, stage a revolution like that? Only a Lenin could do it, and maybe not even him. Personally, I don't think he'd have the balls. When you've planned how you're going to spend aunt Eustathia's will down to the last drachma, what's the point of pretending to be a tough guy? Now what am I going to say? So I turn on the radio. Beethoven's *Eroica* was playing.

Julia grinned at the diabolical coincidence. The radio playing the *Eroica* while I hardly even dared to ... She didn't say another word. Just switched off her light. The ultimate humiliation. I swallowed my words, even though I knew goddamn well that auntie Eustathia had sworn to convince Julia to dump me, the sooner the better. Otherwise, there would be no happy ending for her life. I called auntie "Tartuffe." "He married you for your money, he stays with you for your money, he'll die for your money."

Before I could walk out the door, she'd start up. Maybe she was right. Mind you, as long as I was around she played the saintly martyr. Polite and obliging, to a fault. The whole time she stayed at our place, I can't remember Julia once serving me coffee. It was always auntie. Ten minutes before departure there it was, piping hot. But no sooner was I out the door than the demolition got underway. You figure it out. Wait on you hand and foot; dump mud all over you behind your back. Bizarrely enough, it was Julia who told me. Now that I think of it, she probably did it for fun. She sure as hell didn't take me seriously any more.

I wasn't a hell of a lot better. When it came to auntie, that is. Behind her back, it was anything goes. I'd concoct nicknames for her, to suit every circumstance. Stool pigeon, I called her; snake in the grass, old bag, rag picker, holy mafia. The only one Julia really objected to was "rag picker" The rest didn't bother her.

In any case — don't laugh; I'm serious — auntie's three-storey apartment made me into a laughing stock. And her manic piety made me groggy. Talk about religious, the old hag! She didn't miss a turn: morning prayers, vespers, last rites, you name it. And royalist to boot. My father-in-law's great fear was that one fine morning she would march down to the notary's and sign the place over to some prim and proper matron of the church.

Every morning when he called, his only concern was: "Keep your eyes on Eustathia. Don't let her out of your sight."

Louis did everything he could to convince me to throw Liakopoulos into the fray; maybe he could bring a little light into her life even if he didn't fuck the daylights out of her like he did to Chrysanthi Antypas.

— Really, does he still see her? I asked when I ran into him once in an antique shop not far from Constitution Square.

It was "saint" Eustathia's name day, and I'd gone to pick up an antique. You figure it out ... I even bought her gifts ...

The owner suggested an icon of Saint Kosmas.

— It's not all that old, she said. Maybe one hundred years, for sure.

As I was struggling to bring her down to fifteen thousand from twenty, who should emerge from the back of the shop but Louis.

I hadn't seen him for ages. Everyone had lost track of him. To be honest, I wasn't as pleased to see him as I once would have been. I knew how badly my own half-witted behavior had disappointed him: my marriage with Julia, keeping company with suspicious types, socializing with nonentities ... I'm levelling with you, I mean; I didn't feel so comfortable with him. Besides, I was in a hurry. How was I supposed to explain about Julia ... He'd really give me shit this time, it would be the same old story, why don't I just walk out, who the hell is Julia anyway, was I pussy whipped or what? How was he supposed to understand why I put up with everything, me, in my situation — the house is in her name, a lousy salary, the food bills, not to mention what happens if daddy's and aunty's inheritance doesn't come through — and how was I supposed to get off the hook if I tell him?

So, lo and behold, who should appear at the exact instant that I'm counting out the one-thousand drachma bills onto the counter. As my mouth gaped open in astonishment, he gestured to me not to buy the icon.

He wanted to buy me a coffee, nothing less. As we walked through the door of the Brazilian, I tried to break away.

— I really can't, Louis; I'm in a rush, I said, without adding a word about Julia's hysteria, her nerves.

I was ashamed. It was my ultimate humiliation, let me tell you.

— Kostas, my boy, you're not going to slip through my fingers. You can't even hide behind the telephone.

— Me? When?

— Tell that Julia of yours when she wants to cover for you not to ask who's calling. So get off my back with Julia, OK? As for Saint Kosmas, that icon isn't even ten days old. I paint 'em, for a living.

You could have knocked me over with a feather.

— Come on. You're no icon painter ...

He laughed.

— When I'm not travelling, I paint icons.

Suddenly, as I sat there staring at him, the thought flashed through my mind that maybe Louis didn't really exist at all. That he was more a figment of my imagination, or someone our gang had dreamed up ... As if, in one fateful moment, we had conspired to create him, for the hell of it ... As if he was more like a character, a hero from a book of some kind than a real, living person.

Later, when I mentioned the idea to the group, at one of those melancholy soirées at Lazaris' place, everyone jumped on me.

Liakopoulos was there, I recall. He'd joined up with the "turncoats," as he called us. Those were the Junta days back then; Moschos was a big man, couldn't do without him, no, sir. First there was the little matter of overdue taxes, then the little matter of getting a loan to start up a bottled gas outlet, and gradually one little matter led to another until, sure enough, he ended up on the regular invitation list.

— Manolopoulos, we don't have a shred of honor left to our names, but when you come right down to it, we did what we could for the country. Besides, ideology is one thing, making a living is something else.

For a time, he brought Martha along too. It was all over between her and Agis; she and Liakopoulos were married now, living happily ever after. Three times he brought her, altogether. All three times Martha contrived to sit across from me. At the table, and sitting down, after the meal. All three times she wouldn't take her eyes off me until the gathering was over.

291

She had eyes only for me, and she was brazen about it too, as if she didn't care what anyone else thought, not even Julia. Her attitude was passive, indifferent, almost haughty; all she did was stare at me. The only time she opened her mouth was to ask my opinion.

— What do you say, Manolopoulos? was her refrain.

Always with that good old ironic smile of hers.

Whenever she said it, I felt like gagging, choking. If Julia could have killed her she would have.

— I don't want her around here. Who does she think she is?

It was during one of those arguments that I slapped her for the first time. Julia, that is.

Meantime, Liakopoulos seemed to think he could get back into the group without too many compromises. Maybe he could even get what he wanted without getting mixed up with Moschos and Lazaris.

I remember when Lazaris called to invite him over, saying he'd invited Moschos and me. He broke into a cold sweat.

In a flash he was on the phone, asking me what he should do, how he could wriggle out of it — not to insult anyone of course — without messing up his chances for the loan. Nothing but insinuations, hints.

— Come on, Liakopoulos. Sure you're coming. What are you worried about?

— Are you crazy, Manolopoulos? How? I can't; with my background? Be serious. I don't want to hurt your feelings, I know you're going, but ...

It was all I could do to keep from laughing. I knew that as soon as he hit on the same alibis I had, he would show up, and show up again. So it was. Five minutes later the phone rang again.

— They aren't really one hundred percent Junta people, are they? I mean, Lazaris was an assistant professor from before, and Moschos was already an officer, right? And besides, we're not going to change our ideas, are we, just because we happen to drink a glass of wine with them? The hell with it. They don't even say they support the Junta, if you don't count

292

Moschos. It's not as if we're going for a stroll around Constitution Square with them, is it?

The only person he was afraid of was Martha. He couldn't predict her reaction. Funny thing is that when he did come out with the idea, she raised nary an objection. Just asked him if I'd be there.

— Manolopoulos? You bet he'll be there. With Julia on his arm.

He was dripping with malice as he said it. As if to tell her: "Look how low your old flame has sunk."

I believe that was when Liakopoulos completely lost her respect, because of his maliciousness toward me. Maybe that's why she agreed to come along to our evening get-togethers, to force him to take off the mask, to stop playing the revolutionary, the man who was always judge and jury for everybody.

So, they put in their first appearance. It was probably coincidence; that was the evening I floated the notion that perhaps Louis wasn't real, that perhaps he was a character we'd created, that somewhere along the line our imagination had taken over his life, that he seemed more like a mythical figure than a real, live person with his own wants and needs.

Liakopoulos cut me off.

— Give us a break, Manolopoulos. He's the one who takes his imagination for real life, not us. His stories are all fairy tales anyway. And while you're at it, you can tell him to stop insulting us, stop calling us bourgeois sellouts.

He stopped. Probably regretted saying as much as he did. Maybe he noticed the expression on Martha's face. Probably worried she'll ask him if he really believes he's not a bourgeois sellout. It's all hot air, said Lazaris. He's just a vagabond, a monstrous ego, a pimp, pure and simple, a freeloader and nothing else.

— Still, he's got a job. Painting icons, I said.

As far as Moschos was concerned, he was a nut case. A hereditary nut case. "He's nuts, he doesn't fit in, he's amoral. Always been that way, ever since he was a kid." That's his memory of Louis.

293

Liakopoulos didn't let out a peep. Except for "Well, maybe it is hereditary, I admit, but he knows what kind of impression he makes; it's all to draw attention to himself. He's a prisoner of his own myth — and he knows it."

In Julia's humble opinion, he was antisocial and dangerous.

— Not dangerous, I said.

Martha entered the conversation:

— Why not, Manolopoulos? Sure he's dangerous; not one of you will invite him into your homes. Right?

And she glared at us provocatively, insistently.

— Good for them, Julia chimed in maliciously. They've all found their way, except for him, that is. What did he ever do?

Twiggy was the only one to stay out of the discussion. Julia went on:

— He doesn't give a damn about anyone else; can't even remember he's a father most of the time. Maybe he sees his daughter once in a blue moon, and even then ...

Martha cut her off right there, at the "even then," and turned to me.

— You never answered me, Manolopoulos. Who's right, them or me? Is he a threat to your homes, really?

The boldness of her interruption made Julia fume. Me, well, I was in a fine pickle. What was I supposed to tell Martha? How was I going to defend him? They'd make mincemeat of me, Julia most of all. I broke into a sweat; finally I blurted it out:

— Listen here, Martha. As far as I'm concerned, we're a sorry mess compared to Louis; it's as simple as that. None of us are half the man he is. That's why we try so hard to drag him down. Maybe we're even a little afraid of him. He has a way of pricking our conscience. You're right. We know he's got the goods on us, so we avoid him. Enough of the fine words; sure he's dangerous. But he's the one who's paying the price for his craziness — in blood. If anyone's leading the Spartan existence, it's him, not us. Don't forget, he's done the impossible. I mean, he can fit in everywhere, and still not give up a shred of his freedom, still stay himself, be his own man.

294

When I finished, I noticed Martha looking at me in amazement. Probably she didn't expect me to rush so heroically to Louis' defense, to take on the whole gang. I felt good, proud of myself; there was a swelling in my chest, in my soul. She was still looking at me. Then I glanced around at my friends lounging in their armchairs, their bellies bulging like bullfrogs — double chins, flabby faces, puffy cheeks, dead eyes — balding, nondescript, gross fifty-year-olds. I shivered in disgust. Dirty old men, that's all they were. Then I slipped into deep melancholy.

Martha piped up again.

— Manolopoulos, when I say crazy I mean exactly that. Clinically crazy; not just somebody goofing off.

— Right, said Lazaris. Anybody who behaves like that has to be crazy. Sure, we all dreamed about doing the things he does, but what about common sense, good manners?... We couldn't ...

Suddenly I caught Twiggy's eyes staring at me so intently I couldn't go on. I didn't reply.

The evening limped to an end. It was all I could do to wish them goodnight. Martha was smiling. She seemed to be enjoying the stir her little speech had created.

The rest of them had such long faces you could have sworn they'd just killed their fathers. I tell you, Martha was the only one in good spirits. And Twiggy, in her own way.

When I got down to the sidewalk and caught up with Julia, and when she told me I was an idiot to support a swine like that, I gave her a good smack in the chops. Her glasses shattered and her nose started to bleed. "My little girl!" cried aunt Eustathia when we got home.

Lazaris waited until Julia served the coffee — that's where we left off, if you recall; at the coffee — before he launched into a convoluted, blow-by-blow account of Louis' latest misadventure. Just as he got to Fatmé's death he broke off, and took a long, loud slurp of coffee. Then he began licking his lips. Lazaris drinking coffee, now there's a sight. Slurp, lick, slurp, lick, until you're just about ready to puke if you happen to be watching him.

— So there you have it; but can you imagine Louis, first mate on a yacht? The Dutch girl? He was taking her for a ride, in the old neighborhood. On his motorbike, she was wearing shorts, her blouse was unbuttoned. Right at the corner he threw her off, skewered her on glass at Botsaris' — you know the place. He got off cheap, nothing but a small concussion. He'll be OK. Bike had no plates, no license; involuntary manslaughter, they say. Needs bail money. You're going to pay? But try to remember, Manolopoulos. You saw him day before yesterday, right? He had to tell you about the Dutch girl ...

I couldn't hold back.

— Asshole!

I got to my feet, picked up my briefcase, and walked out the door. Left 'em, mouths agape.

Then came Julia's voice:

— Don't worry; he'll get over it. He always does.

I heard the rest from Louis himself, right there in the hospital. I found him lying motionless in bed, with an ice bag on his head, depressed, silent, and under arrest.

Aside from the concussion, he'd broken three fingers on his right hand. "He'll never paint icons again," I thought to myself.

Before he drifted off to sleep he said:

— That's luck for you, cousin. If only you'd taken Fatmé. But there's more to it than luck. Sure, we can blame everything on luck, makes a nice alibi. But deep down, there's always something wrong. The only lucky part is the size of the mistake; all the rest, nope, luck's got nothing to do with it. Things aren't as simple as I thought.

And after a short silence.

— Maybe they are, after all.

His eyes closed. He was in pain. Then sleep overcame him.

11. AH, WHAT MISERY!

THE PIRAEUS CEMETERY — could you think of a more macabre place? We're burying Agis. The second of our group to go, after Argyris.

First came that shocking letter — the epistle, he called it — then he killed himself. That's right, the coward of the gang — you remember him, right? — killed himself. Went out like a hero. Downed more than sixty valiums.

You might say he finally caught up on his sleep. Insomnia was Agis' eternal lament. It got so bad even his own mother couldn't stand him. "He's my boy, but all night he wanders through the house like a ghost; I can't take it any more. I'm leaving." And she did. Went back to her village. Then came our turn. His nerves were so shot that those friendly discussions of ours ended up in near riots.

That had to be one of the main reasons Martha left him. Insomnia. We always thought insomniacs had to be intellectuals; or guys down on their luck; or gripers, never satisfied; or people who are cornered, trapped by life's ups and downs.

But Agis wasn't cornered, he wasn't down on his luck, and he wasn't an intellectual. On the contrary. He was our resident optimist. Still, he would be wide awake until at least two o'clock every morning, wandering through his dark house. It took a good three kilometers of pacing before he could finally fall into bed, ready for sleep.

For the first hour he'd circle the bed on the chance he could drop off without running the full marathon.

— Get it over with, will you! I can't take it. Go to sleep!

But at Martha's "Go to sleep," he bounced to his feet again and began his wandering in earnest. Sleeping pills, you say? Trying not to bother Martha, he consumed them in huge quantities. No use; they didn't touch him. The only thing that did it was walking. One step at a time.

At first, Martha stayed awake with him, reading, until the end of his nightly stroll. He did the perambulating, she did the reading. Worked her way through every lending library in Piraeus, and that was after she read every single one of Louis' books, and every one of mine.

— Hey, pen pusher ...

That's what Agis called me.

— Martha's looking for a good book.

Agis' route inside the house was immutable: from the bedroom down the hallway, into the office, back down the hallway to the kitchen, then into the bathroom,the living room, the dining room, through the hallway and back to the bedroom.

By the sixth month they'd moved into separate beds, by the sixth year to separate rooms, and not long after, into separate houses. Martha's forbearance finally evaporated.

— Agis, I'm moving out. I can't go on this way.

And so she did. Agis made not the slightest effort to keep her. She rented a one-room apartment, not far from our place.

The move was the beginning of the end of the romance between Agis and Martha. For a while they would meet in the park or at the beach, but rarely at his place, while at the same time Liakopoulos began to insinuate himself into her life. The last act came when, one fine morning, Martha sublet her apartment and moved into Liakopoulos' penthouse. He was the second member of the gang to make it big, after Drakopoulos.

As you might expect, the last one to find out about Martha's new address was Agis. Funny, no one thought to tell him. Not even Lazaris. Or so we thought.

But when he did find out, he consoled himself with the hope that she would come back. He was all but certain:

299

— Martha's not like that; she'll come back, she's got to come back. No way she'll put up with that parvenu, that shit head.

All that discouraged him was the size of Liakopoulos' penis. He was worried the comparison with his might prove disastrous.

Their two penthouses had one thing in common: you could see the same water.

We all knew exactly how their story was going, and how it would end. But no one had the guts, if nothing else, to prepare him for the climax.

Martha actually made a couple of halfhearted attempts. But she quickly realized he wouldn't listen; might even drop dead right on the spot from a heart attack, in fact. She gave up.

Not much later — maybe it was insomnia, maybe it was a premonition that he wasn't long for this world? — his heart began to skip a beat. Martha's attempts to initiate him into the world of literature may also have had something to do with it.

— Come on, Agis, forget the comics; read something with some meat in it.

But comic books were meat for Agis. Maybe his half-finished body was to blame. He was of medium height, but his legs seemed endless, and his arms were more like oars. Agis didn't walk; he rowed along. Picture wedging a frame like that into an armchair, and keeping it still for hours on end.

— OK, Martha. But tell me ... You're reading all the time, and what difference does it make? Let me tell you something: comics have an attraction all their own. Besides, when you get right down to it, it's not as if I've got no feelings or brains. What can I get from all these books of yours that I haven't got already?

She'd been twisting his arm to read some short stories by Chekov. Hoping to kick-start the machine. Wasted effort.

— Maybe if you liked the theater. Anything. But you fall asleep almost as soon as we sit down.

— Why bother with theaters when there's movies, Martha?

Why shouldn't I fall asleep? The picture talks. That's why I like comics. Just turn that ... that Dustyevksy of yours into a comic book and people will eat him up. Why should I waste my time reading pages by the thousands when I can learn the same thing in an hour?

No patience. Talk about patience ... he couldn't even figure Louis out. "A man of adventure and action like him? How come he wastes all that time reading?..."

Agis had a point.

— Listen, my friend. Whatever I read, I swear to God, I get the feeling I've already thought of it, I already know the story. Take *The Lady and The Little Dog.* Martha wanted me to read it. So what happens? You know how many ladies with little dogs I've met right here, in our neighborhood? Anyway, it's got too many pages. How's a working man supposed to plow through it? But with a couple of sketches you can tell the whole story. Martha, what does she have to show for it, all the books she's read?

Maybe that's why Agis had such a weakness for painting. The only books he really enjoyed leafing through — and he had plenty of them — were art books; you know, the ones with pictures by famous painters.

— Me, it's the picture that tells me the story.

Agis may not have been a reader, but that didn't mean he didn't know what was going on.

By the time he got to work at the water company every morning, he'd converted all the newsstands in his path into open-air reading rooms. All he needed to know, he got from newspaper and magazine headlines. Nope, Agis was not lacking in knowledge of current events. Quite the contrary. He quickly picked up the details in discussion; in fact, he'd honed it to a fine art. His technique was to blurt out one of the headlines he'd spotted, dangling it like bait in front of us: "Did you see where Turkish demonstrators in Izmir raped some Greek army wives?" And nine times out of ten, like so many famished fish, we'd bite. Antoniadis most of all; he was our big newspaper reader, so naturally he would start filling in the details.

Now, of course, my example of the Izmir rape incident isn't entirely fortuitous because, as later became apparent, Agis' insinuation — that's exactly what he was trying to do, the S.O.B. — was what finally blew the lid off the latest heart-rending episode in the Moschos and Twiggy story. He was military attaché at the Greek consulate in Turkey back then; and she was the unfortunate victim. Not only did they rape Twiggy, she ended up pregnant.

— No, really?

— No kidding.

— It was that bad?

— That bad? It was worse.

People even say that Twiggy's disgust with Moschos dates from that precise moment. After everything that happened, she asked him to resign his commission and clear out; or at the very least, not to march back and forth and snap to attention in front of the consulate when the Turkish and Greek officers saluted the flag, in the name of neighborly reconciliation. It was the first time Twiggy ever raised her voice to her field marshal.

— Don't do it, she said, almost threatening him.

— It's impossible; don't even think about it. You want me to dig my own grave? Orders are orders, it's a matter of honor.

— That's just what I'm telling you. A matter of honor.

How's that for guts, eh? Moschos was at a loss for words. Couldn't believe his ears.

— You're right, Eleni, only I ...

The "only" destroyed him. In the end, the only concession he made was that she didn't have to attend the ceremony.

— They paid us compensation, what else do you want? What's the government supposed to do?

In all probability the compensation package included paying the abortionist. But with it, Moschos lost his only chance in life to become a father.

But back to Martha and Agis, and their relationship. To make a long story short, I can tell you that Agis adored small talk and comic books. Ah, yes. And writing letters. Make that postcards. Martha sent him a postcard telling him she was leaving: "Dear Agis, I'm sorry, but I think it would be best for us to separate. I respect you too much to try to fool you, or to play games." What she didn't say was that, for all her fine words, she had been fooling him and playing games for quite a while. Her message went on: "... I tried to tell you, but you never let me finish. I've taken what I need. Whatever is left belongs to you. I'm not certain I won't regret it. You never know. Maybe one day. Thanks for everything. Martha."

The postcard showed a sunset at Cape Sounion.

The sunset was just coincidence, Martha insisted. "Agis was wrong to read so much into it, saying I was trying to emphasize our separation."

I believe her. What Antoniadis says is frightfully unfair — he never could stand her anyhow — "Sure there were other things, but that sunset was what made him kill himself."

The fact of the matter is that, as soon as Agis received her card, almost the same day, in fact, he took up a position on the balcony of his penthouse, the very penthouse Liakopoulos had built from Martha's drawings: built him the apartment first, then stole Martha away.

So, as I was saying, he sets up his rocking chair on the balcony overlooking the Papastratos cigaret factory and the sea beyond. He liked the sounds of the port, the ships, the whistling of the trains. Went out less and less.

Louis and Antoniadis were his only visitors. The rest of us

abandoned him to his silence and to his fate. I mean, completely. There's no name day on the calendar for Agis, nothing to make you think of him at least one day of the year.

Later Antoniadis abandoned him too; he couldn't stand the sight of Louis. It was an ultimatum.

— Let that creep, that anarchist, into your house one more time and you'll never see me again.

He never saw him again. Maybe it also had something to do with his suicide. No way he could stomach Louis' bankruptcy.

— What did he ever do to you?

— What did he do, you ask?

As far as Antoniadis was concerned, Louis was dead meat.

— End of the line. This is where I get off. The guy's nothing but a bum. Worse, he's dangerous. Never grew up. So he screwed a half-dozen women more; big deal. For him, nothing's sacred.

— Why should there be? He's a free man.

Agis' last remark showed that he had moved on, to another sphere. A much loftier one. As it turned out, the comic books had a positive influence on him. They had sharpened his mental discipline, which became apparent from the dignity with which he dealt with Martha's departure, and from the letter he sent us. Posthumously, or course. Stunning, extraordinary:

"... I'm going to die, you rats, you dishonorable scum, me, the simpleton of the group, the guy who likes comics and pictures. I'm going to die, and not just because Martha left me. Good for her. Got out in time. If she hadn't left me I would have left her. I wasn't so stupid I couldn't see that she was leaving. Leaving. More and more distant every day. Manolopoulos knows exactly what I mean. That turd, he ought to remember what I told him when I went to his place after Louis' famous flight from the basement apartment, the time Martha slapped him, like Antoniadis told me after. Or maybe he can't remember?"

Did I ever remember! It was true; a few days before I was to marry Julia he looked me up. Did I ever remember!

What a day. He was drunk, filthy, his eyes were bloodshot, like small red onions, and his shoes and socks were caked with mud.

Mom's good living room rug became a dirt road. He stunk the acrid stench of cheap wine and sweat.

— Some fucking cab splashed mud all over me, just outside Carmen's beauty salon. Remember Carmen? She's closed now. Closed when she got married.

He hadn't been home for two days. Hadn't been to work either.

I didn't let him say anything more. First I made him wash up. He stunk so much I couldn't pay attention.

— Pen pusher, sit down, we gotta talk. I ain't as drunk as I look.

I hauled him into the bathroom. Mom brought him clean pants and a clean shirt. She was nice that way. Down deep, a loving soul.

When he looked human again, we sat down to talk. He didn't want anything to eat, no coffee. Just ouzo. Dostoevski describes scenes like that, scenes of impassioned love, impassioned people. I thought of Ragozin, of prince Mishkin and the fly that destroys their silence. It was in *The Idiot*. Only I couldn't tell which one of us was the prince and which was Ragozin.

Of course my mother bustling around with a combination of curiosity and suspicion spoiled the scene, robbed it of the dramatic majesty it should have had.

Finally Agis couldn't stand it one more minute; he asked her to leave. "Leave us alone," is what he said. He said that. Where did Agis find that kind of guts? Anyhow. Now, where were we? Oh, yes, I was saying the scene reminded me of Dostoevski. I must have told him I'd read Dostoevski. He read my thoughts. Mind-boggling.

— I didn't read any of that Dustyevksy of yours — Martha kept banging me over the head with it — but I saw the film twice. I know the scene you're thinking of. Anastasia what's-her-face is dead in the next room — see, I know what I'm talking about — and outside her door, the two guys hear the fly buzzing. But since I'm not planning to kill Martha, will you save me? I don't want to end up in an asylum, or blow my brains out. I'm going crazy, pen pusher. Crazy.

I still didn't know what he was driving at.

— Come on, Agis, don't make such a big deal of it. Couples have fights all the time, but what can I do to help. Want me to talk to Martha? Everything will straighten out.

But that wasn't what he wanted.

— I don't want your help. I don't want you to talk to her. I want you to marry her.

Before I could answer mom opened the door and walked in. At just the right moment. Mom was as un-Dostoevskian as you can get. You never know when she's stepping out of a Greek tragedy and into a comedy. Never saw anyone who could smell the crime before it happened, or let the air out of people and situations like she could. With that entrance of hers — it was one hundred percent planned — she brought everything back to its normal dimensions, if not to reduced dimensions. Give her an enlargement and she'll give you back a miniature; stick around, see what she can do with atmosphere and dramatic tension.

— Did you call me? she said.

— No, Mrs. Manolopoulos, we didn't. And don't go eavesdropping. We're talking serious business here.

She'd done her job — wrecked the scene, that is — so she left, closing the door behind her. Me, I still hadn't recovered. I didn't know what to think. "What did he say, the bastard?"

— You're crazy! What did you say? You know what you're saying?

— Pen pusher, you heard just what I said. Listen, you'd better do what you have to do now, 'cause I'll never have the guts to put it to you like this again. All of you guys, you think Agis can't see anything, can't hear anything. Dump Julia, I'm telling you, dissolve your marriage and marry Martha. I'm losing her, that's for sure; she's leaving, but I don't want Liakopoulos to get her. I don't want her deceiving me any more. It's you she wants. You think I didn't see she loved you when we picked her up from Argyris' place? I fell in love with her later, but you, you always wanted her. She's one hell of a gal, even if she did cheat on me. If she's with you, I can take it. But with Liakopoulos, no way, that putrid little son-of-a-bitch; I can't stand the thought ...

— Agis, you're exaggerating.

— No I'm not, Manolopoulos. He'll grab her right out of our hands. I know it. I'm telling you, she'll fall. She can't resist much longer. Doesn't know what she wants. Not to mention the poverty she's been through. My career is going to hell, and he's making it big, fast. So I'm not right for her, I agree. Martha, she's made for better things. A hell of a lot better than Liakopoulos. You, you're just right for her. No matter how carefully you hide it, you've still got something to say, you S.O.B. Sure, sure, he's got a university degree, read a few books; he's still not up to her. What's he ever read anyway? Shit. All he knows how to do is quote Zahariades. Anyway. You're starting out on your career; get her out of his office, marry her. She's the only woman for you. Listen you pen-pushing asshole, you'll end up with her one day anyway. Don't put it off. It's not only me says it; Louis too. "Listen here, skinny, you better get ready, because Martha is going to check out on you one of these days, and when she does, she'll end up with that writer of hers, you can count on it." Seriously, that's just what he said.

Agis' and Louis' predictions stunned me. The walls were closing in. My stomach was churning, cramping; I was almost hyperventilating. But he kept right on:

— Is it true? Are you writing something? That's why he calls you a writer? Right now, I just want to make sure you don't have any misgivings. You aren't thinking "I can't do this to Agis, I can't treat him like this," 'cause I know if you didn't have misgivings you'd have grabbed her long ago. Liakopoulos can't be bothered with details like that. He'll get her and he's not worthy of her, the scum bag. I'm telling you one thing. Around here, they give you forty percent return on land, and that crook shafted my mother for thirty percent. I mean, is he a rat or isn't he?

As I remember it, the scene ended more dismally than it began.

I was so indecisive, inoculated by my little dos and don'ts and my petty calculations now that father-in-law Nikolaides was covering for me, that I couldn't dare leave Julia, couldn't dare even dream about Martha. I thought about it for an instant, but the idea terrified me so much — who tells Julia, who tells the father-in-law that you're walking out, how do you tell Martha — that I retreated, full-steam.

But what spoiled the scene was my father, who called me to come try on my wedding suit — he was tailoring a new suit for me — when the doorbell rang.

Just as the discussion was about to take a really melodramatic turn — ouzo, cigarets, long silences — just as I was telling him, "No way, Agis, no way Martha's going to walk out on you," drrnnggg went the doorbell.

It was Martha. She'd come to pick up her long lost Agis.

— Come on, let's go home, she said.

— How did you know I was here.

— Antoniadis. Weren't you at his place earlier? He called, told me, "Hurry, before he gets run down by a car." Come on, let's go.

As I saw Agis get to his feet and stumble after her, I could have sworn I was watching a whipped dog, crawling abjectly after its master.

On the way out, Martha remembered to throw me one of those merciless looks of hers.

— I don't know what kind of nonsense he's been telling you. Please, forget it.

— I didn't tell him a thing, Agis cried, terrified that I might reveal his insane monologue.

But as far as I could understand, she knew exactly what kind of nonsense he'd been telling me.

We were to read his epistle after the funeral, in his apartment, in front of his mother, as we were sipping the time-honored cup of coffee she would brew for us. It was Agis' last request.

It struck me as bizarre, him insisting his mother be there for the reading.

Whoever still considers himself a friend — he wrote — should go to his place, minus wives, though — he insisted — to hear his letter. He'd asked Martha to read it; she had to agree, of course.

Almost everybody showed up. Even though we were in tatters emotionally, even though most of us couldn't really stand anyone else, even though we knew the letter would most likely leave nothing standing; in spite of all that, we went.

Talk about a heart-rending spectacle. You know the expression, "Enough to make a horse weep"? Well, that was us. To a man. We were speechless, ill at ease, restive, each of us with millions of lumps in our throat, seething with dread and apprehension, but with curiosity too. No one knew what he would say, how much dirt he had on us. We could hardly breathe. Even Louis seemed nonplussed. Unless maybe he knew what was coming and was simply faking it.

We settled into sofas, chairs and stools, and when his mom served the coffee, as specified in the scenario, and when we finally sat her down in his favorite armchair, the chair he used to sit in as he looked out over the Papastratos sign to the sea — that was also one of his requests — Martha began to read.

Each paragraph began with the same sentence: "I'm going to die, you rats, you no-good scum."

Now back to the letter, right where we left off:

309

"... I can't take it. My bad luck meeting Martha, my bad luck something's wrong in my head. I can feel the pulling and pushing going on in there. Ever ride in a car with busted shock absorbers? That's how I feel. Or like I'm being drained, emptied by a sump pump. Antoniadis will tell you it was the sunset on the postcard that did it. It wasn't. Martha, you can sleep in peace, without regrets. I simply can't take it anymore. I'm not playing the Holy Man who leaves everything behind in disgust. Alright, so I am disgusted. With all of you, with everything, and with myself too. But no, you rats, that's not the reason. If it was, Martha, I'd have killed myself the day you shacked up with Liakopoulos in his penthouse."

So he knew, even though he pretended not to. Someone had spilled the beans. Lazaris — we all suspected he was the one, unconsciously our eyes turned in his direction — interrupted Martha's reading. He wasn't the one, let's not be ridiculous, he swore. He hadn't said a thing to a living soul.

Agis' letter went on to describe the whole scene, as I'd experienced it back then, when he came to my place and begged me to marry Martha. "But the asshole didn't have the balls — again." He described everything, dotting all the "i's" and crossing all the "t's," even where I made him take a bath — he even wrote that! — and where Martha came to pick him up.

He revealed the commission "that animal Liakopoulos" got on the land he ripped off of his mother; and while "Louis talks about the magic of the sea, all that hardhearted money grubber can think about is making money off the sea, getting into shipowning; too bad a girl like Martha let her head be turned by his money and his real estate because there's no way his mind could have turned her head, unless maybe it was the length of his penis." He even wrote that. And again about the "three dirty old men," Lazaris, Moschos and Liakopoulos, and again about the sea, the sea Louis had made into a poem — here he wrote out the verses — was nothing but merchant ships and piles of money for Liakopoulos, who had no com-

310

punction about dealing with the foulest characters if it meant he could borrow money, and borrow some more. His father's memory? Gone. His life story? Going; going; gone.

Rats he called us; rats, rats, rats. He ground us into dust. Words could not describe our humiliation. We prayed for the earth to open and swallow us. Sure, we pretended to be perfect gentlemen. We tried to pretend we heard nothing, as if his epistle had nothing to do with us.

His mother had turned into a pillar of salt, her eyes were so wide you'd have sworn they were about to pop out of their sockets. But she wasn't crying. She was listening. Then I understood. He wanted her to play the role of God, of judge; to mete out justice; that's what he wanted.

On and on he went, until he turned his attention to me:

"... If Manolopoulos is there, which he probably won't be — he likes to keep out of tight spots — tell him that there's a letter of his to Tassoula in the top drawer of my desk. Give it to him to read, and see what an asshole he was. Maybe he can use it for the book he's writing, because that turd — the simple fact he married Julia gives me the right to call him a turd — that turd, he's using us and our lives as raw material for that shit book he's writing. But me, when I die, I'll cut off the tree at the roots. End of the line for Manolopoulos, that ghoul. He invites me over to suck my mind, the rat, not because he wants to see me. For him, we're all corpses, corpses lined up waiting for an autopsy. One at a time he lays us out on his dissecting table, picks up his scalpel — and his distance — and goes to work. Prefers dead bodies, the rat; easier for him that way, no strain, no pain, doesn't have to get involved, get burned. Manolopoulos, you rat, I know which chapter you'll put this scene in. And I even know what will happen in the scene between you and Martha, when finally, years later, the two of you meet in some fleabag hotel; I know exactly what you'll say — word for word; I know exactly what you'll do. Louis was never wrong; whether you admit it or

311

not, you'll want that particular part to be the big scene of the book, you prick, so don't you ever forget for one second that it's us, the gang, who wrote it. Remember that. With our blood and sperm and piss and shit. One time we even dressed up in Greek national costume, Louis and me — did you know that? — partly for fun and partly to make a little money, and screwed some tourist girls in Constitution Square. Louis' father had a scam going with some American aide big shot. Between the two of them they stole whole truckloads of UNRRA supplies, back in '45; did you know that? People thought he was with the guerilla fighters in the mountains, but he was selling stolen emergency rations in the villages. You didn't know it was Tzavaras who got him his job, did you? You didn't know Tzavaras ripped off most of his earnings in the end, and when old man Retsinas tried to get his money back, Tzavaras told him to bugger off, what did he think he was, a black marketeer, a con man — that's hunger for you, Manolopoulos — even though he'd killed old man Retsinas' son-in-law. I'm not accusing anybody. Old Retsinas had to do it — he was out of work, hungry, scared — but I'm not pointing the finger at anybody. Ever go to Lazaris' new place, the one in Psychiko? I'm not mentioning it to accuse any of you of climbing too high, you rats, or because I never went anywhere — I'm not jealous, shit heads — but only so you'll know about the porn jerk-off photos he uses. You heard me. Louis and I peeked through the window one night, saw him doing it. Hides them in books and drawers, stares at them when he jerks off. Martha found them — she's right there, let her confirm it — at first she didn't believe me when I told her, then she saw them with her own eyes when he invited her to his place and made a pass at her. That's right, you rats, he even waved his wang right under her nose. Then came all over her skirt. She pushed him aside — so she claims, anyway — and he comes all over her. But my mom's still living in a basement in the refugee district. That's why I'm telling you, piss, blood,

312

sperm and shit; you should know who you're identifying with, Manolopoulos. And even today, when I'm at the edge, I understand everything, I forgive everything. Just ask Lazaris. Was it him I saw or wasn't it, coming out of the Hilton in 1966 after a lecture by that Junta flack, Konstantopoulos? Ask him. Maybe I didn't tell anyone then — I've got a heart, you pricks — but I saw him. Ask Panagos. Was there a picture of the King hanging on his wall or wasn't there? Antigone knows better than me. And old man Retsinas, of course. Maybe nobody said anything. Panagos was playing everybody's game. You know all that, Manolopoulos, but will you write it down? Know why Antoniadis can't stand Louis, know why? Not only because he was disgusted when he found out about the UNRRA deal — it was his brother-in-law, Drakopoulos, who blew the whistle — but mostly because he found out later it was Louis who knocked up his sister, his saintly Madonna of the seven moons, his Tatyana. You didn't know that either. It was Drakopoulos who raised Louis' kid. If he's there for the reading, he'll be finding out about it for the first time."

There's no describing what he puked up about each one of us, the vermin.

I remember Antoniadis' sister, Madonna of the seven moons. The spitting image of Rita Hayworth. Better looking, in fact. Best looking friend's sister in the gang. We all figured she'd become the Greta Garbo of Piraeus. Funny, she ended up believing it herself. Not without reason. That's how Louis lost her, just when the two of them had something going.

Drakopoulos, the tomato paste canner, was already in the money back then; he was the one who plucked her, so to speak. In a flash.

When, I can't remember exactly. Before Litsa, for sure, but was it also before Aleka, or after Aleka? What I do know is that he'd taken Madonna under his wing, proud as a peacock — "You'll be the next Greta Garbo, Madonna"; it was Louis who nicknamed her Madonna — and set out for Drakopoulos' place.

We didn't have a clue about their relationship back then. It was top secret. So, off they go, hand in hand, to Drakopoulos' cannery. He wanted Drakopoulos to give him a job flogging tomato paste. As soon as Drakopoulos lays eyes on her — it was the first time they'd met — he just about goes nuts. He really wasn't all that close to the group then. He could also see what a basket case Louis was.

In any case, he quickly handed Louis the tomato paste, and plucked Madonna. In the twinkling of an eye. So it was that Louis lost the lady of his life — lady of his life, he called her — and so it was that Madonna lost her chance to become Greta Garbo.

Suddenly, she had to piss. By the time Drakopoulos could lead her to the toilet and show her where the soap and towels were — at the other end of the plant — Madonna crossed over to the far side, toted up the pros and cons with lightning speed, and decided then and there to made Drakopoulos the man of her life.

That was when Louis decided to knock her up. "Revenge had nothing to do with it, cousin," he swore to me later. "I just wanted a kid of mine to be brought up in more humane circumstances."

To be sure, Drakopoulos — it was true, he swore — insisted that he had no idea of Louis' relationship with Madonna, and if he had known, he certainly wouldn't have made a pass at her.

However, that same night, as Louis described it much, much later, when he pieced together what must have gone on in the toilet at Drakopoulos' cannery, he picked up his Madonna, took her down to the beach at the Seashell Club and laid her. Screwed her for the better part of the evening, in fact, saying not a word about his suspicions.

314

Meanwhile, the reading continued, and I was still lost in my
memories.

I only snapped back to reality when I heard my name come
up again. Now Agis was onto the book I was working on.

"I know you, Manolopoulos, you turd, I even know what
page you'll put the scene on. You? Miss an opportunity like
that? Louis keeps on telling you, 'Don't throw your life
away. You've got the keys. Don't just stand there. Open
the doors, and walk into the Kingdom of Heaven,' and you
don't do it. You hold back. What we haul around inside us,
rats! It's not your fault, I know it. It's him, the son-of-a-
bitch, worming his way into our lives, sending us off in the
wrong direction, making a mess of things, who's per-
verting us and destroying us and transforming us into
empty bags, him ..."

Get a load of Agis, will you my friend, look at the pupil
Louis turned out! But that wasn't all. There was more to
come. And I was the target.

"But you, you rat, Manolopoulos, you'll survive one way
or the other. Whether you like it or not, you'll end up in the
Kingdom of Heaven at the right hand of God, the Father
Almighty, right next to Louis."

Martha couldn't take it any longer. Suddenly she broke into
tears. She hung on, hung on, but I could see the sobs welling
up inside her, up from her chest into her throat, her larynx,
her tongue, welling, welling.

"Now comes the outburst, it's coming, coming," I said to
myself and suddenly she opened her mouth and let out a high-
pitched screech, like the safety valve on a pressure cooker,
like a pregnant woman's water breaking. Dams bursting and

315

rivers rushing. Sea water pouring through the portholes of sinking ships.

I was right next to her. Liakopoulos, her husband, was sitting opposite. As she cried out, she fell into my arms, writhing and shaking. And as we all sat there petrified, speechless, breathless, the only thing to be heard was her sobbing. Then Agis' mother got up, walked over to her, slapped her hard on the face and returned to her chair as though performing a sacred duty. Calm, other-worldly.

Again, no one budged. For a fraction of a second. Then Martha asked me for a handkerchief, wiped her tears and snot, got up, picked up her purse, stuffed the epistle into it and left.

I don't know which I regretted most, her leaving or missing the rest of the letter. Who knows how much more dirt it would bring out, how much deeper it would plunge the knife.

No one moved. We sat there motionless, speechless.

We could hear the elevator coming up, its door opening, closing, the noise of its cables, the sound it made when it reached the lobby. We even heard the outside door close.

At the sound of the door Liakopoulos got to his feet. Grimaced, looked at us one by one, and said, "For six months I pay his psychiatrist bills and his drugs, and look what I get. Don't believe a word of it. Too much electroshock," and walked out.

Drakopoulos followed close behind. He stood up and said: "More of Agis' idiocies; Tatyana never went with Retsinas again. He's right here, let him own up, if he's man enough."

He waited for a few seconds. But seeing Louis silent and unruffled, he picked up his topcoat and left. Two down.

I was sorry our wives weren't there to hear the reading. Agis only wanted Martha to be present. The sonofabitch knew she'd be enough to blow everything sky-high. Pure nitroglycerine. One drop was all it took.

Lazaris stood up, looked us over, made a triumphant turnabout and after sticking out his lower lip as if to say something to humiliate us, to spit on us, picked up his leather briefcase and left.

Panagos, just as earthy and crude as usual, said: "So I put up a portrait of the King in a moment of weakness, big deal. What did Agis expect Antigone to do when they fired her? Eat deep-fried air, maybe? We all need a life preserver, right? Isn't that what we're all looking for? Just get off my back, the whole fucking lot of you. You're wasting your time with all this crap. Bunch of dumb shits." And with that, he stalked out.

Antoniadis, well, he got up, put on his gray sport coat — he liked wearing sport coats — let out a bland "bye now" and headed for the door. I hadn't seen him so close up for a long time. He was short and bald, with a double chin and puffy cheeks. There goes Antoniadis' physique. Now I remember his wife at his funeral, she looked like a cartoon character. Nothing but skin and bones. Holding a plastic bag.

That left Louis and me. Suddenly it had turned chilly! We looked at each other without a word. Then came the odor of wet earth. It was fall. October.

— It's raining somewhere. It's going to rain here, said Agis' mother, and closed the balcony doors.

Soon the rain began to fall. In fine, sparse drops.

12. THE OUTING

ONE SUNDAY MORNING Louis got up at the crack of dawn and asked Litsa to press his suit — a gray suit with blue stripes, completely out of style, all but covered with cobwebs from disuse — and his pin-stripe shirt.

When she finished the pressing and he was almost dressed, just as he was tightening his red tie, in fact — where in the world did he unearth that tie? — Litsa mustered the courage to ask him where he was going, what wild idea did he have in mind now. He did not answer. It was only later that she learned of the glorious sequel, from the others.

His first stop was Psychiko, to pay a call on Aleka. Took a taxi, if you please. The gardener opened the gate, a maid opened the door, and finally Mr. Anargyros received him, in his pyjamas. Remember Mr. Anargyros? No? The developer who was going to sell them the apartment cheap? The guy with the red hair and the freckles? The guy that stole Aleka instead of selling them the house? Him.

Anargyros enjoyed Louis' company. One look at him was enough to set his heart-strings twanging. The fact that Louis held nothing against him even though he'd stolen his wife made him more than acceptable; it made him a friend. "Brother, you've got real soul," he would tell him.

As soon as he caught sight of Louis, he began to issue orders: set the table, bring on his favorite roast meats and side dishes, play his favorite music — whatever Louis wanted was his. And if he happened to come in the evening, the pool

318

lights would be switched on, the finest wines would be brought from the cellar. I'm telling you, for Anargyros, Louis' visits were an excuse for a party.

So, first Anargyros would entertain him, and a good deal later, Aleka would put in her appearance. When the first hors d'oeuvres began to arrive, they would look on in admiration as she swept down the staircase in one of those red dresses of hers.

Louis would be rambling on with his customary nonsense; Anargyros would be chuckling things like "You're a prize," and "Aleka, why in the world did you ever give up this walking treasure?" But of late Aleka had stopped laughing at Louis' attempted humor.

Now and again they'd reminisce about Louis' former father-in-law, Mr. Antypas, the goldsmith.

— Tell us, Louis, did your friend, Liakopoulos, really lay her, Chrysanthi, I mean?

But Aleka had stopped listening to them, and retreated into melancholy. Distant, remote, cold, eyes flitting from doors to windows to sky.

— Don't worry about her, she'll get over it. Maybe she doesn't laugh so much anymore, but at least she doesn't cry. Imagine if she started crying on me.

Around that time his daughter, Louisa, would put in an appearance. She was fairly old by now, spoke French, played the piano; a tall, self-assured girl, blue-eyed — Louis' eyes — and smart as a whip. As soon as she saw her father, she broke into a broad smile. She knew how full the day was going to be. "Come here, sweetheart," he said, and took her on his lap.

— Can you imagine, sweetheart ... What if Mr. Anargyros hadn't stolen your mummy and you'd grown up with me? Can you dream of anything more terrible?

— Hold on ... Next thing we know, you're going to claim you sacrificed everything for the kid.

Said Aleka, as she looked at him. Once she fixed her gaze on him, it wasn't easy for her to loosen it. She sat there staring at him, as if petrified. Each time Louis visited their place, she seemed more and more withdrawn. And he would feel pangs of sadness. Or sorrow.

Anargyros made a point of offering him a job, not so much to help him out, he admitted, as to relish Louis' refusal.

First there would be a brief introduction: how could he expect to survive without medical insurance, without pension — "You paying contributions?" — no one will trust you with a yacht; you should be doing something about it; then he came right to the point:

— How about managing one of my supermarkets? Come on, it's the answer to your problems.

Louis never could figure out why whoever found him a job always wanted him to be a manager. "Hell, what makes them think I'm so trustworthy?"

— No, my dear fellow, better find someone else for your supermarket, he replied.

— How much longer can you go on like this, Louis?

That unavoidable question, "How much longer can you go on like this?" was the only subject under discussion at our group's last evening get-together, over drinks on Liakopoulos' terrace.

Lazaris was the first to raise the issue.

— Hey, how much longer can he get away with it anyway, the sonofabitch?

Lazaris had put his guilt complexes behind him long, long ago. He used to be terrified to open his mouth, especially in my presence. And when he did speak, it would always be tactful. But now that everything was out in the open, he could be as crude and as vulgar as he pleased. Why bother to hide anything from us?

So the attack on Louis went on. Lazaris was still speaking:

— ... never even spent a drachma on health insurance. He's not going to get sick, not even once? Not going to look after himself? At all?

Everyone, especially after Agis' epistle, was all but expecting him to fall apart, to see him dressed in rags knocking at death's door, ready to give up the ghost.

— Just let him show up at my door one day, sick and hungry, asking me for help, Liakopoulos continued. That's all I want. Nothing else. I want to see him crawl, beg for help.

Julia, more than ever, was leering with boundless resentment, with almost a sardonic sneer. Her teeth had begun to fall out. But it was she who answered Liakopoulos:

— Yes, but when he had the crash, when he killed the Dutch girl, the two of you posted bail for him, you and my dear husband here.

— Did I know then? Did I know?

I wanted to ask him: "Know what, you ungrateful bastard? What did he ever do to you, anyway?" But, as usual, I stayed out of the dispute; said nothing. So she handed the baton back to Lazaris.

— What the hell's the matter with him, anyway? There's got to be a limit. Either he admits he's a nut case, or he's a write-off. We've all watered down our wine. So what's his big problem? Hey, here's how!

And we clinked glasses. No, wrong; not me. I drank without touching anyone's glass.

It was crazy, but true: every last one of them depended on how Louis would end his life in order to justify their own. I wanted to say, "What's it to you what Louis does and how he dies?" but I held back. But what if I'd said it, what difference would it make?

Most of the time I kept silent. But the odd time, Liakopoulos would corner me. Like today.

— Take a stand, stop talking out of both sides of your mouth.

— I'm not, but I'm no fool either. We'll see what happens at the final reckoning, Liakopoulos. We'll see who won and who lost. How am I supposed to know what will happen? To each according to his mortgage.

— Nothing before its jerk-off time, that's what he means, chimed in Drakopoulos, who had become a regular member of the group after Agis' death, and, of course, a mortal adversary of Louis.

What bound them together was their shared hatred. Well, maybe I shouldn't exactly call it hatred. A mess of confused emotions, really. Admiration, hatred, envy, but most of all a hidden, unspoken sense of awe. No one could forgive him for going up square against everything they had wasted their lives in vain pursuit of, and yet always managing to float to the surface, to remain uninfected by compromise and disgrace.

Martha remained distant and indifferent. Another version of Aleka. Couldn't even be bothered listening to us. She'd settle into a corner of the veranda with a glass of whisky and her daydreams, rotating the glass between her hands, sipping slowly, rocking back and forth, absorbed in her thoughts.

It was Agis' old rocking chair. In that celebrated epistle of his he willed her the chair, and all his art books.

It was a lugubrious sight — Martha sitting there with the glass in her hand, in Agis' rocker — but no one dared to say a word, not even Liakopoulos.

She went herself to see Agis' mother, picked up the chair — and the books — and set it up on the balcony.

Gradually she stopped reading and began leafing through his comics and art books. And in them she uncovered Agis' world, and Agis himself.

Worst thing was that the whisky kept disappearing faster and faster, until she got to a point where all she could do was drink herself into a stupor, then go to bed with a curt goodnight. She didn't seem to care about me anymore, even though the odd time I would catch her glance on the fly. But she wasn't aggressive like before. In fact, she seemed to be calling for help.

But on that day, when everyone was praying for the fall of

Louis the titan, her eyes seemed to recapture their old power.

Julia was talking about Louis: "Let's see how well he manages those icons of his with busted fingers."

As she was speaking, I noticed that her skirt had crept up her thighs. Actually, first I noticed Lazaris eyeing her, then the skirt. He didn't see me watching him. It was one hell of an eyeball job, let me tell you.

Drakopoulos replied: "You think Louis is a painter? You're crazy. I found out some fairy paints 'em for him."

They were lying. Dripping with malice, the scum. But I didn't say a word. I was sick of arguing with Julia about Louis. Sick. Or was I afraid?

That was when Martha turned in her rocker and glared at me. Her eyes were full of accusation, desperation. When I saw that look, I couldn't hold back. I spoke out. Finally.

— Stop talking nonsense, I snapped. He paints 'em himself and you all know it. He painted in school, and pretty damn well at that. Why are you trying so hard to forget. It's absurd the way you want to turn white into black.

— Manolopoulos, don't insult us. You're calling us liars. Sure, you always manage to keep your hands clean, but we know you pretty damned well. Besides, every one of us could draw just as well as that Louis of yours back then.

Liakopoulos was beside himself. I was about to answer when Lazaris cut me off.

— Go on, Liakopoulos, tell him the rest. Tell him he's covering for Louis. Isn't that right, Manolopoulos? Maybe if you weren't so interested in covering his ass, maybe if you told him a thing or two — don't forget, he listens to you — maybe you could have saved him. But you liked him the way he was, a useless delinquent. Maybe he fixes you up with the odd piece of ass. I don't know. Us, whatever we're saying, it's out of compassion. We want to rescue the guy.

— Get off my back, will you. You want him to crash. And make you look good.

I told them off. Couldn't hold it back. There was more:

— Because you want to prove to yourselves that your lives

mean something, that's why. I'm not trying to prove anything. I'm in the same shit, but at least I know it. That's right! I know, I know just how we'll all end up. And more. Compared with Louis, I'm telling you, we're a bunch of dwarfs. Dwarfs. There's a guy who succeeded in doing what he wanted with his life; whatever he didn't like, he kicked aside. That's Louis. But us ...

They all froze. I had them pinned down. They could not respond.

Martha was smiling at me. Something had come back to life inside her. I could feel it. Her smile was like a transfusion of hope and promise. I had done the right thing.

As I finished my little speech, she broke into applause, then looked at me as if to say: "Manolopoulos, you bum, how do you always manage to land on your feet? Just when people start believing you're nothing but another piece of shit, somehow you manage to drag yourself out of the swamp."

I looked at her, and thoughts flashed through my mind: maybe she still loves me, still thinks of me, dreams of me, and I, as time goes by, I feel pity for her, dream about her and curse the biggest mistake of my life, when I lost her.

Then Julia awakened me from the dream. Time to come back to earth.

— That's all you can do, make excuses for your friend. Didn't you ever ask yourself why he never did anything with his life, why he's just a cipher, why his women end up leaving him? All of them. Isn't that right?

Whenever she opens her mouth, nothing but poison comes out, the slut.

— Litsa abandoned him? I asked.

I wanted to say more, but I held back.

— Fine, fine, if you think Litsa's a woman, then ...

She stopped. From the way I looked at her she understood that was it, that she'd gone too far.

I felt a surge of nausea. It was the first time hearing Julia's voice made me want to vomit. And I did. Everybody knew why. Including why I vomited.

324

No one said a word. When I got back from the toilet, they stared at me silent and expressionless. I understood. They had already condemned me. I had been discharged. Julia's expression was the same. She loathed me.

Then the old fears came over me: "If she hands me my walking shoes, what do I do? She and Lazaris can totally destroy me." I'd been stupid enough to buy the house in her name. Mom never forgave me for it. "Fool," she hissed, over and over. "If you separate one day, what will you do? Where will you go?"

In any case — I could see it coming — the moment I tell her, "I'm leaving, I've had it with you," she'll come back with "So what are you waiting for?"

But let's get back to that Sunday morning, back to Louis' unexpected call on Anargyros. So, after relishing Louis' refusal to take a job in his supermarket, he began warning him of black days ahead.

— How much longer is Fanny going to support you, anyway? How many more injections can she make?

Louis was deeply involved in the third great enterprise of his life, but none of us knew a thing about it, what it was, or where he'd found the money to start it. We'd only been able to pick up a few hints. Some claimed he was going to manufacture surgical supports, others said plastic fly traps.

So when Anargyros saw him dressed to the nines, with a serious expression on his face — unsmiling, taciturn — naturally he got suspicious. "He's got to be up to something." Maybe he was worried Louis would ask for money for the business; that was all he wanted to talk about of late. But Louis wasn't in a joking mood that morning, and he wasn't spouting nonsense. Besides, he hadn't visited them recently.

— First of all, Kostas, there's Aleka. Anargyros' earthly

325

paradise just wasn't for her. When I saw her coming down the stairs that day, I just about broke down in tears. That wasn't the Aleka I knew. Now she was fat, like a barrel. Always was short to start with, but this? No waist, no chest, no neck left, even. Her stomach had swallowed them all up. Her throat was puffed, maybe she had goiter. When I see something like that, I want to go get pissed. You can't believe how lousy I felt. Suicide in the making, cousin. The walls started to close in, the dining room, the terrace. "Aleka," I say to her, "what the hell's going on? What's wrong? What are you missing?"

According to Louis' account, he declined the wine, the roast, the music and the flowery compliments. They hardly knew what to think.

— What's the matter, Louis? Got something against me?

— Not at all, my fine fellow; but I'm in a hurry. I just came by to pick up Louisa. Nothing against you.

"Aha," they said, and relaxed. He would take her for an outing; that was it.

— Take her, by all means! She's your daughter.

And so he did. But this time it wasn't your common garden variety outing.

For Louisa, an outing with her daddy was no normal outing; most of all, it was never an outing into the world of make-believe, as you might have thought.

You know how it is with separated parents: take the kids out, buy them ice cream, take them to the playground, to an amusement park, remind them to work hard in school, to be good and to behave themselves, even give them some pocket money; then it's goodbye until next week, when the cycle starts all over again.

But with Louis and Louisa it was just the opposite.

First of all, the whole outing was a desperate effort by Louis

326

to pull her out of the make-believe world, not into it. Secondly, it was Louisa who gave Louis pocket money, not the other way around. Louisa bought him ice cream. Louisa took him to the amusement park, but she didn't go on any of the rides. Louis did! He would ride the bumper cars and the Ferris wheel, and she would look on, laughing.

In fact, just looking at him was enough to make Louisa laugh. She only wanted to come along when they came to the deforming mirrors. The idea was to laugh together.

But when she turned fifteen, suddenly he cut off the amusement parks, and started taking her to the opera and the theater instead.

For Louis, there was nothing like the opera to introduce his child to the world of art. There she would encounter fine music, get a taste of culture, there she would learn how to reconcile the irreconcilable.

— Can you imagine dying and singing at the same time? In opera, everything goes.

What he wanted to show her was that if anything can happen in art, anything could happen in life.

— Art is more than just having a good time, Louisa. It's the key that unlocks all doors.

Then he proceeded to knock down all the sacred cows — parents, teachers, priests, "authorities" in quotation marks — showed her just how relative our so-called eternal values really are, then set them up on new foundations. Even the Ten Commandments; he went over them with her, one at a time.

— Take "Thou Shalt Not Commit Adultery." When your life partner turns out to be a dud, what are you supposed to do? The trick is not to have to commit adultery. When you feel you have to, it's too late to stop. Look, I forgave your mother, even if she did it. And me, your father, "Honor Thy Father,..." isn't that how it goes? What about it? You've got to honor me even if I'm a bum, a crook, a nobody? And me, you? What if you turn out to be a dumb skirt, with dumb ideas and dumb behavior, won't I be ashamed to introduce you as

327

my kid? Just because I'm your father and you're my kid, everything has to be picture perfect? No, criticize me. That's the way to honor me, when you sit me down and criticize me. How you do it, based on what, now that's another story; we'll talk it over another time. Louisa, we've got to take another look at things every so often. Rebuild, renovate. Everything. Stand still and you're dead.

But with that kind of talk, he was leading her onto dangerous paths.

— Hey, Louis, I told him, you can't do that. What'll happen to the kid if you tell her everything?... Are you sure? Aren't you destroying her world.

— The way the world is, I'm doing the right thing. Down deep, I want to stimulate her mind, I want her to start thinking for herself. Better that way than let another rat loose in the world. You commit adultery, or you don't. So, things get fucked up somewhere down the line. People commit murder. Or they don't. At least start asking why. Let her doubt me, cousin. Tomorrow she'll say, "Daddy's talking nonsense." Well, that's a start. Otherwise we'll be stalled at "Judge not lest ye be judged." Is that what you want?

At any rate, every time Louisa came back from an outing with her father, the ground beneath Anargyros' and Aleka's feet slipped a bit more. Apprehension began to creep over them.

— He's a monster, not a human being, Aleka cried. Look what he's doing to her.

— We can't let him see her again.

— Never, that was the last time, they agreed.

But after the first explosions had subsided, Anargyros came around to Louisa's viewpoint.

— That's the way it is, Aleka, just like she says.

And he laughed.

— She's wrong?

And the outings with Louis continued.

But, like I said, this time — this particular Sunday — was a different kind of outing. No ice cream, no chit-chat, no biblical exegesis, no opera. No, this was an outing with a purpose.

This time Louis, dressed in his Sunday best and with a serious look in the eye, took Louisa by the hand and set out to introduce her to his friends. One by one.

It had to be the worst Sunday anyone in our group had ever experienced.

Their first stop was his place, his shack; then it was on to the friends'. For the first time she saw how her daddy really lived. Until then, he consistently refused to show her. "Not today; some other time," was his line.

For the first time Louisa entered into the world of make-believe, but by the rear door, ass backwards, so to speak.

She met Litsa — and saw her limp; met Litsa's sister, Fanny, a dried-up stubby little woman with a mask of bitterness, desperation and strength. Met Fanny's husband too, the man they called Customs.

The three of them looked her over, nicely dressed, cute, with gold jewelry on her fingers, her ears, with her pearl necklace, and fell under her spell. She seemed too good to be true.

— Manolis' daughter! Good God!

Everyone was overcome by emotion. Louisa was embarrassed, it was all she could do to keep from crying. Louis kept his eyes riveted on her.

— This is my life, Louisa. Take a good look. My world.

Louisa touched the masks, the curtains, the swords, the stage settings, leafed through the books, switched the bizarre table lamps on and off.

— But, but it's like a theater here! If only it was like this at home, she said, embracing her father. And broke into tears.

There was an awkward moment when she met her grandfather, lying flat on his back. She gave him her hand. He shed a silent tear. That was all.

Then began the ritual visits to each of his friends. Actually, it was more like he was dispatching them to the firing squad, one at a time.

Unexpected, he rang doorbells; boldly he called out over house phones:

— It's me, Retsinas. I want you to meet my daughter.

But when they opened the door, he didn't present his daughter to his friends; he presented his friends to his daughter.

Let me tell you one thing, though, this ritual was not simply for show, "Get a load of my daughter!" and such nonsense. Nope. Nor was the idea to show off his friends to his daughter. That was not the reason for the visits. It was a good deal more serious than that. Louisa might never see him again.

— Let her judge them — and me — with her own eyes, cousin.

The way I understood it, it was Louisa's initiation into the adult world, Louis style.

— Louisa, I'd like you to meet Mr. Lazaris. A man of means. We went to school together, but he got ahead. Money, a nice house. At university, he was at the top of the class. Now he's a professor. See what a lovely house. Five rooms, isn't it, Lazaris?

Lazaris was smoldering but — what could he do? — he kept up appearances.

— No, eight, he finally managed to say.

Lazaris wasn't lying. There were eight rooms. I don't want you to think Louis was being sarcastic. Not exaggerating, either. All he wanted to do was show her the real world. Nothing more, nothing less.

Next, without a moment's hesitation, he took her to meet Drakopoulos, even though he knew the man loathed him.

330

— Now here is a truly important man, Louisa. Maybe he never finished university, but he made lots of money. He's the industrialist of the gang; moved up a class or two, alright. It all began with some home-made tomato paste. When you grow up, just tell him you're Louis' daughter and he'll make you a queen. His wife, Tatyana, just missed being your mother. Madonna of the seven moons, we called her.

And he pointed her out.

— Still good-looking, cousin. Ageless, he confessed later, when he told me about those mind-boggling visits of his.

"Kostas, my boy, Julia was right when she said I couldn't hang onto a good woman. Take Tatyana, for instance; she could have been the woman of my life. A house, kids, love ... But she's gone.

Louis turned bitter. He'd always wanted Tatyana, even if he'd never breathed a word to Drakopoulos who stole her away from him. He still wanted her.

And as Drakopoulos listened to him talking about Tatyana, it was all he could do to restrain himself. "Do I kill him or not?" he thought. "Who the hell does he think he is? He's got the gall to tell me in my own house that Tatyana was almost his daughter's mother? Those that have ears, let them hear! First comes Agis with his disclosures; now this guy. Is it my kid or isn't it? Guy's got a nerve, rehashing it all right in front of me. Let me get this straight, his daughter might be my son's sister?..." He was speechless, sputtering, couldn't even tell Louis to go to hell. Just as they were about to leave, he finally blurted out that it wasn't his fault if he made a pass at Madonna back then, he had no idea there was anything between Louis and her. "I swear it on whatever I hold sacred," he shrilled.

But Louis was not about to let him off the hook.

— Come on, Drakopoulos, forget the solemn oaths. You knew damned well.

And Drakopoulos began to gnaw his lip. When he starts doing that, you know he's trying to hide something. He couldn't help himself. At the first lie, he began to gnaw. In fact, that habit's been nothing but trouble for him. Can't bluff at cards without gnawing his lip; anyone who knows him picks it up right away. Drakopoulos might have been another Rockefeller if he didn't have that fatal flaw. He couldn't even cheat on Madonna. Just as soon as he started gnawing his lip, "Drakopoulos is hiding something," we would say. It was his Achilles' heel, and everybody and his uncle knew it.

Whichever way you look at it, Louis' round of ritual visits to his friends was one of the most curious events of his life.

— How the hell did he ever dream up the idea? Only a brain possessed by the devil could have invented a torment like that, and for the whole group yet ...

Everybody was convinced it was an act of revenge, a pitiful mockery.

— He just wanted to drag us through the mud.

Meanwhile, Lazaris was wracking his brain for the origin of Louis' satanic scheme.

— He's got to have read it somewhere. Came across it in some book, liked the idea, and decided to put it into action. What else has he done all his life? We know all about him. Whenever he finds something he likes, he tries to act it out. Using us as guinea pigs, of course. But I'll find out where he got it. I'll find out.

He did. In a literary monthly. He found the issue, the page, the author. A Czech, it was. He even read it for us.

After Lazaris, Louis visited Liakopoulos. He was third on the list. When Liakopoulos saw him all gussied up in his suit, sober of mien, the dimples in his cheeks started to twitch. "Is he trying to kid me or what?" he muttered to himself, just as the others had done, when Louis launched into a torrent of fulsome praise. You can imagine what he told his daughter.

— And here we have the self-made man of the group. The perfect example of the Greek who starts out with nothing, and reaches the moon.

Martha could overhear him.

— Louisa, I want you to appreciate just who it is you're looking at. The man you see before you has walked on the moon. He's become a great success, a shipowner, and plenty else besides. Nothing can stop him. He lives off the land, like a hunter. But instead of hunting birds or dreams, he hunts money. An insatiable soul. Take a good look at him, and remember what a man is capable of. But the most important thing is that in spite of his money, he never abandoned his ideas, or his party. Rock steady, a man of principle.

Louis' praise kept on pouring out. He only stopped when he noticed Liakopoulos' eyes starting to glaze over. For an instant, he felt a pang of fear.

Louisa should show him respect, he went on. It would help her understand what a wrongheaded man her father was, how he'd wasted his life, and accomplished nothing — what the hell, maybe he had five or six extra adventures — while all his friends had gone on to greater things.

— If he becomes a government minister, which is bound to happen one of these days, don't hesitate to ask him for help.

On and on he went. He had become a master of rhetoric; a modern day Demosthenes.

At first Martha didn't know what to think. He was so serious not even she could tell whether he believed it or not. Finally, she couldn't help herself; she burst out laughing, laughing so hard they finally had to pound her on the back, throw water over her head, slap her on the face to bring her out of it. She hadn't laughed so hard in ages.

— Don't laugh, Martha, I'm not joking, he said.

That did it. The last straw. The "I'm not joking." That's

when the laughing began in earnest. She laughed until she fainted. When she came to and gradually calmed down, she said to Louis, eyes red-rimmed from laughter:

— God bless you.

Yep, I'll certify that. That's exactly what she said, dead serious now. "God bless you!" and sat down in her armchair on the balcony.

Did I overlook anyone? Everyone got the shock treatment. The scenes defied description. Why, they even paid a call on uncle Tzavaras.

— Louisa, these are the men who set the course of history. Even today. You must respect them.

He was convincing. It came out as though he believed every word. Or did he, really?

Tzavaras was in full uniform. In fact, he was about to leave for a memorial ceremony commemorating the "patriots fallen in the war against the bandits," but Louis' visit delayed him. Tzavaras couldn't tolerate Louis, of course; he nearly fainted from astonishment; couldn't believe his eyes or ears. For the entire scene, he stood there, speechless, until Moschos came along and shook him out of it. He was so astounded he never managed to kick the two of them out, Louis and his daughter.

Twiggy appeared, dressed in her nightgown, still half-asleep. Of course, Louis was careful to present Moschos to Louisa as a great patriot:

— The only pure-hearted man of ideals never to profit from circumstances to make a pile. And he's your uncle too. Ah, and here's your aunt.

And he pointed to Twiggy, who had just appeared at the door.

— And this is the worthy spouse. She who has suffered every humiliation for the sake of appearances.

334

Everyone there flashed back to the incident at the consulate in Izmir.

Let me tell you, if they hadn't been so astonished, they'd have shown him the door then and there. Him and his daughter both. But they were too late. By the time they could begin to react, Louis was long gone.

Only Twiggy dared venture out onto the balcony. Louis spotted her when he turned for an instant to look up at their apartment. Probably knew what he'd see; that's why he turned. He saw her lift her hand with the merest suspicion of a wave, but at that very instant Moschos appeared on the balcony, and dragged her violently back into the house.

How could Louis have possibly known that the visit would be fatal to his uncle? Tzavaras pulled himself together briefly, but as he opened the front door of the apartment building on his way to the memorial ceremony for the innocent victims — it was already underway, in fact — he suddenly collapsed, in thoroughly antiheroic fashion, into a puddle of dirty water. One of the neighbors was washing his car, and the water had collected in a hollow in the pavement, right outside the building. Plaf! he went as he hit the water.

Death came almost instantaneously. Stroke. The first and the last. As the neighbor cursed him for dirtying his car, he passed on.

So, Louis pulled a slip of paper from his pocket. It was a list, with the names of the friends. One by one he drew a line through each name.

Next, he paid a call on Panagos — where else? — at his house of sin, in Kastella. There, I think it was, Louisa met her illegitimate cousin, her daddy's sister's daughter, that is.

— As you can see, each of my friends is better than the next, Louisa. And all of them productive people.

335

Lately Louis used the word "productive" a lot; often in the wrong context, but frequently. The way he said it, no one could tell whether it was an insult or a compliment. Much later, I asked him about it.

— You crazy, Kostas, my boy? Don't you know that the more productive you get, the less there is left of you? That's what our invisible masters want, in any case.

He didn't say "big bosses" any more. He liked "invisible masters" better.

— The more productive you get, the deeper you sink. The fun's over; no more art, no more literature. We're all headed straight for the shrink.

Only then did I realize what a nightmare world Louis carried around inside him, what his world and his life meant to him.

Antigone embraced Louisa. It was the first time she'd ever seen her brother's daughter.

— You've got a daughter like that, you sloth? Impossible. But she looks like you; has your eyes, she said, and kissed the girl.

I won't even bother to describe the visit to Antoniadis. You can imagine.

Take it from me, Antoniadis never doubted for a minute that Louis had knocked up his sister, Tatyana, but he wasn't prepared to tell his brother-in-law, Drakopoulos, about it, not even to mention it. Whenever he was asked, Antoniadis simply denied it outright, ruled it out completely.

— Better to be n good terms with Drakopoulos, right Antoniadis?

That was Panagos' comeback whenever he encountered Antoniadis; the only way to stop him from playing the self-righteous ideologue.

336

One time, even Agis suggested he come clean with his brother-in-law. "You just don't talk about those things," replied Antoniadis. And so it was that the two of them discovered that there are certain things you simply don't talk about.

— I mean, these so-called pure hearts are going around telling us what great guys they are? Get off my back. We're all shit, got it? But no back stabbing ... Drakopoulos would say when he later learned that just about everybody had conspired against him — Louis, Madonna and Antoniadis — each in their own way.

— The scum, they sold me out. Now that's what I call collusion.

He ended up keeping the kid and Madonna — where would he find a living doll like that again? — and kept on supporting Antoniadis.

You really want to know why? Well, he preferred living with his doubts to losing Madonna. "In spite of everything," he thought to himself, "Tatyana may not be lying." In fact until death she maintained her innocence, up until the bitter end.

But no matter how hard you try to imagine what went on at the meeting between Louis and Antoniadis that Sunday of the social calls, there's one thing you couldn't possibly imagine: what Antoniadis told Louis in the midst of the introductions. "Know something, Retsinas?" he tells him in an moment of awkward silence, "the only thing that can save you is to join the Party again. That's the only place you can find yourself, because you deserve it, goddamn it. Pull yourself out of the slime those bourgeois shit heads are trying to drown you in. You'll see."

When Louis asked him what he meant by slime, who the bourgeois shit heads were, and what it was he would see, Antoniadis couldn't say.

337

I was next to last on the list. When Julia heard the doorbell ring, asked who is it and heard the voice saying, "It's me, Retsinas," she became so agitated that her lips and hands began to quiver.

— Don't open the door.

— He heard you. I'm not supposed to open my own door?

So I opened, and, as you can imagine, it was my turn.

— This is the writer I've been telling you about, Louisa. A man of substance. But not like the others. What he's really doing is waiting, in a railway station. Sometimes he pretends to be working, but that's just for show. He's not working; he's waiting.

He was making fun of me, damn him. He had to be making fun of me. He had even brought flowers. I was certain he was making fun. But then again, I couldn't be entirely sure.

I was off balance. Julia didn't know what to think. She couldn't make heads or tails of him; just sat there staring, and listening.

— No, cousin, I wasn't making fun, he told me later.

That's when he explained his reasons for the visits, and told me about Aleka, how she'd gone to fat, and everything else.

Later, I tried to tell the guys in the group that I was beginning to believe that for the first time in his life Louis was not making fun of us, that deep down he wasn't being sarcastic, that he was doing it all for his daughter. In chorus, they all answered that it was high time I stopped being such an imbecile.

— Sure he was making fun of us, Manolopoulos. His life proves it. He thinks we're all a bunch of thugs. Slimy careerists, compromisers, alienated. Why kid ourselves? He doesn't have anything but scorn for us, he loathes us. Don't pretend you don't know what's going on, don't make like you don't know what he thinks of us. Not making fun of us, my ass. Get off our back with that Louis of yours, will you. As far as we're concerned, he's dead.

338

All the while Louisa was staring at me with those huge, sparkling, intelligent blue eyes, as if I were one of the Four Horsemen of the Apocalypse. She didn't know what to think either. Was I really the remarkable person her father was describing, or was I just the pathetic little man sitting there in front of her? She could sense a difference in her father's attitude toward me, but she couldn't understand why he lumped me in with the others.

— Don't ever be like him, though. The perfect split personality. Has the gift of understanding what makes people tick, but he doesn't dare do a thing about it. Is he going to stay there in the same place forever? Or will he cross over to the other side?

It was Louis' longstanding accusation.

— Kostas, my boy, time is running out.

Julia didn't even make a move to offer him coffee. Instead, as soon as she'd regained her composure, she attacked:

— Come now, Mr. Retsinas, who do you think you're fooling?

Louisa was momentarily taken aback by Julia's aggressive attitude.

— What other side? You're crazy with jealousy, you. And that's all there is to it. Just because everybody else made something of themselves and you went nowhere, you're just looking for a cheap alibi ...

— See what I mean, Louisa? Listen to my friends. The lady's right. That's how it is, just like she says. Except, I'm not looking for an alibi. She's barking up the wrong tree.

Julia was at a loss for words. He'd silenced her. It was the last thing she expected. Louis agreeing with her, I mean.

Round about then the phone started to ring. It was the other guys in the group; they'd recovered from the initial shock, and now they wanted to lash out at him. How the hell did they find out he was at my place?

— Who gave you permission to come knocking at our doors, you bum? Maybe we invited you, is that it?

And so on and so forth.

339

Julia acted as their willing representative, and then some. Quickly she recovered and went over to the counterattack.

— How can poor little Greece ever get ahead with people like you, Mr. Retsinas?

Julia was a politically-minded gal. Still, the bit about poor little Greece was the last thing I expected to hear from her. But she kept right on, shooting from the lip.

— It's all on account of people like you, Mr. Retsinas, you and Agis and Antoniadis. That's right, you heard what I said.

As far as she was concerned, they were all backward, under-developed; I can't even remember what else they were.

— So Lazaris is getting ahead — big deal. Is he hurting anybody? Because he bought a place in Psychiko? So what? Go buy a house there yourself, if you can. What was Liakopoulos supposed to do? Ruin his life just because his father goes and gets himself shot? Betrayed his memory, did he? Well, good for him.

And on she went. She knew Agis' epistle inside and out. "Who the hell gave her the information? One thing for sure, I didn't say a word to her about any epistle. That's what we agreed. Top secret."

But Julia kept on. She had still more poison to spit up.

— And if your father stole from UNRRA, good for him.

The telephone rang again; it was Drakopoulos. He kept up the bombardment.

— The fun and games are over, Retsinas. The world's moving forward at lightning speed and you're still diddling your dick. And you even think you're superior. Shit. You're just pulling yourself down, and dragging the whole country down with you. Don't hang up, wait ...

When we met later, I asked him why he hung up on Drakopoulos, why he didn't let him speak his mind.

— I hung up on him, cousin, because he and your wife were just talking nonsense. I can't understand why they think I'm the same as Agis. Did I ever say Agis was vindicated? All of us, me for sure, we're hung up on illusions. You really want to know something? That's what's dragging the country

340

down. But not me, least of all me.

I could tell Louis was serious. He wasn't kidding, not this time.

— Manolopoulos, I showed you guys the way to the horizon, but you're such dummies you never even realized it. Cousin, I belong to the future. Tell 'em that. You know what I'm talking about; but them, they're doomed men. Don't tell 'em that.

And, still fuming, he took Louisa's hand and walked out.

I never saw him so angry before; Louis had never spoken of the future in such prophetic tones before, never with such certainty. We were speechless. Julia for her own reasons, I for mine.

We didn't say a word for the rest of the evening. Not me, not her. "It's not worth calling her by name anymore," I thought to myself. And I never called her Julia again. "You!" I called her. Only that.

13. THE LITTLE UMBRELLAS

BY NOW ATHENA, Panagos' wife, tipped the scales at over 250 pounds.

Take me to the doctor, she told her husband. "I've got a little pain here and ..."

They went. Afterward, as she was getting dressed, the doctor whispered in his ear:

— Another pound and she won't live till Christmas.

It was spring.

— And if she puts on three, doctor?

— She's finished by the fall.

After the doctor's morbid prognosis, Panagos became the most gallant of husbands. Whatever he had deprived Athena of up until then, he now plied her with, prodigally.

— If she's going to go, she's going to go satisfied, he vowed.

For a short while, Athena believed that Panagos had returned to home and hearth a chastened man; he had broken up with Antigone — hadn't he? — and now he was trying to buy out his regrets — Athena calculated everything in cold cash, which is why she used a term like "buy out" — by making her life as pleasant as possible.

The couple had lunch at the most exclusive downtown restaurants. There were Wednesday and Friday buffets at the Ledra Marriott and the Hilton — two thousand a head, all you can eat. And when she was feeling really low, he would take her for ice cream — elaborate concoctions topped with miniature Japanese umbrellas — at an ice cream parlor in New Philadelphia. It was Athena's passion. Not the ice cream so much as those little umbrellas, which she collected. Counting the umbrellas was like counting the happiest moments of her life.

As you might expect, after Panagos' elaborate repentance — by Athena's lights it was repentance — she forgave him.

Naturally, Panagos avoided explaining his curious behavior to Antigone at first.

— Oh really? she said. Falling in love with Athena all over again?

Meanwhile he struggled to convince her that it was indeed possible for a man to feel Christian charity for once in his life.

— I've treated her rotten a hell of a long time, Antigone. I've caused her enough heartache; let her go out with a full stomach at least.

— I'm sick of the same old story. You've frittered away your life waiting for her to die. All for a couple of shitty apartments; why didn't you tell her to go to hell? Our life is wasted.

— One way or another, Antigone, the fun and games are over.

But when he finally revealed the doctor's latest prognosis, "another pound and she..." and so on and so forth, Antigone froze:

— You're insane! So, you're deliberately stuffing the food into her?

Panagos looked at her coldly, remotely.

— But, that's cold-blooded murder ... she whispered.

Panagos continued to stare at her coldly, remotely. Antigone kept on speaking until suddenly she broke off. Everything froze.

— So, it's not regrets ... You're killing her.

— What's it to you? I should put her on a diet? If that's what you want, it's a diet, as of tomorrow. That's what you want?

Instead of replying, Antigone popped a cassette in the video. Then told him to do whatever he liked, and sat down to watch Rock Hudson.

So it was that with Antigone's silent assent, Panagos went right on making Athena's life as pleasant as possible.

As it happened, the doctor was wide of the mark. Athena did not die: not in the fall, not at Christmas time. She died the following spring. She hadn't gained one pound, or three. She'd put on fifteen. It was when she registered that fifteenth pound that the inevitable finally came to pass.

She died happily, while eating — so said the medical report — her one-hundredth, or so, ice cream sundae at the fanciest ice cream parlor in New Philadelphia. Death came after a once in a lifetime eating binge, capped off by the ritual ice cream. The last spoonful was the one that did it. Just as Panagos was about to ask her if she'd like seconds, he saw her lean back in her chair and stare off toward the mountains. Then he noticed the two streams of melting ice cream dribbling from the corners of her half-open mouth.

Athena had taken leave of this vain world.

Panagos rushed to the telephone to give Antigone the sad news. But as he spoke, she felt the disgust flood over her. The house began to smell; her own skin smelled, her breath. She threw open the terrace doors, turned on the fan. It was still there; something was stinking. She didn't say a word; hung up the phone. Panagos didn't know what to think. Before he could get out one sentence, bang, she hung up on him. Suddenly, Antigone felt like vomiting.

In a flash, her entire life passed before her eyes. For no apparent reason, she remembered her childhood, her brother, her father, the old neighborhood, and she started to cry. My God, she muttered to herself, how many years had she dreamed of this day, the day she would no longer be Panagos' kept woman, and now when the great moment finally arrived, how absurd it all seemed; the dream had dissipated so fast she realized it meant nothing to her. Not one damn thing.

344

"Goddamn it, Manolopoulos, goddamn it," she muttered as we stood there side by side — purely by coincidence — at Athena's burial. She was almost delirious. That wasn't the Antigone I knew. "Everything stinks; what's wrong with me?"

Panagos plied her with breath fresheners — flavored with cinnamon or clove — but the smell of disgust clung to her palate like a bitter aftertaste; the same nauseating odor she'd smelt from the first moment lodged in her nostrils. It was a curious stench, something like the sweetish stink of rotten food, of mold, of rancid frying oil.

The doctor didn't take his eyes off her for the entire ceremony. Did he know anything? Of course he did.

"No, I can't take it," she suddenly began to howl. She had snapped. Panagos was at a total loss. He pinched her.

— Shut up, he hissed. You'll give us away.

I was standing right beside them; heard every word. Antigone kept on shrieking. Crime was clearly not her cup of tea. The dream of her life had suddenly turned into a nightmare. Snap out of it? No way. Complete collapse was only a matter of time. Either she goes crazy or walks into the first police station she finds and tells everything, to get it out of her system.

That was no burial. It was more like a third-degree interrogation.

The group was thunderstruck. Well, part of it. Lazaris, Liakopoulos and Drakopoulos were conspicuous by their absence. But Lazaris' mother did show up. She was a sorry sight; half-blind by now, and hunchbacked. Antoniadis was there with his wife. But this time she wasn't holding a plastic bag, like at Agis' funeral.

In the meantime — we're still at the burial — the doctor had his eyes riveted on the couple: Antigone was in hysterics,

345

Panagos was pinching her, trying to stop her; Martha was looking at me, I at Louis, and Louis at Panagos ...

Our glances described nightmarish circles, as if an invisible ball were bouncing from eye to eye, and all the while, Antigone was sobbing and screaming.

Louis finally found the solution. As the burial performance continued — because that was no burial, it was a performance of a burial — he took her by the hand and the two of them vanished among the gravestones, while we, silent and grieving, trailed along behind Athena's coffin.

The only thing that comforted my soul during the whole gruesome ceremony was Martha's gaze. It was still fixed on me. I could feel it, even when I wasn't looking at her.

Julia, standing there beside me, was starting to steam.

— What's with her? She's devouring you with her eyes. A hell of a nerve she's got! Why don't you just go ahead and screw her and get it over with? What're you waiting for?

Me, I was watching the doctor who kept his eyes riveted on Panagos until the ceremony was over; he had an ironic half-smile on his face.

As the howl of the ambulance siren came closer — it had come for Antigone — Athena's casket was being lowered into the ground. Martha's eyes were still fixed on me. Eyes full of dreams and despair. Daring me, maybe. Then I looked at her. Tears came to my eyes.

14. THE LAST GOODBYE

— SOONER OR LATER, cousin, everybody has their day of reckoning. Our turn will come. Won't it? Sure, you can put if off, you can pretend it's no concern of yours, you can tell yourself, "Some live, some die," but every time you have a crisis, it hits you like a sucker punch. Just when you're not expecting it, that's when it hits you. Like a ghost or a bad dream, or like a well-dressed gentleman who suddenly sits down beside you uninvited and begins admonishing you, insolently, and you don't dare ask him where the devil he popped up from or what he wants, whatever ... I don't know how or where, but it will hit you, you can be sure of that. Whenever something happens that you can't explain, say you're looking down over a lighted city or a dark sea from on high at night, and all you can hear is the distant roar of the waves and you're alone, really alone, no alibis, no excuses, face to face with yourself, then, whoever you are and whatever you're doing, it will hit you and there'll be nothing you can do about it, cousin. Maybe you're soused, roaring drunk; maybe you're a beggar or a big shot, the king of kings himself. It'll hit you and that'll be that. It'll hit you like sudden nausea, like gas, like a lump in the throat you can't get down, and that'll be that. You can play the tough guy, you can shrug it off, tell yourself, "Don't let it bother you, just live life one day at a time," but you won't convince anyone. You're whistling in the dark, you don't believe a word of it. So what if you've got a reputation, if you're a big success, if you're swimming in pools of money, bankbooks, credit cards and

347

stock options, if you believe in God and metempsychosis, if you mess around with metaphysics and the afterlife, still it'll hit you, just when you least expect it. You'll be stretched out in your chaise-longue by the pool with bimbos lounging around, with soft music playing and crystal glassware tinkling, with your plans for the future and your big mirrors; but don't worry, it'll hit you. A tiny insignificant little pain just below the heart, an ever-so-tiny pinch deep in the bones somewhere between your kidneys and your liver, that's all it takes; you've got the message.

Maybe the crisis will pass. Then, since you think you're clever, you'll rub your hands with delight. "Well, we got through that one," you'll say, "that wasn't it," and you'll forget about everything. Of course you will. But don't kid yourself. You only got an extension. Don't deceive yourself, don't go thinking, "That was it, it's past. Lightning never strikes twice." Because then, just when you've made it big, just when you've signed that once in a lifetime contract, just when you got the big signature, just when you've got the other guy where you want him, bang, it'll hit you, the fucker, and this time will be the last time, the ultimate, as they say, and that'll be well and truly it; forget the alibis, forget the fancy stories. The well-dressed gentleman? He was you. You didn't notice? Look out for that little pinch; most of the time you won't even know what hit you, most of the time you won't have time to think back over your life, people, things. And of course, you won't be man enough even then to admit how wrong you went. To put it bluntly, cousin, there's no way to escape. Picture yourself driving along in a car down a wide, straight highway, gobbling up the miles and the landscapes and the colors, fiddling with the radio knobs until you pick up the sounds of beautiful music and you're whistling, not a care in the world; "we're going great," you're saying to yourself. "Look what I got, the great looking piece of ass I had my eye on," and there she is, sitting right there beside you. "The stock market went up, couldn't be finer!" and you're singing along and gunning it and whistling and intoxicated and all of

348

a sudden, bang, the pain, or worse, you hit a hole in the pavement just where you least expect it, you never could have believed that hole was made just for you. And in a flash you're a pile of wreckage. There go your plans, the car's lying upside down in the ditch and you with your guts spilling out. Don't even think about it, cousin.

Louis was in a state of rare excitement that day. How was I to know it would be the last time I would see him? It was at Lambros' ouzo joint, the place where we'd agreed years ago to meet as long as we lived, to talk over our troubles: "But we've got to spit everything out, cousin, everything. Can I count on you?" "Everything. Count on me." And we shook hands as we stood there, looking out over the water and he said, "You'll never see it motionless, cousin," and suchlike. There's where I met him.

The meeting had been preceded by one of those unexpected phone calls of his at the most awkward possible times.

— You busy? Come on down, let's talk.

Fortunately I got to the phone first. Julia lunged for it, but I beat her.

I didn't realize he was saying goodbye. I was in a rotten mood. It was after those satanic visits of his, with his daughter, to our homes. I don't know what got into me, but I was feeling rotten. I was seeing less and less of my old friends. There was still the odd brain-numbing get-together at Lazaris'. He'd taken to inviting all kinds of new people, intellectual assholes, university technocrats, arid, angst-ridden people. But it was all public relations, to repay social obligations. He was campaigning full out for a full professorship. A whole lifetime he spent, in pursuit of that chair. Phew! We were fed up with the whole damn story.

The little scum, he had the votes counted. He would invite a potential supporter, with his own personal clique, to every reception. The whole thing had to go according to plan.

Forget it ... Our old get-togethers — just us, the guys in the gang — were almost a thing of the past. But even though life had torn off our masks and our true characters showed

349

through, naked and slimy, even then, still, a minuscule tongue of flame from our "bygone glories" flickered inside us, and sometimes, at those get-togethers, it would flare up.

In any case, something still held us together, maybe remnants of a tiny sense of trust kept friendship alive; those evening encounters still meant something.

And so it was that Louis' phone call found me totally unprepared, feeling out of sorts. There was no more room to turn; even my illusions had vanished. "Lucky we got this far. Mustn't be ungrateful."

We'd buried ourselves in cynicism, in pettiness; we never solved the great mystery of the world; the questions remained unanswered, implacable: How could you live this way, why? You were looking for another road, for another meaning, but you rang the wrong doorbells, knocked on the wrong doors, went down the wrong streets, loved the wrong people, slept in the wrong beds, lived in the wrong houses. Why such contempt for your dreams? Your ideals? What the hell ...

Anyway, as I said, Louis' phone call came at the wrong time. I was unprepared; tried to put the meeting off.

— Can't we make it some other day, Louis?

— Nope, cousin. Last chance.

I hadn't seen him for a while. None of the dirty old men had heard a thing about him. Agis was gone; he was my one source of regular information, even if it was only by telephone. He knew the invisible threads that connected me with Louis.

Slowly but surely, as we talked, Louis gained the upper hand. Something began to awaken inside me, a faraway sound ... At first it was like a military march, then like distant music drawing closer. It reminded me of Bach, or was it a saxophone, playing late at night?...

The sound was getting louder, louder.

— OK, I'm on my way, I tell him.

— I'm ordering, sonofabitch. Time you get here, the ouzo, the food and the moon will be served. It's a full moon tonight. Remember? Remember your first woman, at the corner next

350

to the power pole, beneath the poplar tree?

Nostalgia flooded over me.

Memories, cries, the whistling of trains, coal dust ... He was chattering away, and meanwhile I was facing backward, toward the past, and slowly sinking: Look, Urania! "Urania, it's your father! Telephone!" and there went Urania, heading for the grocery store on the run. Uncle Anestis, auntie Melpo. He died; she killed herself. Gas.

Now he was onto Maritsa.

— Maritsa, dummy! Aren't you listening? Forgot everything?

— I'm listening. I'm listening.

— She's a proper little housewife nowadays, Maritsa is. Got old. I went to see her. She started to cry when she saw me, but she's lost her looks, goddamn it. Lives downtown, bought an apartment. No one knows her there, just another face. Plays cards with a retired teacher, a former prosecuting attorney and an olive oil merchant. She gets her oil at a discount. Pericles, you know, her son ... disappeared, never came back.

Louis' spell had enveloped me. I had begun to take off. I hadn't even seen him yet and there I was, airborne. Louis the great, the endless, the incredible!

— Alright, alright; I told you I'm coming, but you should have called me the odd time, just so I can hear your voice.

He went on:

— Remember Eugenia, the girl I almost married, Krugas' sister? Her brother's getting out of prison any day now, the skag. He's coming after me, going to kill me, he says; says my debt to his sister has to be paid up. In full. I believe him. He means it. I bet you remember when you and Agis ratted on me, and they came to my place and beat the bejesus out of me? Remember?

— Do I ever!

— What ever happened to Eugenia, anyway? Maybe I'm keeping you?

— Go on!

— Know how she managed? Her brother's in jail, the

351

bakery is sold, mother and father on the street. What's Eugenia supposed to do? She starts screwing the clients from a big uptown travel agency. House calls! Modern stuff. At the Hilton, the Grande Bretagne. But a bout of syphilis puts an end to that line of work. She opens a flower shop; that's what she does today — makes her living as a florist. Go see her. She won't recognize you. She didn't me. Those flowers I brought you that Sunday when I came visiting; bought 'em from her. I looked at her, she looked at me, I paid for the bouquet, and she never even noticed. We can't even recognize ourselves anymore, cousin; we've all turned gray. End of the line! Eugenia, she's in her forties now, but she's still a looker, nobody you'd turn your nose up at.

On and on he went, the words poured out in a torrent.

When we finally ended the conversation, just as I was putting down the receiver, I spotted Julia standing there, purse in hand, dressed up to go out. She was waiting for me to finish my call to tell me she was leaving, she wouldn't be late and that if I decide to go out not to forget to lock the doors, turn on the answering machine, arm the alarm system ...

As she talked to me, I stared at her as if I'd never seen her before. Recently even her features had changed, her teeth were longer. I don't know ... I felt like I didn't know her any more, as if ... She was different. Her clothing was more vulgar. She's trying to attract attention, to please. Showing her breasts, her back, her legs. I remembered Lazaris looking up her skirt.

She didn't so much as mention Louis. Didn't even tell me not to go, like she usually did, not even that ...

— You taking the car? I called out.

— Nope, you can take it. But put in some gas.

She left. At last I'm alone. In an empty house.

352

That's roughly how I described the situation to Louis when we met at Lambros' joint.

— What's getting into me, Louis? All of a sudden, I can't even recognize my own house. Everything's strange, the furniture, the paintings on the walls ... Never seen it before. Can you believe it? I don't like the place, nothing about it. The colors give me a queasy feeling in my stomach. No kidding. The brown ceiling, the yellow paint in my office, the aluminum trim, the mauve flower pots ... everything, everything. The chair legs make me dizzy. Julia's taste, all of it. Sure, sure, we picked it out together, but she was the one who ... The chandelier; ugly, cheap. Gives you heartburn. Only thing I could recognize was my books. "What's happening to me?" I said. I blink my eyes, maybe it's only a passing thing, just a bit of momentary confusion ... No way. It's not going away. And there I am, about ready to burst.

Louis was staring at me. We were drunk, and then some. Stammering and slurring our words. That's when he launched into his speech about the day of reckoning, how it'll hit us, when, whether we like it or not.

It was dark now, and we kept on drinking.

The moment of the last farewell was drawing near.

— I don't want to go home, I said suddenly.

What got into me? It just popped out.

— I can't. End of the line. It's all over.

— Come on, Kostas, my boy. Time to go. If anything's over, it's the fun and games that's over.

— It's all over, I'm telling you. It's like she doesn't exist. No way, I'm telling you, I ain't going.

I insisted. And he looked at me with a broad smile on his face.

— I feel like I never lived ... You understand? Never lived. First off, I never did anything really evil in my life, never dared to really hurt someone. Not once. I wanted to hurt someone, just once. To know myself better. Hurt someone, and have it turn into a nightmare, into a straitjacket. Maybe that would relieve me.

353

Louis was getting excited. He looked at me as if he could hardly recognize me.

— At last, Kostas, my boy! Just once, throw off your collar, leave your cares behind.

I was more than slurring my words; I was semi-delirious by now. Him too. The words were coming out in bits and pieces, I could sense it, but I couldn't stop.

— No kidding. I can feel it. Doing evil tempers you, brings you face to face with the universe, with chaos. Maybe then you'll discover how much you want everybody else to do good, how much you want to make sense out of the chaos.

What was I saying? Damned if I can remember. I wanted to say something meaningful; something earthshaking was on the tip of my tongue but mostly I was rambling, the words wouldn't come out straight, I meant something else when I said evil.

Again I'm telling him, "I never lived, never even hit the target, life slipped through my fingers, not life, what the hell, we've had our life, one way or another, it's behind us, in front of us, nope, I mean the other thing, the one you can't put your finger on, the one you leave at the outskirts of your mind, in the deepest depths. Discard it, file it away, forget about it, don't even think about it, even if you know deep down that's where the heart of the matter is. Waiting for you, at the next turn, waiting to hit you, that day of reckoning you're talking about."

— Come on, Kostas, my boy; on your feet. When you sober up, think it over again. Now let's go home.

— No way; I ain't going. I got no home.

— Kostas, my boy, if you're thinking I'm going to put you back on God's road, you've got another think coming. No way I'm going to be your father confessor, no way I'm going to beg you, "Come on, forget the wild ideas and go on home"; no way, I'm not going to do it, cousin.

— Louis, you know what I'm saying?

And I droned on, "I'm not going home, not me ..."

— Look, don't get the idea I'm the happiest guy in the gang

354

just because you all think being happy is my hobby. And get off my back with that "I'm not going" stuff, will you, 'cause you'll only come to grief, you're not ready for it. Forget the fine words.

— It's not fine words. I'm a stranger. I don't belong; the milk's curdled.

— Have to do it your way, eh? Well in that case, don't look back. Can you handle it? Because if you can't, she'll land on you, hard. Make up your mind. Choose which side you're on. Jerk.

I started to stammer again, something about curdled milk. But in spite of my drunkenness, I avoided going into the details of my relationship with Julia. I was ashamed. I wanted to tell him how contemptuously she was treating me, about the time I threw up at Liakopoulos' place. But I didn't. All I told him was that Julia seemed more and more like a whore, that nothing was sacred, there were no limits.

He looked at me as though he couldn't understand what I meant. Then, he lit into me.

— Manolopoulos, just forget it, will you. You and those idiotic fears of yours; a whole lifetime goes by and you, you never got to know your son ... She's dried you up, Julia has? Well, good for her. She's paying for your mistakes too, not just you. Serves you right, idiot.

— I went, Louis, just a second. I went to see him, my son. Comes a time when a man grows up; it takes time, but he grows up. I went to see him.

Louis stopped short. He hadn't expected that. Again he looked at me as if he didn't understand what I meant. Then he spoke:

— Kostas, my boy, I promised I'd never say another word about it again, that night of orgies with Chrysanthi and Liakopoulos. That asshole Liakopoulos, he was a good-looking fuck back then. Problem isn't that people take time to grow up; problem is most of the time they go backwards. Seriously? You saw him?

— Sure I did. What am I telling you? Haroula doesn't hate

355

me anymore, or at least, not so much. She's changed. Maybe she's sorry for me. Probably.

— Kostas, my boy, you're makin' me cry. That's more like it. Would have been the mistake of your life. You've taken a load off my mind. I never told you about the time she came to me with the kid.

— When I want to forget myself, when I want a moment of peace and quiet, I go visit them. She's living in Psychiko now. With her shipowner. They offer me a cup of coffee, or a glass of orange juice. Julia doesn't know anything about it, of course. I've "recognized" the kid. I want him to have my name. Now, in hindsight, I don't regret a thing, Louis Konstantinos was born in a moment of beauty, or more like a moment of passion, I guess that's what I mean. Everything has happened just as it should have happened. Probably. I've been wanting to tell you for a long time, but I lost track of you.

Just then the moon rose. Full, bright-red.

— Whatever I promised is yours, Manolopoulos. Shut up, let the past lie, and look at the sky. All we were missing was the full moon. There it is, all yours.

We were the last customers in the place.

Silence fell; it had turned chilly. Rain was in the air. I wanted to ask him about himself. What was he up to, where was he ... But I forgot, forgot myself.

The two of us stared at the moon. Sad, silent. Then I began to belch.

15. LIFE FRAGMENTS

IT WAS ALMOST DAYBREAK when Louis brought me home in a state of general paralysis. Julia refused to touch me, refused to show the slightest interest. Spitting contempt and disgust all over us, she ostentatiously gathered up her sheets and blankets and stalked off to sleep on the couch in the library.

— You made a mess of him, you look after him, was all she said to Louis as she slammed the door behind her.

He laid me down on the bed, pulled off my shoes and trousers. I'd forgotten my jacket at Lambros' joint.

I didn't want him to leave.

— Don't go. Take me with you. I've got to get out of here; I'm not staying. See her? For a whole lifetime she's been trying to cut me down to her size. How can you love someone if they're always trying to cut you down?

On and on I rambled, until I drifted off to sleep.

I dreamed of a full moon, of Agis, Julia and Martha. She — Martha — was dancing naked on the terrace of her family home, in Piraeus. The moon behind her cast such an intense light that I couldn't make out her face. It was a hard white light, the color of chalk. Not far away a goose-necked desk lamp threw its light over her, a crimson light, the color of blood; she was drenched with blood. The terrace was more like a cabaret. With a dance floor, an orchestra — I couldn't see it — and tables. The spectators were wearing white scarves and top hats. I couldn't make out the faces. The moonlight was blinding me. It was immense. There was a wind blowing too. Far away, I could hear Mahler's *First Symphony*. I'd heard it

357

a few days ago at Liakopoulos' place. Martha had put it on to play. We were chatting away, while she was listening to Mahler's *First*. Was it coincidence? I seem to recall telling her one time how much I liked Mahler, and now there she was, listening to Mahler. Mahler's *First* at that.

Agis was climbing an endless spiral staircase toward the moon. Up, up he went, his eyes fixed all the while on a particular spot on the terrace. I looked as well. But Martha was dancing precisely in front of that spot, hiding it from my field of vision. Slowly I began to make out Julia, seated in the shadows in an armchair; her skirt was pulled up, her legs were spread wide. In front of her stood a man with his pants down. I couldn't see his face. Only his back and buttocks. Suddenly the music got louder. I tried to cover my ears and then, magically, came a strange silence, not a sound could be heard, and everything — people and things — simultaneously came to a stop, turned to statues. Even the moon. Icy, frozen solid. "You won't get away from me now," I thought and tried to stand up, to identify the man standing in front of Julia. Impossible. I too had become a statue. I strained mightily. But no movement came, no sound. Then, in the midst of that immobile universe, Martha began to move once again, as if in slow motion, like when they want to prettify the action in a film. Then she began to disappear. I tried to cry out, to tell her not to go. No use. I was a statue and she was slipping away, vanishing.

I woke up exhausted, in a cold sweat. When I managed to open my eyes, I found a tray next to the bed, and on it, breakfast. "Can't help twisting the knife in the wound, can you, you old slut?"

It was Sunday. No work today. I was cold.

I got up and threw a heavy sweater over my shoulders. I still had my socks on.

358

The door was closed. I opened it a crack. Barely. Silence.

— Julia! I called out.

No one. "What does she care, anyway?"

I left the bedroom. All the other doors in the house were open. It was empty. "Who knows where she's screwing around?" I was still under the influence of the dream. What a dream. My boyhood home was sold years ago, Agis is gone, and a simple terrace turns into a monstrous cabaret!

But even as I thought about the dream, I could feel yesterday's nausea welling up inside me again.

I couldn't touch a thing.

Back in the bedroom. I reached out my hand toward the coffee cup. Then pulled back. "Same old dirty tricks. Been at it for half a lifetime. Breakfast in bed — just what I need."

Panic surged up in me. The stereo was off, but I heard Mahler's *First* playing in the distance, just as in the dream.

I couldn't go on living like this. But what should I do? When we got back to the house the day I vomited at Liakopoulos' place, she announced: "Look, I'm not going to take any more insults. I didn't say anything in front of your friends — but never again. The whole group can't be all wrong and only you right! That friend of yours, he's done everything he can to break us up, to stop us from marrying; now it looks like he's finally going to succeed. But I want you to know, I never could understand why you always backed him up."

Someone was ratting on me. She must have been meeting secretly with someone who was feeding her information. Who told her about Agis' epistle. Who told her about the time Liakopoulos and me put up the money to get Louis out on bail after Fatmé died in the crash? "I found out. Cost you sixty thousand, and you'll never get it back." No way Liakopoulos would have told her. He knows how to keep a secret. So? Couldn't have been Martha; impossible. They never phone one another. She knew about Haroula. "You think I don't know what's going on? That you had a kid with her? That you still see her? That's what I heard. But don't you dare bring that bastard of yours around here."

I pretended not to understand a word. "Who's Haroula? What kid are you talking about?" I denied everything, gutless wonder that I am. Everything.

She made a cutting remark about Martha, but I was still struggling to defend Louis.

— What did Louis ever do to you for you to hate him so much? Maybe you really had your eye on him, and now you're taking revenge because you couldn't get him? Or maybe you did?

— Whatever I did, I'm glad I did it, the old tart replied.

On purpose she didn't deny it, just to give me ideas.

I sat down on the bed. Idly I reached out for the coffee cup, but quickly put it down as soon as I realized what I was doing. "Not even your coffee!" And half the contents slopped out onto the dresser top.

"Who gives a damn what she thinks." She'll give me shit for destroying auntie's embroidery.

And suddenly I realized, for the second time, that I was a stranger in my own house.

"Why else would I feel so terrorized ... a stranger." I felt a slight tightening in the chest. "Guilt, all I feel is guilt, god-damn it."

Mahler's *First* was still playing.

"I'm going crazy, that must be it. That's where I'm headed; where they hear music from nonexistent orchestras."

— How does Lazaris do it without a woman? What's his secret? Sure, he jerks himself off. But for an entire lifetime?

I threw that one in her face, I recall, when she held him up as an example of success in life, in business. Mainly I wanted to test her reaction. He was the one I suspected.

— You're disgusting, she said.

— We're not going to his place again. What does he want with us, anyway?

— You can stop going if you want. Not me. Go to Liakopoulos' place and watch your sweetheart drink herself under the table.

I got up again. Watered the flowers. They were already

watered, but I did it again. I always seemed to end up acting out my anger on the flowers.

"Don't water them again, they'll rot," she said.

"How did I ever manage to live with this woman? How did I make love to her? How ..."

As I watered, millions of how's rushed into my mind. How this, how that? Not too long ago I saw a Strindberg play where a couple keeps on putting off the final crisis of their relationship, until finally they turn into mummies.

I threw down the watering can and went into the house. Stood there, motionless, imagining what I would look like as a mummy, propped up on a footstool in dirty pyjamas, broken-down slippers, unwashed, unshaven, thin, almost skeletal, with a glassy, idiotic stare on my face, perpetually staring at the same painting on the wall as if behind it, behind the wall, far away, lay a world of wonders.

I shuddered.

Around me the walls, the furniture, the trinkets, the photographs awakened nothing in me, no memories, no emotions.

Only nausea. Same as yesterday.

I'm trying to describe my every movement as accurately as I can; I want you to understand my feelings — do I leave or stay? I want to bring all the colliding impulses within me to the surface, panic at the thought of leaving, panic at the thought of staying.

I brought my big suitcase down from the closet, opened it; that touched off the angst.

A hundred times I told myself it's now or never, I'm leaving. A hundred times I held back, uncertain, torn by doubt.

Imagine, me picking up my shaving gear and putting it down. Pulling the underwear out of my drawer and putting it back.

"Where are you going, imbecile?" I wondered aloud. "Where?"

I ran to the phone to call Louis. I had to talk to him. A man's voice answered; all but told me to go to hell.

— Isn't that the Retsinas' residence?

— Yep.

— Louis' place?

— That's right, but don't call for Retsinas, for nobody called Retsinas, snapped the voice, and slammed down the phone angrily.

Strange. We were together yesterday; he hadn't said a thing to me about his house, nothing about leaving, nothing about any quarrel.

I had to do something, talk to someone. Martha. I called Martha. Liakopoulos answered. I hung up.

I rang Louis again.

— I thought I told you? You want me to tell you to fuck off?

I asked to speak to Louis' wife, Litsa.

— She's asleep.

And he hung up again. "What the hell is going on, anyway?"

I sat down again on the stool, the one I imagined myself seated on as a mummy. I stretched my arms, my legs ...

It was all I could do to breathe. I felt like crawling back into bed, sleeping for days, months, years; I wanted to stop thinking, to vanish.

Suddenly I felt the whole house closing in on me; the furniture was growing larger and the house was shrinking.

The walls were closing in, the ceiling was collapsing. Bizarre stuff.

I felt an onrush of panic. "I'm going crazy. That must be it." "What's going on?" I muttered. "Could this be the end of me?"

Meantime, everything was in abeyance. The suitcase lay there gaping open. Shirts, underwear, shaving gear were strewn about.

"If she walks through the door right this minute and sees

362

me like this, God help me.''

She'd help me fill the suitcase herself and throw it out the door. ''No one's holding you back,'' she'd say as she dumped it on the landing. She'd even ring for the elevator.

''If I don't leave now, it's all over. How will I ever find the nerve again?''

''Where the hell could she have gone, bright and early Sunday morning? Doesn't give a shit. Couldn't even be bothered to leave me a note. It's all sweetness and light with auntie Eustathia these days, all billing and cooing, the two of them. They're plotting against me.''

''I'm leaving, that's all there is to it. But where will I go? Fine, so I fill up my suitcase, take along a couple of suits ...''

I felt sorry for my books. She won't let me have a thing. ''It's now or never.'' They're full of notes, ideas, thoughts. Forget about the records, the paintings.

I threw whatever I could into the suitcase. Was the phone in my name? I could put up with just about anything as long as I had a phone ... ''She won't let me have it, the shrew. And we've got two lines. Won't give me a single one. Unless it's in my name.''

I searched frantically for a phone bill. Damned if I could remember. In my panic I could find nothing. I yanked cupboards and drawers open; nowhere, nothing.

And all the while, ''You asshole, time's flying, what are you going to do, stay or go? If you're staying, hide the stuff; at least she won't see what you were doing. Another humiliation you can do without.''

I tried to hide the suitcase. Stopped. Once again I realized that nothing belonged to me. Everything was hers. And she'll demand alimony. Lawsuits, courts, witnesses.

No problem for Louis. He's gone. Wonderful.

''Who the hell was that, the guy who just about told me to fuck off?''

— Cousin, you'll die of cancer, you know that? Decide what you want. If you're comfortable, fine. Enjoy yourself. But one thing for sure, you can't keep walking the razor's edge.

363

— I dream about her death. Or I catch her screwing some guy and spit on her, or I look on as she dies.

Now, bits and pieces of our talk at Lambros' ouzo joint are coming back. Got to go pick up my jacket, the one I left there.

"I'll grab the car; at least it belongs to me. It's in my name."

The thought of the car gave me courage.

"If worst comes to worst, I'll sleep in the car ... make do until something comes along."

I tried to think of a friend, a good friend, somebody I could talk to. Liakopoulos? No way. Things just aren't the way they used to be between the two of us, and I don't want Martha feeling sorry for me. Lazaris? What a joke. Me, show up at his place and catch them in bed, hard at it.

I was sure he was the one. Why? He'll be underneath, and she'll be on top. Her favorite position. "She likes being in charge." That's how Agis put it.

"Gone, Agis is gone." Should I call Antoniadis? Him? No. He'll only look for an opening to go after me, call me a sellout, say I'm no different from the other big shits. What music! Mahler's *First*. I could hear it so clearly I'd have sworn it was a record playing on the stereo.

"Come on, you asshole, get it over with. Don't try to make it look good, don't try to get off easy. No house, no woman, OK; but get it over with, over with."

Imagine, looking for a woman. Can't live without a woman. The world shrinks, you stop dreaming. Wait a second. You dream all that much with Julia? Love-making doesn't even work anymore. So much anger, how can you even bear to take her? And if you go looking for it, you're giving in to her, she starts getting ideas and then it's back to square one, you're doing it on her terms.

It struck me that lately, in spite of everything, the bitch was more attractive than usual. Maybe it was her crudeness that excited me. When I take her, it gives me an unbelievable charge. Maybe because I'm the master of a body I detest. What is this shit called love, anyway; where does it all fit in?

364

Only two women really wanted me. Haroula and Martha.

Call Louis again. Must have been a mix-up, a satanic coincidence.

Now I get it; he mentioned something about cannibals, stuff like that. Then something about his house; but we changed the subject. What was he saying? Ah, yes, "Spend your life trying to find out why we act the way we do, why people turn into beasts, why we get stuck with worthless ideas, worthless feelings, why we turn so rotten, so false ..." That's when I spoke to him about evil.

— Louis, old buddy, I wanted to understand evil. Why does it happen? For people to do it, over and over again, in cold blood, there must be something evil inside us.

I thought of Martha again. The phone rang and I came to. It must have been ringing for a while without me hearing it. I let it ring until it stopped. If it was Julia, what would I tell her?

Look how things change. During the first years of our marriage, she may have raised her voice, but as soon as she saw I was about to raise mine, she started being nice — anything I need, what would I like to eat? — and backed off, but now, nothing could hold her back.

Then I remembered the bankbooks. We had four. All joint accounts. We kept them in a locked drawer in the dresser.

I reached for the key. Vanished.

"The slut hid it! So, she was expecting me to leave, that's why she hid it. And you're still there, with an enemy, an enemy like that, in the same house? You asshole!"

I grabbed the suitcase and started throwing anything I could find into it. Even tossed in one of Migadis' paintings. A boy sitting on a chair. Reminded me of my childhood. I loved it.

"I'm going to leave her with three million?" I thought to myself. "Am I crazy? Half and half. I can get by on that for a year or two until I settle down."

I turned the dresser upside down.

"I'll bust the bottom of the drawer if I have to!"

365

The phone rang again. I answered.

Get a load of this, pal. I dream about Martha, dancing, and stark-naked at that. You're saying, sure, I knew what she looked like. But I only knew her breasts. She never wears a bra, and when she bends over it all shows. Wait, maybe I did see her once. When she was young, at Argyris'.

As I pick up the phone I'm thinking about Martha.

— Yes?

It was her. Julia. Just like I expected. She'll be late, she said. Gone to look at a couple of display cabinets. After, she'd be going straight to auntie Eustathia's. She's ill. Suddenly took sick last night.

— You'd better come and see her, right now.

Auntie had moved into her own place. Sold two pieces of land and bought it outright. To be willed to Julia. Along with the three-storey house in the north end. And another lot by the water. If and when auntie kicks the bucket, Julia's in the money.

— You hear me? What are you waiting for? she shouted. Get over there fast, daddy says so. She's breathing her last. We'll all be beside her. I'm worried she'll change the will at the last minute.

— Daddy says so, does he?

— Don't try to be sarcastic; you think you're so selfless all of a sudden? In fact, you never were really selfless at all, you were always keeping count ... I'll be at her place. I'm late.

I wanted to tell her to go fuck herself, tell her if I was counting on auntie's inheritance it was my mistake, because it would all be hers, not mine.

But I didn't say a word. Only asked her about the drawer, why she took the key.

— No way. You think I'm going to let you use our good money to bail out your pal.

The same old song and dance. I'd sure as hell like to know who ratted on me.

My mind was whirling as she babbled on.

— You hear the latest about your pal? Didn't he tell you

366

anything yesterday? Hiding it from you, is he? Want to know? Well go ask him ...

I hung up. In the meantime, I'd pried the bottom off the drawer.

I found one hundred thousand in cash. Remembered Martha. She had the most gorgeous breasts I'd ever seen. Even today.

Everything came together. Counting the money, her breasts, the *First*, Louis.

"What's he up to now, the sonofabitch? The whore, go ask him if I want to find out, she tells me."

"So I knocked out the drawer bottom. Good for me." Did it with a brass pestle. The one we kept in the living room, for decoration. "Good for me." "No turning back now. I've got to make things happen."

I took the two bankbooks and fifty thousand cash. Exactly half. Counted it.

I only tore the photos I really liked from the album. Including one with Martha. It showed the three of us: me, Louis and her. She's in her swimsuit. Agis is in the picture too. Squatting in front. We're standing behind. It was taken at the Seashell Club. I could make out her nipples; almost smell her.

I ran over to the stereo and put on Mahler's *First*. Now I wanted to hear it, close up, for real.

One of her breasts had almost popped out and you could see the nipple. It was dark, round.

I started masturbating. Why hide it? Julia was late, and the thought only heightened the enjoyment of my freedom.

When it was over I found myself standing there, spent, prick in hand, in the middle of the living room, standing over the photo of Martha with Mahler's *First* playing in the background. For the first time I felt powerful, liberated.

I looked around; satisfaction and triumph welled up in me. The room looked like a city put to the sack by vandals. Closets gaped open, clothes were strewn about, drawers hung out, paintings leaned against the walls.

The car keys. "If she's got 'em, I'm stuck." Couldn't find the keys. "Means she's got 'em." I ran over to the balcony to see if the car was parked in the street. "No, fuck it! Gone. She's got it!" But at least it was in my name. "I'll get the duplicates, if she hasn't taken them too, and come by another day for the car." Fortunately they were in their hiding place, in a jar of cold cream. I grabbed them.

No way I can stay here. When she sees the dresser ripped open, what will she say? She'll put two and two together and my life will be pure hell."

"I'm losing time. What will I do?" "Leave, get out; don't stick around."

I rushed over to my desk and gathered up my writing, all of what I'm telling you now, stuff I've been jotting down on scraps of paper. Almost forgot it. She didn't like that either. Me writing. She even told the gang, or rather, Lazaris.

"He spends hours just writing. What could it be?" she'd have said.

That turd, Lazaris, can't trust the bastard.

And they mocked me. But after the reading of Agis' epistle they also began to fear me; who knew how much of their dirt I'd drag up.

Call mom. "If worst comes to worst, I can stay at her place." Didn't occur to me. No, wait. Voice of caution. "Stay home, don't go doing anything foolish. What did the poor woman ever do to you?" "Forget her, she'll be the last to know."

Suddenly I realize I don't have a friend I can talk to, open my heart to.

I dial Drakopoulos. Without thinking. Just like that. He's home. He hates Louis but he kind of likes me, kind of respects me.

— You're doing what? Leaving? Are you nuts? For years you've been eating shit and now, your aunt is croaking and

368

the two of you are going to strike it rich, now you're ?... Forget it, stay where you are. Isn't it a bit late, Manolopoulos? A few years ago, fine, go ahead, make your move; but now? Won't be long before you'll be getting around on crutches.

I'd told him about some curious blue swellings on my legs. He remembered.

— Get 'em looked after, find out if it's arteries or veins.

— Mom would tell me the same thing; stay.

— Me, I got problems of my own with Tatyana. The kid, whose kid is it? I'm stuck. I stayed, and now you call up to tell me that ...

— What? You can swear mine's not fooling around?

— How do you know? You don't. Even if she does, it's the same as if she doesn't.

— Oh really?

— Damn right. Me, I know, but how can I prove it?... Agis isn't alive, and he's the only one who could prove I'm telling the truth, who could tell me his sources. But just try and find him in the great beyond. Sit tight, forget all about it ...

— Bye-bye, I said and hung up.

Suddenly, through the window I spotted the neighbor from across the way, pacing back and forth on his balcony, wearing gray pyjamas. We rarely greeted one another. A quiet man. Professor at the Technical Institute; retired, alone.

Every few steps he would stop, stare out toward the sea then start pacing again. He would have been visualizing the sea, is what I mean to say. You couldn't see it for the smog, the cloud. "What's he doing? Is he crazy?" Every minute or so he put his hand to his forehead as if to shade his eyes from the sun, and stared off into the distance. What sun? The sky was leaden, dark; it was going to rain any second.

Don't ask me how long he'd been at it. Just spotted him this minute, myself.

"Like you said, Agis, old pal, it ain't easy for your friend to take a seat on the right hand of God, close to Louis. It's tough."

On and on I go and still, here I am. It's as if I can hear him, Agis, giving me courage. "What are you worried about, imbecile? You've got a job, they can't take that away from you. What's the problem? Make your move. What will happen? You're going to die for that place? Me, I'm dead and I don't regret a thing. Why should you?"

The phone rang. "If it's her again I'll curse her out. I just want to be left alone." No, it wasn't. Unbelievable. It was Martha! Now there's a coincidence. Can you imagine! Martha!

— Hi!

That's how she began.

— Martha?

It was the last thing I expected: a phone call from Martha. Mahler's *First* was still playing. The most powerful part. The final movement. She hardly ever called me at home, and only when she was certain Julia was out. Maybe she'd called once or twice in all these years. Damn. And today she decides to call? Strange things going on today, strange.

The smell of her perfume came back to me, her dance in the dream, her breasts ...

— I was looking at your photo two minutes ago. You won't believe it. The one with Louis at the Seashell Club. He called it a porn shot. Remember?

— I had a copy too, but your friend, Liakopoulos, ripped it up. After Agis' letter he tore up all my photos with you and him.

— Martha!

I had so much to tell her, and here I am like an idiot, all I can do is repeat her name.

Look that, will you. Coincidence. Phones me just when I'm thinking of calling her.

My neighbor was still pacing back and forth on his balcony For no rhyme or reason.

But why does life have to have a reason? What's it to me if it does? No reason. Try to give it one and you kill off your natural instincts, you're trapped. I'm sick of searching for reasons. The hell with it.

Him — my neighbor — he's just fine. All he has to do is let himself go. No doubt about it, he'd like to have some reason to live and because he can't find one, look at him. Whether he jumps or not, it's all the same. Even if he doesn't, he may as well have. I won't try to stop him. What would it be like to finally make up your mind and then, just as you're about to jump, someone stops you?

— You're listening to Mahler's *First*?

— Yeah. I'm listening to the *First* and watching the man on the opposite balcony. Been pacing back and forth for hours. For no reason. He's probably about to dive off.

— Don't stop him.

— No. That's what I was thinking. Where are you, aren't you at home?

— Why?

— I hear strange sounds. You've got the TV on? Ah, Martha, I should tell you about this dream I had. I've been thinking about you.

— Me too.

Her voice was still sweet.

— Ah, Martha! I repeat.

— Listen ... Hold onto that photo. I'd like to see it. Send it to me, will you?

What's she saying? Send it where?

— What're you watching? A war movie? I hear planes. No. Sounds like ships' whistles.

— I'm not feeling so great, Manolopoulos.

— Martha, if only you knew ...

— I know, why shouldn't I know? What can you know that I don't?

— What's wrong?

— I'm not feeling so good. Isn't that enough.

— You want to leave, is that it?

371

— Could be. What made you think that? Go where?

— Where? Right?

Her breathing told me more than her words. Heavy. They came out with difficulty.

— He's ready to jump. I can see him. He's leaning over.

— Let him. If it was me, you'd let me go.

— Martha!

There, I was stuck on her name. Not a word more. What was I supposed to say? A whole life gone by, and all the things I should have said, I never did.

Martha was in her forties now. A few dark blotches on her face. She was still good-looking, but the booze was starting to show; her back was a bit hunched, the flesh hung from her arms a bit, her muscles were a bit soft, but her breasts were still breasts. Upright, round, firm.

Liakopoulos must have been jealous of the porn shot; why else would he tear it up? For sure. He was pure reactionary, the creep.

The dark circles under her eyes had grown larger. Always had dark circles under her eyes, Martha did. And when she walks, she doesn't shake and shimmy like she used to. Whatever became of that proud, haughty walk of hers? What a combination! Sensuality and pride.

I was jealous of Liakopoulos. "Don't throw your life away, Manolopoulos." That's what Louis always said. I didn't listen. Back then with Haroula, it was the same line. "Don't throw your life away." It was at "Dorothy's," in Piraeus he said it.

— Are you alone?

— Alone. Why?

— To see you, Martha, I'd like.

My throat is constricting, my words are coming out in the wrong order.

— And what'll come of it, Manolopoulos?

— Right, what will come of it.

A long pause and then I start telling her about the crisis I'm going through, about Julia, about the suitcase lying there

372

open in front of me, me leaving and not leaving.

— Martha, you hear me? Martha. I called your place, but your husband answered and I hung up.

The man is still pacing.

— You know something? I made myself a bet, if he keeps on like that, I'm leaving, not staying. I'm leaving home. Forever. Martha. Martha?

She'd hung up. Wasn't even listening. I step out onto the balcony. Stand there, just across from the man. Look at him. He stops. Our eyes meet for a fraction of a second. Then he starts pacing again.

I go inside. Close the balcony door. It had begun to rain.

"Maybe I should call the police, or maybe his family."

I pick up the phone. Dial Martha. Offhand, almost. Wanted to ask her why she hung up. It rings, rings. No answer. I let it ring.

"Why did she hang up? Maybe she started to cry?" There was a sob in her voice! She couldn't take it; had to hang up. That's it. The phone is still ringing. Just as I'm about to hang up Liakopoulos answers. For a second I don't know what to think. I almost put down the phone, but it's too late, a "hello" slips out.

He recognizes me. I ask for Martha.

— Are you completely nuts, Manolopoulos? Julia didn't tell you?

— No. Tell me what? She's out. I was asleep. Just woke up.

— Here I am tearing my hair waiting for your call, and you pretend you don't know what's going on? Don't give me that stuff, Manolopoulos. Always trying to have it both ways. I was on my way to your place, just caught me going out the door.

"What's he saying? I don't get it."

How is it I didn't tell him I'd just been talking with Martha a few seconds ago? That's my style. Absent-minded, naive, plain dumb; that's me.

— You hear me? he roars.

— I hear you, what is it?

— Can't you understand? Martha left home. Walked out

373

yesterday. Julia didn't say a word about it? What's the matter with her?

The slut. She knew and didn't say a word. On purpose. Figured out the connection; what's to stop him from doing the same thing, she says to herself. One thing's for sure, she didn't forget.

I'd never seen Liakopoulos in quite such a wild state. No, not seen. Heard.

— Didn't she go to the office? I ask.

— Office? What office, Manolopoulos? Quit playing the babe in the woods, will you. She hasn't been to the office in weeks. When she goes out by herself she comes back plastered. The cops bring her in, or passers-by, or neighbors. What else would you like to know? Sometimes they find her down at the harbor, sometimes at the airport, staring at the sea or at the sky. I've had it, up to here. She can fucking leave anytime she wants to; just get it over with. Wait a second, Manolopoulos, you're not going to put one over on me. You're playing dumb, but something's brewing. She always confided in you. Always liked you, even if ... It's all in Agis' letter, isn't it? When she's drunk or when we get in a fight, you know how many times she's come out with it? "OK, so I like him; what of it." Know how many times she's thrown those words in my face?

It was then that I realized how much more easily we puke up the truth about ourselves over the phone. When you're face to face with someone, the doors are closed and locked, you clam up; but on the phone you can talk, you can forget what you're doing, you can get carried away.

After all, it's the presence of the other that terrifies us. The closer he comes, the more frightened you get; you start avoiding him, start backing up.

How many times has it happened lately? I'll be talking with someone and suddenly I forget where I am, my mind starts to wander. Right now, as Liakopoulos talks, my mind is wandering, on and on; I only catch his last few words.

— Speak up! What's the matter with you? I asked you? Who

374

were you with yesterday, Louis or Martha? You've got to know that at least.

— Louis.

— Until the next morning? Get off my back, Manolopoulos. If you were with her, fine, go ahead and tell me, and I won't go looking for her, making a fool of myself. I'll understand; good luck and good riddance. Drunk or sober, Martha's something else; I still love her, but if it ... She never really loved me — it was more convenience — I know. She just wanted to get away from something.

"Get a load," I'm thinking, "of what people will spit out over the telephone. In front of me, he wouldn't dare say a word."

— But if you really don't have an idea ... I'm afraid she'll do something crazy, that's why I'm asking ... do you know anything?

I remember Martha's words when I told her about the guy across the street, "If it was me, you'd let me go."

— Speak up, what do you know! shouted Liakopoulos.

I'd drifted off again.

— No, how should I know anything?

I resist. Don't let on about her call. Did she take the car, I ask.

— What am I telling you all this time? Of course she took it. It's hers. That's what scares me; what if she's drunk, ends up in a wreck? The streets are slippery.

I hadn't heard a word he said.

— Anyway, if you hear anything, call.

Maybe they'd had a little spat, I ask, maybe that was the reason.

— Sure, all the little spats you like ... If I don't slap her around a bit, she'll be wandering the streets all day long. But she's never been out all night before. Everything infuriates her. Me, the gang, your wife. Never invite Moschos to our place again, same for Lazaris. "We're not going into seclusion, are we Martha?" I'm supposed to apologize to Louis, she says. "No way I'm going to say I'm sorry. First he pays me the

375

bail money he owes me then maybe ..." And then the fun starts. Sure I give her a smack the odd time. Hell, Manolopoulos, I bring home the bacon and she ... When you get down to it, Lazaris has everybody kissing his ass. You should know better than me. You think it's easy to get rid of him? Try telling Julia to drop him. You won't even dare.

That "You should know better than me" really kills me. In other words, I hang around him for the same reasons? Is that it?

— So, speak up. Do you know anything?
— No. Nothing.
— Fine. If you hear any news, call me.
And suddenly he hangs up.

As I put down the phone I see a shadow, motionless, on the glass of the balcony door. I freeze. "Game over," I think. "It is finished." I turn slowly and who do I see? Julia. Who else? She's the only one with keys. She and her aunt.

She can barely swallow. Her mouth is dry.

I stare at her. I swallow hard. "Sure, asshole, you diddled around until ... another unfinished job." "Goddamn son of a fucking bitch!" I muttered to myself. "Might as well take a running leap yourself."

No idea how long she's been there listening. She doesn't say a word. Naturally she could see everything. The mess, the suitcase ...

She goes over and switches off the stereo. Sudden silence. That's it for the *First*. Now all you can hear is the rain. Falling hard. I haven't moved; I'm still standing there, motionless. All she says is:

— Auntie's dead. I tried to phone you, to let you know to hurry on over; I need you. I didn't know what to do. The line was always busy. So I came.

376

— Me, busy? I was only talking with Liakopoulos, just now.

— By the way, I forgot to tell you about Martha.

She doesn't say another word. And starts to pick up the mess. Cool, calm, collected. Putting everything right back where it belongs. Impassive.

I watch her.

She turns the dresser back upright and pushes it into place. Lays a thick piece of cardboard at the bottom of the drawer to cover the hole.

Picks up the photo album and closes it. Later she'll discover how many photos are missing. Hangs the Migadis painting on its hook. A little crooked. I straighten it. Then she bends down to pick up my papers, to stuff them into a plastic bag.

— Don't touch them. Leave them just where they are, I snap maliciously.

She leaves them.

Not a word, the slut, about the mess the house. Expressionless, coldblooded.

But I know her too well. She's toting it all up to throw back at me one day when we're sitting there eating, watching TV, me with my slippers and pyjamas on. Julia plans her attacks for moments of calm, when the sea subsides, when exhaustion sets in, when you're unarmed; then she pounces.

— Get dressed. Put on your gray suit; we're going to auntie's. Want me to fix you something to eat?

— I don't want any food.

I don't put on gray, of course. Brown instead. A pair of brown slacks with a cream windbreaker.

She's about to make some comment about the color, how it wasn't right for the occasion.

— What's the matter, you're worried auntie will lose her temper? She's not alive to see me, and make some last minute changes to her will.

No answer. On her way to the bedroom she asks me what I did with the car. Couldn't find it anywhere this morning, she says.

— The car?

Then I remember everything. It was at Lambros', right where I left it. I was so far gone that Louis wouldn't let me drive. I fumble through my pockets for the keys.

— Don't bother. I've got 'em, but I couldn't find the car.

She says nothing else. Just goes into the bedroom to change into her mourning clothes. She's prepared for everything. Bought a classy black dress just for the occasion.

"Somebody's got to die," she would have reasoned. "Daddy or auntie." But she took it for granted that she would be the second.

I sit down on the stool — the one I'll be sitting on when I turn into a mummy — and wait for her.

My neighbor on the opposite balcony is still pacing back and forth. Before long I hear an ambulance coming closer, closer, until it comes to a stop. Must have pulled up in front of his apartment block. But the siren keeps on whining demonically.

I think of Martha again. Her labored breathing, the sob in her voice over the phone.

"She dared. She walked out. Goddamn it. Made her break. She's gone, or," and then I begin to wonder where she might be.

For an instant I'm frightened. My mind goes back to her words, "If it was me, you'd let me go." Panic. Could she?... No, impossible. Martha wouldn't kill herself for anything in the world.

Then I get a crazy hunch.

— I know where she is! I almost shout it out. I know. And she knows I know. That's why she asked me to send her the photo. She knows I know. That lousy old hotel in Piraeus. That's where she is, one hundred percent. There's where she spent the night. Where Agis killed himself. That's where they found him. He took her there for the first time, you remember, when she was just a high school student, when we abducted her from Argyris' place. Later he took her home. That's where we took her, Louis, Agis and me; kept her in hiding for the first few days, so Argyris wouldn't be able to find her and take

378

her back. We were looking for a cheap hotel, I remember. No one but Louis and I know the place.

Everybody knew they found Agis' body in a hotel after the suicide, but I'm positive no one knew where it was or what it was called.

She's still in the bedroom, getting dressed. I've got the second pair of car keys in my pocket.

The bedroom door is about twenty feet from where I was sitting.

"No time left. It's now or never, idiot. So auntie never sees you again, big deal! You'll never see her again either. Go for it. Now. No explanations. You want to come back, you can. You don't, you don't. Not a word. Whether she likes it or not. Just a bit of self-respect, asshole. You've got the bank-books. What're you worried about?"

I walk out. Leave the door ajar so as not to make a noise, and walk out.

When I open the door to the apartment building I hear the apartment door slam. So hard the whole building seems to shudder. Picture her state of mind!

I expect her to appear on the balcony, to hear her yell, "Come back, you half-wit, come back!"

Did it before, in other fights.

But she doesn't. I hear nothing. My neighbor is refusing to get into the ambulance. Resisting mightily!

As I turn the corner I can feel his eyes on me. The ambulance siren is still wailing.

16. DESPAIR, TRAVELLING

"... PEOPLE ARE ALWAYS CALCULATING. Better than any calculator ever invented. And I don't only mean money. Sure, there's money, it's everywhere. But there's more; you set up a kind of invisible measuring stick inside you, one with a million tiny gradations, each representing part of your character, and once it's in place you can't take a step without it. You measure, you count, you act. You slice people and things into a thousand pieces, lead them with consummate ease to the firing squad, cut them down and they never even notice the executioner. Who answers to no one. The victim — your victim — will never know why you did what you did. Miss so-and-so, for instance, she will never know why you promised to phone her and didn't, never find out why you married her when you didn't love her or why you didn't marry her when you did. How are they supposed to know everything that goes through your mind before you chop off their heads? At first glance, everything seems calm, humane, civilized; but beneath the surface, the knife is at the bone. We analyze, weigh and act with mathematical exactitude, with microscopic precision. Within a fraction of a second you make countless decisions with thousands of variations and gradations, some for, some against a particular person, a particular thing. All mistakes, of course. Erroneous judgments, repulsive, ridiculous, inhuman, or the contrary — much more rarely — and all according to your calculations. Sometimes you try to slow down your thoughts. You see how filthy you are, how vicious, how disgusting — 'Why doesn't she just croak?' you say, 'so we'll get the house' — but then you think about it again — 'But if she dies, there goes the pension' — and come to another decision, 'Let her live.' Afterward, your own thoughts begin to terrify you but it's too late, you've already had the thought, it's taken on a life of its own, you can't take it back. Sure, it never comes to light, stored away in your own personal archives, in your most secret hiding place, in your sanctum sanctorum; that's one small consolation. We've killed off spontaneity, truth, I'm telling you. Sincerity? Don't make me laugh. Murdered, with malice aforethought. Fine, fine, that's the way it has to be, I know. That survival instinct of yours, that's what makes you act the way you do. But, dammit, we've distorted it, adulterated it, bound and gagged it.''

Those are my thoughts as I hurry through the rain, looking for a taxi, on my way to Martha.

As you can see, it's always easier to be self-critical when you're among friends. I'm convinced that if Agis were still alive he'd be saying: "Come on, Manolopoulos, forget the fine words and get it over with. You left the best scene for the last, anyway, looking for the best spot, but we're running out of patience; get it over with. You wanted Martha, Martha wanted you, but nothing ever came of it, something was always going wrong at the last minute. You think we don't know those tricks. The one where you pile up one obstacle on top of another to make the story more interesting? But don't overdo it, asshole, this is no fairy story; it's your life. Don't you believe for a minute there's any such thing as an impenetrable hiding place. Everything eventually rises to the surface, even corpses; the sea eventually spits them up. Get off my back, will you. Martha knows you well, no matter now much you pretend to ignore it. Louis told you, didn't he? One of these days the whole thing will end up in Martha's bed, that's where it'll end up. So what are you waiting for? How nice and romantic, how convenient it all turned out. The same hotel where I took her the first time, the same place where I put an end to it all — that's where the inevitable will happen.

Listen to Louis, Manolopoulos! Louis is a comic book hero. That's where he came from. Not a thing he didn't foresee. But me, don't think I don't regret a thing. I do, I do, idiot. I was looking for a bit of melodrama myself, thought I'd move her if I died, thought I … But I figured wrong. I forgot how useless the feeling would be, since I'd be dead and gone. So much for my calculations. Well, I calculated wrong. But you saw what my death did? Made a stir. Look at Martha. What a mess. Took to the streets. Now she's discovered Agis, discovered comics. Problem is, she can't take it. The only thing I regret is the melodrama. Same hotel, same room. Sure, it's a bit much. But what a gimmick. You'll see; that's where she is. And that's where you'll find her, the exact same place. Remember the room? Number twelve. Right next to the bathroom. You went up first to have a look. 'No bath, but a view,' you said, 'sea view.' So get on with it. For once in your life, don't go looking for alibis, don't plan everything, don't kill it. Forget the measuring stick and the calculations, follow your destiny. Idiot! I opened the door. What are you waiting for? You'll reap what you've sown all your life. What's wrong with that?''

Look what's happening to me. Talking with Agis! Standing there waiting for a taxi in the rain, drenched to the skin, talking with Agis, with a dead man. Wrap your mind around that, if you can. Regular dialogue, too. His words almost came out aloud.

In the meantime, taxis aren't stopping. Rain is pouring down. It reminds me of when the Retsinas' basement apartment flooded and we had to bail it out with buckets.

I can hardly see a thing. Every so often I wipe my glasses, but they fog right up again.

The taxis whiz by but I can't tell if they have passengers. One stops, but refuses to pick me up.

— No, my good man. Piraeus in this weather?

That's what Louis called Aleka's husband, Anargyros, "my good man." How come I'm remembering all this? Here I am, waiting for a taxi, and my brain is jumping all over the place. Must be something wrong with me. Look, now I'm thinking of Haroula, of my kid, Constantine.

— Taxi! Taxi!

The lousy bum. No fare, still won't stop.

How old is he, anyway, Constantine? Her son? Our son? Now I remember, when I was lonely I went to see them, that's when Martha had flown, when I thought Haroula might be a temporary solution. But all she felt was disgust at the sight of me. How about that for calculation? By the time I got to "Dorothy's" I'd counted and recounted the dangers, the involvements. On the one hand, I liked her body, dreamed about it, and on the other hand, I figure how much I would have to give in return, how could I make everything as painless as possible. "You tight-fisted creep, keep on counting, lay your profits out where we can see them!" A little bit before the bar it occurred to me to turn around. Do I go in, or don't I? And if I do, then what, how?... Calculation on top of calculation, yardstick of shame. Good for her. Shitting on my head was too good for me.

I'll never find a taxi. Nothing's stopping.

— Hey, sonny, I'm heading for Voula. You want?

— No, Piraeus.

— No, sonny boy, someone else is heading in that direction.

I'm drenched to the bone. Every time I venture out from under the newsstand awning I got a fresh soaking. All at once, in the depths of my despair, I hear a voice calling my name. "Come on, Manolopoulos!" A car pulls up a few paces away. I know the voice. Go over. "Hop in, I'll have you in Piraeus in nothing flat. That's where I'm going. Hop in. Mycenae Hotel! That's where you're going, right? Room twelve?"

Who the hell knows where I'm going? Who in the world can possibly know where I'm going this minute? I shiver. As I

383

bend over to look through the open window, my heart misses a beat. Who the hell! I shake my head. Glasses slip off. I catch them in mid-air. Agis. In person. Smiling, ruddy-faced.

Most of the dead we encounter tend to be on the pallid side, with glassy, motionless eyes. Am I crazy? I'm telling you, it's Agis. Agis!

I know what you'll say — the shape I'm in and all — "You're dreaming; it's your imagination ..." Maybe so, but I swear it's Agis I see at that moment.

Cars horns are blaring. Ambulances, trucks, taxis.

As I stand there staring half-lost, half-terrified, mystified, he cries out: "Come on, what are you staring at? Coming? It's me, what's the matter with you?"

I stare at him. "You're too much," he says, guns the motor and speeds away.

A few seconds later, when I've pulled myself together a little, it strikes me maybe it was someone I knew, maybe I thought I heard Piraeus but he meant something else, a word that sounded like Piraeus. Maybe that was it.

But it takes me a while to recover ... "Something's wrong with me. What's going on? Am I losing my memory? My head? Just a petty bourgeois tight-ass, that's me, goddamn it. I'm not ready for this, this leap, better back up, back to the slippers, the job, back to Julia ... What are you looking for beyond the horizon, you asshole? You'll lose your eggs and the basket, that's what. You'll crack. For sure. You're not ready for this. You don't have the guts. Sit tight, turn back, idiot. What is it you're trying to prove?"

I remembered Martha's ironic smile. Julia was right:

— You're getting worse by the day. You're antisocial, you hate everybody who gets ahead, but deep down, you're the worst of the lot.

"I'm the worst, right? Wait a second. Why isn't Lazaris worse than me?"

The panic is deepening. I try to drive out those trivial thoughts, but they rain down inside me like a torrent.

"You're taking on water. How much longer can you stay

384

afloat? It's leaking through all the cracks, idiot. She's on her way. Lazaris; he's going to make his move. Julia's in the money, as of today."

By then I've sunk to cheap comparisons. Who should I choose, Martha or Julia?

I begin to compare their legs ... Julia has perfect thighs. Now I realize it. That's what was holding me. Plumped up a bit, too; not the charmless billiard-cue she once was. Martha is like a leaf, brittle, crystalline. Julia is a full-blown slut. That transformation of hers fascinated me, terrified me.

A taxi pulls up, and tears me away from my thoughts. I quickly come to.

Another ordeal begins. No sooner am I seated in the cab than I'm in for the scare of my life. Get this for coincidence; you won't believe it.

Between there and Piraeus, he tells me his life story.

— That's how it is, mister!

Driving along like a madman, saying:

— Take it from me, mister.

He was married to a woman called Thalia, he says, but he really loved a girl named Alexandra. It was like red hot rivets in my brain. Thalia this, Thalia that, one complication after another. There I was, trying to concentrate on my own problems and this guy insists on unloading his life story.

— What was that? I didn't hear? What?

So he repeats the whole thing:

— That's right, friend, I left Alexandra and married Thalia, and now my life's a roller coaster ride. That's what it is. I didn't marry my dream girl, Alexandra, the girl I loved; I married the roller coaster instead. You figure it out. Had a house, and a taxi permit in her name. Sold myself for that. And for what? Sure, Thalia was a nice girl, good family and all the rest. Alexandra, she scared me a little, didn't have a drachma, but she had guts, mister ... Friend of mine married her. Guy named Anestis. But he wasn't for her. I was the one. So what happens? She ends up in the nut house and me and Thalia, up to our necks in ice water. But don't knock it; got

385

me a house, got me a permit.

"Shit! Look at that! I mean, this I need to hear right now? I'm in twice worse shape, and here's this guy telling me his life story. He's going to drive me nuts. Here I am, drowning, and this guy ..."

— Want to hear some more, mister?

And on he goes.

— Get a load of this. Maybe I'm calm and collected, you think? Well, I'm going nuts. Fifty-five, mister, going on sixty. Me, I wanted a little love, a little affection, and instead I'm going nuts. On the brink, let me tell you. I've lost everything, mister. Everything.

"Anyway, if we finish this run in one piece it'll be pure luck." The windows are misted over from the rain. He can't see a thing, can't hear a thing; he's driving like a man possessed.

— Don't worry, I'm being careful, he keeps on repeating. Where am I, where am I going, what's going to happen anyway, mister? The house, it's hers, her property, and here I am ready to blow my brains out. Why? Because just one hour ago as I was driving up from Piraeus on Syngrou — that's why I'm taking the long way, so I can retrace my steps — what do you think I see? No, you tell me. I'll show you exactly where. Wait. Here, right here, in front of the medical clinic. See it? The yellow building? Here, what do you think I see? You tell me, mister. It's Thalia. In my friend Dendrinos' little Fiat. Me, Anestis and Dendrinos, we go way back. Outings, tavernas. Sure he's a little creep, Dendrinos, a bit of an operator, but still, we go way back. Yessir, right there in his little Fiat, it's Thalia. You hear? Arm around her shoulder, hand further down, under her blouse, feeling her breast. Fondling her. You realize what I'm saying? I'm her husband and I can see this going on and there's nothing I can do about it, can't yell out, can't say a word. Yep. That's where we've ended up. I left Alexandra, took the roller-coaster, and look where I ended up ...

On and on and on he goes, and suddenly I become aware

386

that this man is telling my life story; not his life story, mine. I rub my eyes. I can't be sleeping. The only difference is the names. Instead of Julia, his wife's name is Thalia. Instead of my dream Martha, it's Alexandra, the girl he wanted, the girl he left behind.

Am I going crazy? Lazaris, my boyhood buddy, had a Fiat; he was a little creep too. One coincidence after another. What am I saying? It's my life story. Listen, listen to the rest.

— And, mister, when I left this morning she told me she was going to the dentist. I tried to get closer, so they could at least see I'd spotted them, because she'd deny everything that night, she'd make me crazy, I know her: "What do you mean you saw me; that's disgusting! You were dreaming." She'll make me crazy. But some damned truck cut right in front of me, I couldn't see. I begged him but he just laughed. They vanished. I turned at the next corner, called home. No answer. Called the dentist and asked for Thalia. "No, Mr. Antoniou, her appointment is for tomorrow." And I come to the simple conclusion that my dear Thalia has put the horns on me, but good. What else could I expect? What else could she do? Nothing but ice water between us, didn't I tell you? Good for her, I had it coming. A deal's a deal, right? Of course, it all seemed simple and easy back then, real easy, just give Alexandra the boot, look out for number one and tie the knot with Thalia. Nothing to it; what did I know? "Don't worry about it," that was my motto back then. But you'll pay for it all one day, mister. Pay dearly. In blood.

Naturally, the taxi crashes. A total loss. But us, not so much as a scratch.

— On your way, mister, go on.

He's stammering. Doesn't want money. Stammering, and weeping.

— On your way, mister; he repeats.

I leave him sitting in the wreck of his car, weeping. No way he'll take money. It happened just in front of the Mobil station; a Rover was pulling out. They collided. The Mycenae Hotel is just around the corner. I could walk.

17. YES ... YES ... YES

I CAN HARDLY WALK. The crash, the cabbie's life story ... it's all too much for me.

The rain has stopped. It's damp, bitter cold; mud everywhere. The cashier at the gas station tries to look after me.

— You're white as a sheet. Here, sit down.

— No, no. I can't.

— Are you hurt?

— No.

And I wobble off, in the direction of the hotel.

I met her again when I revisited the place, much, much later, to refresh my memory for a book I was working on.

She remembered me.

— Aren't you the man who?...

And she treated me to coffee and a sesame roll. Olga was her name.

People! Sweet, tender, warm people. Meet them for a few minutes, a few seconds, then they're gone, you never see them again. But they never vanish entirely. They travel on, inside you. Imagine, they could have been a part of my life, another story.

That was Louis' old refrain: "Stories, cousin, action! Have something to remember, something to tell your kids, your friends." "Yeah, but when you run out of stories, you end up melancholy, empty. The more you load your memory, the emptier you feel. I think." "Maybe so, but that's another kind of emptiness. Don't ask me. Like silence. Except it's never really pure silence. Is it?"

He was right. Silence is never pure.

I turn the corner, head down toward the harbor. It's all I can to keep going. My legs can hardly hold me. I'm still haking.

I sit down on some marble steps covered with muddy footrints, try to revive myself. "Terrific," I think, "what if omebody I know comes by and sees me in this state. I'll make spectacle of myself."

The idea that Lazaris — that prick! — might see me is too uch. "That'd really be the day. I'd never live it down."

Doesn't Antoniadis work somewhere around here?

I turn up my windbreaker collar to hide my face; I don't ant anyone recognizing me. The dampness of the marble enetrates the fabric of my trousers, my underpants, my skin. m cold. Then I notice where I'm sitting: on the steps of a novie theater. I look at the posters. Nothing but nude women. orn stars on parade.

I could smell Martha's perfume again.

I get to my feet. One more left turn and I'll be at the Iycenae. But I take a different route, through a narrow lane nat comes out at the harbor. I want to see if the fake eoclassical facades are still there, where the whores used to ounge in the sun on their tiny balconies. That old two-storey uilding has to be somewhere hereabouts, the place with the rooden staircase, the colored glass, the old lady at the en-rance; Louis' name day gift to me, when he took me to see assoula. I remember her rubbing her hands above the erosene heater, how she turned, and saw me.

Suddenly it occurs to me that maybe Martha hasn't gone to ne Mycenae after all. Why that particular hotel? She may ist as well be on her way to Australia; an aunt of hers lives nere. Mentioned her once, always said she wanted to get as ir away as she could.

— I want to leave, Manolopoulos, just leave.

Couldn't get any farther away than Australia. The kind of ountry that's too far away to dream about.

— That's where I want to go, somewhere too far away to

dream about. I don't even want to have dreamed about it
There you can change your skin, your cells, your thoughts
Australia, that's where I want to go. I've got an aunt down
there. If she'll put me up.

That was my first serious exchange with Martha. Funny, I'
forgotten all about that particular conversation. How did
manage that? She was alone on the balcony; I wanted some
more details about the rest of Agis' epistle. She wouldn't talk
I wanted to know if he said anything about Julia and Lazaris
She wouldn't say. How did I ever get that idea? Don't know
Don't know why she's chasing me either. It was as if the
answer held the secret of my life.

— Don't try to find out, Manolopoulos.

She knew what I was looking for.

— You too, Martha. You've changed since Agis died. You're
searching for something too. What is it?

She looked at me with those bright, piercing eyes of hers.
went on:

— Why do you drink so much? Why so withdrawn?

Her eyes weren't like Fatmé's. Remember Fatmé? Anyway
Martha's eyes, they weren't crystal clear, innocent, limpid
Sharp eyes, in the positive sense, I mean; always seemed to be
concealing something enigmatic, thoughts that would neve
be revealed. You could tell.

Martha kept a small piece of her world for her own private
use. She would never open her gates wide.

— Manolopoulos, I never regretted leaving Agis, if that'
what you mean. No. Not marrying Liakopoulos either. Jus
mistakes you realize after the fact; in fact, when you get down
to it, they weren't even mistakes. But now? I don't want to
end up in the insane asylum, I'm not going to give the lot o
you the pleasure, but unless I do something fast ...

— Stop drinking, to start with. If you want to take deci
sions, you'd better be clearheaded.

That's when she shot back with:

— And you, what are you going to do?

I turn into the lane way. "So, could be Australia? Maybe it'

390

all a wild goose chase. Maybe that's why I thought I heard airplanes over the phone. Was it the airport? But there was the sound of ships' whistles, for sure. No, no. It had to be the harbor.''

These are the very same streets I used to stroll with Louis.

I try to bring those days to life inside me, back when he tried to haul me into the brothel. No use. The magic is gone. Most of the neoclassical buildings have long since been demolished and replaced by faceless apartment blocks. Only the Yannoulatos building is still standing proud, imposing, solitary, amidst that wasteland of destitution. The new buildings are sordid, ugly, filthy. Here and there you can make out the ruined remains of one of those glorious old structures, reminding me of my own past glories.

In front of me the Chicago Hotel looms like a huge, threadbare ghost. It was the first place we'd looked for a room for Martha. Back then. "No room," said the hotel keeper.

Today it's closed, dark, covered with cobwebs. The entrance way is full of garbage; the doors are chained and locked. Nothing but rust, filth and gloom.

I reach the Mycenae. Or is it the Mykene? I can't remember. Nothing has changed. Same color, same door. Same peeling paint on the window frames, same cobwebs in the upper reaches of the hallway.

Suddenly, at the entrance, I have an attack of anxiety. I step back. "No you don't, idiot! Don't hold back, keep going. If she's inside you'll find her. If she's not, you won't."

I stare at the corridor, the steps. They are marble, foot-worn, grimy. A naked bulb is gleaming dimly.

I lean against the outside wall.

"Don't give me anymore of that shit logic of yours, Manolopoulos. I've had it."

"Louis, old buddy."

"No way, Manolopoulos, you're impossible. You turn your back on Haroula and call it logic; you avoid Martha for years and call it logic; marry Julia, you call it logic; we both lose Fatmé, you call that logic? Don't give me any more of that shit."

"The second I walk down that corridor, everything's possible. Do I take the chance? Logic, logic, sure. But what if something's happened to Martha. You never know, the condition she's in. The clerk will talk; a man came here to see her. They'll show him photographs, he'll recognize me. Then what? You lose the goose, and the golden eggs, right?"

"Ain't no such thing as life without risk, Manolopoulos. For once let things come to a head. Go on. Just once. If that isn't how it is, why would Oedipus go looking for the man who killed Laius, when he knew all along that everything would turn against him?"

Maybe she's left for Australia? The thought flashes through my mind. I'll be off the hook then; someone else has made the decision for me. "Who are you trying to kid? Your ideas stink, they reek. What a gutless wonder. Before too long you'll start hoping she's dead, just to get yourself out of a bind. What kind of bind, idiot? That's not your problem. Problem is, can Martha be your happiness, the poetry in your life, when you've spent a whole lifetime killing her in cold blood? That's the problem, not how to return to your hell, fool!"

I move ahead as quietly as I can. I don't want the hotel keeper to spot me. I can hear him talking on the phone.

"And so I find Martha. What do I tell her? What can I say? She should go back to Liakopoulos? That's what I want? What?"

"Now, idiot, now. He's got his back turned. Straight ahead, room number twelve. If she's at the hotel, she'll be in that room."

Suddenly I'm certain. Martha is still there. There in the Mycenae Hotel. I'm absolutely certain. Martha has climbed these stairs. One hundred percent. I can smell her perfume from here.

"Here I am, keep coming."

Seriously. The stairway was redolent with her perfume.

"Get moving." And I do. Hurrying up the stairs, I'm there in front of the door to room number twelve and the hotel keeper is still on the phone. Never heard a thing. The door to the toilet is half-open. The sound of women's laughter from another room snaps me to my senses. "Don't wait. What if a chambermaid shows up and asks what you want."

I knock softly, fearfully. Silence. Knock again, louder this time. Still silence. Now, I think, what if she's killed herself. "Then what would I do ..." And panic surges through me. That was all she could talk about lately.

Didn't she say, "And if I wanted to jump, you'd let me go?"

But how sure is it she's in room twelve? Maybe she asked for twelve but it was taken and they gave her fifteen or twenty instead. Are you sure she's not in twenty? The thought calms me.

I knock again. Suddenly I'm certain she's there. Her perfume is seeping under the crack at the bottom of the door. "She's there. Get it over with." I put my ear to the door. Silence. "No such thing as pure silence." Louis, you again. I think of you a hundred times!

I take the knob, barely turn it. The door is locked from the inside. "It's all in my imagination? That strong a smell of perfume, all in my imagination?"

I try again. Nothing. Locked. Then I hear her voice.

— Better go home, Manolopoulos. Go home.

— Martha!

— Go back to your shit, Manolopoulos. You're late. One of us is paying, that's enough. Why two?

— Martha, listen to me.

I don't want to shout, don't want the desk clerk to hear me.

— Are you alright?

— If that's what you're interested in, I'm fine.

— Come on, open up. It's useless to keep this up; no sense ...

— It's too late, Manolopoulos. It's true. Too late for everything. Don't bother.

— Martha, please.

— If you keep on, you'll regret it. This isn't for you. Forget it.

She has to be there, standing right behind the door. I picture her, disheveled, pale, tear-stained, drunk. But she isn't slurring her words as she was doing lately when she drank.

— Martha, whatever's past is over and done with, please. Anyway, if you phoned me ...

— I didn't call you to ask you to come. I only wanted to call. Nothing more. Call you and hear your voice. When I get really down ...

— Please, Martha.

— Maybe I'm even sorry I called you; it was all a mistake, I apologize.

— Come on, Martha, please, it's not worth the trouble.

— I said I'm sorry. Isn't that enough.

— No, Martha, it's not enough.

Silence. The woman down the hall is still laughing. Suddenly, I hear the key turning in the lock.

I don't enter immediately. For a few seconds I hold the doorknob. I know that as soon as I open the door a new chapter in my life will begin. Before Christ and after. You get my meaning?

I feel at that instant that as soon as I cross the threshold I will be entering another century.

I open the door. When I enter the room my glasses fog over. Can't make out a thing. Room warmth suddenly hitting them, coating them with mist. I take them off, wipe them on the lining of my windbreaker.

The windows are misted over, you can't see the harbor. A table, two straw-bottom chairs, a wooden closet, the sink, the bed — an iron bed, wide, but not quite double — made up the furnishings.

At the foot of the bed lie her shoes. Black high-heeled pumps. Martha never wore flats. Always heels. Maybe that's why she swayed so provocatively when she walked.

I find her on the bed, under a gray blanket, her back to me, facing the wall. She had time to lie down again.

On the night table is a small bottle of brandy and a half-empty glass.

I don't know what to do. I sit down at the foot of the bed. Then I slide more toward the center, and she edges over to make room. I'm cold. Pick up the glass and drain it. Warmth. Her hair is dyed red, cut short, boyish. That's her cut, her style. Liakopoulos couldn't forgive her that either.

Then I notice her dress thrown over the back of a chair, her stockings, her bra. White.

Her shoulders are uncovered. Naked, white. I want to touch them. I look at her. As she moves over to make room for me the blanket clings to her, outlining her body beneath.

Her body is stretched out on the bed as if drawn by invisible forces. It seems immense, endless.

I look at the bottle. Almost full. "Hmm, hasn't been drinking."

— No, I'm not drunk, if that's what you're worried about. I left without taking a drop. Haven't had a drink here either.

Surge of shame; she's read my thoughts. "Fuck!"

— When I left it was warm and sunny. I don't have a thing. No overcoat. I've got a chill.

I want to touch her shoulders.

— You squealed on me to Liakopoulos, that I called you?

Her manner of speech, her words irritated Liakopoulos of late. He'd begun to feel uncomfortable. Stopped taking her along to official functions. But me, they won me over, drew me toward her, charmed me. "Jerk-off artist, stool pigeon, shit head, pud-face, queer." Words she would use every day, as part of her normal discourse, no matter where she was. "Martha, I beg you," Liakopoulos would plead, "what kind of talk is that; you're not living in a whorehouse, you're living in a home."

She ignored him. And kept it up, only worse.

— Manolopoulos, why aren't you answering? I asked you if you squealed on me?

My mind is wandering again.

— No, I didn't squeal on you, not to anybody; but he's looking for you like a wild man. Everywhere. The police, your friends, me.

I look at her hair.

— How come you cut your hair like that.

— For him. He doesn't like it short. That's why.

Then I tell her the taxi driver's story, about his wife, the crash, how I can barely walk.

— Hurt yourself?

— No.

I want to touch her shoulders.

— Where did you get the guts to come?

— Don't know. All of a sudden, while Julia was getting dressed, it hit me.

I want to be honest with her, not hide anything. To be myself. I tell her.

— No matter how crummy and pathetic it is, I'm going to tell you.

— Know something, Manolopoulos, I can't even call you by your first name. I want to call you Kostas, my boy, like Louis does, but it comes out Manolopoulos.

Then I touch her shoulders. Barely. My hands remain there, motionless, steady. She freezes. As if holding her breath.

— I knew you'd come. You had to come. Just another guy drowning in his own shit, that's what I'd have said if you didn't come.

— But I came.

— You came.

Everything motionless. Her shoulders, my hands, time, words.

— There's another blanket in the closet. Bring it. It's cold.

The ice breaks.

I bring the blanket. Cover her with it. Then, she lifts it up by the corner.

— Come on, lie down. Take off your clothes, lie beside me.

I'm not expecting that. I'm totally unprepared for such a proposal. My hands begin to shake. The cold of the room, the confusion, the distress.

396

— Come on, no one's watching.

As if to underline my indecisiveness. Of course, she still has her back turned.

— Remember the compositions we had to do in school? "One Day Alone at Home?" Or something like that. And you told me what to write, remember? I've been thinking about it all morning, here alone. Come on, lie down.

First I take off my shoes. Then my jacket. I hesitate with my pants. I turn to look at her. "She's got to be naked," I think. Take them off, hang them over the back of the chair beside her clothing. I unbutton my shirt but keep it on. I'm cold.

Again she lifts the covers to make room for me underneath. She holds them until I lie down.

— You're cold as ice.

— Sure am.

My hands begin to shake. It isn't only the cold now. Her body is hot. But with the warmth I start to revive. I don't know what to do with my hands. I want to reach out, touch her buttocks, but I don't dare.

— Don't worry. I'm not going to hold you responsible, for anything.

— Martha, that's not what I was thinking, honestly.

And I relate all the tragicomic events of the day at my place. My fears, my changes of heart, am I leaving or not, the dresser drawer, when Julia showed up. Only thing I don't mention is me masturbating. But I promised to tell her everything, didn't I? That too.

— In front of your picture, looking at your nipples.

And she takes my hand, my left hand, and puts it on her buttocks, exactly where I want.

Then she edges toward me. Her body close up against mine, taking on its shape. A shallow curve, like a bent bow.

But in spite of this, I still have a case of nerves. No sign of arousal. She senses it.

— Don't worry, it'll come on its own. I know. Better that way. When you stop worrying about it, it'll come. Anyway, what does it matter?

397

— Martha, I've always dreamed about your body. Dreamed about it; dirty, obscene dreams, call it whatever you want.

— I know.

Then, slowly, she turns toward me. Now, one body opposite the other. Eye to eye.

— No, Manolopoulos, I don't believe it, the obscene part. No. That's what I love about you. That's what's been haunting me for a lifetime, that's what's bringing me to you, I can see it in your eyes. I know how you look at my body. You think it's obscene but not me, because at the same time — maybe you don't even realize it — you give it an identity, you send it back through my own thoughts, my own eyes, my laughter, back through everything I am, my whole story. You can see me from the inside. Not many men can see women that way. At first glance, you look just like any other human being, but then, nothing happens inside you if you can't breathe soul and fantasy and thought into it.

Come to think of it, that's probably true. Now that she mentions it, I can see for myself. That's it.

She looks at me with those perpetually smiling eyes of hers and slowly I feel something melting inside me, feel things becoming fluid. Put sugared honey in the hot sun and it won't be long before it starts to melt, to run.

At that moment Martha is melting inside me, like thousands of threads of liquid honey.

I want to tell her how frightened I am, how terrified I am of that moment. But all I can say is:

— Martha, we're not kids any more.

— I know, Manolopoulos.

— On my way I was wondering if you'd be here, wondering if we'd make love, I was worried you'd see my flabby belly, my messed-up eyes, my little hesitations, my way of putting things off. But I was wondering the same things about you. I didn't want to be disappointed by your wrinkles, your varicose veins. I tried to imagine your legs, to compare them with Julia's.

— Your wife has good-looking legs. But no, there's no way

398

you could make love with a woman unless you knew she really wanted you. I call that soul, Manolopoulos. There had to be something deep between you and your wife, something that bound you with her body. You can't convince me. Maybe you never tried to find out why. No, it's not just her legs. That would be awful.

— There's nothing between us any more, nothing. Not even her legs.

Silence. We look at one another.

— So, what do you say? Are you disappointed? But you haven't even seen me.

And abruptly, with a gentle movement, she lifts all of the covers. She's wearing only her panties. They're white.

— Here, have a look at me, get to know me. That's me.

I look. Martha! The dream that's pursued me for half a lifetime, and now here she is, lying naked, in front of my eyes, slender, fragile. And for me, it's the same. I'm just as naked, just as exposed, just as fragile before her.

Silence. We look at one another.

— OK. You approve?

She's still holding up the covers.

— You're beautiful, Martha.

— No more, Manolopoulos. You want me to be.

— You are, Martha.

— Just like then, at the Seashell Club, in the photo? Like that?

— Just like that.

She lets the covers fall.

— The performance is over. No more peep show.

I stretch out my hand and take hold of her neck, my fingers entwining in her hair. I caress her. I'm slowly starting to relax.

— So? You didn't tell me. Where did you find the balls to come? I'm the one that did it? Managed to drag you out from behind your walls?

My lips are probably making a tiny expression of bitterness. She notices it.

— No, I'm not trying to make fun of you. I know the way you are. I understand that shyness of yours, I love it.

She stops, looks at me, then continues.

— Manolopoulos, you bastard. What clowns we are. What a mess we've made of everything. I never saw anything like it. You made a million compromises, but you were always different. You never fouled your own soul. You managed to keep it intact, unpolluted. The sad thing is that I'm the only one who knows it, me and Louis. Agis knew it too, but he's gone. You've only got the two of us left. Take care of us. We're your alibis. If anything happens to us, you're stuck. For everybody else, you'll just be another poor shit intellectual, no more.

— What about my writing?

— Yes, I forgot. Your writing.

I see her left nipple. My eyes come to rest on it. It's just like in the photo.

— Remember Drakopoulos' wedding, with Madonna? I never could get that white stain off my skirt. I left it there, something to remember you by ... Ah, Manolopoulos!... If you hadn't chickened out, and run. How I wanted you then, when I felt you come ...

I'm not listening. She keeps on talking while I stare at her nipple. Suddenly Mahler's *First* starts playing. No. First it starts to rain. Heavy, fat drops drumming against the window panes. Along with the rain, along with the sound of Martha talking, Mahler's *First* comes into the room. Like an uninvited guest. More than just comes in; rushes in like a torrent.

She sees where my eyes are riveted. She stops talking, looks at me. It's small, pink, round, erect — her nipple.

Slowly, ever so slowly, I creep down the bed, brush it with my lips. Barely. So gently. Then I begin kissing all around it, on the fly, like birds swooping and darting over fields and valleys.

Now the rain and the *First* are fading away.

She grabs my hair, I start to suck her breast. She pulls me up toward her.

— Rat, Liakopoulos told you. That's why?

As I continue nibbling and sucking, she pulls me toward her head. Everyone in the gang knew her secret. From Louis, who got it from Agis. "If Martha ever makes the mistake of letting someone touch her nipples, or worse yet, kiss them, it's unconditional surrender."

— Rat, rat, she whispers as she pulls me toward her by the hair. You knew it.

— I knew.

We embrace, tightly, tenderly.

Suddenly I feel my penis coming erect.

The rain has turned to hail, beating against the window panes, and I hold her tight against me.

— If you only knew, Martha.

— I know.

She is crying.

— If only, I repeated.

— Shh, don't say a word.

Hold her tight. Her eyes are agleam with tears. I start to lick the teardrops, salty, delicious, as they roll down her cheeks. They remind me of the sea, of the waves, of Louis.

Then she begins a low-pitched, wild monologue, saying how she melted when I came, how I figured out where she was and came, how I remembered the Mycenae.

— You made me melt, Manolopoulos, melt.

Then she starts cursing herself for being so emotional, what the hell's wrong, maybe she was wrong to call me.

— I took it all back. I begged you not to come, I didn't want you to come. Shit, shit. Let's get it over with, Manolopoulos, over with. Can't go on this way.

Her body is arching, touching mine, and I want her like I want nothing else in the world.

My penis is hard now, brushing up against her, and she talks and I hold her tight and I want to shout, to cry out, at last I exist again, I can, I can!...

My insides are heaving, heart pounding, puffing out like a sail in a fair wind, the world is too small for me, my body can't hold me, finally, finally, not everything is dead, not everything is finished. I can feel — can you believe it? — sails filling, doors and windows opening, the wind rushing in, carrying us before it, and we're travelling along atop the bed, I can hear the lapping of the waves rushing through the doorway. The Mycenae has weighed anchor ...

Slowly she falls silent, looks at me with her enormous eyes, wraps her arms around me and pulls me on top of her while with the same movement she rolls over onto her back and spreads her legs. Reaches her hand down, takes hold of my penis and brings it into her. I hardly move. Lie there atop her, all of me.

— Yes, yes, yes ... she whispers as she kissed my lips, my throat, my cheeks.

I look into her eyes. It's as if my penis is not deep in her vagina, but in her eyes ... I'm having intercourse with her eyes. Travelling deep, deep in them.

— Yes, yes, yes, she goes on.

The "yes" says everything. All the world's love words concentrated in that "yes" of hers.

I lie motionless. And she, motionless.

— I'm ready.

— And I.

With hardly a movement, with a small, simultaneous spasm, we come.

I hold her tight, tight. She holds me.

— My love, she says.

— My love, I say, and everything becomes as it had been.

The wind drops, the lapping of the waves and the salty sea taste in my mouth, gone too.

Once more I can hear Mahler's *First*, the drumming of the rain, and her, breathing.

18. THE EXECUTION

WE LAY ON OUR BACKS, staring at the ceiling. Me next to the wall, Martha on the room side of the bed.

Sadness crept back into her eyes, like a morning dew enveloping roofs, trees and streets. Damp, dark, amorphous.

For a long time her "yes, yes, yes" echoed in my ears, until it too gradually died out. The rain had stopped. The sun had come out. A tattered, yellowish curtain and two ugly brown shutters blocked half the window.

We said nothing. Avoided speaking. Suddenly she got up, still naked, walked over to the window, lifted the curtain and pulled it over to one side against the wall. Light flooded into the room. Something seemed to be stifling her.

— You'll catch cold, I said.

She touched the radiator.

— The heat's on. It's warm.

She stood there in the corner, halfway between the wall and the window.

— If you lean over, you can just see the water from here.

She peered outside. I could see the varicose veins on her thighs.

But she must have been cold, because in a few moments she came over, took my jacket, and threw it over her shoulders, then returned to the same place. Now my windbreaker was blocking the view of her breasts.

We had so much to say, yet neither of us could begin. Like school kids trying to write compositions, not knowing where to start, what to write.

She stared out the window, while I counted the little squares on the curtains. She was first to speak.

— I'm not so innocent. I was ready to leave, you know, but ... I cut her off.

— Why did you come here, Martha?

— I wanted to think. I don't know, really. I couldn't go on. He makes me sick. When Agis wrote about how Liakopoulos took him for the property, that's when ...

— You never call him your husband. Always Liakopoulos.

— Never. I can't.

The windbreaker was too big for her. It had swallowed her up, completely. She went on:

— That did it for me. Back when I started to work in his office, I had no idea. But you think that was the only time? Later, he and Lazaris were thick as thieves. It was Lazaris who told Agis — did you know that? — that I'd moved in with Liakopoulos. Did it for revenge. We thought he didn't know a thing. He knew everything. I would have told him gently. I didn't want him to hear it from someone else.

She turned toward me. I caught sight of her breasts again, under the jacket.

— What made you leave home, Martha?

— Leave home?

She said it as if she didn't know why herself. Then walked over to the sink, took a glass from the shelf above it, and came over to the bed. Poured a little brandy and offered it to me to drink. I sat up, shoved the pillow up against the iron headboard and leaned back. Took the glass. Still wearing my jacket, she picked the other glass up from the night table as it was, half full, curled her legs up under the blankets, laid the other pillow up against the headboard and sat down beside me.

"Is it possible I could spend the rest of my life with her?" I wondered. She tossed it down in one gulp.

— You're not drinking?

I drank. A moment of awkward silence. Then, as if talking to herself:

— One way or the other, Manolopoulos, we've made a mess of everything. But I don't want you to think I'm all that innocent. I'm not.

She took my hand and looked at it.

— I always loved those hands of yours.

— Martha!

— Don't say a word. I know, you wanted me, I wanted you. But look what a mess we made of everything. If you hadn't run out on me there at Drakopoulos' wedding, when you came all over my dress. I tried to find you, you were gone. Why? You knew I wanted you, you wanted me. Why? How absurd. My God!

I drained the brandy from my glass.

— Where's it all going to end. Shit.

She grabbed the bottle and filled both glasses to the half-way mark.

— Know something, that night I fell into the trap. Told him, yes. Liakopoulos. He trapped me, the rat. He had to know how desperate I was when you left, he had to. Probably even eavesdropped on the scene, even if he never did admit it. But don't worry, I got back at him, and how. One step at a time, deep in the shit. Let's get it over with, over with.

She kept repeating "over with" as though she wanted to believe it, herself most of all.

I looked around the room. It had lost its spell. Now it was full of ghosts, of bitterness. The air was heavy. As if the oxygen had been depleted, the air smelled of faded flowers — rotting lilies and roses, was more like it — days without fresh water. I told her so.

— Yes, like something rotten. You're right.

— But he loves you, I said, bringing us back to Liakopoulos.

— He hates me. Only my body is good for him, but he knows he never really possessed me, never made it his own, and that kills him. He hates me, the bastard, uses me. But I'm not the only one who's trapped. So is he.

She paused for an instant, drank two gulps of brandy, and went on:

405

— You probably all think he's worried about me, that it bothers him, my drinking ... Not in the slightest. He enjoys it, the brute. The deeper I sink into the alcohol, the livelier he gets, the better he likes it. That's the only way he can get it up. Can't even stand to touch me when I'm sober ... And I can't stand him. Won't be long before he learns about his good friend, Lazaris, how he screwed me at his place.

— But he already knows, from Agis' letter. Doesn't he?

— Nope. When we got back home and he asked me if it was true, I denied it, but now when he sees what his friend is really like, he'll crap in his pants. He may be a brute, but he won't be able to stand it. It'll be curtains for their friendship.

I shivered.

— How's he going to know?

— I sent him a letter. Describing everything, the whole works. All the details.

— A letter?

I was taken aback. Again I felt the apprehensions, the hesitations creeping back. "If she wrote him where she is now, that means he could show up at any second with the whole sideshow, Julia, Lazaris and Company."

I wanted to ask her if she'd written anything about us. I held back. "You asshole! You've left home, crossed over to the other shore. So they find out where you are? What difference does it make? Let 'em come. So much the better. Let's get it over with. You're gone. Maybe you don't know it yet, but you're gone. Gone for good."

She turned to me and looked at me, most likely read my thoughts.

— So, getting cold feet? Worried about the letter? Think again, Manolopoulos. The hunt is about to start. Things aren't so simple. You escaped from prison. You understand? Escaped. Not just a change of neighborhood. You're gone. For good. Or not?

— What can she do to me? Sure, I'm gone.

— Julia? She'll get revenge. First thing she'll do is have Lazaris get you transferred far away. Right to the Turkish

406

border, for instance. What about your salary? Can you live on it?

The ghosts had become almost brazen. I could almost see them walking barefoot there in the room, taunting, obscene, grimacing.

— I want to talk, before the brandy carries me away.

She stopped, drank two mouthfuls, and went on:

— Manolopoulos, you're not cut out for a tragic hero. That's how it looks to me. After a lifetime of compromises? You're too used to the routine. Tragedy and compromise just don't mix.

— What about you?

— I paid dearly. For both of us. Now it's behind me. I'm ready for anything. Whoever likes me, that's fine with me.

It had begun to get dark. The blanket had slipped down, and now I could see her belly. A soft fuzz began at her navel and worked its way down, like a little brook, toward the thicket of her sex. I liked it. Started to caress the fuzz.

— Know what I'd like? To make love to someone I don't know, a stranger, a tormented man, someone with scars on his face, puffed eyes, someone who's suffered. One look at him and you'd say, "Now there's a man devoured by life, by sea salt, by pain." A ruined man. That's the only kind of man I could love. I'm sick of careerists, of successes, of businessmen and accountants. I want someone who walks with a limp, someone who's exhausted, clumsy. With the veins standing out on his hands and on his forehead. A wise man. Someone who doesn't keep track. I'm fed up with men who keep track of everything. All the counting has made a wreck of me. A tormented man, but built solid. Not necessarily tall, but looks tall. Someone who gets taller as he speaks. Who doesn't dream any more. Enough of dreams, of illusions. Enough of

407

the shit, enough, enough.

On and on she went, while I, the model citizen, all I could think of was her letter to Liakopoulos. What was in it, did he ever get it, did she ever send it ... Maybe he's already read it, maybe the phones are humming, the lines smoking. "Who? What? When?" "Did you hear, Martha and Manolopoulos?" Alley cats they'll call us, bums. Suddenly I was calm. I remembered it was Sunday, which meant the mail would be late, which meant ... I came to.

Martha had stopped. She was looking at me. Finally she asked me where I was, where I'd been.

— Seriously, Martha, you wrote him everything?

— Everything. I've had it, Manolopoulos, I told you. Cleared it out of my system once and for all. See that bottle over there? It's my last. I'm clean. End of the line. I won't give the lot of you the satisfaction of seeing me go out like a candle. As for you, time will tell. Will you ever let all the crap come out? Will you ever let the seas and the rivers and the memories flow? Will you ever let it all out into the light? You've damned up your whole life, you bastard, thrown up walls, barriers ... You don't see the trap, you overcame it, you're fine, is that what you want me to say? That's your life story, neither here nor there, moving back and forth, somewhere in between, nothing to lean on. Sometimes I think maybe you were sent to mess up my life. Asshole!

It was almost night. She got up to turn on the light. For a few seconds she stood there motionless, in the center of the room, then took a deep breath, as if a weight had finally lifted from her shoulders, a soul belch, if you can call it that, then switched it on.

Then she came back and sat down on the bed, in the same spot. Turned and looked at me.

408

— Know something? I read the first chapter of your book.

— Impossible.

— I read it, Manolopoulos. Your wife brought it over one day when you were in the hospital for some operation you ended up cancelling. Liakopoulos read it; he was the only one who could read your writing. He liked it. I think. I could see how you were trying to work through your guilt, your remorse.

— Seriously, Martha, you read it?

— What am I telling you all this time? I heard it, to be precise. You wrote about a girl named Fatmé, who gets killed. Everybody laughed, except me. Most of all when you write about auntie Eustathia and the three-storey house downtown. Of course, the aunt you mean isn't really called Eustathia, and the house isn't downtown, but everyone figured out who you were talking about, and about the house. I don't know what you're going to call me in your book when you finally get to the scene we're experiencing now, or should I say, playing, eh?

— For sure I'll call you by your real name.

— So, I'll be hung out to dry but good. Tell me, at least, will you be fair? Your wife was happy you didn't go with Fatmé, that you chose your home instead ...

— I chose?

— She never said a word to you about the reading?

— Never. Not a word.

— But it's clear what you think of her.

— Not always. When you write, you change characters, names, relations, events. Sure, deep down ... But the idea is to ...

— I know. Show what's invisible.

— That's the idea. That's what you want, the invisible. Not the nonexistent. That's the magic. And the danger.

— It hurt her, your wife I mean. And she never said a word.

— She knows how to keep a secret.

— You don't describe her with such kind words.

— Anyway, it's all over now.

— Over?

I turned and looked her in the eyes.

— It's all over.

The bare bulb gave off a sallow light. Coated everything with frost. I was sleepy, the sickly yellow light made the curtains and the walls and the furniture even uglier, more tasteless; my mood turned sour. Slowly I began to sink, to hide the inhospitable space from my eyes, and put my lips to rest against her belly. She began to stroke my hair. Then I felt my eyes closing, blinking.

— Better you'd never come, Manolopoulos. Better you should have stayed at home.

She stroked my hair as she talked.

— You remind me of Hamlet. Nothing you did in your life matched what you wanted to do. Never balanced. Same for me. No, we never did what our little hearts desired.

When Martha said "our little hearts" she suddenly turned tender, erotic.

— But Hamlet doesn't hesitate at the finish, I said.

— No, but you? Still, you remind me of him.

Gradually her voice was becoming a lullaby, the smell of laurel, music.

— You know — she went on — what I said to you before, that I'd like to love a tormented man. I found him. Found him. Day before yesterday. Pure chance.

At the word "chance" my lips came to a halt on her belly. Froze. I held my breath. "There you have it, you asshole. While you're still counting the pros and cons, the go's or stay's, she's already on her way, far, far away. Asshole, asshole!"

She kept on stroking my hair while she talked to me about the man she'd met by chance.

— He tunes pianos, builds furniture; married. Whatever he makes, he spends. He's bald. I didn't notice whether he's good-looking or ugly. All I remember is how wide his hands are. Reached right around those fat beer glasses, the ones shaped like little barrels. Right in the palm of his hand. The whole world fitted into the palm of his hand. He took me to show me

410

his workshop. A basement. Pure enchantment. He doesn't give a damn about his work, his orders; spends all his time on wood carvings, just for the hell of it. Most of them show a rowboat, with Death at the oars. He carves sea sprites too. An acquaintance of Louis. That's how we met. He brought one of his sculptures to a bar; a special order. "I know you," he said. "Weren't you living with Agis?" And so I started to tell him about my life. At one point his wife, a real shrew, came down into the basement, spat on him and walked out. They lived right upstairs. He was laughing. "My wife! That's her, take a good look. Nothing more, nothing less. Nothing to hide. That's her." And laughed. "Comes down here once or twice a day, spits on me and walks out. If I tell her bye-bye, we're separating, she'll drop dead. Can't live without me, and still, you saw her."

"Then he caressed my hair and kissed me and said, 'Sweetie, let's get the hell out of here.' There was an old diploma on the wall, from the Academy of Fine Arts; it was covered with fly specks and old telephone numbers. 'Sweetie, if you're not in love why bother living; I mean, where will you find the urge to live? I want to do wood carving, I want to make a living carving wood, and all she can tell me is that I'm a cabinet maker, to forget that wood carving nonsense, 'cause I'll never make money carving wood. She draws a crappy pension, and wags it under my nose, if it wasn't for her pension, her pension! That's why I'm telling you, let's get out of here, sweetie. Let her drop dead. If you're not in love, you're not alive. See her? Comes down here, spits on me, and leaves. Doesn't matter what she has to say, she still spits on me.' And all of a sudden I fell in love with him. He even had a piano, sitting on top of a pile of wood shavings. Just sitting there. You can't imagine what was in that basement. Washing machines, boats, anchors, broken furniture, paintings. She left him a plate of food, spat on him and left. 'The hell with you, you no good loafer,' she said. Didn't even see me. First he said, 'Sweetie, let's get out of here,' and then he sat down on a three-legged stool and started to play the piano. A sad,

411

sad piece. I can't recall the composer, or the title. 'I can't remember, I don't want to remember, what's the point,' he said. But he remembered the melody. 'First I went to music school, then art school. Then I met the old battle-ax and everything changed.' And all of a sudden I fell in love with him. He seemed to be growing taller in front of my eyes, like I said. I went over to him. He took my hand. Now he was playing with one hand. Then he stopped, propped the chair up against a wooden beam to keep it from falling over and lifted me onto his lap, on top of him. I sat down. Why resist? He looked like you. Sometimes I can't tell the two of you apart. And his wife looked like Julia.''

''What's she saying?'' And I came back to reality. Was this all happening or wasn't it? Was she just talking off the top of her head, or remembering? Reality or imagination? ''What's she saying?'' I couldn't believe my ears. Suddenly I felt a surge of jealousy. A knot surged up from my chest into my throat, jealousy. But she went on, inexorable, unchained, relentless, talking about him.

— ''When you're not in love, you don't betray anyone, my darling,'' he told me and just like that we made love, there, on the chair. He was unshaven, sweaty. The door to the basement was wide-open, and the cool dampness of the night came in through the broken glass of the high windows, and we made love. Rivers must have overflown their banks somewhere close by, rain must have been falling; the smell of rain was in the air. And my head began to reel, I began to confuse his face with your face, his hands with yours, his life with yours. We agreed to meet here, at the Mycenae. We would both leave home, he was going to pick me up and we would leave, the two of us, for a voyage somewhere in the Aegean, without baggage, without memories, no more rags and tatters any more, we said, no more castoffs. ''Right from the very beginning, honey, from zero, from alpha. Coming?...'' Was it you talking, or him? I couldn't tell. Were you holding me, or was it him? Didn't know. Maybe once I thought you'd treat me that way, but you never did. But he never came. The night

412

went by, he never came. Dawn came, he never came. He dumped me. That's when I called you, and your face started to come into focus. Was I dreaming? Love-making in a chair, him, you? Did it happen, didn't it, Manolopoulos? Did that magical basement ever exist?

Then I fell asleep. Maybe I caught a few more fragments of her story, but my memory couldn't hold them, my drowsiness swallowed them up, words without meaning, pictures without color. Over and over again I tried to remember. I could not. She said something, I answered her, but ... Maybe we were talking about us, about what would happen to us. "You're still hesitating?" Maybe I said, "Why don't the two of us leave for the Aegean, an Aegean of our own?" But maybe I didn't dare to say it, maybe I held back, didn't say it in time. I'm telling you, I can recall fragments of sentences, words, colors; but, fuck it, I fell asleep. What I mean is maybe we said earthshaking things, but I fell asleep. That much I can remember, I fell asleep with my head there on her belly. No, it can't be; imagine it's the Crucifixion, Christ is rising from the dead, and you fall asleep, I just can't believe it ...

I was awakened by the sounds of ships' whistles, horns, engines roaring, a radio far away playing Maria Callas singing an aria.

When I opened my eyes I noticed that the curtain had been drawn across the window, to keep out the light. Then I saw a bouquet of lilies and roses in a glass on the night table. "Those flowers weren't there yesterday; no way I could have

413

missed them." In any case, there were only two glasses. Everything was neatly put away. The other glass had been washed, and was sitting upside down on the shelf over the sink. The brandy bottle was empty. There on the chair were my pants, my jacket, my socks, all hung carefully. The light had been turned off, daylight shone through the cracks. My head was on the pillow.

I awoke. At that moment I became aware of the situation. Martha was gone! Her skirt, her blouse, her shoes, nowhere to be seen. She was gone!

The pain began deep down and rose up into my guts, then lodged somewhere in my chest. I was choking. She was gone.

I got up and yanked open the curtain. It was true, just like she said. If you leaned over a bit, you could see the water.

The pain in my chest became unbearable. Just then, as Callas' voice sang on, someone flushed the toilet next door, a vacuum cleaner started up in the hallway, and a white cruise ship blew its whistle as it sailed out of the harbor; just then, for the first time in my life I felt as though I'd ceased to exist, felt like a piece of trash thrown on a rubbish heap, like time had ceased to exist inside me; my feet had lost contact with the ground, I was cut off from the universe, for the first time beyond borders, beyond my own present.

Afterward I searched the room, thinking maybe she'd left a note. Now that I think of it, good thing she didn't, it would have been absurd for her to have written, "I'm leaving, see you some other time." Better this way. The only thing worth writing would be to tell me to go back to my shit. That would have been worth it, for sure.

When I went downstairs and asked the desk clerk, I still had one last hope that she'd gone out for awhile, that she would come back; after all, since she got up first, maybe she'd gone out for a sandwich or a coffee. "Otherwise, what's the point of the flowers?" I thought.

Then it occurred to me they were lilies and roses, just what I'd told her. I was stunned. So, the flowers were the note she didn't leave? "Lilies and roses in stale water" is what I said. I almost collapsed. Had to catch ahold of something, keep myself from falling. It was all I could do to speak to the clerk. My words were slurred. I leaned against the glass wicket across the desk to keep myself upright. When she finally managed to understand my question, she told me, "The lady paid and left. Someone came this morning and ..."

— Someone? A bald man? Unshaven? Big hands?

— Yes, someone like that. He picked her up, they left.

I turned around and headed up the stairs.

— There's a couple and a gentleman here to see you.

She lifted her hand to point. I didn't have time to turn. As I raised my eyes I saw them standing there glaring at me, erect, cold, pale, unwavering.

I slumped against the wall, caught a glimpse of their guns as they took aim. Heard the shots. They were executing me. In cold blood.

First I fainted, then rolled down the stairs. Like a dog. They left me there and walked out. Worse than a dog. Without a word. It was enough that they'd seen me.

From far away came the sound of Callas' aria.

EPILOGUE

19. SUN ABOVE THE WHOREHOUSE

REALLY, IT WASN'T A FIGURE OF SPEECH. The last time I saw
Louis was at Lambros' ouzo joint; when you get right down to
it, we parted for good then. That was the last I saw of him.
Trains and boats took him, clouds, horse carts, and God knows
what else took him; he disappeared. I no longer had anything
to do with anyone from the gang of "dirty old men"; there
was nobody I could ask for news of him. They disappeared; so
did I.

After my "execution" at the Mycenae Hotel, I quickly
found myself posted to a small town near the Turkish border,
exactly as Martha had predicted — but it helped obliterate the
last vestiges of whatever contact I still had with them. From
then on distances grew greater, memories turned rustier,
faces began to lose their definition; when I happen to meet one
of them I pretend not to notice, or cross to the other side of the
street and walk right on by.

As for my job, well, I didn't last long up there. The combination of isolation and boredom made me so desperate that one
fine sunny morning I heroically tendered my resignation and
returned to my old haunts.

Naturally, Julia married Lazaris. The day our divorce came
through they got married, almost to the very day.

Everyone attended the wedding except me, despite the fact
that they — the pricks — sent me an invitation, not out of a
sense of humor (I'd have gone then) but out of pure cynicism,

416

pure indifference to what that invitation meant to me.

From that day on, only one question continued to prey on my mind. If they hadn't caught me in the act at the Mycenae Hotel, would I have had the nerve to stage my heroic exodus? I wanted to know: I mean, say they hadn't caught me, would I have gone back home? Maybe I'd have spent the rest of my life as a mummy, sitting there on Julia's footstool? I needed to know: was I the one who precipitated events, or was I only a little rubber ball that ended up bouncing out of the game? Had the showdown begun inside me, or was the whole escape a matter of chance, a pure coincidence? Who's pulling the strings of this story, anyway? Is it possible to be caught between the millstones without knowing who threw you there?

Up until today, up until the moment I'm relating to you this story of mine, no one has ever seen Martha again; not Liakopoulos, and not me, for sure. No one. Martha has gone, vanished, just like Louis. But you never know, do you? It's not only the criminal who returns to the scene of the crime; it's the victim too. They come back, sometimes. Maybe one day she'll get it into her head — although it's pretty damned unlikely she will, — to come back. Maybe one day the memories, if she happens to hear Mahler's *First*, if she thinks back to that Sunday at the Mycenae, if ... if ... You never know. Maybe one day, as it was with me, she'll return to the scene of the great crime. Maybe. I know her affair with that weird guy, the one she ran away with, was more an act of panic and despair than real love. So I'll wait — who knows? — it's the only thing that gives me some hope, some zest for living, a reason to tell you my stories.

As for Liakopoulos, her husband ... well, I heard later that on that eventful Monday when he discovered me at the Mycenae, he returned home, gathered all her clothes, all her photos and her records and her books, and that rocking chair of Agis', stacked it all up and stuffed it into a storeroom and there it stayed — he wants it that way — as if she'd never passed through his life, as if she'd never existed, as if she'd never lived in his house. But now, the way I hear it, he's set up a chair on the balcony, can't go to bed unless he's plastered — just like she used to do — but, swine that he is, I'm certain he'll get over it, just like he gets over everything else.

But the prime missing person, the great enigma, is still Louis. Things — my transfer to the Turkish border, my divorce — happened and I never even managed to find out what went on that fateful weekend when I fled; who was the son-of-a-bitch who told me to go to hell when I called his place.

Much later, I got some answers to the question — question? call it a mystery, better — of what happened to the bastard, from Drakopoulos when I encountered him, ages later so it seemed, one midday in the public urinals in Omonia Square. In fact, I was taken aback.

— Drakopoulos! I didn't know industrialists pissed in public urinals.

— When you gotta go, Manolopoulos, you gotta go.

And when we got back to street level, once we'd cleared away the reminiscences and the small talk and the "Hey, remember when's?" and the "What happened to you, where'd you disappear to's?"; once the discussion touched on Louis, he launched into an account of everything he knew:

— The day you called his place and a madman answered, the guy who told you to go to hell, know who it was? It was Customs, his brother-in-law. Louis had evaporated, as you know. Ever see him again? No? Evaporated, turned to mist, rose up to heaven. Yes, indeed, it was Customs, his wife's — Cissy, remember? — sister's husband. That's who. Fanny's gone, my friend. Kaput. Remember Louis' fly trap venture? How we kept trying to figure out where he got the money? From Fanny, that's where, my friend. Her life's savings, the poor woman; he conned her, took everything. It's all gone, the business, the idea, her money. His partner, a Frenchman, ripped it off. The money and the idea, both. But if you go to France, you'll see the very same plastic fly traps on sale everywhere, just like Louis designed them. So he wasn't pulling our leg the way we thought. A couple of days before you called his place, they buried Fanny. Killed herself

418

Manolopoulos. Couldn't take it. Louis couldn't take it either. If Customs didn't kill him, Krugas would; he had to clear out. He did. But if you want more details — you, you like details — hop in a cab just as you are and go straight to Piraeus, to his shack, and see Cissy. She's one hell of a whore now, Cissy is, Manolopoulos. Did you know that? I'm just filling you in so you'll know what to expect. A whore. One thousand a shot.

— Come on, don't go pulling my leg ...

— I went myself. You think I don't know what I'm talking about? In Marguerite Gauthier's boudoir, that's where she entertains. Customs sits outside, on a throne from one of the Richards, and takes the money. His father, old man Retsinas, still lives there; he's half-paralyzed. They capped the well. Old Retsinas won't live with Antigone after the murder of Athena — don't tell me it wasn't murder pure and simple — he can't hear very well, keeps the Philips on high volume. That way he can't hear Cissy screwing. I wanted to find Louis, so I went myself. I had to find out. Had to ask him, whose kid it is, his or mine, just get the whole business over with, I want to know, anyway, I couldn't get over it. They took me for a customer, didn't recognize me. I paid, fucked her and left. Straight up. Go on, she won't recognize you. She's near-sighted but she won't wear glasses, they don't look good on her ... And, just between us ... you'll have a good time, listen to me.

That was the last thing I expected to hear from Drakopoulos. Louis, old buddy. How was I to know back then, that night at Lambros' place, when I was suffocating with my own torments, how did I know you were stuck with worse, and it didn't even occur to me to ask.

I didn't wait for another word. Gave Drakopoulos a wave and left. He called out after me:

— Just a second! Where are you going? I've got more about Louis, that's not all.

I stopped in my tracks, turned back.

— Take your choice, Manolopoulos. It may be all mirages, of course. I even heard he was working as a street musician

419

not far from here, along with a mad composer, a guy called Asimos, and a woman who looks like Twiggy, Moschos' wife, only with longer hair, dirtier, who passes the hat. Did you know Twiggy dumped Moschos just around the time Louis disappeared? She was playing a drum, Louis the guitar, and the composer was playing some other instrument, I can't remember, some kind of wind instrument, maybe. But I doubt it would have been Louis. More likely he's somewhere in the Aegean islands; Paros, that's what I heard. Shacked up with a wealthy old woman who hired him as a gardener. A guy I know saw him there, someone who looked like him, with a beard, long hair, drunk. You figure it out. Some people say he went to Australia. What do you hear?

— Nothing. A friend of mine got a card from him, no address, telling her he had opened a restaurant in Johannesburg.

— What Johannesburg? I heard it was Australia, but Aleka swears he's parking cars for some nightclub down by the airport. I went, but it wasn't him. But for a while he did work for a theater in a provincial town, painting stage sets, that much seems certain. I went looking for him. Bad luck, though, because just the day before, he'd left for an unknown destination. They didn't have the faintest idea where. But the way they described him, it had to have been him, for sure. With a false name. Their guy was called Kanellos. There was a woman with him, they said. From what they told me, it sounded like Twiggy. But as far as I can tell, the most reliable information is that he's washing dishes in Brooklyn. Also heard that he blew his brains out. That would suit everybody just fine. A fitting end, don't you think?

He stared at me, waiting for my reaction. And then I really cut loose. Really let 'em have it, him and me and everyone else; good for him for not letting us know how it ended, good for him for sticking it to us. What didn't I tell him! That Louis was the one who broke the sound barrier, the one who turned our shitty ideals inside out. Maybe he's screwing old ladies or washing dishes or parking our cars, he's the one who broke

420

the sound barrier, who made a mess of all our stinking alibis, and even if we finally admit he's dead then there'll be birds chirping on top of his grave, like the poet says, whose name escapes me.

— Assholes, we're all assholes, I told him at the end of my diatribe. Christ walked right by us and we never noticed; Ulysses, Kolokotronis — whoever you like — walked right on by us, and we never noticed. Never noticed. What a bunch of mindless assholes!

Not a peep out of him. He stared at me vacantly, his eyes almost crossing. I remembered what Louis said the last time I met him at Lambros' place: "Manolopoulos, every book I read has gotten me in trouble. I can't help it. Corrupted me, cast a spell over me. Isn't that the way you want it? Well, that's the way it is. But you guys, you smart-asses, you got it worse, and then some. You can see 'em coming, the turkeys, the gutter rats, the braggarts and the boasters and instead of standing up to them you fall right in step. 'Us too,' you say and jump right into the shit. Those ideologies of yours, those big words about country, family and religion, nothing but alibis, nothing but bullshit and excuses. Smoke and mirrors and bullshit. But you never really identified with 'em, at least then I could say to myself, OK, at least you're trying to get something out of it. Not you, you pretended to be above it all, pretended it was all far, far away. Neither one thing, nor the other. Fingers in every pie, braggarts, amphibians. You know amphibians, eh? You thought you were climbing the ladder, but look what happened to you. You were climbing underground stairs. From one level to another, cousin. And when you make it to the top one day, what do you think you'll find? You'll find a sewer hole cover and you won't even have the strength to lift it, to come out into the light, into the air. Pity, cousin, pity, 'cause mankind is such a fine, tender invention, as some writer put it. Pity. All you did was make the whorehouse bigger."

Drakopoulos shook me out of my recollections; he'd finally recovered and was speaking to me, but I hadn't heard.

421

— Come on, Manolopoulos, you're off in a dream world. I'm talking to you. Know what I remembered? Got to hand it to him. Back in high school, in 1950 it was, the principal brought some police forms into class and asked us to write down if any of our friends or teachers were Communists. Wanted to make stool pigeons out of us. Remember Louis? Picked up the paper, got up from his desk, walked to the front of the class and tore it up in front of the principal. Never set foot in school again. That's why he dropped out. The only one. Some of us even filled them in. Isn't that how they caught Katsikaros? Remember?

Did I ever! That was what made me get out of there as fast as I could.

— Just a second, he called out, we've got to get together sometime. Just a second, I've got more ...

I didn't answer. I was in a hurry. I wanted to find out all I could, fast. So I grabbed the first cab I could find and headed straight for his shack.

I found the situation exactly as Drakopoulos had described it. It was true, Customs was sitting on an imperial throne. He had it tilted back against the wall; didn't even look to see who I was.

— A thousand, he said.

I gave him two and went in.

When he saw the two bills, he got up and opened the door for me. Even bowed. Still didn't recognize me. Litsa didn't either. Took me for another customer. There was still something attractive about her.

She took me into the bedroom with the heavy red drapes. Nothing had changed since my first visit. The table lamp, the perfume, everything was the same, everything was red. Only it was more threadbare, unwashed, dirtier, even her housecoat was frayed and dirty. Underneath she had on a rose negligée. Didn't even look forty. She must have been quite young when Louis married her. Still good-looking, desirable even, just like when I saw her for the first time. She noticed my hesitation, asked me if I wanted to lie down with her.

422

— No, I'd rather talk, I said.

She was surprised, but didn't ask for any explanations.

I don't know if Louis will ever read what I'm telling you, but if he does, I'm sure he'll call me hopeless, say that for once I had a chance to do something evil, to sleep with my friend's wife, and I didn't do it.

I began to talk. Told her I knew Louis, asked her if she had any news of him, if she knew where he was. She didn't.

— Did he leave because of Fanny? — I asked — after she killed herself over the money? He couldn't take it? Is that why?

— I don't know. Maybe. One thing's certain, he left before anybody knew a thing. I didn't even know. Customs was after him to pay back the money, and one day as we were talking he gets up, grabs a beat-up old suitcase, stuffs whatever he can find into it. "What is it, Manolis, where are you going?" I ask him. "I'm leaving," he says. And he leaves. "Wait," I yell. "Wait!" And he leaves. That's it. Never saw him again. His father was asleep. Didn't even tell him goodbye. "I'll be back," he says, and leaves. Someone told me he went off with his brother's wife, someone else told me he's living with a poet, someone else ... Later I found out that the Frenchman ripped him off, stole the money and the fly trap idea. Later. Oh, yes. I got a card from him, too, showing just the sea, no name, just the sea. The postmark was all smudged, you couldn't tell where it came from. It had to have been from him. Just a second, I'll show it to you; see for yourself.

She showed it to me. As I was looking at it I remembered Agis, the man who corresponded with nothing but postcards. It's as if I can hear him: "Get it over with, Manolopoulos, wrap it up, don't try and tell everything, you can't tell everything, you don't know everything. Whether you like it or not, it's your life finale, so get it over with."

Agis was right. A book, the ending of á book, it's like a kind of life finale, in a way. So, period. I've put you through enough.

423

Anyway, so I tell you all this, and I still don't really know why I did it, or whether I told it to you, or to me. After all these hours, I honestly still don't know who I'm talking to.

Maybe I told you all I've been through — all jumbled, and clumsy to boot — just so it would all take on another weight, another meaning for me, but also so you can judge us from a distance with more understanding, with less sentimentality, as if we weren't, neither you — which you weren't of course — nor I — which I was — in the thick of things.

Now, whether I like it or not, you will pass judgment on me, and I welcome it, now that the illusions and the lies are over with, now that a whole era is gone, even though I still don't believe anything really ever ends, that anything ever begins. It only seems to be ending, seems to be beginning. In reality, everything finds it own path, everything balances out, inside us and around us, for people and for things. Constantly changing, coming into equilibrium. Balancing, becoming calm. Like the sea. That's why Louis loved it so much. "You'll never see it motionless, cousin. But you'll see it calm," he'd say over and over again, every time we'd meet for a drink of ouzo at Lambros' place, up on the hill, as we watched the sea, far-off, gently moving.

KOSTAS MOURSELAS

Kostas Mourselas was born in Piraeus. He studied Law at the University of Athens and worked as a civil servant until 1969 when he was dismissed by the colonels' junta. Since then he has given himself totally to writing: for theatre, television, cinema and journalism. His plays have been staged in Greece, in Cyprus, in France and in Germany.

The present *Red Dyed Hair* is his first book of prose which has immediately become a best-seller.

FRED A. REED

Fred A. Reed is a self-taught neo-hellenist. He translated Nikos Kazantzakis' *Journey to the Morea,* and translated and adapted Kazantzakis' *Comedy, a Tragedy in One Act* for Canadian television. He has lectured on Kazantzakis both at Canadian and Québec universities, and on Canadian radio.

He has written extensively on modern Greece and its literature. Fred Reed currently works as a free-lance journalist and makes his home in Montréal, Québec.